THERE IS A
TOMORROW
REDUX

DAVID NAZAR

authorHOUSE®

AuthorHouse™
1663 Liberty Drive
Bloomington, IN 47403
www.authorhouse.com
Phone: 1-800-839-8640

Published by AuthorHouse 9/7/2012

ISBN: 978-1-4772-0928-8 (e)
ISBN: 978-1-4772-0929-5 (hc)
ISBN: 978-1-4772-0930-1 (sc)

Library of Congress Control Number: 2012908793

Any people depicted in stock imagery provided by Thinkstock are models, and such images are being used for illustrative purposes only. Certain stock imagery © Thinkstock.

This book is printed on acid-free paper.

Because of the dynamic nature of the Internet, any web addresses or links contained in this book may have changed since publication and may no longer be valid. The views expressed in this work are solely those of the author and do not necessarily reflect the views of the publisher, and the publisher hereby disclaims any responsibility for them.

David Nazar is also the author of
The Romantic Psychedelic Revolutionary

This book is dedicated to
Giordano Bruno, Thomas Paine,
And all those who have contributed
to the evolution of Humanity

Many thanks to Garry Tucker,
Nancy Bertrand, Donna Landry,
Monessa Guilfoil, Barrett Taylor
and Karen Claypool
for their help with this work.

WHAT HAPPENED

John's mood had been dramatically transformed by the incredible bliss he had just experienced. He felt really great. Light as a feather, relaxed and wonderful. Yet he was very puzzled. What just happened to him? Never in his life had he experienced anything like it. The lights, the sounds, the ecstasy - what was that? It had seemed to go on forever. He closed his eyes again, hoping to be transported back into that ecstatic state. After a few moments he realized that it wasn't going to happen again, and he reopened his eyes.

"What was that? And where am I?" he said out loud.

John looked around, then stood up and turned around in a complete circle. In some ways he seemed to be in the same place. He could see the Bay and the bridge there, but now he saw that several of the ships had colorful sails. Some looked to be of cloth; some more rigid. There were myriad trees on the hill now, some sixty to seventy feet high. John walked up to one and, yes, it was a young redwood. Through the trees he had a view of what used to be the industrial section down by the bay, although he no longer saw any signs of industry. The whole area seemed to be a park filled with foliage.

He could see the downtown area through some of the trees and yes, there was the pyramid building, a San Francisco landmark. And what were the colorful flying things he saw above him in the sky? John looked up overhead, and one flew over the gap in the trees not more than a hundred feet above. It looked like a hang glider with a propeller up front. He could hear the sound of its propeller as it buzzed by. "Hey," he yelled as he waved up at it, but got no response.

A little to his left there was a worn path leading down the hill.

John walked over and looked down it. Flowers were growing in the sunny areas. He decided to head on down.

"I must still be hallucinating," he said out loud. He wondered if it was safe to be walking around. His steps were cautious at first. The path came to a circular clearing. He looked up at the sky, now a beautiful blue and perfectly clear. Just then about seven different colored flyers passed overhead in a V formation. "What the hell is going on?" he wondered out loud.

In the center of the clearing was some kind of a statue, but he couldn't identify the large, obese, roly-poly woman depicted. Several bouquets of flowers lay at the statue's feet. As he rounded the figure, he saw a young woman sitting in a meditative posture with her eyes closed. John stood there for about a half a minute wondering what he should do. He wanted very much to talk to her, but he didn't know if he should disturb her meditation, or whether it was even a good idea to be seen by or communicate with anyone in this amazing new world. Then the young woman opened her eyes and looked right into his. There was a powerful energy between them that seemed to keep either from speaking for another ten or twelve seconds.

"Hi." She spoke first.

"Uh, hello," John said rather tentatively. He took a few steps towards her. "Um, you're not going to believe this, but I just had the most incredible experience of my life."

"A good one I hope, but why wouldn't I believe it?"

"Yes, it was way beyond good," said John, "but, incredibly confusing. When I came up this hill a little while ago, none of this stuff was here. There were no trees. The sky was gray and polluted. And there weren't any ships with sails on the Bay."

"Well, I've been here for almost an hour," she said looking at a bracelet on her wrist, "and nothing has changed."

"But everything has changed! What time is it?"

"About twelve-thirty. Are you sure you aren't polluted? Have you been drinking or getting high on something?"

"No, no, nothing like that. Unless someone slipped me some LSD or something. No, there's no way. What day is it?"

"You're really lost in space, aren't you. It is Friday, June nineteenth."

"June nineteenth. That's right, but this is a Saturday."

A chill ran down John's spine.

"What year is this?"

"Twenty-ninety-five, of course."

John almost fell to a sitting position. His expression became even more bewildered than before.

"Uh, no! That is impossible!"

"Well when do you think you came up here?"

"Would you believe Nineteen-ninety-three?"

"Of course not. That's impossible. Though, I must admit your outfit is authentic, from old videos I've seen. You're period dressing, right? And you're out here playing games with people, or is this some new kind of line?"

"No, I swear!" John exclaimed. "I'm as amazed as you. More so."

John got up and walked closer to her and said, "My name is John Berry and I came up here on a Saturday in nineteen-ninety-three. I was feeling terrible, having a real crisis of faith. I was really upset. I prayed to God that I could have faith again. Then all of a sudden I had this incredible experience of bliss and light and color and sounds like I've never heard before. It was awesome, amazing, beyond anything I had ever experienced. It was as if my whole body was in ecstasy, and my mind was merged with a whole universe of light and sound. I don't know how long it lasted, but, I can't believe it lasted for a hundred years."

John sat down again across from the young woman. Though she wore no makeup, she was rather pretty. Her clothes seemed to be hand-made and not quite like anything he'd seen before. They were rather sweet and attractive though, and maybe the cloth was hand woven. She looked lovely in her little peach top, and she had long sandy blond hair that was braided into pigtails. Her eyes were either blue or green, John couldn't tell for sure. There was a knowing smile on her face that showed she seemed to be quite skeptical of the truth of his story. She looked down at his feet and said, "Where did you get those old leather shoes?"

"I sent off for them through a catalogue that carries wide sizes. Why? Don't people wear leather shoes anymore?"

"Not much."

"Would you pinch me or something? This is just crazy."

John reached into his pocket. He took out a quarter and a nickel, looked at them, and handed them to the young woman. When he gave them to her, he pressed them into her hand just to verify that she was a real flesh and blood person.

"Maybe this will prove I am telling the truth. These coins are from 1987 and 1991. Back in 1993 coins over a hundred years old would have been very rare. What's your name?"

"I'm sorry. After your incredible story, I've forgotten my manners. My name is Crystal."

"Well, Crystal, I believe you. I can see that either I'm not in the same time, or I've gone totally crazy."

"I can believe that," Crystal said with a laugh. She looked at the coins, turned them over in her hand, and said to John, "This is a joke. I'll give you credit for a good job. The clothes look good, the shoes, and coins. But many people collect old coins. I guess you didn't know we haven't used coins for over sixty years. They were used on the black market for a while. That's why they're not around except for collectors. Most were rounded up and melted down. Listen to me. I don't really believe you." She looks up from the coins in her hand, staring at John with a skeptical smile on her face.

"Well, I can't say that I blame you. I don't believe it either, but I'm living it. I guess I'm alive. You're so beautiful; I could believe I've died and gone to heaven."

John was smiling sweetly at Crystal, and she returned his smile as their eyes met and stayed in contact for a long moment.

"Now I know this is a line," said Crystal with a laugh, "but I think I'm going for it. I get it. You're acting in a play about the Twentieth Century, right?"

"No. I swear, I came up here in 1993."

Crystal shook her head gently, but she was still smiling.

"What do people use if you don't have money?"

"OK, I'll play this game with you, that you are from the past, but if I catch you, game over. We use credit accounts and computers to keep track of everything. Not having any cash money cut down tremendously on crime. That and the fact that every major purchase is registered to the owner, so your property can't very easily be stolen either. People do barter a whole lot, mostly for hand-made, non-registered things like clothing and food. Didn't they have credit cards back when you say you are from?"

"Sure. I even thought it could come to this, but we would think that that kind of a system was too much like Big Brother taking over."

"Big Brother?"

"Yeah, you know, George Orwell's *1984*, when the government controls everything and limits everybody's freedom. So what's the government like now?"

"Oh, we still have a democracy. America has the same kind of government. It's not perfect, but it works pretty well. I believe back in the time you claim to be from the government was rather corrupt. It was amazing how people of that era let campaign contributors have so much power. That was what caused many of your ecological and economic problems."

"So that doesn't happen now?"

"Nothing like back then."

"Is there a world government?"

"The United Nations is still in existence, but they had that back in the Twentieth Century, when you claim to be from" she added with sarcasm.

"Still don't believe me," John said with a sigh. "Ask me some history questions."

"History is not exactly my strong suit," Crystal said smiling, "but I'll think of something."

"Well, I have a lot of questions to ask you. What happened to the world, the environment? Obviously, we people are still here. That is tremendous news! Incredible!"

Tears welled up in John's eyes and he found himself balanced between laughing and crying.

"I can understand your deep appreciation of that fact. The fate of the Earth and humanity were in serious doubt for decades after the excesses of the Twentieth Century. There were horrible droughts and serious destruction of the environment. For a while it looked as if it were too late to recover. And the truth is, we lost a fabulous wealth of species, never to be brought back."

"Well, what happened?" he asked.

"Humanity had to make many difficult lifestyle changes. You guys were living as if there were no tomorrow. But by moving to sustainable energy production, and through decades of work, tree planting and reforestation all over the world, combined with discoveries that helped us reverse or eliminate some of the pollution, we are now a healthy planet, and becoming healthier. Our fields are getting more fertile, not less. Our forests are larger, and much of the native animal life has been restored. There are some notable exceptions. Serious exceptions. But at least our problems are confined to a few relatively small areas, whereas when you say you lived, the fate of the whole Earth was in danger."

"We made it. Well, that answers a significant part of the questions

I was asking God when I got zapped. I just didn't think there was any hope for the world."

"So, did you get your faith back?"

"Gee, um, well yeah, I feel much better anyway. If I only knew what was happening to me. Things are a lot better? You say there is less crime?"

"Compared to the late Twentieth Century, you bet. It was practically anarchy back then. We probably have less crime in the whole country than was in the Bay area back then."

"I saw blood on the street from the shooting of a child, just this morning. A hundred and two years ago, I guess."

John's face became more serious. Crystal was noticeably moved herself.

"A CHILD! That's terrible!"

"Tell me about it. It was common back then." John stood up and walked a few steps towards the statue, then turned around slowly again.

"These are redwood trees, right?"

"Yes, San Francisco led the way in replanting trees. And most of ours are set aside to become permanent and ultimately will become ancient trees. There is very little space left to plant a tree in this city. Look, you can even see greenery on top of some of the houses with flat roofs, except for the ones with solar collectors."

Crystal stood up and pointed through a space between trees on the downhill side. Sure enough, John could see that many of the houses and apartments did have small trees or other foliage on their roofs.

"I must admit, John, when I came up here this morning I had a feeling something extraordinary would happen. I thought I might have a powerful spiritual experience. I have learned to trust my inner guidance."

"So what does your inner guidance say about me?" John asked.

"It says that, incredible as it seems, you are telling me the truth. I believe that you think you are from the past. But time travel is completely impossible. The past is dead, and the future nonexistent. It is just impossible. No one has ever done it."

"Then I must be the first." said John with assurance, quickly realizing he wasn't sure about anything. Just then three flyers flew so close overhead that John could hear them laughing and talking to one another over the hum of their propellers.

"What are those things, Crystal?"

"Power gliding is a very popular sport."

"Power gliders. In the city?"

"Sure," answered Crystal. "Nowadays we don't have commercial aircraft overhead."

"What about power lines?" asked John.

"All buried in the ground to shield their electromagnetic fields. It cut cancer rates down noticeably."

"What powers the gliders?"

"They all have lightweight, high-charge batteries and high-speed lightweight motors. Most have the new flexible solar voltaic material on the tops of their wings. That can sometimes double their time aloft,"

"Incredible," said John. "How long can they stay up, and how fast can they go? Do you do it? Gosh, I'm sorry about all the questions."

"Well, you're staying in character very well. They can stay up two to four hours, but with thermals, all day. Flat out, they go sixty to maybe a hundred kph. Much faster in a dive."

"Wow," said John.

"There is a big flight park up on top of Twin Peaks. I do fly on occasion. It's great fun,"

She said with a smile.

"Who is the statue of?" John asked.

Crystal got up and handed John back his coins. They walked more to the downhill side of the statue so that they could see the front and face better. Her head was covered with little bumps, and she had no features on her face.

"It is an ancient goddess that was found in a cave in Europe. She is perhaps the oldest goddess ever discovered. The group that planted this tract of redwoods years ago was given permission to erect this large statue and dedicate this circle. She's know as the Willondorf Goddess. I love it up here. Usually there are even more flowers blooming, and since this is rather high up and many people don't relate much to this particular goddess, there are usually few people up here. It just shows you that beauty is in the eye of the beholder. Probably way back in the Ice Age when the original goddess was made, this was the ultimate idea of feminine beauty."

"Now how could that be?" Asked John.

"During the Ice Age people had to eat animals and game was often sparse. A woman who could endure a famine, have a baby, nurse it, and bring both of them through the ordeal would be very highly prized. Plus her obvious wealth denotes high status."

"Is there still status nowadays?"

"Of course, John. Some human qualities will never change. However, what gives status has changed since your time. Wealth, beauty, and fame still give a certain status, but without a loving heart and positive social and spiritual values, they are not very respected."

"I don't quite understand."

"For instance, having a huge mansion that drains away an unfair share of resources and causes unnecessary pollution is not something most people look up to anymore. Though some people do push the environmental laws to the edge, those people are not highly regarded."

"What is highly regarded?"

"Achievements that uplift humanity, and a wealth of generosity and intelligence in the distribution of the rewards of such achievements."

"I don't quite follow you." John replied. "Rich people are not respected unless they distribute their wealth?"

"Well, they can't take it with them, can they?"

"In my day they left it to their children."

"John, you have a lot to learn. Look, it is getting on towards one and I have a two o'clock class at Berkeley. I just have to go now. It was fun. Good-bye, John, whoever you are."

John stood there with a blank stare. Crystal seemed to be a little sorry she had to go, he thought, and he had no idea what was happening or what he should do. He let her turn and take a few steps down the hill before he shouted.

"Wait, Crystal"

In a few steps he was even with her, walking down the hill.

"Please, let me go with you. There must be some reason that you were here. You said so yourself. I need a guide. I need help. I don't know anything about these times."

They walked together slowly down the hill, with Crystal looking thoughtful.

"So what is your major?" asked John.

"I am a teacher," said Crystal. She turned and looked at John.

"Please. I don't know anyone but you. I need to find out what's happened to me."

Crystal took a full breath and let it out with a soft sigh. She looked at John for a long moment, then spoke. "I'll tell you why I came up here, John." Another pause. "I had a very amazing and vivid dream last night. In my bedroom there is a large mirror on one side of the bed and a large picture on the other. I dreamed I awoke and got up on the side of the bed with the picture. I looked across the bed at the mirror and instead of seeing myself standing there I saw an angel. It had bright shimmering robes of white that sparkled like diamonds. Beautiful golden wings, and a very incredible face, well, like an angel. It was looking at me with love and energy. Then its left arm went up in front of the picture and I felt my right arm raise. When it passed in front of the picture, it changed, and there was a lifelike picture of me, in these same clothes, sitting up on this hill meditating. I turned to look at the picture behind me, and then woke up."

"Wow, so you had a incredible experience too. Why didn't you tell me?"

She tilted her hear and gave him a little smile. "Your story is rather unbelievable John, because you aren't saying you had a dream, you're saying you time traveled. I don't readily see the connection."

"Both are amazing experiences," said John.

"I did have a very powerful experience. I'm a bit frustrated because I feel there was more to it that I somehow don't remember. Something wonderful was happening or going to happen. There seems to be a space there. Well, that is about all I remember. I had a client over here on Burnal Heights this morning anyway."

She looked at John, shook her head gently and smiled.

"OK, John. You can stay with me until I can see that you are really from the present. Surely you'll do something to give yourself away. Then not only will I know it, you'll have to admit it, too."

They walked on down the hill together. John thought that it was greatly improved, and he said so to Crystal. When he came up it was barren except for some antennas and grass. Now it had trees all over it except for the paths and numerous flower beds. About fifty yards down the hill they crossed what seemed to be, by the fertilizer along it, a bridle path.

"Is this a bridle path, Crystal?"

"Yes. There are stables at the Bay Shore Park down the hill."

"Where the industrial section used to be?" John asked.

"It's been a park for a long time," Crystal replied.

Just then, they came upon a raccoon.

"A raccoon in San Francisco?" It doesn't seem to be afraid of us," John said.

"No, all the wildlife in the city are tame, and often a nuisance because of it. I actually saw a bobcat up here last month. It wouldn't let me get too close, so it must have been new to the city. I should have reported it for relocation, but I figured it would be okay up here."

"Isn't there a problem with rabies?" he asked.

"No. An oral vaccine was developed years ago and they use bait to administer it to the wild animals. Rabies is almost completely eradicated now."

"That's incredible Crystal. You said you are a teacher? What do you teach?"

"I'm really a healer. But I was asked to teach at the university because I have a gift for energy healing. I was tested as part of a carefully controlled scientific study, and it proved that I could speed the healing of many kinds of ailments. Not just me, but many spiritual and energy healers were shown to be effective. I seem to have a special gift for being able to facilitate others to be able to heal with their hands. I had dropped out of college when my practice became too large for me to be able to do both. Besides, I was already actualizing my special gift and had a career in full swing. I always knew I would be a healer. I started with my pets, then my friends and families. By the time I was in my teens I was helping people. I found some techniques through my inner guidance and have had a very good success rate ever since."

"That's incredible. I was studying to be a doctor myself."

"Really? You'll find that medicine has changed considerably since that time. What kind of a doctor did you want to be?"

"An alternative one. I thought that radiation treatments and a lot of the chemotherapy employed back then were a mistake. Plus most doctors weren't the least bit interested in prevention."

"You were right. Radiation therapy has gone the way of bleeding and bypass surgery."

"That's gone now too?"

"You mean bypass surgery? Yes, it is quite rare now. Few people let their hearts get all clogged up anymore, and those who do know that only a lifestyle change will permanently improve things. We don't have alternative doctors any more, as in your times, when I believe allopathic doctors controlled medicine and pretty much kept everyone else out. All effective styles of treatment are utilized nowadays."

"That's great! The Clintons, our new president and his wife, are supposed to reform health care and make it universal. Did that happen?"

"Not in their time, but we do have a system now where everyone has access to medical help. It's rather hard imagining it any other way. Health care is so essential."

They passed through another clearing with a statue of the Buddha. By this time they were almost back to the street. John saw that it had a tree canopy over most of it, as there were trees planted down the middle and on both sides of the street. He could see bicycles going by in both directions under what seemed to be a cover of some kind under the trees. When they reached the street he saw a covered lane with people walking along one side and riding bicycles and what looked to be motorized skateboards along other lanes, under the shade of a curved roof extending all along that side of the street. The other side of the street had a narrow two-lane road. Both wound themselves through a beautiful park that took up the rest of what once was a broad boulevard.

John saw fountains, flower beds, and a basketball court with a three-on-three game in progress. In the other direction John saw a swimming pool with many people of all ages swimming and frolicking in it. On past a large modern looking sculpture of some kind were a couple of tennis courts. The two of them walked down the last fifty yards of hill as John took in each new scene, with his mouth hanging open.

"Wow. Everything is so different."

"Nineteen ninety-three you said, I guess so." answered Crystal. She unlocked her bicycle from a large rack at the bottom of the path.

"I guess you don't have a bicycle?"

"Of course not." Replied John with a smile. "Where would I have put a bicycle for a century."

"If you needed to, you could use one of the green bikes. They're for everyone, and it is against the law to put a lock on them. See, there are a couple in the other rack. I need to take the sub anyway," Crystal said as she walked up to the street corner and pushed a button on a post next to the covered bike path.

"The subway?" asked John.

"No, they are trains. A subus is a bus that runs below the street.

They're more versatile than trains on tracks. An express subus can pass a local. We have to cross the ped. When the gate opens, it turns on a warning light."

John could see an amber light flashing in the middle of the ped, hanging from the curved roof about eight feet up. Within a few seconds a six foot gate slowly slid open.

"You still have to look both ways before you cross. The speed limit is twenty-five kph."

Just as Crystal stepped in to look, three skateboarders came whizzing down from the uphill side at a rapid rate, squatting so low on their boards that they couldn't be seen over the meter-high padded walls. Right before the youths got to John and Crystal, yellow lights began to flash along the tops of the walls, keeping pace with the kids but slightly in front of them. The skateboarders seemed to slow down slightly and the lights went off.

"They were going for the yellow. If they had gone five kph faster, red lights would have come on, and within fifty feet they would have had their licenses scanned and been fined a credit for every kph over twenty-five, every tenth of a meter."

"Wow. No slack to this system."

"Well, they could hurt someone. You don't have a credit account either?"

"All I have is the clothes on my back, about seventy-five cents in change, and an empty wallet."

John pulled his wallet out of his back pocket.

"Let me show you some of the stuff in it. Here is my address book with phone numbers in it. Here is my social security card."

Crystal looked at the card.

"That's interesting," Crystal said, slowly looking at both sides of the card. "We don't have those anymore. All my personnel records are in my PC."

They walked down a wide ramp to an underground stop next to a roadbed set about a foot below their level. Before entering the waiting area, they came to a pair of turnstiles, and a gate more than a meter wide. John heard a soft humming sound and turned around to see a man sitting on a box about a meter square. To steer, he was using controls on a long handle that came up from the bottom of the box in front of him. When he reached the turnstile, he hopped off and turned the grip on the end of the handle around so he could control the box while walking in front of it. It had wheels under it and seemed self-propelled. He waved his hand over the scanner on the wider gate and then steered the box, which was obviously self-powered, through it and up to the edge of the waiting area ahead of John and Crystal.

"What is that?" asked John.

"That's a lug truck. It's battery powered and can go about ten kph, tops. People often ride them to and from the subs in non-congested areas. We have to have some way to move big things around, so we use carts, hand trucks and lug trucks, depending on how much stuff we are carrying. They are all standardized to half and whole meter dimensions so they can be secured to the stow bars on the subus."

Crystal walked to the gate, passed her wrist over what seemed to be a laser scanner, and passed through the gate with her bicycle. Then she passed her wrist over the scanner at the turnstile and told John to come through.

" It costs more to take a bike or hand truck, so you come through the turnstile," Crystal added.

"People with bikes, trucks and carts use the back doors, and people with nothing to stow use the front."

A wide vehicle resembling a bus pulled up to the stop. Doors opened on both ends and little draw bridges came down to the platform. The fellow steered the box on to the subus and John could see him pull it up to a row of bars set about a foot apart. He did something with the controls, pulled the handle to check how well secured it was, and then took a seat along the double row of seats by the windows. John saw many other trucks of different sizes secured to the bars, and through the back door John could see several bikes in a bike rack at the rear of the subus.

"We want to wait for an express." explained Crystal. This one will stop every four to six blocks."

The subus pulled out, and within seconds another pulled in. Crystal led John onto the subus and put her bike into a place on the bike rack, then stepped on a round button on the floor.

"That secures it."

A row of twenty double seats along the windows lined each side. Along the wall there was an area with stanchions, and many had carts or hand trucks attached to them. About fifteen other people were on the subus.

"The carts are standardized to a half meter square. Some have motors, and some don't."

They took the first pair of open seats.

13

"And hand trucks are a whole meter square. All of them have motors. The height of both can vary"

"So when you take something somewhere, you use one of these gadgets to haul your luggage or whatever? Cool."

"Cool, what do you mean by that?" asked Crystal.

"Oh, it's an old slang term meaning really good. What are you wearing on your wrist, and what was the deal with the turnstile?"

"This is my PC. It keeps track of my finances and can do just about anything. See, this bracelet is actually a screen on this side, and the underside can interface with scanner registers."

Crystal turned her wrist up so John could see the underside of it. The device seemed to have a computer bar code like what was used in supermarkets in John's time, with some sort of sensor on one end and a little red light on the other.

"You can ask your PC, or look at the screen to see how much you have spent."

"Credit accounts for buses!" he quipped. "In my time you only needed them to rent a car. I had to cut my credit card up to avoid an early bankruptcy. I've been paying it off ever since. It was tough being a struggling medical student. I didn't need the temptation of easy credit. So how much do I owe you for the bus ride?"

"Don't worry about it. It was just a credit. We pay for everything through our accounts. If you have a line of credit, you can charge things the same way. There is a movement, which I support, to get completely off the account exchange. The people who are really dedicated to the movement make their own clothes, furniture, bikes and whatever else they need. They barter for as much of their necessities as possible. Most all of them grow their own food. There is no tax on anything as long as there is no computer record of the transaction. As soon as anyone keeps any kind of a record, taxes are charged on the transaction."

"I would imagine that would be a hard law to enforce."

"Actually, it is much easier for the government to tax everyone, as there are instant records of every payment, and they tax us immediately. Most people still get most of what they need the old fashioned way. Through their account. I guess that isn't the old fashioned way to you. You had money."

"I guess barter is the most old fashioned way of all. How does this bus run?"

"It runs on electricity. The electricity is produced by a mix of ecologically sound sources. We have a lot of wind, solar, hydro, ocean currents and even geothermal here in California," she explained.

"There isn't any nuclear power anymore.?"

"NO! Nuclear power was a disaster. We are still cleaning up the mess from the nuclear power plants from the time you claim you are from."

"I was always against them," John said.

"Well, it's too bad there weren't more of you back then. In three days I am going on a mission to do something about the incredible mess left to us by the nuclear nightmare. This particular problem was caused by the building of nuclear weapons, not nuclear power. But the nuclear power legacy left us more than 150 areas in America alone that have been ruined for human or animal habitation. Most of them are only a few square miles in size, but that is a lot of wasted earth, and we are not sure we can contain it at that level for the tens of thousands of years it will be dangerous. Where I'm going is over a thousand square miles, and its size has been enlarged five times in the past century. Now they are talking about the need to write off even more land." Crystal paused for a moment. "I've said too much. Let's talk about something else."

John wondered what she meant about a mission, but she wanted to change the subject, so he didn't press her. He asked if the covered bicycle and pedestrian trails went up and down every street, and she replied in the affirmative.

"Everyone looks trim and healthy. I can't believe these covered bicycle trails on every street. Where are the cars?"

"There are no individual autos allowed inside the city of San Francisco. Some of the suburbs allow limited access, but most car travel is done in the countryside. Only service and emergency vehicles are allowed in town. Most people don't drive much, if at all, and when they do, they rent cars for a few days or weeks. Cars are just too expensive and unnecessary."

"Is it like this everywhere?" Asked John.

"No, but most cities in America don't allow cars in most areas. That is why there is so much less pollution and noise. More free time, too. Back in the car era people worked about one day a week to maintain an automobile. Toward the end of the era it was getting closer to two days work a week to pay for an auto. That era burned up most of the oil in the world in one century. It was crazy. Sure cars were somewhat convenient, but compared to the time spent earning all that money, the little extra time people sometimes saved wasn't nearly worth it. And there was so much traffic and gridlock. I can get around faster now than you could before with cars. When we take the magna-train to Berkeley, it will only take ten minutes and deliver us right to the campus."

"I sure love the clear air you have now."

"Yes, it's much better. In your time the air quality became so bad it was killing people, and still nothing changed. It was so stupid, considering that simply driving more efficient cars or sharing rides could have helped so much. We are still amazed by just how polluted people allowed everything to become back then."

The subus had reached a rapid speed, and John could see patterns of illuminated colors whizzing by through the windows.

"Wow, that is beautiful."

"That is a new art form, John. The windows were originally there so people could see in and out of the subus at stops, but then some artists had the idea to use the speed of the subuses to create patterns of colors when seen from the inside."

Just then the subus started to decelerate rapidly, and they pulled into another station. They got up and off, with Crystal wheeling her bicycle onto the platform.

"No drivers on these things, Crystal?"

"No, they are sensor and computer controlled. Do you want to go up and take a look at Market Street?"

"Sure, Crystal."

They went up through a much more crowded ramp and were soon at street level. The bike paths had many more people on them. He saw some trucks passing by down the open and uncovered lanes. What looked to be an ambulance sped by.

"So you still have ambulances?

"Yes, of course. People still have accidents and illness. Not as many traffic accidents, obviously. We also have delivery trucks. Way too many if you ask me, but people don't want to have to carry things home themselves. I think trucks should only be used for heavy stuff."

"Boy, San Francisco has changed a lot. There seem to be many more races here than before."

"San Francisco has changed less than most cities due to the temperate climate here. Wait until you see L.A. or any of the cities in the Sun Belt. You won't recognize them. There are more races living here now, but a lot of these are foreign kids here for the International Youth Festival this weekend. San Francisco is hosting it this year. A quarter of a million people will ultimately come through here on their way to the festival. I'm working at it. It would be an incredible experience for you, if you're really not from this time."

"Crystal, I swear."

She tilted her head and gave him a little smile. "My PC can function as a universal language translator. Can you speak any foreign language?"

"A little Spanish," John replied.

Crystal spoke softly into her bracelet held close to her mouth, and asked John to say something in Spanish.

"La casa de las marinas."

"The house of the sailors." The computer repeated in a low but clear voice.

"That's incredible. How many languages does it interpret?"

"Every language and most of the major dialects on Earth. I'm going to get the new chip soon that translates all dialects. Everyone can communicate now. Televisions have language chips, so you can watch programs from any country and understand them. See those people over there? They're wearing ear sets, so the translation is quietly given in their ears while they talk."

Crystal pulled a little earpiece out of her waist pack that had a small microphone projecting forward a few inches and showed John.

"So I could use this to talk to anyone in the world? Amazing! This must be really good for international relations. What's with that guy sitting on the bench over there with the goggles on?"

"I must say, you're very good at staying in character." Crystal looked at John intently for a moment. "Some people still prefer virtual to reality. He could be playing a game, visiting some place, or learning something." Crystal replied.

People with bikes were walking them now. They were flowing with a lot of other people to an entrance with a descending ramp, while from the other direction many other people were coming out, some with bikes, some with little wheeled carts, a few leading the bigger hand or lug trucks, some just walking with brief cases or packs. There were many different styles of dress, though the colors seemed more muted than in John's time. Hardly anyone was wearing a tie. John saw that when they got to the covered bike lanes, bikers would mount up and ride off. John observed that many of the bikers weren't pedaling.

"How do those bikes run without anyone pedaling?"

"It is legal to have up to a five hundred watt electric motor as a booster. Now with the latest in lightweight batteries, lots of people use them most of the time. I don't use one, though. You stay a lot healthier if you always pedal."

There was the din of people talking, but the street noise John had been accustomed to was gone. The trucks seemed much quieter. John could actually hear birds singing in the middle of the city. When he and Crystal went inside the ramp way, he saw that it was well lighted and that there was lovely art work along both walls. There was no graffiti on the walls.

"This is really nice. In my day kids scribbled graffiti all over everywhere."

"Yes, I've seen the pictures. It's become a trademark of your era."

A lovely indoor waterfall cascaded down natural looking rocks that had been set in the wall at a turn where the ramp continued down in the opposite direction. After another descent of about the same distance, the two of them came to a long platform, very much like subways of his time except they had only one large rail down the middle of the track.

"You can take your bicycle anywhere?"

"Yes," replied Crystal. "Bicycles are the most efficient mode of transportation. For a while they were used extensively, but nowadays no one has to walk more than a few blocks to catch a subus, or train, so they aren't used as much as they once were."

"Do all the streets have covered paths on them? Like y'all can ride bikes anywhere and not get wet in the rain?"

"Pretty much," she answered. "There are covered peds between all cities too. You can ride your bike across the country without ever getting rained on. Out in the country, many of the covers are made out of clear plastic so you can still see the scenery. In most of the parks, too."

They were moving down the platform with the other people with bikes or carts.

"The first two cars are for pedestrians only," she explained.

John watched another train heading the opposite way across the tracks pull in. It was very streamlined and amazingly quiet. People were getting on and off. Just then he noticed the lights of the train on their side of the tracks, and in a moment it was alongside them. When the doors opened he saw that the car had racks for bikes, trucks, or carts, and were set up pretty much like the subuses, only longer.

Crystal pushed the front wheel of her bike into a space for it, and they took a seat. The train started up and accelerated rapidly, then rapidly slowed down. In a minute they were at another stop. Some passengers got off; others got on, and in another minute the train was off again. In a matter of seconds the train was out into the light, and John could see it was on a bridge heading across the Bay. He could see another level above them through the large, wrap-around windows of the train. There were three other train lines with wide rails down the middle on their level, and intermittently a train flew by traveling in the opposite direction.

"Don't tell me this is the Bay Bridge?"

"Yes. The upper part is used for service vehicles and bicycles. Some people do walk or run across, though."

The train was still accelerating to a speed much faster than anything John had previously experienced. Within a few minutes they were across the bay and at a stop on the Oakland side.

"That was the fastest trip I've ever made across that bridge. The last time I crossed the bay, it took David and me about 45 minutes due to the traffic."

"All in all, transportation is much faster now without the use of automobiles. It was just crazy when everyone had their own individual vehicle. It just about ruined this state. Really, the whole world."

"We couldn't even persuade anyone to carpool. How did all this change come about?"

"As I said, John, we almost didn't make it. Humanity had a crisis, and we absolutely had to change to survive."

"Well, what all happened?" John was so curious about so much, he didn't know where to start.

"I don't think we'll have time for me to explain all that to you now. We will be at the campus in just a couple of minutes. I'm afraid it would cause a disturbance for you to come to my class with me. Why don't you go to the library while I'm teaching and learn some things for yourself. I'll meet you back there after my class is over."

"You promise me?"

"Yes, John, if you haven't taken another leap in time by then."

They arrived at their stop, and Crystal and John got off the train.

"The library is over that way. Follow that path up to the center

19

of the campus, and take a right. You should see the library then. If you can't find it, just ask someone. I have to go this way."

Crystal unfastened a sparse helmet from her bicycle seat, put it on, mounted her bike and with a smile, turned and started to pedal away. She looked back and could see that John had a dejected look on his face.

"Don't worry. I'll meet you by the main desk at three." She turned back around, stood up, and started pedaling faster.

I think I've just been brushed off, John thought. God, she was nice. Maybe she will meet me. I sure hope so. She is so lovely and sweet, and I really need a friend. She did say she was expecting something special to happen to her today.

How John's Day Began

John stood by the window in his small, crowded apartment. The little patch of morning sky visible through the canyon of buildings was gray. He looked out at it for a while anyway. How utterly bittersweet to dream of her, his first love, his only love. In dreams he could almost experience her love again, but the memory of her recalled the deep sense of loss and despair he felt about her death. It seemed so unnecessary, so unfair for someone so young and alive to be torn away from life, from love. His love. Familiar emotions welled up inside, feelings he hadn't allowed himself to have for a time.

"Good morning, John," David emerged from the bedroom looking tousled.

"Good morning, David."

"How's the weather look out there today?"

"Pretty dismal."

"What do you have planned for today?" David asked as he started cleaning up the mess of dirty dishes in the sink.

"I'm going to spend the day with Ishmael. I promised I'd take him to the Giants game this afternoon."

"The kid from the Fillmore district you got connected with through the Big Brother program?"

"Yeah David, here, let me help you with that mess. You do more than your share of keeping this apartment together."

John didn't feel good about David doing most of the cleaning. He did insist that David take the only bedroom in the tiny apartment, and that was some consolation. But then, with John working at the restaurant four nights a week until well into the morning, that was pretty much a necessity.

"Talk about doing more than your share, I'm not ready for you. First sponsoring an adopted child through Save the Children, and now you're a big brother. For someone who's working his way through med school, and barely staying in, I might add, don't you think you're overloading yourself? You don't want to get yourself burned out before we even start our internship," David said with a smile that masked his genuine concern.

"Why wait until then?" John joked in return, but he couldn't quite laugh. A weak smile was all he could muster. "If anything is needed to demonstrate that modern medicine doesn't have all the answers, the intern and residency ordeals where we're due to be systematically overworked until we can't possible do our jobs right, should suffice."

"You're right about that."

"I want to help people now, David. I don't want to postpone doing anything until I'm a doctor. Besides, I'm not so sure I'll ever be a doctor. I really don't have much faith in the kind of medicine they are teaching us. Damn prevention; just poison the patient with chemotherapy or irradiate them with multi-million dollar equipment and hope only the cancer dies. That's what they did to Faith, and the end of her life was a living hell."

"I can't blame you for being disillusioned with the scene at school, John, but you knew what they would be offering when you started."

"Yeah, but I guess I thought I could make some kind of a change."

"And you can, Man, but not in med school. That argument you gave Dr. Jenkins really pissed him off. You can't just tell your professor that what he has been doing to his patients is crude. Damn, I mean, the veins on his neck stood out. I don't think that is going to help your grade any, and if I remember right, you're flunking his class already."

"Everything I told him is true. Lots of studies show that alternative healing methods have just as good success rates in curing cancer as chemo and radiation therapy, and starting with sicker people, too. Many of them had been totally abandoned to die by conventional doctors, yet they still recovered using, to quote Dr. Jenkins, "unproved, unscientific quackery.""

"I know John, but you just can't argue with the professors. You have too much invested in your education to blow it over some pointless fight you can't win. I suggest you apologize to Jenkins next class, and if you really want to pass his course, do it in front of the class."

"Well, I'll just have to pass it anyway, because I'm not going to apologize."

"I don't want to be negative, John, but you flunk it and you're out." David got some milk and a peach out of the fridge, took a bag of granola out of the cupboard, pushed some books and clutter aside, and sat down at the table. He finished cutting up the peach and was pouring milk onto the cereal.

"Mary's best friend Sandy arrives today, John. I know I said I wouldn't bug you, but are you sure you won't reconsider a date with her? I know you've got plans for today and you're working tonight, but you are off tomorrow night."

"I absolutely have to study."

"Well how about Wednesday night? I tell you, she's really cute."

"Got to study then, too."

"Come on Man, you haven't had a date, you haven't had any fun since I can remember. You need this, John. You have to get yourself out of this mourning thing and start living again."

"I just don't think I'm ready for dating yet," John said with a break in his voice.

"Well, when, John, when? It's been six months."

"I dreamed about her last night." John was getting noticeably upset now. Tears welled up in his eyes.

"I guess this is a bad time to try to get you a date. I'm sorry."

John regained his composure and said, "It's not your fault, David. I mean, the dream itself was great. It was like before we knew she was sick, when we were so full of love and hope. We were even laughing together. Then I woke up, and it was like losing her all over again."

John's voice started to quiver. He stood up and walked over to look out of the window so that David couldn't see the pain and sadness on his face.

"Then I couldn't help remembering the end. I should have known. I should never have talked her into it. I could have waited."

"Come on, John. You are a young man. You were in love. You were engaged, for God's sake. There was nothing wrong with your making love."

"I knew she wasn't ready," John shot in. "She was raised a strict

Christian. She wanted to wait until we were married. And because of me."

John broke down. He cried as if his heart were breaking. David got up, walked over, and put his arm around John's shoulder.

"Come on, here, sit down."

They both sat down on the couch John used for a bed. John cried with his head in his hands while David sat there, his arm still around John's shoulder. As the crying began to subside, David started to speak in a very soft voice.

"It wasn't your fault, John. You just have to get over this guilt trip you are on about this."

David went into his bedroom and came back holding a piece of newsprint.

"I didn't want to show this to you because I didn't even want to bring up the subject, but look at this. You said that Faith lived outside of Denver and went to grammar school and high school there, right? Well, this article shows that the leukemia rate around the Rocky Flats Nuclear Plant is three times the national average. Three times as much! That suburb she lived in was close to Rocky Flats, right? Faith didn't die because you made love a few times. She died because we humans are crazy enough to build atomic bombs and gave greater priority to that than people's health."

"Yeah, I already thought of that, but even if that's true, it's my fault she died feeling guilty."

"No, Man, it's not! It was her parents who laid that guilt trip on you guys. There is nothing wrong with two people in love wanting to have sex."

"I thought I knew what was right and wrong," John said, interrupting David, "but I don't know anything. All I know is that she is gone. Three weeks after we first made love she was diagnosed. Why Faith?"

John was crying again. "Her beautiful hair." After his crying started to subside, David started to talk again.

"You said Faith looked beautiful in the dream."

"Yes "

"Hold on to that, John: hold on to that. I think this dream was supposed to be a blessing to you, John, so you would remember Faith as she was before the sickness. Don't buy into that guilt trip. Don't let her parents' bitterness and blame ruin your life."

David got up and went back to his bowl of cereal.

"You know the latency period for leukemia, John. She obviously actually had it before you even started dating. I met her parents, remember? And I think if you were from a family with money, their attitude toward you would have been much different."

John started to take some deep breaths. He remembered what he learned from the few yoga classes he attended about deep rhythmic breathing helping one calm down and cope with stress, and it seemed to work.

"You've got to cut yourself some slack, John. You really need some time off."

John looked at the clock and realized that he had to leave if he were going to arrive at Ishmael's when he said he would.

"I have to get going," said John.

"If you can wait a few minutes, I'll drop you off."

"No thanks, David. I've had it with inconveniencing you every time I go somewhere just because I can't afford a new transmission. I'll walk."

It was about twelve blocks from John's apartment house to the little apartment in the Fillmore district where Ishmael lived with his mother and two sisters. John was really in the mood to walk today, to walk and think and not really have to be with anyone. He knew that his motives for volunteering to be a big brother were not all unselfish, for he knew he needed to get out of his thoughts of guilt, self-pity and sorrow. To find others less fortunate than himself and help them seemed good advice. Well, today would be the proof of that, he thought to himself. "By God, I'm going to get myself out of this funk," he said, thinking out loud. "David is right. I should start going out on dates again."

The day itself wasn't helping in this cause. There was a heat inversion over the city, and the sky wasn't just gray, it had an ugly brown undertone from the pollution. About half way to Ishmael's, John saw some commotion up ahead. As he neared it, he could see it was a crime scene. He asked some of the onlookers and learned that an eleven year old boy had been shot dead. There had been a running gun battle, and the poor kid had been shot through the throat. An ambulance had taken his body away, but there was still a pool of fresh blood glistening on the sidewalk. Supposedly, the kid had nothing to do with the battle, had been running away from the shooting and was almost a block away from the fighting.

John remembered that what he thought had awakened him from his dream was distant gunfire. Jesus Christ, John thought, what a pathetic and terrible waste. I knew these streets were dangerous.

John had already faced the fact that he would have to go deep into the ghetto to be with Ishmael. He had already been frightened by the looks he had received from some of the young men on his other visits. He had told himself that it would be safe as long as he always went in daylight. The reality that Ishmael had to face these fears every day and night sank deep into his consciousness. It seemed that John's short rally into a more positive head space was at an end.

When John arrived at the fruit stand, he looked into his wallet. Aside from bus fare and a couple of bucks for something to eat later with Ishmael, he had maybe five dollars he could afford to spend on fruit. He bought some apples, oranges and bananas, and a small bunch of grapes. John always brought some fruit or vegetables when he went to visit Ishmael. On his first visit, he found that the kid seemed to subsist on Kool-Aid and junk food. John thought that Ishmael's mother pitifully mismanaged the food stamps and welfare money they all lived on. She always seemed to have cigarettes to smoke, somehow. She would buy white bread and bologna, prepackaged convenience food, chips and snacks, and very little fresh produce. John had already found that his attempts to steer the family finances into more wholesome foods were not welcome. The realization of what an incredible task it would be to just get this one family eating better had already become apparent.

When John arrived Ishmael was sitting in front of the TV eating Cocoa Puffs. John was in no mood to go through another rap on the virtues of whole grains verses junk food with Betty, Ishmael's mother, so he just put the fruit on the table and said hello to everyone, forcing a smile. In a couple of minutes Ishmael grabbed the baseball glove and ball John had given him and they left.

Ishmael seemed to be in as quiet a space as John, and there was little small talk on the bus to Golden Gate Park. They walked along the sidewalk without saying a word until they reached the gate of the arboretum.

"Let's go in here," John suggested, as he turned and walked through. He wasn't really ready for playing catch. John was taking Ishmael to his favorite place in San Francisco, and was very glad he had saved this place until today. He really needed a lift. The two of them talked as they walked about the profusion of birds that hung out around the pond there, but there seemed to be little joy taken by either of them.

They arrived at the entrance of the Isle of Fragrances. It was a small circular walkway with plants planted at waist level in a meandering circle. There were plaques in Braille for the blind, placed near each species, inviting people to touch and smell the lovely scents of the plants. Tucked into a corner was a life-sized statue of St. Francis. Water flowed from his hands into the little pond below, and birds would sit on his hands and drink.

John loved this place. He had found that very few people in the city knew about it, though St. Francis was the city's patron. The walls around the walkway were made from stones taken out of a fourteenth century Franciscan monastery, and John always thought he could feel the spiritual vibrations they had undoubtedly picked up over the centuries. In the middle, a large bell hung without a clapper to prevent people from ringing it.

John always felt comforted in this place and often came here alone to meditate and think. Each time before leaving, he struck the bell with something, because he felt it shouldn't be eternally silent. The bell had a wonderful ring. They sat down on the bench under the old mission bell, and John remembered something he wanted to tell Ishmael.

"Ishmael, what do you know about Dr. Martin Luther King?"

"He got shot dead. Why do you think he got shot?"

"Well, uh." John wasn't really ready for that question. He wanted to tell Ishmael about the time he had visited Dr. King's grave in Atlanta. "I guess I don't really know. I visited his grave in Atlanta. I was really moved."

"What you mean?"

"Well, I really have great respect for Dr. King. I think he was a great man. He was a very spiritual person, and was the champion of nonviolence."

"It didn't seem like nonviolence did him any good. Some white man shot him anyway."

John immediately felt defensive, and before he had time to censor himself blurted out, "Well, the person who shot his mother was black."

This news seemed to shock Ishmael. Great, John thought to himself. What a stupid thing to tell the kid. That's really going to help. I don't need to be defending white people.

"I'm scared my momma will get shot. I'm scared I'm going to get shot, too. I ain't going to be nonviolent. I'm going to get me a gun."

"Nah, Man, you don't want to do that. That's not going to help. That kid that got shot today didn't have a gun."

"What kid that got shot today?"

Jesus, John thought to himself, why had he brought that up? He wanted to show Ishmael that even if he had a gun, he couldn't protect himself from random bullets, but was that going to make a difference to Ishmael? John was frustrated.

"A boy about your age was shot by a stray bullet from a gunfight not far from your apartment this morning. He didn't have a gun or anything. He was just trying to get out of the way. It is the guys doing the shooting who kill people."

"It's better to kill than get killed."

"No it's not, Ishmael. What about your soul?"

"I don't know about no soul, but I know I ain't letting nobody shoot me. I'm going to get me a gun and shoot they ass first."

"Martin Luther King was a man of God," John answered. " He knew the risk he was taking. He believed in nonviolence."

"If he was a man of God, why did God let him get shot? And you said his momma got shot too? I don't believe in God. Why would God let a good man and his momma get shot?"

Emotion welled up in John's throat. He wanted to answer. He wanted to say that God is good, but he just couldn't find the words.

"Don't say that, Ishmael. Who do you think created all this stuff?"

"Nobody."

John had to get up and move. "Come on Ishmael," John said walking away. He didn't ring the bell today. He tried to stay a few steps ahead of Ishmael so the child couldn't see how bummed out he was. He wanted desperately to answer Ishmael's question, to be able to straighten him out, to inspire him. What did he know, he thought to himself as he fought back tears. The only answer he could think of was that everybody dies, but what did that say? God, maybe the kid knows more than I, he thought. I need him more than he needs me. Benevolent white big brother, bullshit! God, I wish I could just be by myself for a while.

"Ishmael, do you know anybody who would like to go to the game?"

"Larry probably. Why?"

"Here, here's the two tickets."

John took all the money he had except his last dollar and gave it to Ishmael.

"I really have to study for an exam today. I've got a big test, and I'm afraid I'll flunk out if I don't."

They walked back to the bus stop in complete silence. John was so anxious to get away from Ishmael that he didn't get on the bus.

"Just take the same bus as we did last time."

Right before getting on, Ishmael turned to John and said, "Can I go by myself and sell the other ticket?"

John was taken back, but after a moment was impressed that Ishmael had bothered to ask him.

"Sure, Ishmael, if that's what you want to do. Be careful."

Ishmael got on the bus with a smile on his face. As it pulled away, John felt guilty about not going to the game with him. Good grief, what am I thinking? I can't just let him go by himself. I'm supposed to be responsible for him. Damn, what a fuckup. And just as bad, I failed the child by not giving him a good answer. Maybe the kid is more right than I am. At least he was honest. I lied to Ishmael just to get rid of him. Now John felt terrible. Guilt and worry added to John's already terrible mood.

John took the next bus that came along. On the seat was a newspaper someone had left. He picked it up, thinking he might find out something about the shooting that morning, but the shooting was so fresh it hadn't made it into the paper yet. He did see a story about a child's being killed, one with a photo as well. A child, fatally shot by a Bosnian Serb sniper, lay in a pool of blood. That child had been deliberately targeted.

John put down the paper as a lump formed in his throat. There is something about blood, John thought. It has the power to deeply touch our emotions. "The world was a veil of tears." His mother had quoted him that in her attempt to help him through Faith's death. He thought back to the funeral, where Faith's parents had made him feel like an unwelcome guest. She had been their only child.

When the bus arrived at Market Street, he transferred to another bus, one he had never before taken. At the end of the line he got off and started walking. He could see the top of a high hill, where there were no houses, just some antennas. He started walking in that direction when a young man walked up to him with a pamphlet.

"You should read this. The time of the rapture is drawing near. Jesus is returning soon."

John stopped for a moment. Today he was in the perfect mood to hear some good news.

"The chosen ones will fly up into the sky to be with Jesus. The rest of humanity will stay here and go through the tribulations described in Revelation. Accept Jesus Christ as your personal Savior now, before it is too late."

"Well, what is going to happen to the rest of humanity?"

"Haven't you ever read *The Book of Revelation*? Those who do not have fellowship with Christ will be left here on the Earth and will be destroyed. The Earth will be covered with bodies. The beast will rule, and all kinds of plagues and stuff will happen."

"What about good Jews or Arabs, or other good people who aren't Christian?" John asked.

"Those who have not accepted Christ will not be a part of the rapture."

"And that's when everyone flies off into the sky to be with Jesus. I find that very hard to believe. And I find it even harder to believe in a God who would destroy everyone left on Earth."

"Oh, God doesn't destroy them. They destroy themselves, as the evil destroys itself."

"Good-hearted Buddhists too?" John asked.

"They all will have had a chance to accept Jesus Christ."

"It still sounds rather negative to me. Anyway, if everything is going to hell here on Earth, and Jesus has to come back to take some people away so that they won't be destroyed, what's the point?"

"It is not something to be sad about. Those who reject Jesus had every chance to accept him, but they didn't. They stayed in rebellion against God, just as they were when Satan led the rebellious souls out of heaven."

"Ah, man, that's hard to buy," John said angrily. "You're telling me that all of us here on Earth are the souls Satan led out of heaven? Look, take your pamphlet back. You're bumming me out even more than I already am. That is the most negative thing I ever heard"

"I'm sorry if I can't explain it right, but it is a good message." the fellow added. "You should read the pamphlet. Accept Jesus as your Savior now, before it is too late."

"I don't understand a God who would save some souls, but let everybody left on Earth, even good people who, according to you, don't pronounce his name right, be destroyed. Nor can I understand or believe in a God who could let anyone burn in hell for eternity. And I sure as hell don't want to believe that we're all the rebellious souls who supposedly followed Satan out of heaven."

"If you would let Jesus into your heart, you would understand," said the fellow.

"Hey, don't you think I want Jesus in my heart? What the hell do I have to do? Beg, cry? Well I've tried all of that and more, Brother." John was getting so worked up he was poking the fellow in the chest. "If you really had something together and knew what the hell you were talking about, you wouldn't need to be out here on the street trying to prove something. If God is willing to let everyone who doesn't agree with YOU be destroyed, you can have Him."

John turned and briskly walked away. He turned back and said, "Jesus is coming back and you're going to fly off into the sky with Him. Give me a fucking break!" He left the fellow speechless.

John just couldn't think of anything uplifting. The world was so full of problems and pollution, injustice and evil, how could a benevolent God have created it? What loving God could allow it to remain so? Could it possibly be true that we are all the ones who followed Satan out of heaven? Well, that would explain a lot, but what a terrible thought.

John had been raised a Catholic, and had always been a rather devout person. He thought that there was a lot of bullshit in the church and all organized religion, and he didn't believe in much of the doctrine, yet he nonetheless felt there was something valuable behind them. He had thought of himself as a rather spiritual person, and he had certainly believed in God, until Faith's illness and death. It was all so horrible. The treatment made her sick and caused her hair to fall out, and she became so emaciated before she died. Then the extra trauma of her parents and the blame trip. Why did she have to tell them that she and John had made love? They were so attached to the idea of their daughter's still being a virgin at her marriage.

John finally reached the top of the hill where he thought, what a scene. To the extreme left, thousands upon thousands of tract houses, all alike. Then Pacific Heights with its mansions, some of them four stories tall, some with walled gardens. The rich always take the high ground.

Below them, the ghetto, with thousands upon thousands of people crowded into a few funky, dirty square blocks. If you're born there, getting out, getting to Pacific Heights, is almost impossible.

Then John looked over to the downtown and its skyscrapers. People pushing paper around keeping track of everybody's money, he thought. The tall buildings certainly look dingy today. The bridges and bay are barely visible, seen through that gray-brown film. The industrial section to the right with noise, and yes, even more pollution pouring into this already disastrous sky.

"God, what a mess," John said out loud. "Why are we killing so many animals and cutting all the trees to produce more of this? Why am I such a failure? I couldn't even help Ishmael. I don't have any faith. Why should I have faith when the world is a mill for suffering? For every rich person there are thousands of poor. There is no justice on this planet! So many people say they are Christians. How can they let people starve? People in this country just want more, more, more, and they spend more on cigarettes or dog food than on helping people, and what they squander gambling could save the world. My adopted family in Bangladesh has to live on two hundred and thirty-five dollars a year. Six people! Nobody here gives a damn about people starving in Bangladesh, but what I really want to know," John's voice was breaking, "what I really want to know is, does God care about them? Floods them all the time. God! Are you there God? Do you care? Oh God."

John's voice choked, he became overwhelmed with emotion. The repressed feelings of days, of months, all spilled out, and John fell weeping to his knees. He reached into his pocket and took out the one present he had received from Faith, a Swiss Army Knife she gave him because he had told her how much he enjoyed watching McGuiver, who never used a gun, and solved all the worlds problems with his little knife.

"Yeah, like that could really happen," John voiced sarcastically.

He opened the big blade on the knife, and his mind flashed to Juliet taking her life with Romeo's knife. Perhaps he could solve his problem.The fact that it seemed an attractive option scared him to his depths. Though it seemed to have been lurking in the back of his mind, he had never before seriously thought about killing himself.

"The whole world has been flirting with suicide for the last fifty years. Or should I say murder, because no matter how they do it, they'll take all the creatures down with them. They didn't have the guts to do it with nukes, so now they're going to just commit ecocide, self-poisoning, the slow painful way."

John put the knife to his wrist. "I can't face another tomorrow." He collapsed back onto his haunches, with tears returning to his eyes.

"Oh, God, help me. I want to believe. I want so to believe that You are good. I want to have faith. I want so to know that there is a reason for all this suffering, that there is some good behind it all. We aren't just born and it's all luck and then we die. God, if You are real, help me to believe. Help me to have faith in You, in myself. Why did You take my Faith?" John sobbed. "God, I want so much to have my faith back."

John buried his face into his hands and wept with a heart-rending intensity. Suddenly, he felt different. Strange. His crying stopped as he wondered what was happening. Maybe he was going to faint. Then in a moment John was transported to a world of brilliant light, intense swirling colors, and transcendental sounds. His body seemed filled with an amazing ecstasy. Infinite vibrations of pulsating color and energy swirled around and through him. Sounds such as no human ear has ever heard filled his being. It could have been an instant, it could have been an eternity, as there seemed to be no time, no up, no down. Just an ongoing, infinitely unfolding experience. Then the vibrations began to form back into shapes and a vista, and he was again kneeling on the hilltop; but everything, however, was different.

BACK TO THE FUTURE

John had been on the campus at Berkeley before, so he knew where the library was. As he started walking toward it, he could see that the University had changed very little. There were even more races represented than before. Caucasians were in a minority. Many of the students had on jeans and T-shirts, not unlike in his time, but many had clothes similar to Crystal's that looked hand-made. The weave of the cloth seemed rougher and the colors more muted. Some of the students had on clothing that looked like native garb from other countries. When John reached the plaza, he saw a young man standing on a box with a small circle of people gathered around, listening to him. The fellow had on colorful, well-worn clothing that looked hand-made, and he had bare feet. John decided to listen in for a while.

"It is time to end our addiction to the monetary exchange system. It is time to get out of clothing made by soulless, mindless robots!"

"Not any more mindless than you," someone heckled back with a smile.

"To be fully human, to fill our lives, bodies and spirits with energy and life force, we need to abandon mass produced merchandise, to abandon the concept of monetary exchange. Create the things that give your heart joy, with love and artistry, and share, not trade them, generously with those who need them. Let go the game of accumulating credits and live in the moment. Take your account bracelets off and throw them away. Join our movement to make all mass transportation and communication free." The young man stepped down to a mixture of cheers and jeers.

Then a young woman in a brightly colored business suit stepped up onto the box and said with a smile. "Brilliant logic. We eliminate the possibility of taxation yet we make all mass transportation free. How does he believe that can be accomplished? Well, I for one do not believe that an army of dedicated civil servants will spring out of the ground and willingly run all our communication and transportation equipment for free for very long. And even if they would, do you believe the systems would run well indefinitely with volunteer labor? I can see it now. Without that credit transfer to keep them disciplined and responsible, we'd have anarchy. Our subs and trains would fall into disrepair, and people wouldn't show up for work."

"Not true," the barefoot fellow piped back in. "In Toronto, where the Com-Union has taken over, everything is working great."

"Sure, one demonstration project has worked for a couple of years. But we all know that they have had help from all over North America. It is going to be different if all these services are converted to Com-Union personnel everywhere at once, and no one can expect help from outside his own areas. It is foolish to expect volunteer labor to run everything efficiently forever. It is just not going to work. People have a right to fair exchange for their labor, and there is nothing sinful about it."

Berkeley is still a haven for radicals and free speech, John thought to himself. It appears that there is some kind of a movement to make everything free. That sounds a lot like the old hippie ideal. John remembered the stories his cousin Bob had told him about the anti-war protests here in Berkeley during the Vietnam War. He described the fear and anger the students had at an army of police with gas masks, clubs, and shields shooting tear gas all over the plaza and Telegraph Avenue. John wondered if there were still wars and decided that would be the first question he would research in the library. The speechmaking seemed to be over, so John decided to stroll around the plaza and check out the other activities.

He came upon a little push cart with a young lady selling tofu sandwiches and lemonade. She seemed to be doing a brisk business. Tofu! It was the most maligned food in the country when I left, John thought to himself with a smile. It reminded him that he was hungry, but he had no account to use. I wish that free stuff were happening already, he thought. John walked on down the line of street vendors, and he could see only one of them was selling anything with meat. He figured that he should head to the library.

John walked into the library and found it was totally different.

There were no books. There were hundreds of little booths with computer terminals and fairly large flat screens. Most of them were occupied by students, some of whom were reading off the screens and some had their little ear phones on. In the center of the library was a large square desk with what looked to be a large amount of computer equipment. He went over and stood by the desk to see if he could learn how to access the information he wanted. One of the ladies behind the desk was talking to a student and he heard her say; "I don't know why you can't find Shelly. You must not be pronouncing it right. Ask for Nineteenth Century British poets."

The young man nodded his head and walked away. John stepped up to the counter.

"I'd like a history book and the World Almanac for last year."

"World History?"

"Yes."

"What period."

"The Twenty-first Century."

The librarian answered, "Well, have you tried just asking for it?" she said somewhat condescendingly.

John stood there for a moment with the librarian looking at him. "I don't have an earphone."

"Just keep the volume low."

"I don't know how to use your computers."

"What do you mean? What's to know?"

John wasn't sure how to reply, so he turned around and walked away. She can't even imagine someone who can't use a computer, he thought. He found an empty booth and sat down in front of the computer. He could see where one might insert a disk or plug in an earphone, but he didn't see a power switch. He sat for a minute, puzzled, then he figured that he should watch someone and see if he could learn how to run these machines. John stood back up and went to stand quietly behind someone. After a minute or two, he heard the fellow talking to the computer.

"Voice activated," he said out loud. The fellow turned around and put his finger to his lips. He went back to his work and after another minute turned back around to look at John, who smiled and moved on.

Just then John saw a young lady sit down at a station and say, "Computer on."

"Aha," John thought. He went back and sat down in front of the computer screen and said, "Computer on." The computer immediately turned on and said "Good afternoon, would you like to be addressed by name?"

This is great, thought John, and he responded, "sure, I'm John."

"What would you like me to access for you, John?"

"How about the World Almanac for twenty-ninety-four?" John answered as that book came first into his mind. Soon he had the index for the World Almanac for 2094. Pretty cool, John thought, overwhelmed by the possibilities. What to look at first?

John remembered back to the last time he had used the almanac, when he and his dad were researching crop production figures. His dad was trying to make money investing in the commodity market in grain futures contracts. Having just finished a project on world hunger with his church youth group, John had been shocked to discover that each year Americans fed billions and billions of bushels of grains to animals, eighty-plus percent of the grain that was grown, while millions of people were going hungry or starving around the world. He decided to look at the crop production figures, and asked the computer to give him the crop report for 2094. Sure enough, the computer instantly brought up the figures.

"Could I compare these to 1993?" Those figures were instantly put next to 2094.

It seemed that America produced more wheat, a good bit more soybeans, and vastly less corn then they had one hundred years earlier. The whole Midwest used to be covered with corn, John thought. What had happened? He looked at the figures for the number of people engaged in farming and saw that it had grown considerably. When he saw the production figures for meat, he understood better. Beef, pork, and poultry production figures had shrunk considerably compared to in the past. Looking back to 2000, he saw that meat production was now less than twenty percent of what it was then. Turkey production was still a half or so of past figures. So, John mused, they are no longer mining the Midwest for corn to feed to animals. If they weren't growing all that corn, then what is growing there?

John asked for life expectancy charts. Incredible, he thought. Life spans had leveled, then fallen slightly for a time around the 2020s, but had begun to rise again in the middle forties. They had risen steadily from then until the 2094 figures. They now stood at 87 years for women and 85 for men. We still don't live as long as women, John noted, but the gap has been narrowed, and look at those figures! Those are world figures. Now that's incredible. The

United States of America's figures were slightly higher, with an average life-span of 89 years. That's about 14 years longer that it was in 1993, John realized.

Looking at the mortality charts, John saw that deaths from cancer had risen steadily through the end of the last century, peaking in 2035, then leveling off for a decade before they started to plummet. Only one person in ten died of cancer now, he saw. Heart disease related deaths were now down to about a quarter of the year 2000 figures, and accidents were way down as a cause of death. Suicides were way, way down. Automobile related deaths had fallen until about the middle of the century and now were no longer listed as a separate category. That surely makes sense, he pondered. Mass transit was now saving tens of thousands of lives a year. What fabulous progress! It looks as if people are eating more soy foods and way less meat. So it really does work to save lives. I wonder if I'll ever be able to tell David? He was so sure that most people would never give up meat and start eating soy foods.

For a while John got thoughtful. Remembering David brought John back to the realization of his present situation. What is going on? How is this happening? Will I be here forever now? Is this some kind of vision I'm still having? A dream? Yes, that is possible. That's a good theory, he thought, but this is vastly longer, more complex and much more real than any dream I have ever had. I'll try giving myself a good pinch. It hurt. Probably that theory was out anyway. And that ecstasy experience, what was that?

John got a cold chill when he entertained the thought that he might indeed be dead. He remembered the knife. What had happened to that knife? He didn't remember actually cutting himself.

Could this be… heaven?

John thought that it would be very much like heaven if he could have heaven be any way he wanted. What could be better than a regenerated world and humanity living in peace and harmony?

Well, how much harmony is there? John wondered. He asked for the crime statistics for 2094. The murder rate for the whole of the USA was 1,396 last year. Well, there is still murder, but what an incredible improvement. Some cities had almost that high a murder rate in 1992. All crime categories were amazingly low compared to the past, except white collar crimes. While many fewer than before, they were still significant. It is not perfect here yet, but good and getting better all the time, John thought.

The figures for education were also dramatically improved.

Ninety-three percent finished high school, and seventy-seven percent finished college, art, or trade school. That's a great achievement, John thought. How did they turn that around? God, life is so much better now. Without the stress of all that crime, without the worry about pollution or atomic annihilation, people must be much more secure and relaxed. Folks do seem far cheerier and healthier now. His mind was about to boggle.

John got up and walked over to a drinking fountain he had spied. He needed a trip to the rest room, so he found it and relieved himself. That's one thing that hasn't changed very much, he thought. They had motion activated toilets and faucets some places in my day.

He went back to the computer and asked it for a world history book for the Twenty-First Century, and soon he had an index of history files to chose from. He picked one that seemed to be the most comprehensive. He looked at the time on the bottom of the screen and saw it said 2:45. Oh my goodness, he thought, I don't have much time to look into this. He started by looking up what was the last war in the index. It was in 2044 and had been an war of independence for the Kurds. The United Nations had become involved, and settled it by holding elections, and the nation of Kurdistan was established after the results were in. John quickly scanned through the following years and found no sign of any other wars. There has been over 50 years of world peace. Tears again flooded John's eyes, tears of joy and happiness. He felt the bliss again, but not as strong, without the lights and sounds, and it only lasted a few seconds.

Not having much time left, John went to the period when Crystal said there had been a world-wide crisis. Sure enough, times had been quite difficult in the early part of the Twenty-first Century. He discovered that America had fought a war in Iraq and Afghanistan after an incredible terrorist attack in New York that had brought down the World Trade Center's twin towers. John was skipping rapidly through early Twenty-First Century history. There had been a massive nuclear meltdown in Japan after a huge earthquake and tsunami. I knew it! John thought to himself. When I heard about Diablo Canyon I thought, what kind of fools would build a reactor at the oceanside on an earthquake fault? Obviously they did the same stupid thing in Japan, even putting many reactors at one site. I bet there were some powerful lessons learned about power -political, financial and nuclear - because of that fiasco. God! It wasted a large part of Northern Japan and caused a massive evacuation, then migration out of the area. There was an earthquake with a tsunami in California that caused massive damage and a reactor meltdown. Give me a break, John thought. Even after the disaster in Japan, they didn't shut down nuclear power? Incredible! John discovered that there were hundreds of thousands of nuclear refugees who had lost everything in the meltdown, yet were never compensated until they organized, demonstrated and protested for years, sometimes even threatening terrorism.

John found a section on global warming and climate change. This should be interesting . He had been an early advocate for preventing global warming. The planet had really heated up, and climate change had caused numerous droughts and extreme weather events. The melting of polar ice in Greenland and the Antarctic had raised the level of the oceans. The need for drastic change was recognized, and at a World Conference on the Environment, strict rules were passed by most countries, but not the United States.

John knew it was getting close to three o'clock, so he skipped ahead a few pages. Though it had nothing to do with the 9/11 attack, America had invaded Iraq and fought a long and bloody war there. John skipped ahead. Strife in the Middle East had caused a disruption of oil coming out of the Persian Gulf for a couple of years. There was a massive world wide depression, and the chaos of the Middle East seemed to be spreading to the streets of the developed world. He looked down at the time and saw 2:58. John was totally fascinated, but turned off the computer and went back to the librarian.

"Is this the main desk?"

"Of course."

He took a position close to the desk to wait for Crystal. Three o'clock came, then ten after, and he was very worried that he would never see Crystal again. He didn't know her name or address or anything. What difference did that make, he thought, if she doesn't want to see me anyhow? Who could blame her? It does seem like a ridiculous story. I know I'd never believe it.

Just as John was preparing to leave, he saw Crystal walk in with another fellow. They walked up to John, and Crystal introduced him to a gentleman named Barry Rogers, who she said was a professor of history. She suggested they step outside, and they sat down on a bench not far from the front door.

"Barry is going to ask you some questions about the time period you claim to be from."

John could tell from her tone that she was more skeptical now than when they had parted.

"OK, John, who was president George H. W. Bush's Vice President?"

"Dan Quayle."

"That's very good. No one gets that one. OK, a couple of years before you say you left the past there was a war in the Middle East. The United States led the fighting against Iraq, and the operation was called Desert Storm. There was another operation that was a predecessor to that one. What was it called?"

"Why, Desert Shield. Professor, can I ask you a question?"

"I guess that would be fair."

"I was just looking at a history book for the Twenty-first Century and I was thrilled to see that there hasn't been a war in fifty years. Is that right?"

"Yes. There was a wonderful worldwide celebration last year to commemorate it." Barry hesitated for a moment. He rolled his eyes and said, "But you knew that. What shall I ask you? Here's one: the man elected Vice President in 1992 had written a book on ecology. What was it called?"

"*Earth in the Balance, Ecology and the Human Spirit*. I read it. I thought that I probably knew more about ecology than Al Gore, but I was impressed with the breadth and depth of the book, and I learned a lot. I can't say the Clinton Administration is doing much about it though."

Barry looked a little agitated. "This doesn't really prove anything, Crystal. He said he's been in there studying history. He probably looked all this information up."

"In less than an hour?" John interjected.

"Look, I have to go. Got a three thirty class. Good-bye Crystal, John." Barry got up and walked away.

"Thanks anyway, Barry."

"I have a lot of questions I'd like to have asked him," Said John.

"He's just annoyed because he told me he could stump you for sure. John... I just don't know what to think of you."

"Please try to put aside your doubts, Crystal. I need a friend in this wonderful new world. I swear I am not trying to put anything over on you. I know it's unbelievable, but it's true."

"I want to believe you, John. I feel your sincerity. Come on, let's go."

John got up and followed her to the bike rack. They started to walk together down one of the paths.

"I'll be happy to push the bike for you, Crystal."

"That's OK, John. It's practically a part of me."

They walked quietly for a while and then John spoke. "I learned a lot in the library. People live much longer than before. They eat much less meat. I saw a girl selling tofu in the plaza. Do people eat a lot of soy foods now?"

"It is one of our staple foods. It is good for the soil, because soybeans fix nitrogen"

"There are more people farming now."

"Yeah, we just couldn't sustain the agriculture of your day, using many calories of polluting fossil fuel for every calorie of food produced. And all that meat production created a large part of the greenhouse gases that were driving up the temperatures. We needed to plant billions of trees, and the only place we could was on the farmland that was growing all of that feed grain."

"And the way they grew it, added John, "pumping in chemical fertilizers and never putting back any organic matter was more like mining than farming. I knew that couldn't last. But people are, I mean were, so attached to their meat."

"The climate changes created a period where there were great famines," said Crystal. "Oil had become so expensive and food costs so great that the poor of the world were starving while the bulk of the grains being produced was still being fed to animals. It was totally immoral. A world wide movement led to people's eating much less meat so humans could eat."

"It was so obvious that the American lifestyle was very unhealthy," replied John, "and that excessive meat consumption was a large part of the problem. You couldn't watch TV without being bombarded with commercials for double and even triple bacon cheeseburgers. David and I, he was my roommate, called them triple bypass burgers."

"Nowadays people want food that is lovingly produced," Crystal continued. "Many people, even in the city, grow gardens for themselves or for barter. People don't usually work at just one job, like in your time. It is common for someone to work at home using a computer and grow a little garden. Food does take more of our income now, but it isn't subsidized by the exploitation of the Earth or immigrant labor. Many farming areas were almost completely destroyed by droughts and dust, caused by what you called mining the soil. That's a good term for it. Those areas had to be planted in trees anyway to end the dust storms."

"I was telling David that people should eat more soy foods just yesterday. He said it would be a hard sell."

"When the Earth was going through the crisis it became apparent that we couldn't continue exploiting Her the way we had been just to put meat on the table three times a day. It had been well established that heavy meat eating was unhealthful and took years off one's lifespan. Then it was linked to mass starvation due to the poor not being able to afford the grains the wealthier nations were still feeding to animals. There were several pandemics in the early part of the century that were linked to the poultry and swine industries. After the enormous death toll they caused, large scale poultry and hog farms were limited severely. That also eliminated the source of most flu strains as well. We rarely have a bad flu season anymore. Now meat is much more expensive, and hardly anyone eats it more that three times a week."

"Well that's a big change. I thought of that back in my time because the CDC used to have people in China to keep track of new flu strains as they mostly came from swine production there. David and I talked about how much disease could be eliminated just by people not eating pork, what with it also being a huge source of saturated fat. I noticed that turkeys were the only category that didn't plummet," John said.

"Yes, people just didn't want to give up the Thanksgiving or Christmas turkey. They are raised mostly outdoors and there is a limit on the number a farm can have at any time. I ate it myself until I was fourteen. Now most people usually only eat meat on holidays or Sundays, or at least only a few times a week. Dairy products are still eaten, but they are not as large a part of people's diet."

"Like ice cream?"

"Well, ice cream and frozen yogurt probably account for much of the milk usage, and people still like cheese. I haven't had any of that stuff since I was sixteen. Do you eat meat?"

"I haven't totally quit, but I was heading in that direction. The restaurant I worked at to pay my way through med school didn't even have a vegetarian entree. Good tips though. I did feel like a hypocrite working there, but maybe med school itself was worse. Is cancer still treated with chemotherapy?"

"Drugs are used for some kinds of cancer. The chemicals go specifically to the cancers and don't effect the rest of the body. It is not like it was many years ago, when sometimes the treatment itself would kill you," she replied.

"Or make you wish you were dead. God, that's great! I saw that cancer rates were way down."

"It is still a hard ailment to cure. The best way to deal with cancer is to prevent it, and we've learned a lot about how do that. Also, when scientists discovered the genes that caused susceptibility to different cancers, most people chose to have children that didn't carry such genetic risks."

"How did they do that?"

"With donated genetic material instead of using their own eggs or sperm," she answered. "That helped eliminate almost all inherited ailments and put an end to a tremendous amount of human suffering. There are still people who have their own offspring, even knowing that there is a high probability of the child's having problems. That is a high price to pay for having a baby that looks like you. It is frowned on to have a child that will have a short and painful life or be a burden to society but people are still free to do it."

When reached to the Eucalyptus Grove John said, "This has always been my favorite place on this campus."

"So you've been here before."

"Yes. David's girlfriend used to attend school here. I really wonder if I'll ever see them again. This whole experience is truly unbelievable to me, too, Crystal. I don't understand it at all, except that when it changed, I was down on my knees praying to God to restore my faith - in God - in there being some good purpose to life - in myself. This wonderful future without war, with less crime and disease, with people seeming to live in harmony with each other and the Earth, it is an answer to my prayer."

"You must not have lost all your faith, or you wouldn't have been down on your knees praying. Would you like to stop here for a while?"

"Yes, very much. One of my fondest memories is of an hour Faith and I spent here together waiting for David and Mary. We were so in love and happy. I haven't been here or even to Berkeley since. The trees are much bigger than I remember. A hundred years can make a huge difference. They were great then but they are fabulous now."

They sat down together on a bench and looked at each other quietly. John thought she was one of the prettiest women he had ever seen. Delicate features and a small beauty mark on the left side of her chin. Her eyes were a blue green. Her figure not spectacular, but very trim, athletic and quite nice. It wasn't her good looks as much as the vibrant energy she seemed to radiate that made her so attractive. He felt strongly that he had known her, or that she was very familiar in some way, but he didn't think it was her looks.

"You are a healer and a teacher?" John asked. "You don't look old enough to be a professor at Berkeley."

"I just turned 22 last February. Though I never actually graduated myself, they wanted me to teach because they recognized that I have a unique ability to be able to pass on my healing gifts to others. It was a major concession for them to let me teach a class without my even having a degree, and a professor is there in the classroom with me. So how old are you, John? And what is your birthday?"

I'm 23, and I was born on March eighth, 1970. Gee, I guess that makes me 125," John said with a smile."

Crystal laughed a sweet little laugh and then added, "So you are a Pisces."

"Are you into astrology?" He asked.

"A little. I just thought your horoscope might have some explanation for your phenomenon, or perhaps even prove your story. If you could tell me about your Twentieth Century horoscope, I'd be very impressed. I'm an Aquarius with Scorpio rising and a Pisces Moon. Do you know anything about your horoscope?"

"I'm afraid not, Crystal."

"I really do want to believe you, John. Perhaps looking for proof is not the answer." She spoke quietly into her computer bracelet, then looked back at John. "Just tell me, John. Are you telling me the truth? Are you really from the past?"

"Yes, Crystal. I will never lie to you."

She looked down at her PC, then back at John and added, "My PC has a voice stress lie detector. It is pretty reliable, and you pass. My intuition was telling me the same thing. It doesn't prove you are from the past, but it does confirm my feelings that you are sincere in believing that you're from the past."

"Crystal, I don't know anything about this time. I am not just some deluded person."

"I'm not saying you are, John. Please forgive me if I implied that. It is a totally amazing concept for you to have just turned up after over a hundred years have passed. Maybe I'm afraid people will think I'm deluded if I believe you."

"I can understand that, Crystal, and it is a lot to ask."

They sat silently looking at each other. John so much wanted

Crystal to believe him, but he realized that he could not blame her in the least for her doubts. He felt such gratitude that she would even try, and that she hadn't already told him to get lost. Maybe she didn't because she thought he was some poor mentally sick soul whom she should try to help. He smiled at her, feeling admiration and a strong sense of love. She returned his smile, and joy permeated his being.

"So you were just born with this gift of healing?"

"Yes. Floyd Farmer, the best psychic in the Bay area, told me that I was given the gift of healing because in my last life I died a tragic and somewhat unjust death as a result of mass karma. I had contracted an illness that caused great suffering, and my death was very painful. It was because humanity needed to learn an important and powerful lesson. He thought it was about radiation. God knows we needed to learn about that. Unfortunately, many people had to suffer and die before we learned that radioactive elements should stay deep in the earth where they belong. Since it wasn't my personal karma to die young and tragically, I have been given the gift of healing to balance that out."

"I'm not real sure I understand karma, but isn't it things that you created that has to happen to you? How could something happen to you that wasn't your karma?"

"Group karma is real, and if we collectively create karma that will affect a random number of innocent people, then it has to happen. It is a bit like the story of Job in the Bible. Did you ever read it?"

"Yes. But I don't remember it well," replied John.

"Satan convinced God to let him test Job to prove that Job was only spiritual because he was so fortunate, and his life was so good. Even though Job had done nothing to deserve it, God allowed Satan to inflict a lot of dire difficulties on him. Job didn't understand why so much tragedy was happening and never believed he deserved it, but he didn't curse God because of it either. He prospered even more greatly after his trials. It seems that his attitude, accepting his lot without blaming God or himself, was a good one for making his life work well."

"Perhaps, though karma is real, that's not all that's going on," Crystal continued. "We live in both a physical and a spiritual universe, and each has rules. Cause and effect work on both levels, but somewhat differently. Within the physical world, chance might very well exist. We can't expect that the only things that happen to us are the ones we create. The rest of the universe is creating all the time as well. Bad things can happen to good people. In those cases, it is balanced by some equally great good. Everything is ultimately balanced perfectly. It is good to realize that just because something hard or painful happens to someone, it doesn't necessarily mean that they are somehow guilty or deserving of it. I don't really know the answers to life's great mysteries. I'm just searching for meaning and understanding, like all people, and these are the best explanations I have. Whatever my past karma was, I am so grateful for the ability to help others heal. It is a tremendous joy. I'm also very grateful for the ability to pass this gift on to others."

"Amazing concepts, Crystal. And you have a hard time believing me?" They both laughed. "All kidding aside, those are some very interesting ideas. So you believe in karma. Do you believe in reincarnation?"

"Yes. What are your beliefs, John?"

"I was raised a Catholic, but I don't believe much of it any more. I can't accept limbo or papal infallibility, or eternal damnation, for instance. Back in my time, we were in the middle of a population crisis that fueled all the other problems we had, and the Pope wouldn't even let people use birth control."

"I believe that changed early this century when many people couldn't have their own children without passing on genetic weaknesses. There was a great pressure from population growth as well."

"Well that's good," said John. "Most of my science professors were materialists who believed that when you're dead, it is all over. I don't like that idea, but I have a hard time believing what the church teaches. Eternal damnation has always seemed a sinister concept to me, and I find it difficult to believe that one. What kind of justice is that? One mistake and you suffer forever? No human parent would burn his own child to death, no matter what the kid had done. I certainly can't believe God would burn his children forever. I don't think there is really a devil either. Do you take the Bible seriously when it has the devil talking to God in the beginning of the book of Job?"

"No, I think the story, like the devil, is a metaphor. Who was there to report the conversation between Satan and God?" Crystal answered. "But it does, I believe, illustrate spiritual truths."

"I can relate to that," added John. "If the devil is a metaphor, what does he represent?"

"Perhaps the material side of life, or our ego, the part of us that thinks it is a separate being."

47

"Then is God just a metaphor, too? Does the God concept just represent the part of us that is eternal and spiritual?" asked John.

"Sounds good to me," Crystal said with a smile. "Except God is not a part. God is everything."

John thought for a moment, then got a smile on his face and spoke.

"I have thought about reincarnation, but I can't say I believe or even understand it. My fiancée Faith, died of leukemia that might have been caused by radiation. She went to school and lived very close to the Rocky Flats nuclear weapons plant."

"Rocky Flats?"

"Yes, why?"

"It is one of the larger wasted areas, unusable due to radioactive contamination."

"Faith's death really changed my belief in God. I just couldn't believe a good God allowed such a sweet, wonderful person to suffer so much and die so young. She was so idealistic. She was going to be a doctor, too, and planned to help the downtrodden. She was incredibly generous. It seemed totally unfair and unjust. I still wanted to believe, but I just couldn't. Yet not having faith in God was terrible. So tell me about reincarnation, Crystal. How does it work?"

"I'm so sorry, John. It sounds as if your Faith was a very beautiful soul. I can't say that anyone knows for sure how reincarnation works. I believe God made death a mystery for a reason, and it is supposed to stay that way."

"It's supposed to be a mystery?"

"I think that is why there is good evidence for the materialist who thinks it is all over when the brain dies, and equally compelling evidence, past life memories and near death experiences, not to mention the word of many great spiritual teachers, that suggests we have souls that survive our deaths. We're not supposed to know for sure. If it weren't a mystery, why, then we wouldn't really have free will."

"I need to think about that one for a minute." There was a pause for several seconds. "I don't quite understand what you mean. Interesting concept, that death has to be a mystery in order for us to have free will, but I don't see it. Wouldn't it be better if we knew about our past lives and knew karma was real. Then people would be good," added John.

"Perhaps so, but then a new life wouldn't give a soul a really new opportunity. That is the wonder of death, that it can give advancement to a soul who had a successful life from a soul growth standpoint, and give a fresh start in a new environment to a failure. I think God does want us to know about karma, but not necessarily about any past life. Also, maybe God wants us to do good out of love, not to manipulate karma. Perhaps the faith and love we develop without having any assurance of karmic rewards, perhaps that faith and love are the point of it all."

John was quiet and thoughtful for a moment.

"Could you explain a little more?"

"I'll tell you what I believe and why."

"Please," said John.

"I believe in soul evolution. I think that our individual souls emerge from the matrix of collective soul life in the minerals, plants, and lesser creatures, and that is another of life's great mysteries. I believe that our souls evolve, just as the physical vehicles that they inhabit evolve. We experience countless lifetimes as lesser creatures and animals, learning to manifest more and more complex bodies, developing our soulware, as we call it. We finally evolve to a level where our souls can start understanding the results of our actions, perhaps even before we get human bodies. Once we can reason what results will follow our acts, we come under the influence of karma. Karma is God's way of teaching us and keeping everything fair. Everything that we create we will ultimately have to experience, if not in this particular life, in another. Karma tries to manifest quickly, and in a way that will help us to connect it with the act that created it, so we can readily learn the lesson. Some of us think that one sign of spiritual advancement is that our karma becomes almost instantaneous. God's grace can intervene to change or mitigate our negative karma."

"How does that work?"

"Perhaps a person creates a lot of good karma too, or maybe some very evolved soul helps him with it. God isn't vengeful and doesn't want us to suffer. God is just and wants us to learn, and the main lesson being taught is that what we do to others, we are ultimately doing to ourselves. I agree with you that people are better off if they know about karma. Grace is also real, and grace keeps karma from being totally fatalistic, or there would be an endless chain of negativity from every bad act. It is also a manifestation of God's love for us."

"Would having faith in God's grace through Jesus Christ work?" asked John.

"Of course, because our faith is God's grace. It is our change of heart, though, that allows us to have that faith. Grace and faith can come in many ways, through many religions and traditions."

After a moment of silence, John exclaimed, "I think I get it!"

Crystal continued. "After our souls have evolved as far as they can in animal forms, and probably after association with humans as pets or work animals, we are ready for human bodies. That is a great gift, because these bodies have great powers, and in these bodies we can come to know God. Then evolution changes from physical to spiritual. We slowly learn the difficult lessons of human existence. We learn to overcome the greed, selfishness and ignorance that would allow us to countenance the suffering of others. Finally, after many lifetimes and many karmic lessons, we evolve to the place where we can manifest the mental and spiritual powers necessary for the completion of our soul's journey. It takes a great deal of psychic energy to realize God. Psychic powers are never given to someone who would misuse them. Have you ever wished someone harm or maybe even dead?"

"I guess harm, in a moment of anger."

"So it would have been a tragedy if you had had a high level of psychic power then. Do you see what I mean?"

There was a silence for a moment. Then John replied, "Yeah, I think so. Well, what is the completion of our evolution?"

"When we have exhausted our karma, and by having surrendered the fruits of all our activities to God, stopped creating more. When we have gained enough spiritual power to be able to handle the much greater energy, and we have seen through the illusion of our separateness, we are ready, when we want, to consciously surrender our individuality. Individuality is never taken away from us; it has to be consciously given up. At least that is what I believe. Then we become one with God."

"And what happens then?"

"Well, I haven't actually reached that point yet, so I can't answer authoritatively, but I believe we experience God's eternal bliss, knowledge, and peace. So, I believe reincarnation gives life justice through the workings of karma. It also gives life a noble purpose, the conscious evolution back to the oneness from which we all emerged. And best of all, this philosophy gives that wondrous end to every creature, even the humblest. No souls are lost forever, and every being will ultimately see, and consciously be, God."

There was another even longer silence. John was very impressed.

"That answers many of my questions. It makes a lot of sense. I have to admit, it makes much more sense than the eternal damnation and heaven theory."

"People can and do experience heaven and hell worlds, or planes, in between lifetimes. Maybe we can work out some of our karma that way. Back in your century, scientists discovered that they could affect the outcome of their experiments by their expectations. Perhaps we can affect our after-death experience by our beliefs. For instance, some people believe that we can only obtain final liberation into God-consciousness while in a human body. Maybe that's true for them. Some believe we are offered liberation in the form of the clear white light after every life, otherwise, our desires draw us back into incarnation. I don't know, though. These are just my favorite theories. It could be that there are almost infinite possibilities awaiting us after death and in our future evolution. The only thing I'm relatively sure of is that it's supposed to be a mystery."

"What religion is that, Crystal?

"Aldous Huxley called it the perennial philosophy, because the idea that we are one with the ultimate - God, if you like - and that the end goal of our existence is to realize that oneness, is the heart of all religion, and has sprung up independently in many cultures and many forms. It is a very old philosophy."

"I think I like your philosophy, Crystal, and it might hold the answer to why I came here and met you."

They sat looking at each other for a long time. John experienced a feeling he had never had before, nor did he think he could describe it, except as a sense of wonder. He did once again flash that he could be dead and in heaven. It didn't change anything though. He was feeling great love for Crystal and happiness at being with someone who could just somehow be his Faith. He wanted to believe her ideas about reincarnation so he could believe she were Faith, and he also felt great inspiration because of the beauty and power of the concepts. What a beautiful philosophy, and what a different one. Life has a purpose. Everyone is saved; everyone sees God, even the animals!

Crystal spoke. "I know what you are thinking, John. And I just don't know. You do seem very familiar. I'll admit, when I first saw you, I thought I knew you, but I couldn't remember from when. Then you told me your wild story. I just...I just don't know what to think."

Would you like to see a picture of Faith?"

"I don't know, John. Sure, I guess so," Crystal said hesitatingly.

John took a picture out of his wallet and handed it to Crystal.

"Oh, she is very lovely, John." Then Crystal realized what she had said, yet was too embarrassed to change is to was. After a moment she said, "Such soft and sweet brown eyes. She does look a little familiar. Yes." Crystal looked up at John with an amazed expression on her face. "She looks a little like the angel in my dream."

"Wow!" said John.

She handed the picture back to John, looking very thoughtful. After a long moment, Crystal stood up. "We should go. Are you hungry? You haven't had much to eat this century," she said with a smile that broke the ice.

"Yes, I am." John beamed brightly as he got up and followed Crystal.

CRYSTAL'S HOME

As they walked to the subus Crystal told John more about the new world. John learned that there were no gasoline or diesel motors used anymore, not even in lawn mowers.

"All engines that were causing pollution were outlawed after a phase-out period. By 2025, all manufacturing that released or created polluting toxins was outlawed. We were in the middle of a terrible crisis, with many drought-caused famines, dislocation due to rising sea levels, and extreme weather had become normal. There were also some terrible epidemics."

"What ever happened with AIDS?" John asked.

"It became very widespread and killed millions of people. Better ways of coping with AIDS were discovered, so that not everyone who contracted it would die within a few years. More and more people were leading almost normal lives though they were infected. Humanity finally learned that the best way to deal with AIDS and all of the sexually transmitted diseases was by taking personal responsibility for sex and not engaging in practices that created disease or unwanted pregnancies and abortions."

"You mean confining sex to marriage?"

"At least keeping it to committed, monogamous relationships or using protective devices. It ended up being a very positive change because the loose sexual morality of the late Twentieth Century was causing many more problem than just AIDS. It also created poverty and crime. One change that really helped was the Coming of Age Ceremony movement."

"What is a Coming of Age Ceremony?" he asked her.

"Every baby born into this world needs two parents who love

each other and want a child together, or it just doesn't work out very well much of the time. People started having Coming of Age Ceremonies when their children got to the age where they could create a life. Ceremonies that were all about respecting the power to procreate. There already were Bar Mitzvahs and Confirmation Ceremonies in our culture, but they had left the central issue of coming to that age out of the teaching. The fact that at puberty one is capable of creating a baby. I am attending one this evening. Have you heard of Confucius, John?"

"I've heard of him and have seen a few quotes, but never read anything he wrote."

"He wrote the commentaries for the *I Ching, The Book of Changes*. Twenty-seven centuries ago he taught that the family was the backbone of civilization. If there is no order in the family, there will be no order in society."

"So there isn't any extramarital sex any more?"

"Sure, there is still extramarital sex. There is even some prostitution still, but it is legal and regulated now. However, now almost nobody has actual intercourse outside of a committed relationship without using contraception or wearing a protective device. Unwanted pregnancies are quite unusual. Ever since genetic testing allowed the government to establish who both parents of a child were and hold them both responsible for the support of the baby, people started acting more responsibly."

"You mean that they could tell who the father was?" John asked.

"Yes, and he would have child support deducted from his credits until the child was through school, and he would also use up part of his inheritance share. So, men have to be just as responsible as women in creating babies. I believe in your day women had a hard time getting men to wear condoms. Nowadays, if a women is in love with a man who doesn't share that feeling, and they have sex, she can't get him to take the condom off. Most people are turned off by condoms and empty sex, though. We have day-after and day-before pills, but most people would rather not mess with that karma. There are still some sexually transmitted diseases, but much less than in your time."

My time, John thought. Maybe she is beginning to believe me.

They arrived at the subus stop, and within a minute one arrived, and they boarded.

"You have credits now instead of dollars?" asked John.

"You can read out your funds in International Credits or dollars. It doesn't really make any difference. But some people didn't want to give up that dollar label."

"Tell me more about this crisis period, Crystal."

"Well, one of the great incentives to action was that the weather became more and more extreme; it got much hotter, and the oceans started to rise. That really started causing serious problems, and scientists were predicting that oceans would rise over four inches between 2020 and 2030, then rise out of control as the global heating continued. Still, there was significant resistance to making the change to sustainable, non-polluting power generation, and it looked as if the world were doomed to warm up so much that most species would not be able to adjust and survive. There were powerful forces that opposed the transition to sustainable power, and even the denial of what by then seemed to be obvious climate change persisted well into this century. It all looked hopeless."

"Well, then what happened?" asked John.

"Then there was chaos in the Middle East that caused a major disruption of oil production. The whole World was thrown into a deep economic depression. There was almost a world war. Thanks to some great leadership at just the right time, common sense prevailed, and that is when the crash program to create sustainable electricity and a nationwide high energy grid really took off. Most historians believe that without the chaos in the Middle East and the long cut-off of oil from that area, we would have never have made the changes necessary to save this planet from the worst of climate change. That would have been devastating for all life on Earth. Once solar and wind really took off, the costs came way down, and they soon replaced all fossil fuels."

"Amazing," replied John.

"There was a movement to replant the world's trees. A moratorium on tree cutting was put into effect that lasted for over thirty years. Cities were islands of heat, so they had to be covered with a layer of foliage. It was thought that it would take a half a century to stop the process, but by the grace of God, the scientists were wrong about that, and the oceans leveled off back in the fifties at ten inches higher than in your day. That created tremendous problems, but they could be dealt with. Sea levels have actually receded an inch or two inches since then. This is our stop coming up."

Crystal retrieved her bike from the rack and the two got off the subus. John could see a large complex of baseball and football fields at the corner, and all had games going on. The baseball game they were closest to had both kids and adults playing together. John could see up the street, and as in the city, the ped and a two-lane road wound up the street through a veritable park, with flower beds and a volleyball court on a lawn visible right up ahead.

"Gosh, people are really into sports," said John. "I am amazed at the number of facilities I've seen so far."

"Yes. People are participating more than just spectating nowadays. Many philanthropists donate funds for different kinds of sports and artistic facilities. They want to know where their money is going before they die. I live a mile from here up into the hills. Why don't you let me ride you?"

"No, Crystal. I'd be too much of a burden. Besides, it looks as if we are going to be heading uphill."

"Get on the back of the bike, John."

John jumped on her back rack, and was soon amazed at how powerful a biker Crystal was. She stood up and peddled right up the open road at a brisk clip. John could see that most of the houses had gardens filling the yards with vegetables and flowers. Many people were working outdoors, and Crystal seemed to know them all, as everyone gave a friendly wave and a greeting. In about five minutes they pulled onto a path that led through a little patch of woods into the yard of a small but charming cottage.

"I was so lucky to find this place out here on the edge of the city," Crystal said after stopping. She was barely breathing hard.

"That was something, Crystal. I must admit, if I rode that far uphill by myself, I would be gasping for breath."

"Biking is one of the best activities in the world for you. My patients who bike around regularly heal much faster than the constant subus and train riders. I rode across America in four weeks once with a group. And I'm talking pedaling all the way,"she boasted.

"That's incredible."

"Well, there were five weekends, so we did have thirty days. We only rode about eight hours a day. The record for cross country bike rides is eight days, six hours. When you've been riding all your life, you become very strong. Several people in our cross-country group were over seventy."

They walked on a winding pathway through a well kept garden, and up a ramp, then Crystal hung her bike up on her porch.

"You have handicap access to your house. Neat," said John"

"Neat? Because of lug trucks, even physically challenged people who still need a wheelchair have access everywhere now."

Her little house was made of brick and when John went inside he could see that the ceiling consisted mostly of white opaque glass. Plants were everywhere, and John could see an attached greenhouse that was right off the kitchen area. The floors were tiled, except for the kitchen floor, which was of wood.

"I just had this recycled wooden floor put in last month," Crystal said. "It adds a lot of warmth."

"I've never seen a glass ceiling like this before. Doesn't it get too hot on summer days like this, and let out too much heat in the winter?"

"No," Crystal replied, "do you feel any heat coming in through it?"

"Well, maybe a little, yet there is a good bit of light."

"I'll show you why. Thena, she is my computer John, increase transparency slowly, and close shutters ninety percent." First the glass became brighter, then became completely clear. Then panels began to unfold above the glass ceiling from both ends of the house. They reached a point where only a small section of the glass ceiling was visible, and stopped.

"I can program them to open up for part of the day to let some sun in for my plants without overheating the house. They are well insulated for their thickness, and they keep me quite cozy in the winter. Of course, Berkeley doesn't get that cold and has very little solar gain in the winter. I just like the beautiful view of the sky. Places that are really cold have thicker shutters that are usually mounted on the outside. These were mass produced for eco houses, but the builder of this house mounted two of them like a conventional roof, instead of vertically."

"So there are a lot of solar houses now?"

"Oh, yes. We use almost all available solar heating because it is by far the most economical and cleanest way to heat a home. With light activated shutters, solar energy can be a major contributor to winter heating almost everywhere. Back in your time people wasted almost all the available solar energy. At the turn of the century, there were few solar houses being built, even in areas where it was practical without shuttering. In your time people wasted almost everything, and it ended up almost wasting the planet.

"What do you mean by without shuttering?" asked John?

"Passive solar energy can be used most everywhere if you use insulated shutters to keep the heat in at night or when it clouds up. A sensor controls the shutter, opening it and closing it when needed. If you are on the south side of a city on a cloudy winter day, you can see most of the windows opening and closing with the sun, rather like sea anemones opening and closing their tentacles. That development alone created enough new energy to shut down hundreds of power plants."

"Cool idea," said John.

"Actually," Crystal chuckled, "that would be better classified as a warm idea. I'm going to check my home PC. Thena, cue PC, messages please."

A large flat screen lit up with a picture of a beautiful white owl sitting in a fir tree in a very pretty, snowy wood.

"Hello, Crystal. You have messages from your mother and Sally Knight."

A picture of a woman in a living room came up, and she spoke. "Hi, sweetheart. Just wanted to chat. Give me a buzz when you have a chance. Bye."

"Crystal," an attractive middle aged woman was on the screen, "I had another dream where I communicated telepathically with Ungma. Call me when you get a chance, and I'll tell you all about it. I'll talk to you soon, I hope."

The owl came back up.

"Is there anything else, Crystal?" asked the owl.

"Yes, Thena, I want to show John some VR. John, sit down here next to the PC."

John sat down while Crystal pulled two helmets with goggles out of a cabinet below the screen.

"Thena, put both VR one and two on the same channel. Here, John, put this on."

John put on the helmet and so did Crystal. He saw her pull down the goggles, so he did also. He found himself in that beautiful wood with Thena in her tree in full, vivid living color and depth. He was amazed.

"I see we have a guest today, Crystal," said Thena.

"Yes, this is John. John, Thena."

"Nice to meet you, John."

John was too amazed to say hello. Thena turned back to Crystal, whom John could see was a fairy-like version of herself in VR, complete with gossamer wings.

"Where do you want to go?" asked Thena.

"Thena is my personal guide, John. You can have one of almost any lifeform and personality you can imagine. Pull up my body scan, Thena. Put us in my, oh, stomach."

In an instant John and Crystal were in her stomach in living 3D.

"Cruise us slowly down the intestinal tract," she ordered, and they started heading towards a valve which opened just when they got to it. John was mind blown.

"This is incredible, Crystal! It is just like being there!"

"Yes, this is a wonderful technology for medicine. I bought this for one of my classes at the university. They're not that expensive, actually. Reduce size, Thena."

They took on a much smaller size relative to the tubing which they were traveling along.

"The color isn't perfectly accurate, though the program can detect and adjust for inflammations and such. Want to see something different? Thena, take us to Venice."

In an instant they were disembodied entities free to float all around Venice. It looked absolutely real, including people and pigeons going through their day.

"Incredible! How do they do this?"

"Some of the cameras are more like radar than traditional cameras, and they are coupled together with computers to produce this totally lifelike world. Take us up at ten feet a second, Thena,"

Soon they were rising above Venice.

"See over to the left, John? That is the dike and levee system that protected Venice through the sea rise."

"Crystal, you're a fairy in VR?"

"Yes, John, and you should see yourself. Are you still hungry? I'm going to pick some greens and things for a big salad. Does that sound all right?"

"This is incredible," replied John. "Sure, that would be great."

They took off the helmets, and John followed Crystal outside again and watched as she picked some green onions and radishes. Her tomato plants were big and healthy and held giant ripe tomatoes.

"That virtual reality was just incredible. You can go anywhere?"

"Well, only places that have been scanned. Next month there will be a program released of a district in London that will allow people to pass through the walls and enter rooms to watch people in living plays. I'm almost out of lettuce in this bed. I'm going to have to pick some out of the rabbit patch, if they left us some. Otherwise, it'll be mostly spinach."

She stepped over the short wire fence into another unprotected patch that, sure enough, had a pair of rabbits in it nibbling on the greenery. They didn't seem to be afraid of her.

"You fellows mind if I get some of your lettuce?" She asked of them, while picking a couple of plants.

"Pet rabbits?"

"No. I just put a patch in for them to keep them from breaking into my garden. It works better than fences alone. I don't have any pets. These guys are free. My mother loves cats and had three. They killed off most of the mice, moles, chipmunks, lizards, and even a lot of the local birds in our area. Our little local eco-sphere was quite disrupted by them. One thing I like about this neighborhood is that most people don't have cats or dogs. It's much different having a pet now. If you don't register and pay a two hundred and fifty credit fee for a breeder's license, your dogs and cats must be neutered before you can get tags for them. There was a lot of resistance to this law, but we are no longer putting millions of animals to sleep every year, as was done in your time. I really enjoy the wild critters that wander around regularly. I see opossums, raccoons, skunks, even an occasional fox or bobcat. Coyotes are not uncommon, and Jacob, one of my neighbors, said he saw a wolf last spring."

"A wolf! There are wolves now?"

"Not in the city, but occasionally a wolf, bear or cougar will get under or over the wildlife fencing and have to be relocated back into a designated wild area."

"Wolves were gone from the whole country back in my time. We were about to destroy the last of many species all over the world. I saw a public television show about how the tigers would be gone in ten years, and it really devastated me. I couldn't imagine a world without them."

"Me neither," Crystal agreed.

"I was up all night after that show writing a poem about it. You want to hear it?"

"Sure, John."

"It's called *I Stand with the Tigers*."

John struck a stance and after a short dramatic pause began his poem.

I stand with the tigers as they make their last stand.
I stand with the tigers against the ravage of man.
I stand with the animals pushed to the wall.
The rhinos, the pandas, I stand with them all.
I stand with the great apes. The gorilla's my kin,
and I wouldn't want to live in a world they're not in.

I stand with the wolves, the she-wolves and cubs
against steel-jawed traps that would leave just a nub.
I stand with the whales. I stand and I weep
over all of their blood that was shed in the deep.
I stand with the elephants, noble and bold,
who are killed for their tusks that are hacked off and sold.

I stand with the animals. I love one and all,
and I think to myself, surely this is Man's fall.
We're burning the Garden. We're cutting her trees.
I stand and I beg; I plead, people **stop, please**!
Yet my heart knows that this won't be enough.
If we stand with the Tigers, we'll have to get tough.

For this is our last stand. We're all on the brink.
We just have to stop it, and take time to think.
We must face the truth that we're killing ourselves.
We must learn to treasure our planet's true wealth.
It's not in the gold hidden deep in her soil.
It's not in the steel and it's not in the oil.

It's not in possessions that these things will build.
What good is it all after everything's killed?
What joy in a world if we're in it alone,
With her beauty destroyed, and our hearts turned to stone?
Oh, we might still live on, but surely not well.
For our Garden most fair we'd have turned into hell.

"That was really great, John." Crystal had tears in her eyes. "I'm very moved. It is hard to imagine what it must have been like to live through all that destruction. It was terrible. I'm so happy to tell you that all those animals made it."

"All right!"

"Maybe in some way your beautiful poem helped. Like a prayer put out into the collective consciousness."

61

"Well, I read it to a few people, and I did leave some copies back then, but I thought it would make people too sad to ever be popular."

"We have much more woods and wild land now, and as many animals as possible have been reintroduced. Nature can actually function in balance again. Cougars do on occasion attack a person, but wolves have never been known to kill anyone. When there is a problem with a wild animal, the local hunters have a lottery to see which ones win the right to hunt it with tranquilizer darts. Those guys just love it. I've seen wolves in the wild both up in Mendocino and at Yosemite. I just love to hear them howl at night. At Yosemite there used to be so many people howling back at them that it was made against the rules."

Crystal had loaded John up with salad stuff and they went into the greenhouse, where she had a special sink for washing her vegetables.

"I have to attend a Coming of Age Ceremony this evening, John. I'm sure it would be all right for you to come too, if you want. I'm sure you would find it interesting." Crystal was washing the greens while she spoke. "I am going with a good friend of mine. A man named Stuart."

"Is he your boyfriend?" John was somewhat taken aback by this news, but with a wonderful woman like Crystal, what did he expect?

"Not really. He is my best friend. Stuart says he is in love with me and has asked me to marry him. I love him, but not like that. You see, I took a vow of celibacy when I dedicated as a Star Voyager. I believe it is also one of the reasons why I am a successful healer. Sexuality takes so much energy and time and is quite distracting. There is just so much to tell you about, John. Many things have changed since your time. Every time I tell you something I can see how much more I need to explain for you to understand."

A quiet filled their space for a few minutes.

"What's this Stuart fellow going to think of me?"

"I think he'll tell me I'm crazy if I believe you, and he's never very happy about my being with another man. But he's learned to keep that under control, and he won't say anything about it. He's quite brilliant and loving and he is a dedicated Greenpeacer and Com-Union officer."

"Greenpeacer!" John exclaimed. "As in Greenpeace? You still have Greenpeace?"

"Yes."

"They call themselves Greenpeacers now? I thought you didn't have any ecological problems anymore?"

"We still have problems, some very serious problems. Greenpeace is actively trying to finish the job of cleaning up the planet."

"You said something earlier about a mission you were going on that had something to do with radiation. What is that all about?"

They were now in the kitchen and John was drying lettuce while Crystal cut up the other vegetables.

"I really shouldn't have said anything about that. I'm sorry. How are you feeling, John? I know that if I'd have been flashed a hundred years into the future, I'd be pretty overwhelmed. What do you think of our world, and what do you think is going to happen to you?"

"I don't know what's going on, but I like it. I feel great. I'm blissed out by all this good news. You know, I used to belong to Greenpeace. I never thought it would last for over a hundred years. Heck, I didn't think the world would last for another hundred years."

"I'm going to make some fresh tofu dressing. I make my own tofu. Would you get that jar of sprouts off of the window? Just add a handful to the salad, and I'll have the dressing ready in a minute."

While Crystal was making the dressing, John looked around the kitchen. Nothing was made out of plastic, and many of her utensils and bowls seemed to have been handmade.

"Gosh, everything here looks handmade. I don't see anything made out of plastic."

"Plastic is not used much anymore. Everything is made to last."

A couple of minutes later they were sitting at a little kitchen table. Crystal reached her hands across and said, "Let's ask a blessing."

John took her hands in his and she closed her eyes. God, she is so beautiful and so sweet, John thought. Her hands felt so very good in his.

She squeezed his hands gently and prayed, "Father Mother God. We thank all the forces that have brought us this food. The Sun, the blessed Mother Earth, the winds that bring the rain. We thank all the creatures, even the bacteria, that give the soil its fertility. We thank the spirits of the plants for the gift of their lives, which will now merge with our lives. And we pray our lives will be worthy of such gifts. Ho."

He squeezed back slightly harder and the warm and wonderful sensation of connection seemed to increase. She and John opened their eyes and they looked deeply into each others as they continued to hold hands for about half a minute. The energy was apparent. She smiled more broadly and released his hands, looked down, and began to eat. John just sat there for a minute with the realization that he was already very much in love with this amazing lady from his most incredible day. They ate in silence, savoring each bite, though John did highly compliment her salad and dressing. Their eyes met many times, and John wondered if his eyes were sparkling in the same wonderful way that Crystal's were. He knew they were smiling. When both had finished eating, their eyes again met and stayed in another smiling, steady, loving gaze.

Just then the spell was broken by Stuart's entry. "Hello," he said to Crystal, giving her a smile and a kiss on the cheek. He looked at John with a somewhat more serious expression. Crystal introduced them and they shook hands.

"Well, Crystal, I didn't know you were having company this evening. Is John going to the ceremony with us?"

"I invited him, but he hasn't said whether he is going or not. There is some salad left if you're hungry."

John couldn't stand the idea of letting Crystal out of his sight, so he added, "Sure, I'd love to go to the ceremony."

"What do you do, John?"

"I am, um, I used to be a med student."

"One of Crystal's students?"

"No. I used to attend U. C. San Francisco Medical School. It doesn't look as if I'll be able to continue."

John was looking at Crystal for some clue as to what to tell Stuart. She looked slightly apprehensive for a few seconds and explained, "I met John on the Goddess part of Redwood Hill today. I went there after my session with Ann's mother in Bernal Heights. It seems that John time-traveled from over a hundred years ago to now."

"Is that what he told you?" Stuart looked at John skeptically. "You don't really believe that ridiculous line, do you?"

"Well, he has clothes, money, even an I. D. from the past. I have a strong sense he isn't lying, and he passed my PC's voice stress test."

"Let me see some of this I. D., if you don't mind," he said looking at John.

"Here is my driver's license. Look at the dates on it, and my picture. Y'all have anything like that now?"

"This doesn't prove anything. This could have been made up. What's your game?"

John felt Stuart's rising anger.

"This is not a game. I find it very difficult to believe myself, but here I am."

Shaking his head, Stuart looked at Crystal and said, "Crystal, you can't really believe this. Come on. You just met this guy today and you've brought him home with you after that ridiculous story? You've got to be kidding."

He looked at John and ordered, "Get the hell out of here, whoever you are."

"Just a minute!" Crystal exclaimed standing up. "You have no right to order anyone out of my house!"

There was a silent tension that filled the room.

"Believe what you will, and let me live my life as I want," Crystal continued in a softer voice. "Come on. We've got a beautiful Coming of Age Ceremony to attend, and I don't want to hear any more of this or have any more bad vibes. I know it sounds impossible, Stuart, but communicating with the inhabitants of other planets was thought to be impossible. Most people still think it is impossible, but we know it has happened. I'm going to change. I don't want to hear any fighting while I'm gone. You'll like John; he's a very nice person."

With that, Crystal got up and left the room. Stuart folded his arms, looked at John, and let out a sigh, shaking his head. John stood up and said, "I think I'll look around outside some."

John got up and walked out the front door. This is getting very complicated, he thought. I wish she hadn't told him about my being from the past. I guess she didn't want to lie to him.

The sun was getting lower in the sky and John walked down the entrance pathway back to the street. He walked along the uncovered part of it down hill for a few houses and then suddenly something stopped him. There were several large marijuana plants in the front yard of one of Crystal's neighbors. He walked over to the fence. No doubt about it. It was pot. Things certainly have changed, John thought.

He remembered back to when he had tried to persuade Faith to smoke some pot to help the nausea her treatments caused. She was staying in her parents' house, and when they smelled it, they were furious. He explained to them that a survey of cancer specialists showed that over half would prescribe marijuana if it was legal to do so, and a majority of them had already suggested to their patients that they get some.

"I saw a doctor from the Harvard Medical School on television who had said it was safer than aspirin," he told them. It was true, but Faith's parents wouldn't believe him. John implored them, but they were very angry and insisted that no illegal drugs were allowed in their house. This was one time that John fought back because he believed Faith really needed the herb. But he didn't have a house he could take Faith to, even if she would have left. It was a bad scene, and definitely finished any good will John had had with Faith's parents. He didn't want to think about that painful memory, though.

Discarding the sad memory, he figured he'd better walk on back. He didn't want to be interrogated further by Stuart, so he wanted to time his return to the moment Crystal was ready. When he got back he could hear the two of them arguing.

"Stuart isn't happy about our taking the subus." Crystal turned and said as John walked back inside. "We usually ride our bikes everywhere around here. Stuart is in the Com-Union and only uses public transportation when absolutely necessary. I told him you didn't have a bike, nor were you ready for a long bike ride. I guess you'll be meeting us there then," she said turning to Stuart.

Stuart walked out looking intense, got on his bike, and peddled off. Crystal looked back at John and said, "Actually, I'm glad not to have to change clothes at the school. Let's walk to the subus. We have plenty of time, and the ceremony isn't far from a stop."

"Gee, I'm sorry. I seem to be making trouble between you and your friend."

"He'll get over it. Don't blame yourself. Stuart has to learn that even though we are close friends and co-workers, I am not his girlfriend."

"I can't blame him for not believing me and wanting to protect you."

"You men! I do not need protecting. Come on, let's go."

Crystal led John out the front door and started down the path. She was wearing a very lovely sky blue dress with points all around the hem line. John was feeling rather foolish and thought he had made Crystal mad. He thought about asking her whether she had locked her door, but decided against it. When they got to the street, John caught up with Crystal, and when she turned and smiled, John gave her a big grin back. They walked quietly until they reached the house with the pot plants.

"Is marijuana legal now? In my time the police would put you in jail and take your house away from you if you grew pot in your yard."

"Take your home away from you for growing a plant! I knew it was illegal, but that's too much. Nowadays it is legal to grow marijuana or tobacco for your personal use, but it is against the law to sell either of them. Keeping drugs and alcohol illegal just never worked."

"So what about harder drugs?" asked John. "Are they still used?

"When the change was made away from money to the credit system it cut way down on drug use. Now you just have your drugs confiscated and pay a fine relative to the quantity and dangerousness of the substances. The fines can be financially devastating for large quantities of the harder drugs, but nobody ever goes to jail just because of drugs."

"That sounds like a big improvement. Putting people in jail because of an addiction just seemed to make things worse," said John. "As bad as many drugs are, alcohol was just as bad."

"Drug use has come way down, but it is still a large healthcare problem. Free treatment has done a lot of good, and most people manage eventually to recover from a more serious addiction."

"So some people still use drugs?"

"Yes. Beer, wine and harder alcoholic beverages are still legally sold most anywhere. That's the biggest drug problem. This isn't quite a perfect society yet. Tomorrow, when I help out at the medical tent at the International Youth Festival, you'll see that undoubtedly many of the problems we'll be dealing with will have been caused by drinking."

"That was the greatest problem back in my time. They'd take your house for growing pot, but they'd let drunk drivers keep their cars, even though they killed over 20,000 people a year."

"It is hard to believe, but I read that intoxicated drivers killed millions of people worldwide during the Twentieth Century. I'm really sorry you can't go to the festival, John. They are incredible experiences. Young people all over the world bought lottery chances to win tickets and charter flights to come to the festival. There will be 125,000 young people from other countries attending, with 125,000 kids from America. There is an international festival, continental festivals, and national festivals held every year."

"People get tickets by lottery?" he asked.

"Right. Tickets and plane or train rides as well. Many of the out-of-country or state attendees will find someone to stay with on the festival internet site. There is also a large camping area close by. The festivals have done much to help bring about a real sense of unity to the world. So many people make friends from all over the world and travel around to visit them, that they end up knowing people from just about everywhere. When a crisis occurs somewhere, everyone feels as if it is in the family and are glad to help out."

Crystal and John were hailed by an older fellow standing in front of his garden manning what appeared to be a small produce stand.

"Hello, Roger. Beautiful evening, isn't it?"

"Yes, Crystal. Do you need any zucchini? It's free today."

"Are you kidding?" answered Crystal with a smile.

They walked over to the edge of Roger's fence.

"Roger, this is my new friend, John."

John and Roger shook hands and exchanged greetings. Roger looked back over at Crystal and said, "Crystal, you are looking very lovely tonight. Don't usually see you walking."

"Thank you, Roger. I probably should walk more. It is more conducive to visiting. Do you need any more tomatoes?"

"Mine are coming along, but I could use some to tide me over. Crystal's are so big and sweet, John, I eat most of them myself instead of selling them."

"I told you, it's that composting toilet I had put in last year."

Crystal and Roger both laughed heartily at that, and John joined in, though he didn't quite understand the reference. They all said good-bye and the two started back down the hill.

"Roger gardens and runs that little exchange for extra retirement income. He'll barter or buy and sell. There are many little produce stands like his," said Crystal.

"That's neat. So what is this Com-Union?"

"I guess neat is a slang word for good?"

"Right," responded John.

"The Com-Union is an organization of idealistic people who have a plan to make everything on Earth free and to create a perfect world. They live a very disciplined life and strive to barter, well, not even barter, for everything. Their ideal is for people to create what they feel they are meant to, then share it without even trying to make everything come out even, as in a trade. I support the Com-Union's taking over the communication and transportation equipment and making it free, because I'm sure that the corporate interests that control them now are not fair and impartial in the dissemination of information. I think maybe in the future we can evolve to a place where no one has to buy or trade for anything, and all will be given with love, but I don't think humanity is that evolved quite yet. Surveys show that we'd have an inordinate number of artists, musicians and actors if everyone just did whatever they wanted to."

"Well, it would be a very entertaining world then." They both laughed at that. "Are you in the Com-Union?"

"No. Hi, Sally, Fred," Crystal yelled while waving to friends on their porch.

She turned back to John. "I want to be able to support the whole program if I'm in an organization. I work with Com-Union people frequently because many of them are in Greenpeace, and we share many common goals."

Crystal and John passed by a large swimming pool with many people swimming and diving off the two boards.

"There is so much to explain to you, John. We think that some of the radiation waste areas are much more dangerous than they are reported to be. There is a conservative element that wants to maintain the status quo and just leave all the nuclear mess to leak, to spread, and to contaminate more and more land and animals. It causes a lot of suffering. Pathetic creatures are turning up at the edges of these sites all the time. It is not well reported, and we believe there is outright lying going on about the radiation levels at some of these places."

"It is interesting to me that you are dedicated to fighting radiation contamination, Crystal."

"Yes, and I think I know why, John." A short pause. "We believe if the truth ever were honestly reported about some of these sites it would cause a groundswell of support for us to go in and finally clean up these places. We think we've found an answer to the long term problem, but the establishment scientists say it will not work. Their line is that it would cause more contamination and that it would be fruitless to try to clean up these places, and, more important to them, cost a whole lot of money. We admit it will be very expensive but are convinced it will only become more expensive and more intolerable. This is the only moral way for humanity to handle this problem."

Upon their arrival back at the ramp to the subus stop, an older woman approached them and spoke. "Crystal, so good to see you."

"Hello, Marge. This is my friend, John."

Marge and John shook hands and greetings.

"Crystal, you would be perfect for a part in my new play. We will start practice next week and are having casting Monday night. Please try out. I assure you, you'll get the part."

"I'm sorry, Marge, I can't this time."

John and Crystal went down the ramp, and Crystal waved them past the turnstile as she explained that there were community amphitheaters in every neighborhood, and they had plays, concerts and dances most every night. Some were free; sometimes donations were requested, and sometimes the most popular performers charged. Crystal showed John how to display the estimated times the various subuses were expected to arrive at this stop on a small terminal in the waiting station. Their subus would arrive in one minute and fifteen seconds. She explained to him how she could get this information on her own screen at home, or even on her PC, for any stop in the system. The bus arrived, and they got on.

"Gosh, Crystal, that is a really great innovation. So people don't have to wait long for transportation. When I came from, people were totally addicted to their cars. They loved them. Their wheels were their most prized possession and status symbol."

"There are still car nuts who put everything they make into owning and maintaining their own automobile. They get out and drive them as much as they can."

"How about motorcycles?"

"Yes, there are even electric motorcycles. So, John, you don't have a place to stay for tonight, I suppose. Maybe I can find you a place at the party after the ceremony."

"Crystal. Please don't tell anyone else I am from the past."

"Why not?" Crystal returned, with perhaps a note of suspicion in her voice.

"It is just such a big deal to have to defend myself and explain to everyone I meet. Stuart will probably tell everyone anyway, and say that I'm lying. Well, that's life. I guess I had better get used to it."

The two transferred to another subus at what Crystal called a sub-hub and were at their stop in a couple of minutes.

Coming of Age Ceremony

John was somewhat apprehensive about meeting the people at the ceremony, but his fears soon subsided. Everyone he met was friendly. A couple of people did ask Crystal where Stuart was, and she told them he was coming on his bike. John felt a little underdressed. Everyone else wore elegant handmade clothing of many designs and styles. Uniformity seemed to be out of fashion. When he and Crystal were alone for a moment John turned to her and spoke.

"Are these wonderful garments hand-made?"

"Yes, John, many of them are. Now that we have robots doing most of the manufacturing work people have much more free time. In some ways, it seems as if we've gone back to the lifestyle of tribal people. Many people spend a good deal of time making beautiful things to wear. Almost everyone's best clothes are hand made. Human energy is our most valuable commodity."

"The colors seem more muted than in my time."

"We don't use dyes that create any toxins, and most people prefer natural colors," she explained.

They were in a large round room with a domed ceiling gently sloping up to a large, round skylight of mostly clear glass that had seven narrow triangles of glass in the colors of the rainbow radiating out from the center. As the sun was lowering in the sky, the light and colors played against the white marble floor off to one side of the room. In the center of the room, under the skylight in the middle of the floor, was a beautiful and fairly realistic mosaic of the Earth as seen from space. Lovely music played, and the room smelled of rose incense. John relaxed in the ambiance and beauty of the setting.

John was glad that all the conversation had stayed mostly to greetings, introductions and small talk. Stuart entered, and after greeting people, came over to where John and Crystal were. He smiled at Crystal as if to say I'm sorry, and gave John a nod. About this time people were beginning to take seats in the block of chairs placed before a large table decorated with flowers and candles.

Stuart, Crystal and John walked about half way down the central isle and took seats on the left side with Crystal sitting in the middle. John heard Stuart ask Crystal what she had planned for after the reception, and she told him that she thought she would show John around the rest of the school.

"If this is part of a school," John said to Crystal, "it must be a very expensive one."

"Not at all. It is a free public school. All schools get equal funding by law, and they are all this nice."

"Wow, now that's a change," said John.

Six people went up to the front of the table and stood in three groups, one couple to the left, one couple in the center, and another couple on the right. The music changed, a door opened on the right, and a lovely young girl walked in, hand in hand with an older woman. They were both beaming and radiant. They walked into the center in front of the table and turned to face everyone. They smiled at the guests for a few moments and then the woman spoke.

"Hello, I'm Sally, Amanda's friend. We are here today to celebrate the coming of age of Amanda Josephine Parsons. After being given the wondrous gift of life, Amanda has now been given the awesome power to create life. This is the most important responsibility given to a human being. The proper stewardship of this great gift is one of the greatest challenges of her existence. It is as difficult as the taming of a tiger or the riding of a wild horse. In the handling of this challenge, she needs the complete love, support, help and understanding of everyone important in her life."

Sally and Amanda turned to face the couple in the middle. "Roger and Gwendolyn Parsons, do you promise to help Amanda by setting an example of the proper respect given to the great gift of human sexuality? To instill in her a reverence for the power to create a life? To help her to understand fully that she now has other potential lives to consider and is not free to make decisions based only on her needs, her wants, her desires? To love her unconditionally even if she fails in this universal test of our human values?"

"Yes, we do," the couple said in unison, beaming smiles at their little girl.

They then turned to the couple to the right.

"Roger and Tina Owens, do you, Amanda's Godparents, promise to help Amanda by setting an example of the proper respect given the gift of human sexuality and the power to procreate a life? To help her to clearly understand the tremendous responsibility she has been given and only allow the possibility of the creation of a child if that child will have the two loving parents and the stable home every child needs and deserves? Will you help her maintain this highest of human values, yet love her unconditionally, even if she fails at this difficult and challenging task?"

"Yes, we will."

Sally and Amanda now turned and faced the couple on the left. "Daniel Chen Chow and Conchita Lopez. As one of Amanda's current teachers, and the minister of her chosen faith, do you promise to help and support Amanda, by demonstrating to her the high standard of respect given to the power of human sexuality to create a life? To educate her, and inspire in her the strength of character, self confidence, and self esteem required for her to succeed in fulfilling her pledge of responsibility?"

"I do," said the man. "I do as well," said the lady.

Amanda and Sally turned and faced each other, holding each other's hands.

"Amanda, I have taught you all I know about human sexuality - the physical realities involved in mating and procreation, with all its dangers and possibilities, joys and responsibilities. I have shared with you, as best I could, my knowledge of the deep emotional and psychological energies surrounding human sexual behavior. I have also given you all I know of the spiritual side of human love. Know that I will always be your friend and will always welcome an opportunity to talk to you, with love and understanding, about this very important subject. Know that I will always love and support you unconditionally.

They both turned to the attendees. "In order to succeed in keeping her pledge of respect and responsibility in the handling of her power to procreate, Amanda will need the help and cooperation of everyone in her life. Do you, the friends and family of Amanda, promise to set a proper example of the respect given to the responsibility of human sexuality, and help her in every way to live up to her pledge?"

"We do," rang out from the group.

Sally and Amanda turned back to her parents and something was given to Sally. "This pendant, with its ruby and sapphire symbolizes the feminine and the masculine, desire and control. When we procreate a life, we join fully in the ongoing drama of human unfolding. The effects of our failure to express properly our power to create another human life can live on for generations after us. In truth, the mating of a man and a woman joins them to much more than just one another. They are joining with the whole of humanity in the ongoing dance of life. The platinum of the pendant and the rarity of the gemstones symbolize the very high value humanity must place on our power of procreation."

Amanda was handed the pendant, and she turned to face the attendees. "I pledge and promise that I will do my very best to live up to the responsibility I have been given." She put the pendant around her neck, looked at it and smiled, then raised her head and spoke again. "I thank each and every one of you for your love and support and for coming to my Coming of Age Ceremony."

Everyone stood and applauded.

"That was wonderful. When I was confirmed they taught me a lot about my religion, but sexuality wasn't even mentioned," John said to Crystal while they were applauding. The applause died down and people began going up front to greet the folks in the ceremony and to congratulate Amanda.

Crystal took Stuart's hand and John found that Stuart wasn't the only one who could feel jealousy. She said, "Let's take John up and introduce him to everybody," then she took John by her other hand as they walked up front. They said hello to a few people as the circle around Amanda thinned out.

"Amanda, this is my new friend John. He's never seen a Coming of Age Ceremony before."

"Really? Where are you from, John?

"The past," Stuart shot in.

"The past?" Amanda said as Crystal gave Stuart a wary look and let go of his hand.

"I've often wanted to take on a persona from the past," said Mrs. Parsons who was standing right in back of Amanda. "When I first met Roger, he was dressed as an ancient Greek, and he stayed one until I was pregnant. Period dressing must be coming back into vogue. From the outfit, I'd say late Twentieth Century."

"That's right Ma'am, 1993 to be exact."

"What did you think of the ceremony, as a person from the last century?" Mrs. Parsons asked whimsically.

"I thought it was wonderful. This is something we sorely needed back then. When my girlfriend came of age, she said that all her mother told her was, 'Don't let any boy touch you down there.' Can you believe that?"

Everyone except John laughed heartily, even Stuart smiled, then chuckled.

"It's true," said John seriously. Another round of laughter followed.

"That was a good one," said Sally, and she introduced herself to John.

Crystal led John and Stuart away from that group over to where Mr. Chow, Amanda's teacher, was talking to some younger children. On the way she said quietly to Stuart, "This is not the proper place to make controversy."

Crystal introduced John to Mr. Chow and told John she had been Mr. Chow's student herself at this very school. She asked her former teacher if the rest of the school were open so she could show John around. He said that some areas were open and that he would be glad to join them and open up any part she wanted to see. Stuart asked if John and Mr. Chow would excuse he and Crystal for a moment, and they walked twenty or so feet away and talked. After a minute Stuart turned and left, looking unhappy while Crystal returned. She told Mr. Chow to stay and enjoy the reception as she was sure that she and John would be able to see enough of the school.

"I think you were right about not bringing up your being from the past," Crystal said as they headed towards a double door. "I can't say I'm the only person who might believe you, but I think it would be greeted with a lot of skepticism and endless questions. Stuart conceded that my guidance is usually right. He could see that you are sincere, but he thinks you should see a psychologist."

"I guess he is handling everything pretty well," John said, "considering he is in love with you, and the whole situation is unbelievable. Time shifting doesn't fit into my belief system very well either."

"What is your belief system?"

"Well, like I said, I was raised a Catholic and was an altar boy and very much a devoted Christian for years."

They passed through the doors and were walking down a hallway. As they moved, lights came on ahead of them and turned off behind them.

"What's with the lights? Are they automatically controlled?"

"Yes," answered Crystal, "sensors turn all lights off if a room is empty and turn them on when someone enters. It saves a lot of energy."

They entered a beautiful, well lit space that contained an Olympic size swimming pool.

"I grew away from a strict belief in Catholic doctrine as I got older and studied science," John continued. "When Faith died, my faith seemed to die with her. I began to suspect that there was no purpose to life, nor a God - just or unjust. And if there were a God, He wasn't the least bit concerned with what happens to us. Now my mind has been blown by this whole experience. I can't help believing that God did answer my prayer. Dream, vision, heaven, whatever is happening to me, it is good. It's wonderful. I also believe that you were up on that hill today because we are connected." John stopped walking, turned and looked into Crystal's eyes. "I believe, at least, I very much want to believe, that you are my sweet Faith, alive and with me again." John reached out his hand for hers.

Crystal's hand moved slightly towards John's, but was drawn back. "John, I believe in your sincerity. I like you very much, but I can't tell you I am Faith." She took a big breath and let it out slowly. "Maybe Stuart's idea about you seeing a psychologist is a good one."

John sighed, wiped a tear from his eye, and turned towards the pool. After a minute he mused, "So all schools have swimming pools like this?"

"Yes. Schools are very different than in the last century. They are not funded exclusively by property taxes. They also get funding from the inheritance share. That helps level things out so all schools are more or less equal. Kids aren't fixed into rigid grade structures and are allowed more freedom to progress at their own pace and concentrate on the subjects they are currently interested in. Nowadays schools have no more than twelve children per teacher." Crystal led John into another beautiful room filled with computer booths, tables and a small stage. "Schools are so beautiful and pleasant that children love to come. Since they aren't coerced into learning, but are instead guided through it, their natural curiosity isn't destroyed. When children are actually curious about a subject, they learn ten times faster, and they retain what they've learned."

"The last time I was home in Georgia, they had just started a state lottery to help fund schooling," John Said. "You could never get the voters to raise their taxes for better schools, but they would gamble away lots of money in the hope of getting rich."

"What a terrible value system to give children. We value our children above anything. Gambling is legal now, but the government doesn't promote it. When the Inheritance Share Law was adopted, it was decided that a part of all the money collected would have to go to education."

"What's this Inheritance Share?"

"I'll explain, but here comes Mr. Chow."

Just then Mr. Chow, who was a slender and slightly graying Asian, walked up and joined them.

"So what do you think of our school, John?"

"It's just incredible. Back in my time our schools were in pretty terrible shape and there was far from equity in education."

"Back in your time. What do you mean John?"

"Well, Mr. Chow, to tell you the truth, just this morning I was in the Twentieth Century. To be exact, 1993. I was having a terrible day, so I went up on a hill and prayed to God to restore my faith in Him, in myself, in the goodness of life. Then I had an incredible experience of bliss and lights and sounds. When it was over, there I was in the same place, just 102 years later. I know it sounds incredible, impossible, but here I am. Crystal and Stuart think I am crazy."

"John, I never said that."

"Well, emotionally disturbed anyway," John continued. "And I can't blame them one bit."

"I don't know what to believe, Mr. Chow," said Crystal. "You know I am a member of the Star Voyagers, and lots of people think we are crazy. I know John is sincere. I really want to believe him, but time travel isn't supposed to be possible."

"Well, let's take the scientific approach," said Mr. Chow. "John, can you prove you are from the past?"

John took out coins and his ID and gave them to Mr. Chow who looked at them carefully then returned them to John. He turned to Crystal and spoke.

"Crystal, do you have any reason to believe that John isn't from the past, other than the supposed impossibility of it? Do you have a motive for why he would play such an elaborate hoax?"

"Well...no, except maybe to pick me up," answered Crystal. "Professor White asked him some history questions and John answered them right. He passed my voice stress analysis test. Do you think time travel is possible, Mr. Chow?"

Mr. Chow looked at John, then back at Crystal and said, "We

have a human being here, not a theory to be debated. John deserves our trust in him until we have solid evidence to the contrary."

The somewhat distressed look on Crystal's face changed to a serene smile. "You are absolutely right, Mr. Chow. Forgive me for forgetting one of your most valuable lessons, and forgive me, John," Crystal reached out her hand and took John's, "for insinuating that you might have mental problems."

John could see a moisture in Crystal's eyes, and his eyes started to fill. This time, however, the tears were joyful. As the two looked into each other's moist eyes, John felt a warm and wonderful sensation flowing from her hand into his being. He wanted so much to hold her, to embrace her in a long hug, but he refrained. He had already asked so much of Crystal. He did not want to push her any more in any way. Then he had an idea.

"Mr. Chow, would it be possible for you to give me a place to sleep tonight? I don't know anyone but Crystal and I don't have a bracelet PC or an account or anything. I'd be very content to sleep on the floor."

"I would be honored for you to be my guest. My son is with the Com-Union helping to organize the next big public works takeover in Cape Town, South Africa, and I'm sure he wouldn't mind your staying in his room."

"That is so kind of you. Thank you so much." John felt good about himself, having removed the responsibility for his welfare from Crystal. She seemed surprised by the development. There was a moment of quiet.

"Have you seen everything yet, John?" asked Mr. Chow.

"No, but I've seen enough to know that your schools are vastly nicer than in my time. Crystal was just going to tell me about how they are funded."

"Yes, much different from how they were a century ago," said Mr. Chow. Let me show you something rather unique to our little school. Have you been out to the gardens yet, Crystal?"

"No, sir."

"Well, let us go out and see. John, many schools have gardens created by the children, but we have something a little different." They went outside to a garden area where both flowers and food were growing. "One of our students was interested in creating a pond with fish and lilies and other water plants, and his idea spread like a contagion. Now we have several different ponds with different types of plants and fish, all put together by the children. Then some of them had the idea to try growing spirulina here in a small pond." John could see the pleasure and pride in Mr. Chow's face as the teacher showed him the different little ponds. Some of them had little fountains, some had lotus blossoms or water lilies growing in them. John could see large goldfish in one. The trio came upon a group of kids who were working on building a pond.

"How is it coming?"

"Great, Mr. Chow. We are putting the liner in now. This raised design is really nice, but the stone work was a challenge," one of the kids replied.

"Yes, it looks beautiful and you all did a fine job laying the stone." The three kept on until they came to a larger pond that did not have any plants in it. Mr. Chow walked up to a boy squatting at the side of the pond. "How is it going, Freddy?"

"Contaminated again, though we do have a lot of algae growing. Dr. Post is right. We'll have to put a cover on it for it to be successful here in the city."

"Do you know what spirulina is, John?" Crystal asked.

"It's a one-celled blue green algae that is supposed to be highly nutritious. I've tried it, and it did seem to give me a burst of mental energy. You could get it in health food stores back then."

"I eat it everyday," said Crystal. "Since I don't eat any animal products, it is my source of vitamin B 12, but it is so energizing that I'd eat it anyway. It is 70% protein, and full of beta carotene."

"I eat both spirulina and nutritional or brewer's yeast every day myself," said Mr. Chow. "The bottom of the food chain, the tiny one celled organisms that support all other life, contain the greatest nutrition."

They continued to walk until they came to a beautiful gazebo in the flower garden area.

"Would you like to sit and talk for a while?" Mr. Chow asked.

"Yes."

"Sure." Crystal and John answered.

The gazebo offered a wonderful view of the gardens with the rest of the city and the Bay in the distance. The sun was starting to sink towards the San Francisco skyline. Many birds were singing, butterflies fluttered by, and the moment was quite lovely.

"That ceremony was very beautiful," John said. "I suppose that there are very few teenage pregnancies."

"Yes. We have few unwanted pregnancies by people of any age." Crystal replied.

"You were telling me about the Inheritance Share. So just how does that work?"

"Let's let Mr. Chow explain that. Do you mind, Mr. Chow?" said Crystal.

"Not at all. In the past," said Mr. Chow, "people left their money to their children, and they can still leave a total estate of three million credits, though after estate taxes, only a little over half a million can be passed on. All inheritance after three million credits goes into the Inheritance Share pool. Before, a few were born into vast wealth and power and many others were born with nothing, as their families had no property. They were destined to have to work and pay rent just to have a place to live. Those who inherited lots of money often didn't do much good with it. They either led self-centered lives, using up vast resources on themselves, or they used the money to give themselves tremendous competitive advantage over everyone else so they could make even more. They were also in a position to exert a lot of political power with all that wealth. It wasn't good for democracy."

"I can appreciate that," replied John. "I didn't think it was fair for a multi-millionaire to be able to spend a fortune to get elected. But wouldn't people want to be able to leave their business to their children?"

"You see, John," added Mr. Chow, "just because someone is the heir to a fortune or business empire does not mean that they are the best suited to manage it. Today, if you are very wealthy, you cannot leave your business empire to your children. If you aspire for them to gain control of it, you have to train your childen very well indeed, so that when you die and your enterprise is put up for sale, your childen are the best qualified to manage it. If that is so, then they will be able to get the financial backing to take it over. If they are not perceived to be best qualified for the job, someone else will gain control. This has been a tremendous improvement over the free enterprise system of your day, and the countries who were the first to institute such rules prospered. It is not good for society for a few to use up great quantities of resources leading lazy, self centered lives. Free enterprise works so much better if wealth that used to be squandered on lavish personal lifestyles is left in more productive enterprises. It is also not good for people without the proper skills to be in control just because of their birth. It is certainly not good for many to be born with nothing and to lack the opportunity to get a good education to start their lives. A lot of wonderful businesses and innovations have come from young people who in the past would not have had much opportunity."

"That sounds like socialism or something. Back in my time people thought they had a right to do anything they wanted with the money they earned, and most wanted their children to be at least as well off as they were."

"When the Inheritance Share was first proposed, the critics of it called it Utopian Socialism, as an insult, a put-down. The system of some inheriting vast wealth seems to us today very much like feudalism, where some are born lords and others serfs," explained Mr. Chow. "Great wealth is not created in a vacuum. It usually takes a great amount of human labor and natural resources that rightfully belong to all people. The system we have now is a better balance between individual and collective values. We have learned that we must want the same good things for all children that we want for our own or social harmony is impossible."

"That is a rather major shift in values," said John. "It is hard to imagine, as everyone used to be so concerned with their own children and grandchildren."

"If that were true, then why did they despoil the environment so?" asked Crystal.

"Just stupid, I guess. There were many people saying everything would be alright, that environmentalists were extremists. But now, you have to just leave everything to the government?"

"No," replied Mr. Chow. "A spouse can inherit all the couple both earned while they were together, or at least a quarter of their estate, regardless of circumstances. A person cannot pass on more than 540,000 credits to their children, which is usually enough to allow for a median family home, farm or business to be passed on, and all of their remaining assets are sold and the money put into the Inheritance Share pool when both members of a marriage die. People can give their money to tax exempt charities, up to ten percent of their income a year. Tithing a full ten percent is very common, as it does give people an opportunity to distribute their wealth personally. This school has benefited from many such gifts. Of course, someone can give all of their money to charity before they die if they want. All of it will not be tax exempt, but that does give them the opportunity to personally give away over half of their money, as the highest tax rate is fifty percent."

"People can give their children a good home life and good values." Crystal added. "When people could no longer leave all their money to their children, they seemed to do a better job of giving them time and love. I think people today appreciate that being well-off has little to do with money and much more to do with character. But in actuality, over 97% of kids receive more than they would have inherited from their parents alone anyway."

"I can understand that. Back in my time, about two percent of the people owned over half of everything."

"There's much more equity now," added Mr. Chow. "All inheritances must, by law, be passed on to the next generation and can't be spent for anything else. It must go to education or to the pool that all children share. Even the cost of administration of the Inheritance Share comes out of general taxation. Every family gets two full shares of the inheritance pool that can go to their children, one share from each parent, but if they have more than two kids, their family share is reduced accordingly."

"How does that work?" asked John.

"For instance, if you have four children," Mr. Chow continued, "their share of the pool will only be half as much as those who only had two children. This is one of the main ways our society encourages people not to feed population growth. We could never have brought the ecological problems under control without halting the growth of our population."

"That makes sense. World population was growing out of control in my time," John interjected. "Well, how does the share work? Do you just get a bunch of money at some point?"

"No," said Mr. Chow. "When you are ready to go to college, you can access funds from your share of the pool for that. You can also use the money to purchase a home, or start a business, once you turn twenty-one, but only if you have a good business plan."

"And you said that all transactions using PC bracelets are taxed?"

"Yes," replied Mr. Chow, "and theoretically, any transaction that is not a direct and immediate barter of food, crafts or clothing. Only consumption is taxed, and on a graduated scale. The more you consume, the higher the rate of taxation. People who don't spend much money on themselves don't pay a lot of tax. It is good for society for wealth to be left invested in businesses. Although consumption creates jobs in the short run, it is not good for society for wealth to be consumed excessively. We have learned that the person who creates the wealth is the best suited to administer it, as long as it is invested in creating products and jobs. When wealth is spent lavishly to create an opulent personal lifestyle, then it is highly taxed."

"Well, I can't argue with the results," replied John. "Life seems to have improved so much in so many ways. I can see how having a level playing field for all children would be a lot fairer. I never considered that such an idea might be a superior economic system. I remember a story of a wealthy man who returned to his inner city school and promised all of the children in a class that if they finished high school, he would pay for them to attend college. Most of those kids did end up going to college, though normally kids from that school didn't even finish high school. I guess it would make a huge difference if all children knew that they would be able to go to college and even to own a home someday. I suppose most people own homes now?"

"Home ownership is very high, though after college there is not usually enough for more than a good down payment. We don't have utopia yet, John, but it is a better and improving world. So tell me," continued Mr. Chow," what do you think has happened to you, and do you think you will be staying in this time?"

"To be honest, sir, I myself have to consider if I am still having a dream or vision. Or I might be dead, and this is heaven."

Mr. Chow laughed.

"I certainly can't be unhappy about Crystal or Stuart thinking I'm crazy because perhaps the least likely theory is that I am actually here in the future. I have no idea how long it will last." John's look became more serious. "I must admit though, the idea of not seeing my parents again is hard. I guess they are long dead now. Wow."

They were all silent for a moment.

"If so, I'm sure they had a full measure of life. You know, John," continued Mr. Chow, "there are records you could look up. If your alternative theories are right, then Crystal and I are just mental projections... or angels." They all smiled. John and Crystal looked at each other. "It would be good for you to do some research so you can settle your own mind. So you can really find out where you stand. I've enjoyed talking with you. I have to lock up much of the school now. I only live a few blocks from here. Crystal, would you walk John over to my house when you two are ready? John, we will be having dinner at seven, and you are both invited."

"I'd better not tonight, Mr. Chow," said Crystal. "I have to get up at five so I can get in my practices and still make it to the festival grounds by opening. I'm volunteering at the medical tent."

"Then good evening, Crystal. It was so nice to see you again." Crystal and Mr. Chow shared a short hug. Mr. Chow turned to John. "Crystal was the finest student I ever had who started college but did not go on and earn a degree. I still hope she finishes her studies, even though she has such a great gift of healing."

"I am learning all the time, Mr. Chow," answered Crystal.

The teacher turned and walked off.

"He'll never give up on me getting a degree. We have some time, John, and I can't imagine a better place to spend it then right here. I love this garden and the gazebo. It holds many fond memories for me."

"Sure, Crystal. This is a beautiful spot." They were both silent for a moment. John looked around and took in the beauty of the garden's many blooming flowers, then spoke again. "So what kind of practices do you do in the morning?"

"I do a little stretching and some breathing exercises and then I meditate for an hour."

"I took a yoga class for a while," John added, "and we did breathing exercises and a deep relaxation at the end of each class. I tried meditating a few times, but I was terrible at it."

"You have to stick with it."

"I'm fascinated by how this Inheritance Share works. Have you received yours yet, Crystal?"

"Yes, John, that's how I was able to buy my home. The Share was 77,000 credits for my birth-year, even though the inheritors here in America declined our share of the International Inheritance Share."

"What's that?" asked John.

"Ten percent of all Inheritance Share pools are given to a world wide pool, then split among all the kids of age on the planet. Most years, kids in the wealthier countries vote to decline to take a part of it so that poorer countries can get more per person. There is talk of raising that to 20% in the year 2100."

"Incredible! World wide sharing. That's great," said John. "I guess that is a good way to help the poorer countries get ahead."

"It is slowly helping to level things out. Please tell me more about yourself, John. Why did you decide to study medicine?"

"Well, I really wanted to be a poet. Still do. Did you ever read or see Dr. Zhivago?"

"No."

"It is a beautiful story that takes place in revolutionary Russia in the first part of the Twentieth Century. Dr. Zhivago was an idealistic and romantic man, as well as a poet. He studied to be a doctor because he thought a person should have a real profession, too, not just composing poetry. He also wanted to help people. I found that idea very inspirational. I like to fancy myself to be like Dr. Zhivago."

"I know you are a good poet, John. I loved your poem."

John was smiling and looking into Crystal's eyes with great love.

"Mr. Chow is a pretty wonderful man, isn't he? So trusting, and he gives that trust to every student he has. I feel ashamed for my lack of trust in you, John."

"Nonsense. You've been wonderful, Crystal." John reached over and took her hand in his. She squeezed it back, and gave him a beautiful smile.

He slid a little closer to Crystal until their shoulders touched. They sat together holding hands, listening to the birds sing. Two butterflies flew into the gazebo and performed their little mating dance there in front of John and Crystal. One of them landed on Crystal's bare knee, then the other landed on John's Levis. The couple turned to look at each other and both laughed a joyous and gentle laugh.

Soon the butterflies were gone, but John's knees and legs were still touching Crystal's. She felt so incredibly good to him. It was as if he were melting into her warm body. Then the wonderful tickling spread to his groin and he felt himself becoming aroused. In a minute she would surely be able to see that. John started to panic somewhat, as he didn't know how this supposedly celibate lady would react. Maybe he was a little embarrassed. Before it could become noticeable, John got up. Being at a loss for words, he said, "Maybe we should head on over to Mr. Chow's house."

Crystal sat there and gave John what he thought might be a wistful look, then said sure. They stood up and walked away from the gazebo, with John feeling somewhat shy about taking her hand in his again. He didn't know how to treat a woman who had chosen to be a celibate. He didn't think he was ready to deal with his own sexuality anyway, as he remembered the tragic effects of his relations with Faith.

DINNER WITH THE CHOWS

On the way over to Mr. Chow's house the energy between John and Crystal was pleasant, but a little awkward. John wanted to take Crystal's hand, but just couldn't. Crystal seemed to be a little put off by John's slight withdrawal, and was staying a little more distant. Yet the magic of the moment wasn't totally lost. They talked about the beauty of the neighborhood and the evening light. John had always loved this time of the day, when the light mellows and casts shadows. Tonight seemed more golden and radiant than ever. John noticed how most of the houses looked a little smaller than in his time. Crystal pointed out that while that was so, the yards were now a little bigger. Crystal told John how her PC was also a phone. She wrote her number down and gave it to him. When they got to Mr. Chow's house, John desperately searched his mind for a reason to keep Crystal there longer, but came up empty.

"So tomorrow you are going to be a volunteer at the medical tent at the festival. It sounds like Woodstock."

"All these festivals trace their ancestry back to Woodstock, John. Woodstock has achieved legendary status. Tell me, John, was it really as outrageous as they say?"

"Oh, yeah. My uncle Bob went, and he told me all about it. There was a movie about it. Did you ever see it?"

"No. I guess the festival here would seem tame."

"Crystal," John said as they walked up the steps to the porch, "can I see you tomorrow night after the festival?"

"I'm sorry, I can't, John. I have an important meeting tomorrow night and I wouldn't have any time in between."

"Well, how about Sunday? Church maybe?" John said church as it was the earliest thing he could think of.

"Stuart usually spends Sundays with me, and though we don't have formal plans, I don't want to upset him any more. I am attending something Sunday evening that Stuart never participates in. It is the Summer Solstice, and I am assisting in a ritual to honor the occasion. If you like, we could go together, and then have dinner afterwards."

"I'd love to." John was beaming from ear to ear.

"I'm going to pop in and say hello to Mrs. Chow."

Crystal stuck her head in the front door and said, "Knock, Knock." Mrs. Chow came out of the kitchen and gave Crystal a big hug. She was a pleasant looking older lady with black hair just turning gray, sparkling blue eyes and a wonderful warm smile. Her apron seemed to be hand embroidered with vegetables and vine designs. They stood there with one arm around each other as Crystal introduced John to Mrs. Chow. "Did Mr. Chow tell you he had invited a dinner guest?"

"Yes, he just called me. No problem. I have plenty of food. You stay too, Crystal. He said you had declined, but your excuse is not too good."

Crystal looked at John with a big grin, then looked back to Mrs. Chow and said, "How can I refuse. I learned some of my best recipes from you."

Mr. Chow arrived a moment later and within a few minutes they were seated in the dining room having a wonderful meal of Chinese dumplings. John was happy that most of the conversation was about what Crystal had been doing since she had seen them last. Mr. Chow hadn't said anything to his wife about John's being from the past, and he was glad that that was not dominating the conversation. Mrs. Chow also told Crystal that she should continue with her education, and Crystal countered that she studied and read all the time.

Mrs. Chow said that she was going to make fried plantains for dessert, and Crystal went with her to the kitchen to learn how.

Mr. Chow asked John how he met Crystal, and John explained how he had been on top of the hill when the incredible experience happened to him, how he met Crystal, and what he had been doing that day. The ladies came back into the room with some freshly fried plantains emitting a wonderful cinnamon smell. Mr. Chow offered Crystal and John a cappuccino, which they declined. He made himself a hand-pressed espresso from a beautiful little brass machine that was in the dining room.

"Well, John, I think Mr. Chow is preparing to talk your ear off," Crystal said with a grin.

"Crystal doesn't approve of my little vice. I gave up my evening cigarette, Crystal. What do you want from me? I am not ready to be a perfect person like you and the Star Voyagers. Or let us just say, I pursue perfection in another direction."

"You're doing a wonderful job, Mr. Chow. I'm still learning important things from you. I'm going to step into the other room and check the subus time estimate."

"Sure. And Crystal, I have learned some things from you, too."

Crystal left for a moment and then came back and announced that she had about seven minutes to catch the bus, so she had better say good night. John said that he would walk her to the stop. Crystal hugged Mr. and Mrs. Chow, thanked them again, then she and John left together.

"How far is the subus stop?"

"Just three blocks," Crystal replied.

John knew that it was by the grace of God that he had another chance to regain some of the closeness that they had experienced earlier in the gazebo. The sun was getting ready to set and the colors over the Bay and city were breathtaking.

A deeper thought entered John's mind. That it was by the amazing grace of God that he was actually here, having another chance at love. Could it be the same love in just another form? Could this even be real? Life itself was such a great mystery, such an incredible miracle, that anything could be possible.

"I was just thinking, how could this be real? Then I thought that life is such an awesome miracle, that the fact that anything exists at all is such a miracle, why shouldn't it be possible? Of all the miracles, for God to roll away the stone of nothingness, and bring forth such an awesome universe teaming with life, with trillions of stars, wow!" John's outburst both surprised him and filled him with the bliss of the moment and the joy of poetic expression.

Crystal stopped and turned to face John. Then they could see that in the other direction, the moon had just risen above the trees almost full, big, bright, and beautiful. John reached out his hand. Crystal took it in hers. What a moment! Deep feelings of love poured forth from John's heart, from his soul, from the deepest core of his being. A wonderful warmth permeated his whole body. Crystal's eyes also shone with the light of love. The moment was so perfect, nothing further was necessary.

How long did it last? Perhaps too long, because suddenly Crystal heard a sound and said, "Oh my gosh, the subus. Come on." She turned and they both ran together hand in hand. John laughed like a child, and so did she. They got down the ramp and to the turnstile just as the subus pulled in and opened its door.

"They only run every 15 minutes going to my house now." John was breathing heavily, but Crystal wasn't even winded. She looked at John quietly for a moment and then said, "I got my first kiss at that gazebo." She gave John a quick hug that was over before he could catch his breath or even hug back, and then she was in the subus and gone.

What a day! What a night! What a life! John couldn't contain his joy as he headed back to the Chow's. He danced. He swung on tree limbs. Even without her there, he was having a fantastic time, high on love. When he got back to the Chows', Mrs. Chow showed him their son's picture. Then she showed him to his bedroom and bathroom and where the fresh towels were.

"My husband tells me you are from the past. I have hosted children from all over the world, but this is a first even for me," she said with a smile.

John was invited to make himself completely at home. Mrs. Chow even came back in his room and gave him a new toothbrush, still in its box. John thanked her repeatedly, and said that he would like to take a shower. Mrs. Chow opened one of her son's drawers and closet, gave John some fresh clothing to wear, and insisted on putting John's in the laundry.

"It would be no trouble to wash them," she said.

John enjoyed the shower immensely. He wondered if everyone in this time was as generous and outgoing as the Chows. Then he thought of David and of his parents. He was no longer saddened by the thought of their being long dead, but was worried that his disappearance did cause them all some distress. Well, there was nothing he could do about that. After he had bathed and changed clothing, he went back into the living room where Mr. Chow was sitting in front of a big flat television.

"So, you still have television."

"Yes, but it has changed a great deal since your time. People aren't as faithful about watching shows when they are aired, as our TVs can be programmed to record any show for watching at our leisure.

There are fewer advertisements, as the public just won't watch them. No matter what they try, everyone soon finds a way to delete them while recording. I was just catching a little local news."

"That's interesting, having very little advertising on TV. I was wondering if the trend would ever reverse. TV advertising was completely changing our whole culture. I didn't notice a lot of the old chain fast food restaurants everywhere. Do y'all still have them?"

"Not as many, and they build them to look like a part of the local architecture. Good observation, John. When television advertisements lost prominence, national chains lost their main competitive advantage and many more small, local businesses sprang up in their place. You can also get programming in 3D, but I soon get tired of the glasses. You have a southern accent. Not just southern, but old southern. There is so much travel today and mass communication that accents are not as prominent as in the past. Where are you from?"

"I was raised in a small town not far from Atlanta. My parents still live there. Or did."

"If your journey from the past to now was made public, John, I think you would create quite a stir. You would probably become very famous. You could even become very wealthy, if people believed you."

John thought about that one for a while. Was Mr. Chow suggesting a motive for deception? Did he want to become rich and famous? Mr. Chow had trusted him, he thought.

"Mr. Chow, do you really believe me about being from the past, or are you just humoring me to find out what's going on?"

"I enjoy your directness, John. I believe in your sincerity. I believe that it could be possible to somehow come from the past to the future, but probably not the other way. I know that there are other possible explanations. But I am not playing a game with you, if that is what you suspect."

"I'm sorry if I suggested that, sir. Your kindness is outstanding, no matter what you think. I think I am going to go on the working hypothesis that I am really here, by some miracle, by the grace of God, and I am incredibly grateful. You see, I lost my fiancée to a tragic illness, and it put me in a depression I just couldn't shake. I was even thinking about going on some kind of antidepressant drug. Now I am here and I've met Crystal."

John wanted so much to talk about Crystal and his love for her, but he didn't. He had just met her, and in very unusual circumstances. And he was just shy about really letting his feelings out.

"Crystal is a very special person," said Mr. Chow. "She has helped many people when no one else could. She helped my own son, when they were both still children. With her great gift, she could already be very wealthy."

"So she doesn't charge a lot for her help?"

"That is right, she only takes love offerings. And she does no advertising. She doesn't even have herself listed anywhere. She gets all of her patients by word of mouth. She does demand a lot from those she helps. Good diet, exercise, meditation, positive affirmation. Yes, Crystal is special."

John smiled, and felt another wave of love.

"Do you have any plans for tomorrow, John?"

"I'd like to go to the International Youth Festival, but I guess there aren't any tickets left at this point, and I don't have any money except these coins." John reached in his pocket and handed the coins to Mr. Chow.

"Coins like these are very rare. Many people still collect them. I bet you could sell them for a good sum."

"That's a great idea. Can I look in your phone book's yellow pages for a coin dealer?"

"You mean the advertisements?" Mr. Chow asked the television to turn back on and in a moment had up the listings of several coin dealers, one right there in Berkeley. "Tomorrow morning you can call them and see what they will offer. You will probably have to pay a scalper a high price, but you could probably find a ticket to the festival if you want."

"Thanks a lot, sir."

John sat back and thought about the incredible day he had and the amazing world he was now in.

"Mr. Chow, back in my time we thought that by now there would be space travel and high tech highways and fusion reactors or some other source of cheap, clean energy. Everyone sort of envisioned a more technically advanced world, with robots doing all the work. If anything, things seem simpler than they were."

Mr. Chow chuckled. "Yes. The people of your time could never seem to get enough. They wanted more and more, yet they already had all that they needed to make the world a paradise. We haven't abandoned material progress, but our main priority now is improving ourselves and society. Fusion was achieved, but like other big, centralized sources of power, it had many problems. You know, when nuclear power was first conceived, it was supposed to make power 'too cheap to meter,' but the eventual cost was tremendous. The myth of unlimited, inexpensive power becoming available was a big part of the reason everyone wasted so much energy back in your time. It would be alright to burn up all the oil because soon we'd have cheap nuclear power or cheap fusion power. People thought technology could overcome any obstacle, but this attitude almost ruined the environment. It was finally realized that more could be done with other, less complicated sources of energy and through conservation. I have a theory that if a fair share isn't enough for you, or for your society, then nothing will ever be enough because you have already exceeded a balance and are out of harmony with the Earth and all the beings on it."

"Some people work a lot harder or are more talented than others. How can you say what is enough?" said John.

"It is what you need to be able to have a comfortable and enjoyable life, but not so much that everyone else couldn't have the same if they worked as hard as you. There is a limit to the Earth's resources. Exceed that balance and you will go on wanting more and more and never find the peace of contentment."

"That sure seemed to be the malady of my age."

"Yes, and a sense of isolation from family, community, nature, and even God. You know, your little automobiles of your time were a major contributing factor to this sense of separateness. Everyone in his own little space. They didn't seem to notice that they were ruining the world with their cars and oil. There are many reasons why people today feel much more connected to each other, to nature, to community. Getting out of the individual automobile is one very important one."

"My car broke down about six weeks ago," said John, "and I couldn't afford to get it fixed, so I've been using mass transit. You do get used to it. Now it is so good. I imagined it could be better, more like you have it now, many times while waiting for a bus."

"About space travel, we have sent instruments all over the solar system, and you can now visit many places in virtual reality. We have made many amazing discoveries. You have a lot to discover yourself, John. Perhaps I can access some space exploration files for you."

"Crystal said that machines do most of the manufacturing work, yet I've never seen so many people working in gardens, even in the Georgia countryside."

"Robots do most of the manufacturing and heavy industrial labor, but it is very difficult to grow some foods with machines. For a long time food was very expensive, so people got into the habit of growing some of their own food. People do work much less than in your time. Twenty-four to thirty hours a week is usual. But if machines did everything, what would we humans do? It is now known that food grown with loving care creates the healthiest bodies. Many people nowadays will not even wear clothing that was mass produced."

"Yes. I've learned a little about the Com-Union and their goals. They sound like our old hippies. Do you think they can succeed in creating the utopia they want, where everything is free?"

"Probably not anytime soon." said Mr. Chow. "Perhaps utopia is in the striving to achieve it. I do believe we will continue to evolve towards greater perfection. There is still greed, lust, and the anger they create in many hearts. This is where we will build our utopia. In our hearts and minds."

"I am still curious about this Inheritance Share. How did it ever come about? It seems like many people would have resented the idea."

"Yes, but they were in the minority when it was implemented. Early in this century, it was discovered that many people carried genes that predisposed their offspring to disease. So many people were having children that were not genetically their own that it seemed to help us get over our basic biological drive to enhance our own gene pool, even at the expense of others. It was a powerful drive, but counterproductive in every respect. We have evolved beyond the jungle, but still have many drives left from that era, like the fight-or-flight mechanism. Good for jungle survival, but in modern society, it only makes us stressed out. Like the urge for revenge, that caused us to punish our criminals instead of trying to help them. Understandable, but counterproductive."

Mr. Chow continued. "Leaving a lot of money to your children is the same thing. Probably most of the time you are not helping them to have a better life. Perhaps a wealthier, but probably not really a happier life. When my great grandfather came to this country, he and his family worked very hard. They managed to buy a home, pay for a business, and put my grandfather and his sisters through college. One lawyer and two doctors. They made a lot of money. Their children did not do so well. They knew they would get all this money, and so they didn't try very hard. Many of that generation had problems with drugs or alcohol, or other psychological problems. Only a few of them accomplished very much, and most had less or no money when they died."

"I've seen the same kind of scenario," said John.

"Today I was looking at a history file in the library and it said that there was a meltdown of four nuclear reactors in Japan that was caused by a major earthquake and Tsunami. Then later the same thing happened in southern California."

"Yes. Of all the stupid things we humans did, that tragedy was perhaps the worst," Mr. Chow exclaimed. "It is hard to comprehend a reactor filled with so much poison being built on an earthquake fault. Even after the tragedy in Japan, we Americans still did not even close down our reactors that shared the same danger. And the way that the victims were treated. Just last night I was watching a program about that era and the struggle of those people for justice. A large area is still filled with ghost towns."

"What happened to them?"

"Before the earthquakes, people of your era were using up everything, and running deeply into debt both economically and ecologically. Every problem was put off until tomorrow. When tomorrow came, there were even bigger problems and no resources left to deal with them. Though hundreds of thousands of people lost their homes and businesses, no one wanted to give up any of what they had in order to help them. In fairness, we were in the midst of a terrible economic and ecological crisis. It does seem that without the terrorism that some of the nuclear refugees resorted to, nothing would ever have been done to help them. They were eventually compensated somewhat for their losses."

"It was a long, hard struggle to repair the problems of the past and then begin to build a better future. I think it is by the grace of God that so many survived and that we did not destroy the ecological balance permanently. One of the reasons the nuclear refugees had such problems was that people did not have much hope that any of humanity would make it, and there were already many people made homeless by poverty and by the dislocation of the rising seas. It was necessary to solve their problem as well. Nowadays, the Inheritance Share is used to help everyone have a home of his own, and we have virtually no homelessness."

"That's fantastic. I guess it was worth all the difficulties and struggle if it helped humanity get to here."

"Yes," said Mr. Chow, "It was inevitable that humanity would

THERE IS A TOMORROW REDUX

push the environment to a crisis due to our lack of any international organization to control the greedy exploitation that was occurring. It was an anarchistic feeding frenzy consuming the Earth. Our inability to work together, our ceding of control to giant vested interests, our lack of any foresight beyond the next election or profit report, created the very crisis that forced us to remedy all these things. Humanity finally had a common foe to face, a monster of our own creation, the climate change crisis. And yet, without it, we probably wouldn't have made many of the important social changes that have created so much more equity and opportunity."

"Well, that's fantastic. Are there still poverty-stricken countries in the world? Or starvation?"

"No. Some countries are better off than others, but no place is in desperate poverty. There has been no major famine in over forty years. The Earth's resources are much more equitably distributed. Beverly and I have hosted youngsters from all over the world and this festival will be the first in a long time that we didn't sign up as hosts. People have so many friends from so many places, humanity does seem to be a big family, and every crisis is responded to with love and generosity. I have many history files that you could look at John. Would you like me to get them up for you?"

"Not tonight, sir. I have plenty enough to absorb. I'm not sure I'll be able get to sleep, but I know I need it. Golly. I wonder where I'll wake up?"

"I assure you I am not a dream, John, and if you go to sleep here you will wake up here. Unless you are a sleepwalker." They both laughed.

"Crystal thinks that just because I have a little espresso I'll not be able to sleep, but I think I am ready for bed."

Mr. Chow showed John how to access the TV programming on his computer and then said goodnight. John just wanted to go and lie down in bed and think about Crystal, her beautiful smile, her kindness towards him, her warmth at the end of the day. He wondered if she would have let him kiss her at the gazebo or when they stood there in the moonlight. He was a bit rusty in the love department, but after her remark, it did seem like she would have. He decided that he would try and attend the festival so he could see her again before Sunday evening. Maybe he could ride home with her or something. Just to see her would be enough. It took him over two hours, but he finally did fall asleep.

THE FESTIVAL

When John woke up, the Sun was shinning in the window and birds were singing sweet melodies. It only took him a moment to realize where he was, and a giant smile grew across his face. He lay there for a few minutes thinking with wonder about the amazing circumstances he found himself in. He closed his eyes to say a prayer of thanksgiving, and then, with the tremendous gratitude he felt, got up and knelt at the window to finish. What he saw made his heart fly even a little higher. A beautiful garden. A beautiful morning. Birds and butterflies dancing and singing. He was still there. This wasn't a dream. Maybe he was really going to stay in this wonderful new world.

And Crystal! He felt so in love. To come to this time and find such a woman, such a wonderful woman. The most sincere prayer of thanksgiving of his young life was sent winging its way to God. And he couldn't help ending it with a small request. Could he see her today, even for a moment?

John went into the bathroom, washed his face and shaved. He found the Chows in the kitchen. Mr. Chow was making himself another espresso, and he asked John if he would like an espresso or cappuccino.

"Yes sir, I'd love a cappuccino."

"In your time they probably used cow's milk. Now many of us use soy milk. Is that all right?"

"Soy milk froths up? That would be great. You know, I was trying to get people to use soy foods before I, I guess 'shifted' is a good term. I was going to medical school, learning about the options for people with cancer, none of which in my time were very good."

"They were still using radiation then, right?"

"Yes, and chemotherapy that made people deathly ill. I read an article that reported that eating soy foods could cut your chance of getting cancer or heart attacks in half."

"Yes, soy is very good for you. Cancer is unusual now except in old age."

Mr. Chow frothed up the soy milk and served John his cappuccino. Mrs. Chow apologized for not waiting breakfast for him, but they thought they should let him sleep. There was a bowl of freshly made granola on the table, and John could still smell the wonderful, sweet aroma from its baking. Mrs. Chow invited him to have some with some fruit, and asked him if he'd like some orange juice. When John saw that she was going to squeeze oranges right then, he tried to get her to let him do it.

"No. You are our guest. It takes only one minute."

John couldn't help but feel a lot of love for these kindly people who had accepted him with so much warmth and hospitality.

"I hope I can find a way to repay y'all for your kindness."

"Nonsense. You know, John, Chen and I decided that since Lee, our son, was no longer living with us, we would take a break from hosting kids for this festival. But now that it is here I miss the excitement of children from other lands filling our home. You are a very welcome guest."

"Thank you so much. Amazingly, here I am eating granola and soy milk, and it is delicious. I was disappointed when my roommate wouldn't try some soy milk on his granola, a few mornings ago, 102 years ago."

Mr. Chow had taken his espresso into the living room, and in a few minutes came back to the kitchen to report that there were many tickets to the festival available for that day, and there were even a few people selling tickets for both days. The festival had started off well yesterday evening and the weather outlook was excellent.

Mr. Chow told John about his first international festival in Singapore. He was 28 years old, so he only had one more year to be eligible to attend. He'd just about given up hope of ever winning a ticket, as the festivals were for youths from 18 to 29 years old. After the festival, he had spent four months traveling all over Southeast Asia staying with people he had met, and then with their friends. Everyone was so nice and generous to him, even the families of very modest means. Thirty years later he still communicates with many of the people he met then.

"Being able to talk with your old friends with life size pictures of them on the screen really does help you maintain a closeness to them. We can take a hand held camera around and show our friends our family and our homes and projects while we talk. I've even taken my friends on long sightseeing trips around the area during a call. That can get expensive though, because it still costs a lot to transmit a picture to the relay station. Then it is forwarded by fiber, which is relatively inexpensive, the rest of the way."

"Why is that?" asked John.

"Pictures take a whole lot more bandwidth than audio to transmit live. Do you understand what I mean, John?"

"Actually, no," said John with a grin.

"The whole world is linked up with wideband fiber optic cable. As it has been used for a long time, it is paid for and relatively inexpensive. Calls transmitted over the very crowded airways cost much more, and a video picture takes a lot of bandwidth to send live, so the charge is much greater than for live audio calls."

When John had finished his breakfast, Mrs. Chow went out to work in the garden, and Mr. Chow took John into the living room to call up the coin dealer. They soon had the dealer on the line with a life sized picture. He was a pleasant looking fellow of Indian extraction named Mr. Patel. He asked John to put the coins in front of the camera built into Mr. Chow's TV, and seemed very excited when he saw them. He would be very happy to purchase them.

"I cannot go with you to the coin dealer, John. I promised I would help some of my students get our new pond stocked with plants and fish. I will give you a map to help you find it. You don't have an account registration number, do you?"

"No." John said.

"This could be a real problem, as he will expect to transfer payment to your record. Frankly, John, I'm not sure how you can overcome this problem. An account registration number is almost essential in our society. Some Com-Union people don't use one. They ride bikes and barter for everything. Perhaps Mr. Patel will have a way to deal with this. Here is my number. If this gets to be a problem call me."

"When did we stop having money?" asked John. "I don't think that idea would have went down well back in my time."

"There was a lot of resistance to the change," replied Mr. Chow, "and there still is. When the idea was sold to the public, they were frightened of any more terrorism, and it was also supposed to help with the drug wars and lower taxes by eliminating cheating. It did make a big difference. Follow me outside John."

They both went outside and over to a small storage area.

"You can use Lee's recumbent bicycle to get there, and not have to deal with the subus, which you can't pay for. Take good care of it and use the lock. If yellow lights go on next to you, slow down immediately, or you will get my son's account fined. See the license plate?"

John looked at the back of the bike and saw a license with a computer bar code on it.

"The code for the lock is m-a-c-k. Our society is not quite perfect. One time someone borrowed this bike out of a bike rack for two months. Lee had to get hundreds of dollars of speeding fines taken off of his record. So follow the blue trail to your left to the University Avenue exit. Watch out, some of the jocks around here cruise at 25 kph in groups, and the skateboarders can swerve in front of you in a heartbeat, so be careful passing them. Even the skaters have motors, so don't be surprised if they speed up going uphill. Once we made the breakthrough to lightweight, all temperature, super conductors, wonderful small lightweight motors followed. That invention also gave us a big energy dividend, as it virtually eliminated the waste of power in transmission. You have a lot to discover, John."

John sat down on the seat of the bike and looked at the controls. "So there are super conductors now. I knew they were working on them in my time."

"This right handgrip controls the speed of your motor," Mr. Chow demonstrated. "Just push this tab and roll it backwards and it will engage. These handles are front and rear ABS brakes, to help you to stop without skidding. Think you can handle it?"

"I think so. It ought to be fun. Thanks a lot, Mr. Chow."

John had seen bicycles like this one on television, but he'd never ridden one. The rider sat leaning back against a plush seat with a back rest, and the small front wheel was way out in front. It was quite comfortable, but he was rather wobbly for the first few blocks. Mr. Chow had told him to gear down to go up hills, and it would help to pedal then. After a few minutes he was having a ball, riding down the bike lane with no automobiles to worry about. There were lots of folks out riding and skating or skateboarding in the two one-way wheeled vehicle lanes, and walking in the pedestrian lane. The beauty of the city was so enhanced without the din and fumes of thousands of cars. He did have to dodge a dog chasing a skateboarder. He didn't think dogs were supposed to be on the ped.

He found that the ped wound around a lot, had banked turns, sometimes went over access roads and sometimes went under them. All in all, everyone on it seemed to be having fun. Many people did still pedal, and he was passed repeatedly by athletic types running mostly in the yellow. Soon he was to University Avenue and at the coin shop.

Mr. Patel was a very nice fellow who still had a slight Indian accent. When John showed him the coins he smiled and said, "Very good."

"Where did you get these?" he asked.

"You're probably not going to believe this," John answered, "but I am from the past."

John told him the whole story of how he was bummed out and went up the hill, had prayed, and had the experience. Mr. Patel listened intently, and then was quiet for a minute after John finished.

"You are sure of this?"

"Yes, very sure. I know it seems impossible, but I am telling you the truth. Not only that, I don't have an account registration number from this time."

"This is an amazing story. I will have to check to see if any such coins have been reported stolen. Please do not take offense. I would not be a responsible citizen if I did not."

"Sure, go ahead. I know these coins were not stolen. By the way, here is my driver's license and social security card. I know they don't prove anything, but they do suggest that my story is true."

"Amazing." Mr. Patel went to his computer and in a few minutes returned and said that there was no reported theft of such coins, nor was he wanted by the law."

"Mr. Patel, is there any way that I could get my own account and PC? Will I get enough for that?"

"These coins are quite valuable. When all coins were rounded up and melted down to end black marketing, only the coins in registered collections were exempted. There weren't a lot of coins of this type in collections then, so they are now rarer than even some old gold coins.

He brought a price list up on his computer and studied the pages. Here is the list price. I can give you nine hundred credits for them. I am offering you sixty percent of their retail value. I can also sell you a PC. I'll have my bank open an account for you. We will transfer the credits to your new account and you'll be set up. The only problem is that you do not have a registration number. I have an idea. We will use your social security number. It has the same number of digits. First we will see if anyone has this number." He entered the number on his keyboard. "No, it is clear."

"That's great." said John.

"There is still a problem. Your number is not registered. When you use your card you will get a message prompting saying for you to report to a social registration office due to the discrepancy. As you will have credits and an account, you will be able to use your PC to pay for things for two weeks before the government cancels it. At that time, you must clear up the discrepancy in order to resume using it."

"By then maybe I'll know what's going on. How much is nine hundred credits worth?" asked John.

"Coincidentally, it is about two weeks average pay. Let me call up my bank. They are open this morning. We should be able to do everything from here electronically."

Mr. Patel sat down at his computer and set up the credit transfer to a new account they opened for John. He then explained to John how he would have to use a voice print for purchases over twenty credits, and a voice print and thumbprint for purchases over a hundred. Tax is automatically deducted every time you purchase something. John signed the signature recorder that Mr. Patel had to have as a merchant He sat still for a picture, took a thumb print, gave a voice print of his name, and it was all sent immediately to the bank. Then they called the telephone company and got John a number. John signed up for the least expensive phone plan.

"Any merchant can call up your photo," Mr. Patel added, "so there is little theft of credit. The phone company will deduct the charge for calls automatically. Now you are all set up. This is an older, used PC so I can sell it to you for one hundred and fifty credits."

"Does it have an interpreter chip?"

"Of course. An IT36 chip."

"Is that a good one?"

"If you have an accent like me, it is the best."

Mr. Patel spent a few minutes explaining how to use the many features of his new PC.

"This PC doesn't have a camera, but it can receive picture calls on the screen. You can encrypt any call if the person you are calling

101

knows your code. It has an automatic interpreter program and a voice stress tester."

John was amazed that a small computer the size of a large wrist watch could do so much. A voice activated computer that could give you data verbally or on the small screen, which also allowed incoming picture calls. An interpreter and stenographer could send data to a home PC to store or make hard copies. A little earpiece that fit over one ear gave better sound than the little speaker in the PC, and was superior for interpretations. What an incredible device. John could even pick between 60 different voices for it. He picked a very sexy lady's voice.

"The cost for air time is also deducted from your account, so don't talk too long from this portable PC. It is cheaper to use a home phone. I have been thinking, John. At first I found your story hard to believe. But it is possible that you went into Samadhi, a state of complete absorption into the oneness of the universe. In my native India, it is not unusual for mystics to go into Samadhi for weeks or months at a time. In that state they need no food or water, nor is breath perceptible. Maybe you went into cosmic absorption for that time."

"I guess that is possible, but if so, how come no one saw me sitting there all those years."

"Perhaps you were vibrating at such a high level that you were invisible. In the Yoga Sutras it is said that one can acquire the power to be invisible and unable to be felt. It is a good mystery. If you ever find the answer, please call me and let me know." Mr. Patel gave John a business card. "It is too bad you did not have a pocket full of coins when you came. We could both make a lot of money. Now give me your PC and I will debit your account for the one hundred and fifty credits, and there will be a fifteen percent tax.

"Can I use your computer to find myself a ticket for the festival today? Mr. Chow said there were many listed."

With Mr. Patel's help, John found one held by a student in Berkeley, and he made an appointment to meet him at a disk store on Telegraph Ave. John found that Telegraph was the same hip little strip of stores and restaurants that it had been in his time. Everyone seemed cheerier than before. He saw a street vendor selling silver jewelry, some kids dancing for tips and several street musicians. There were stores selling disks and mini drives, which evidently now could play holograms of bands and such on tabletop holographic projectors. John spent a few minutes watching one in the window of a store. It wasn't as good as Virtual, but pretty vivid and the 3-D was excellent.

There were restaurants selling food from all over the planet. John read some of the menus in the windows, and saw that meat dishes were in a small minority. He considered buying himself some new clothing but he decided to wait until he was heading back to the Chow's.

He had to pay 250 credits for the ticket. The fellow told him he had just lowered the price from 350, as the festival had already started, but it was for both days. John was very glad that he now didn't have to tell anyone he was from the past, unless he wanted to. They concluded the deal, and both made thumb prints on both of their screens. He saw that he was charged a fifteen percent tax and a half percent transfer fee. He got a prompt that said there was a problem with his number and to report to the social registration office by July fifth. Fifteen percent tax is pretty stiff, he thought, but if they don't have any income tax, probably a pretty good deal.

John decided to leave the bike locked up in the plaza on campus, and get it on his way back to the Chows, as getting to the festival required a subus and train transfer. His PC could give him directions to anywhere. Shortly he was back on the train to San Francisco. He saw that some folks were using their PCs as phones on the train, and he wondered if he should call Crystal. It would be better to surprise her, he thought. He knew where she was working. He wondered if he would have to be injured to get into the medical tent. Though it was approaching noon by the time he got to the festival stop, there were still many young people who got off there.

The mood became much more festive when they got back up above ground and saw the brightly colored pendants and heard the music emanating from the festival grounds. There were hundreds of the power gliders of all designs and colors circling around in a giant clockwise rotation, and it was an incredible sight. They seemed to be spiraling in from up high and to the east and coming out the bottom to the west. It was an amazing and colorful scene. By the time they got inside, he could see that everyone was beaming with smiles and happiness. There was a giant field shaped into a perfect amphitheater sloping down to the stage with a huge screen behind it. Sometimes, the screen had a fantastic light show, sometimes it showed the musicians. The energy was electric, and everyone seemed to be having a wonderful time. John felt somewhat alone though, not having any companions or knowing a soul except Crystal.

Even if I get to see Crystal, he thought, she's working today and probably won't be able to hang out with me. He needed some new friends. John saw on his program that in the exhibit area there was a tent set up especially for meeting people from other countries. He decided to give it a try. When he got there he discovered that it was a computerized information center that had everyone who was looking for companionship, a date, or a place to stay, listed by countries. When John sat down and accessed the list, he could see that most everyone had already connected up, and not too many people were still looking. He decided to look for a friend from Bangladesh, as he had sponsored a child there through Save the Children. He was surprised to find that there was someone listed who had the same name as his child, Shashir Kanti. And the fellow was still looking for companionship. John didn't have to leave a meeting time and place. He could just call him up.

It took a while for the phone to work, then John asked for the number listed, and soon had Shashir on the line. He could speak perfect English, so John didn't need the translator to talk to him. They decided to meet by meeting pole 25. John wondered what he should tell this fellow, and decided that the truth was best. He was curious as to how he had the same name as his sponsored child, and that was worth exploring.

Shashir was easy to spot with his white clothing and green day pack. He had a bushy head of black hair, a fair complexion for someone from the subcontinent, and a wonderful, big smile. John found out that he was also 23, and this was the first festival he had ever attended outside of Bangladesh. He had been having a fantastic time ever since he arrived in San Francisco two days earlier. He had found a place to stay with a couple who were childless. They said they hosted kids for every festival, and any time any of their young friends needed a place to stay, they would put them up. Shashir had arranged a date for himself for that evening and encouraged John to try and get one, too.

"I just met this wonderful woman named Crystal yesterday. She is a very beautiful and special person. She's working at the medical tent today because she is a gifted healer. Do you believe in reincarnation, Shashir?"

"Yes, John, I believe I have had many lives."

"I think I was in love with Crystal in her last life."

"Yes, John, I have thought that about almost every girl I have ever been in love with."

"Well, Shashir, I know I'm in love with Crystal now." It felt good to be able to share that with someone.

"I am very happy for you, my brother. I suggest that we go on over to the medical tent so you can see Crystal and find out if she will be able to spend any time with you, so a date could still be an option."

John got cold feet and suggested they listen to the next group first. They went down as far as they could towards the front but were stopped by virtually wall to wall people at over 100 feet from the stage. The sound was still great. Probably too loud if we got any closer, John thought.

The band really had everyone going. They were from Australia, and had some dancers dressed in native, Aboriginal style garb, dancing up front. The band soon had everybody up on their feet and dancing blissfully. John tried mimicking the Aboriginal dances and was really enjoying the experience.

It seemed to him there were good looking girls everywhere. The summer heat had everybody down to shorts, T-shirts, halters or bare skin. It didn't take long for a wonderful endorphin high to kick in, maybe a contact high too, as lots of folks seemed stoned and he smelled pot smoke. He was enjoying a sensuous bliss of another kind, this time shared by thousands, the ecstatic joy of dance. John could see that Shashir, too, was having a fantastic time.

The band played two encores and left everybody feeling great. John and Shashir sat down and found themselves inside a circle of people who were all tuning their PC's to the same frequency. They invited John and Shashir to join in and John found that he was getting interpretations in his ear set. Then there were 14 of them sitting in a circle, taking turns talking, and everyone got a translation through their earpiece. It worked well as long as they didn't all speak at once.

John found that there were kids from all over the world just in their little group, even a young lady from Tibet. He had so many questions to ask them, but he didn't want to expose that he was from the past, so he restrained his curiosity. There was a fellow from Scotland with a girl from Amsterdam who were raving about the next band up. It was a group from Scotland who took traditional Celtic songs and rocked them.

An American fellow pulled out a pipe, told everyone he grew the herb himself, then lighted it up. John could see that not everyone was smoking. A few passed the pipe on. When it got to Shashir he took a big toke and passed it to John. It had been a while since he had smoked any pot. He had neither the time nor money for it as a struggling student, and that last experience with Faith was a huge turnoff. What the heck, it's legal, he thought, and took a small toke. Shashir was now pulling out a pipe of his own and telling everyone about the great Nepalese temple ball hash he had brought with him. That seemed to excite all the smokers, and in a minute Shashir was handing John a smoking pipe full of powerful smelling hashish. John said, "One more," and took another toke. He didn't think he could feel any better, but he was wrong.

John got a case of the giggles, and his laughter seemed to start everyone else to laughing. He regained his composure for a moment, but when Shashir looked at him and said, "What is so funny?" he started up again louder than before. Funny, he thought, this is way beyond funny. This is miraculous. His laughter spread around the circle until all of them, even those who hadn't smoked, were laughing. It got to the point where John and several of the circle had tears streaming down their faces from laughing and it probably would have continued on except that the next band took the stage.

When they began to play, everyone was soon up and dancing gleefully. John had always loved Celtic music, and found that the addition of a bass guitar and drummer rocked it out in a wonderful way. Everyone was dancing and laughing or at least had big grins on their faces. John danced to every song, and was glad when they did a slow one so he could rest. He was having a lot of fun. Friends were certainly easy to make. These festivals were a wonderful idea, he thought.

John learned that seasoned festival-goers always carried food and a lot of water. Shashir was willing to share his, but by the end of the Celtic group they were out and needed to refill Shashir's bottle. On the way to the water fountains John told Shashir the story of how he had lived in the past until just yesterday.

"But surely that is impossible. No one has ever traveled from the past, nor from the future back to this time. I have studied the Yoga Sutras, and there is no mention of the power of traveling in time. They do say that the yogi can gain the power of movement as rapidly as the mind. They also say that one can become omnipotent and omniscient. Perhaps time travel is covered by that."

"I guess omnipotence would cover about everything," John replied. "Mr. Patel, the gentleman I bought my PC from, said that he thought I might have gone into Samadhi for that time and been invisible."

"Yes, I guess that is possible. The Sutras teach that one can become invisible and not be perceivable to any of the senses. What is a hundred years in God's mind? You must be a very high soul, to have obtained such a state," added Shashir with wonder.

"I sure can't claim that, Shashir. The truth is, I felt very low yesterday morning when it happened. I was about as bummed out as I'd ever been. I don't know why this has happened to me, but it is wonderful. My prayer has been answered. This new world is like a dream come true. I never thought such a peaceful, equitable world was possible. Hell, I didn't even think we would survive this long."

"Then it is a wonderful blessing. In some lifetime you must have done something very good. Perhaps you are a more evolved soul than you think."

"Shashir, do you mind if we don't tell everyone about me at this point? It just brings up questions and makes me the center of attention. Crystal knows and so do the people I am staying with. I'm not ashamed or trying to hide anything. I just don't want to have to deal with explaining it to everyone."

"Sure, John. No problem."

"Tell me, Shashir, I wanted to ask Nan back then when we met her. Is Tibet liberated from China now? It wasn't back in my time."

"The Tibetan people are getting along well with the people of Chinese ancestry living there now. They have both made compromises. Because there are so many Chinese there, the Tibetan people could not win the election to become a separate nation again. They have the Dalai Lama and their own system working within the state, and democracy has helped them very much."

"How about Bangladesh? You know, I sponsored a child there for about a year. He had the exact same name as you. The country was very poor at that time and had terrible floods regularly."

"That is incredible. My great grandfather had my name, and he was the first person in my family to go to college. He received help from your Save the Children."

"Do you know the name of his sponsor?"

"No. But it is possible my grandmother might know. I'll give her a call." Shashir asked his PC to give him his grandmother.

"You're calling Bangladesh?" asked John with amazement.

"Yes. Bangladesh is doing very much better now than one

hundred years ago. Hello grandma. Yes, I am having a great time. Do you know the name of the person from America that sponsored your father through Save the Children?" There was a pause, then Shashir said, "Thanks, I'll call tomorrow. I love you. Goodbye. She said she'd see if she could find out."

They got to the line for water and in a couple of minutes had filled up Shashir's bottle and decided to sit and talk for a while before going to the medical tent.

"Bangladesh was the beneficiary of one of the first big United Nations joint improvement projects. After helping our people through many disasters, and with the level of the sea rising, it was decided that it would be better to help our country build a series of dikes and levees to protect it. Though it would cost a lot, I believe it was thirty billion International Credits, it would save thousands, perhaps millions of lives, and ultimately save money. The influx of money and jobs helped our little country to pull itself up by its bootstraps. We have prospered more and more ever since. I am the fourth generation to attend college in my family. We have a very fertile country, and now that the floods are not a problem, we can feed ourselves and more."

"That's another dream come true for me, Shashir."

"Thank you so much for your dream, and your help to my great grandfather, or some other person from my country if that is so. This is an amazing thing John, very amazing. Would you like to smoke some more hashish?"

"No, thanks. I'm still off from those last tokes, and I want to be rational when I see Crystal. I guess it's about time I did that. I must admit, I'm nervous."

"Do you think she cares for you?"

"Yes, I do, but my story is so outrageous. She already has kind of a boyfriend."

"What do you mean, kind of?"

"She is a celibate."

"Is she a yogi?"

"I guess, sort of. She meditates every day."

"What a blessing to find such a high soul. But is she celibate just because she has not met the right man?"

"That is exactly what I'm curious about. Let's head on over to the medical tent."

The medical tent was not very busy, and there was no problem getting in. There were a few drunks who had banged themselves up, a few bad trips and a few other kids with assorted problems. Not at all what John expected from such a large crowd. He saw Crystal sitting on the ground with her hands on a young woman's swollen ankle. She had her eyes closed and seemed to be deep in prayer or thought. In a couple of minutes she opened her eyes, and when she saw John, a big smile spread across her face. The girl thanked Crystal and said her ankle felt much better.

Crystal got up and walked over to John. He saw that she was going to give him a hug and was thrilled to be able to return this one. Her embrace was soft and close. Though it didn't last very long, John savored the wonderful warmth of her body and felt himself, no, the both of them, melt into one another. Her energy actually made him somewhat weak in the knees and very blissful. John introduced Shashir, and Crystal hugged him as well.

"Well, how did you get here?" she asked.

John told her about his morning and how he had sold his coins and now had a PC himself. He also explained to her the story of Shashir and his great grandfather and how thrilled he was to hear about Bangladesh's recovery from poverty and disaster.

"Yes. John has told me a most amazing story. I am a student of yoga, and it is not unusual to hear of masters who have lived for centuries, but his experience is unique to my knowledge," said Shashir.

"So you believe him?" asked Crystal.

"Yes, I think so."

"Crystal, how long are you going to be working here, and do you ever get a break or something?"

"We can talk for a while now, but I don't want to leave the tent because you never know when I might be needed. I have to leave at six-thirty and grab a quick bite to eat before heading for my eight o'clock meeting."

"What kind of a meeting is it?" Asked John.

"My Greenpeace action group," she answered.

"I was a member of Greenpeace. Can I go with you?"

"No, John, I'm sorry, but this is a closed meeting of my action group."

"Well, can I eat with you and keep you company on your ride to the meeting?"

"You'll miss a lot of the festival. The best bands are on tonight."

"If they are any better than the two I already heard, I'm not sure I could take it. I danced to every song."

"Sounds like you've been having a good time."

"That would be an understatement. And the Chows are really wonderful, generous people. This whole experience, from meeting you until now, has been beyond my wildest dreams. Shashir is a great guy. He has a date at six and was hoping that I'd get one too."

"I wish I could just stay here with the two of you. But this meeting is crucial."

"You are very dedicated to Greenpeace, Crystal," Shashir added, "to miss a festival night for a meeting."

"I made a commitment, and I must follow through,"Crystal stated.

John agreed to return and meet Crystal a little after six, and then he and Shashir went back out into the crowd, and headed down to hear some more music. The next band seemed a lot like a Cajun band from the past, and John never was very fond of that style of music. Their enthusiasm and the crowd's response were infectious, though, and John found himself dancing again. Later, John asked Shashir to walk around with him to see some of the exhibits.

There actually was a Greenpeace tent, and John decided to check it out. Maybe he could learn something about this mysterious meeting and mission Crystal had told him about. He and Shashir were given a pitch about being recruited into the corps that were finishing the replanting of tropical rainforests around the world. John was thrilled to find that they had developed techniques to re-grow the forests. Though it would take hundreds of years for them to regain their magnificence, the rainforests were growing back. They were also working at rebuilding the populations of many of the animals that were endangered and nearly wiped out during the world crisis.

There was a table with literature about their program to reclaim all radiation contaminated land. John was amazed to find that they claimed that they had discovered a method of transmuting radiation that neutralized it completely. It had to be diluted to the right level and then it was composted with organic matter and a special strain of bacteria that could supposedly transmute the radioactive elements into harmless elements.

A soil bacterium was discovered that thrived on radioactivity and used it as energy. These unusual and miraculous bacteria could also actually change elements from one into another. The bacteria were discovered in the earth where there were high levels of natural radiation and had somehow evolved the ability. Amazingly, the end product was a mass of very fertile compost. Many industry and government scientists claimed that it would never work with the higher level waste. However, they had not tested the theory, nor had they allowed the Greenpeace people to try a demonstration project to prove it one way or another. When John expressed some excitement about their project to the person sitting at the table, she hinted that their methods for reversing radiation contamination might be proven soon.

John and Shashir walked around the exhibit area and saw art from all over the world on display. There were contests for best-in-show in all the different media, and young artists could win cash prizes and a lot of recognition if they did well. Being able to communicate with anyone from anywhere was a new and wonderful experience for John. He learned from talking to many people that life was pretty good everywhere. Democracy was universal, and most countries had fairly similar governments. The idea of an inheritance share had caught on almost everywhere in some form or another, as it created the most efficient and competitive, as well as the fairest economic system.

They came upon the Com-Union tent, and John wanted to go inside and learn more about it. Shashir told him that he had thought about joining as he admired their dedication and the simple, somewhat ascetic lifestyle they had embraced, but the Com-Union wasn't as big or popular in Bangladesh and some of the other less affluent countries.

"If the Com-Union succeeds, it will be like the whole world being a giant ashram. Even as a sincere practitioner of yoga, I am not sure it will be possible to create the utopia they envision with no credit exchange. It will take a big percentage of the population living with a high level of discipline and dedication. This is asking a lot," said Shashir.

"The world already seems like utopia to me, Shashir. I know there are still crimes and even murders, but much less than in my time. And no war for over fifty years! No hunger or starvation. I am amazed that they aren't satisfied with everything like it is. I guess it is just human nature to want to keep making things better."

John expressed those ideas to a young lady sitting at one of the information tables. She did not share John's sentiment. She thought that corporations held vastly too much power and were using it in a way that helped their shareholders and owners at the expense of the collective good.

"The communications networks are corrupt, and there is a conspiracy between them and other corporate interests to limit and control what information gets to the people," she said.

"Can you give me some examples?" John asked.

"Safety studies on some products aren't reported. Important research on some alternative treatments and the dangers of drugs and combining drugs are either not reported or are downplayed. Environmental problems are ignored."

"Like the spread of radioactive contamination from some of the old nuclear sites?" asked John.

"Exactly. But our goals and aspirations are much deeper and more meaningful than just these concerns. We hope to create a society where everyone can have completely free expression of their talents and abilities. A society where everyone lives in complete equality. We hope to replace greed and self-interest as man's main motivation, with love, service and spiritual development."

"You sound something like the communists from the past, except they weren't into spirituality."

"In some ways, we are similar. They also wanted to create a utopia, but they were willing to use force to do it. We will create a egalitarian society within this corporate culture and steadily win the people over until there aren't enough people left within the old system for it to function. We will then have helped humanity move to the next level of cultural and spiritual development. A level of true unity and oneness. An enlightened humanity."

"Are you sure this is going to work?" asked John.

"It is already working for more than seventeen million Com-Union personnel all over the planet. A large percentage of them are living without the credit exchange now. We will slowly take over all communication and transportation. When we've done that, all people will be free to go off the exchange without having to use only bikes for transportation, and they'll be able to use phones as well. Our people, and all people, will be able to drop out of the competitive, corporate culture. As more of the truth is communicated and more people begin to demonstrate a life motivated by love instead of competition, more and more people will join us. It is inevitable for everyone ultimately to rise to the Christ level of conscious oneness with all life. We are here to facilitate that happening."

"Yes, that is the inevitable end for each individual soul," added Shashir, "but I have a hard time believing that it will happen to all of humanity at once."

"It won't happen at once," the woman replied. "It will take a long time, but without this work it could never happen. Over two thousand years ago a small sect of Jews in Israel shared a similar goal. The Essenes. They didn't use money and shared everything. They would travel from one of their homes or centers to another so that they could function in the society, Jewish and Roman, that they were within. They had a high degree of discipline and morality and a very good work ethic. They believed that it was their function to pave the way for the coming of the Christ. They were successful, and Christ consciousness manifested here on Earth in the body and soul of Jesus of Nazareth. The early Christians also shared everything in common. We believe that the Com-Union has a similar work. Our work is to facilitate the ascension of all of humanity to Christ Consciousness."

"Then you are a Christian organization?" John asked.

"Not exactly. We use the concept of Christ Consciousness in a more universal sense, the spirit of conscious oneness with all life obtained by the Buddha, Lao Tse, Jesus, and all of the enlightened teachers of all ages. In another culture we might refer to it as enlightenment, or Buddha mind. This same spirit of universal oneness can be, and should be, shared by all humanity. The system of corporate ownership and credit exchange corrupts people, and makes it very difficult for them to function and think in this way. By its very nature, it is set up to preserve inequity. It works against the consciousness we hope to create universally."

"Amazingly lofty goals," said John.

"Those are the only goals worth having," the woman added with a smile.

"I must say," added Shashir, "you people do have very high goals. I am almost ashamed to admit that my goal is personal enlightenment."

"Individual enlightenment is a wonderful goal, but once you have attained that goal and are still here and alive, what goal would you have then?"

"Very excellent point," mused Shashir.

"We in the Com-Union believe that the very best way to attain individual enlightenment is to work towards the enlightenment of all souls."

"So, you are karma yogis?" Shashir asked.

"Yes, exactly. Our path to individual enlightenment is through selfless service towards the enlightenment of all."

"I have never heard the Com-Union's plans and goals presented in such a way," said Shashir.

"That is because governments and corporations have a very large interest in keeping our message from you. That is exactly what we mean."

All of the Com-Union people looked very clear, healthy, high and happy. That was probably the most impressive thing about them. They were very excited about the impending takeover of Cape Town, South Africa's services, as this time they would be running many other civic and governmental services as well as transportation and communication. Though it was not free from problems, particularly the displacement of many workers, many communities, especially smaller ones, had signed on the Com-Union waiting list to have their transportation, communication and many governmental functions taken over by Com-union volunteers.

John's first impression of the Com-Union was not so positive, and he didn't think that their goals were any more possible than the utopia the hippies had hoped to manifest. After talking to many of them, his opinion changed. Perhaps they could actually pull it off. They certainly were sincere and dedicated.

He learned that a large group of youngsters would spend the night in prayer and fasting and be initiated into the Com-Union the next morning. It was preparation for the life of selfless service they were committing to. The Com-Union wouldn't sanction kids going off the credit exchange until they turned 21, so many who had passed that birthday would be taking off their bracelets. Many of the Com-union people weren't wearing PCs, and John thought he could detect a bit of pride in that accomplishment.

It was almost six now, and Shashir needed to go and meet his date. He and John made plans to get together the next morning at ten o'clock at post 25. Perhaps he could get Crystal to change her mind about spending the day with Stuart and come with him. John had become very fond of Shashir's affable nature, friendliness and enthusiasm, and was glad Shashir seemed to like him as well. Shashir told him to come back after he spent time with Crystal, but John didn't want to interfere with his date. Besides, he told Shashir, he had to go and get the bike back to the Chows.

CRYSTAL LOSES FAITH

John headed back to the medical tent to meet Crystal. He was very excited that his prayer had been answered and more. He didn't just get to see her, he got a hug, and now he was going to spend some time with her. After that remark about her first kiss last night, John was hoping that, celibate or not, maybe he would even get to kiss her.

But just to be with Crystal is such a wonderful thing, he would be willing to be a celibate and make do with hugs. Maybe that's a real good idea, he thought. Sex complicates things so very much. Yes, it would be a liberation to just forget about it totally. Just to be with her and love her is enough.

Crystal was ready to go when he arrived. She gave him a big smile, but no hug. They would have to catch a quick bite there, Crystal said, as they didn't have time to go to a restaurant. As they walked towards the food area, John asked Crystal if she had ever attended a festival.

"Oh sure, John. Never an international one, but one national and many smaller festivals. There is one held in San Francisco every other year. This is the third time I've worked in the med tent, and they always give us free passes."

"Then you have a pass for tomorrow?" John asked.

"Yes, but I'm not planning to use it. Stuart turned thirty last year so he's not supposed to attend, though he does have a pass as a Greenpeace staff person. He won't use it to attend the rest of the festival, as he thinks that would be wrong. Last night when he said 'I guess you're going to the festival Sunday,' he sounded so unhappy that I said I'd spend Sunday with him, as usual."

"Well, that was very nice of you." John certainly had mixed feelings about that. He was impressed with Crystal's caring and sweetness. As a matter of fact, it made him feel like she loved Stuart so much that his chances were slim. He wanted to ask her to give up those plans and come to the festival with him, but when she put it like that, he was reluctant to say so.

"Crystal, um, has Stuart ever been to an international festival?"

"Yes. When he was nineteen. He bought five hundred chances. It was a very special one, in Jerusalem. He spent a year traveling all over the Mideast and Europe. He had a wonderful time. That was before he joined the Com-Union. Now he thinks that the festivals should be free and that the lottery system that pays for them is corrupt. The Com-Union doesn't think gambling is moral. Stuart also thinks the foundation that sponsors the festivals pays its executives too much."

"What do you think?"

"These festivals do a wonderful thing by helping to build a global community. Maybe they aren't perfect, but they don't harm anyone. They are nonprofit, and the salaries they pay are equivalent to what other top executives get. I don't charge a set fee for my work, but I don't want to judge people by what they make. That is one of the reasons I'm not in the Com-Union. I pretty much live by their values, but I don't hold any negative energy toward other peoples' values."

"And the Com-Union does?"

"By the nature of the organization, they have to criticize the culture and values they hope to regenerate. I like to leave things a little less organized."

The aroma of Chinese food caught their attention, and they decided to eat at that tent. John noticed that with the exception of two fish, one shrimp and one meat dish, everything was vegetarian. He ordered a veggie egg roll. That was out for Crystal because she was a vegan and ate no animal products. Her Buddhist style vegetables and rice looked great, and John got the country style spicy tofu and rice and a hot tea. He insisted on paying for the meal, and got the prompt about the discrepancy again when he used his account.

"I see that though you have a PC, you're getting the discrepancy prompt. A few years ago you wouldn't have been able to use your account if there were a problem. Every time someone at registration made a mistake, some poor person would have to pay for it by being stranded without the use of an account until they could get to a registration office. A movement to liberalize the system used the petition process to get on the ballot, and it won overwhelmingly. Now you are given two weeks to clear it up before you have your account suspended. Unless you try to buy anything over three hundred credits."

"Well, it sure helps me out. In two weeks maybe I'll have figured everything out, and I'll know what I should do."

The tent was rather crowded and noisy, so they ate without talking very much. John swapped Crystal some of his tofu for her Buddhist veggies. Crystal told him that the meeting was in Oakland and they took the same train as before, but they transferred at the first stop over the Bay.

"Are you sure you want to leave just to ride over with me? I hate to think of you missing the festival."

"Crystal, it is your karma. You are planning to miss the festival tomorrow to keep Stuart company, right?"

"You're right," Crystal said with a smile.

"Besides," John said, "I'd rather be with you any place than be anywhere else, anyhow and at any time."

Crystal's eyes brightened and she smiled a real beamer at John. She does seem to like me, he thought. They finished their supper and left for the exit. John took her hand and they walked together holding hands. It was pretty hot and their hands were soon sweaty from it, but neither he nor Crystal cared enough to let go.

Then he heard, "John, Crystal." They looked around and there was Shashir with a lovely lady with long, flaming red hair. Her name was Cynthia and she was from Kansas. Shashir was very happy and excited, and after introducing them, asked Crystal if she wouldn't change her mind and stay.

"We could have so much fun," he said.

"I'm sorry, I just can't." She smiled and looked genuinely regretful.

"We're sorry too," said Shashir. Then he added, "Perhaps tomorrow you and John can join us at the festival. Cynthia has told me that she is free tomorrow. Don't say no, as John will be very unhappy. I do not think he will find another date."

John was very glad that Shashir had said the things that he had forgone saying. Crystal seemed to be having a difficult time mouthing an answer. She actually seemed pained.

"Crystal already has plans for tomorrow, guys, but if there is any change, I have your number, Shashir. And I'll see y'all tomorrow for sure." He looked at Crystal and took her hand again. "Crystal and I are having a great time. Doing your duty can be fun, too."

"Yes, your dharma. Yes," said Shashir, "we should always take joy in fulfilling our responsibilities. You two continue to have a very good time, and Cynthia and I will, also. Goodnight, my friends."

"It was a pleasure meeting you both. I hope we see you again," said Cynthia.

John and Crystal said goodnight, turned and continued on their way.

"Crystal, I swear we didn't plan that."

"Wait, let me get my voice stress tester up." Crystal said lifting her bracelet PC towards her mouth, only to laugh and grab John by the arm. "He's a real nice guy, John, and you're lucky to have already made a friend who genuinely cares for you."

"Yes, and in such good psychic rapport."

They were all smiles as they walked arm and arm out of the festival site and boarded the train.

"It isn't just that I don't want to hurt Stuart's feelings. I must confess, I'd love to attend the festival and have a great time with you and your friends. This meeting is about a mission that we have been planning for over a year, even before San Francisco was selected for the international festival. John, I am leaving early Monday morning for the other side of the country. I'll be gone at least two to three weeks, and all things considered, I guess I can't even be sure that I'll ever see you again after that."

John was shaken deeply by this news. It challenged the very reason he believed he was there. His expression became serious. He knew she had some kind of mission, but he never considered not seeing her for weeks.

"I want to go with you. Can't I play a role of some kind?"

"That's impossible. I shouldn't even be telling you this much."

"Well, can I call you while you're gone? Can't I come to the area or something and see you when you're not doing whatever it is you'll be doing?"

"No. It could not work. John, you don't even know me. I like you a lot, and I feel your warmth and sincerity. But even if there is some kind of special connection between us, I just can't explore it at this time. We will just have to wait until I come back in three weeks."

"Three weeks! God, Crystal. I am here by the amazing grace of God! And I have no idea for how long."

The smiles were gone. They stood quietly in the crowded train car until they got to the train transfer station. Right before they got there, John smiled and said. "If God's grace brought me here and allowed me to meet you, I'd better start having more faith in it."

The smiles returned to both their faces, but it was obvious that John's was somewhat forced.

"You see, John," Crystal said as they walked arm and arm to the other train line, "I still have a lot of things to get together and pack up. We will have a great time at the ritual tomorrow night, I promise you. They always leave everyone with a wonderful energy. It's at six. If we didn't go to a restaurant, if we took some food or ate back at the festival grounds, we could be there by nine, and see the last couple of shows and the closing ceremony."

"All right!" exclaimed John.

On the way over to the Oakland stop, John told Crystal how he had gone to both the Greenpeace and Com-Union tent. They talked a little about the progress that had been made in restoring the rainforests and all woodlands.

"God, I am so very happy to hear that there are still rainforests."

"The world as we know it can't survive without them" answered Crystal.

"I was totally devastated when I thought that, not just the forests, but all of the animals that live in them would be gone."

"Boy, that must have been really intense. You know, some animal species were brought back only because scientists had frozen fertile embryos that they could implant in surrogate mothers, once there was a safe habitat for them. That's how close we came to losing them. Everything has been improving ever since I've been alive. It is hard for me to imagine going through that period when things were getting worse, and the fate of the whole world was at stake. You are lucky, in a way, because things got worse after 1993. There were about fifty years, which would have been most of your adult life, where the planet was in severe crisis and the fate of humanity and most of the species on the Earth were in jeopardy. It took a long time to recover to where we are today."

They arrived at the Oakland stop and transferred to an Oakland train. Once they had taken seats, John spoke.

"Will you call me while you're gone? I've never received a phone call on this phone."

"I don't think so, John."

"Crystal, can't you tell me where you are going, or some way I can contact you?"

Crystal thought for a minute before answering. "I'm taking the bullet train for Atlanta Monday. I'll arrive in Atlanta about nine AM Tuesday. Thursday, I'll be leaving there, and after that I will not be able to communicate with you for about fourteen days. Please don't ask me any more about this. I'm sorry I can't tell you. It's not because I don't trust you. Nobody knows about this except the people directly involved." After saying that, Crystal got a very serious and thoughtful look on her face.

"Our stop is coming up in a couple of minutes," said Crystal. "I guess you should just take the train back from there."

"Well, how much further do you have to go," said John.

"It's a four block walk."

"Please let me walk with you, Crystal."

Crystal still had a serious look on her face, and did not answer John.

"A lady at the Greenpeace tent said that they expected to have proof of the effectiveness of the method they developed to transmute radioactivity soon. Your mission wouldn't have anything to do with that, would it?"

Crystal eyes widened. She looked surprised, almost shocked. Then she got thoughtful again for a few minutes. John found the silence uncomfortable.

"So, can I walk with you?"

"Just who are you really?" said Crystal with an intensity.

Now John was surprised. God, she's paranoid about me. She thinks I'm some kind of a spy or something, he thought.

"What are you thinking? Gee, I'm sorry if I.....Crystal."

Crystal had gotten up and was heading towards the door. John followed. Crystal wasn't smiling any longer. They both got off the train, and without hesitation, Crystal started walking briskly up the ramp and then down the sidewalk.

"Crystal! Please! Stop a second." John almost reached out to grab her arm but didn't. She stopped and turned to look at John.

"Now I have a good explanation for all of this," said Crystal, with a grim look in her eyes. "I don't think you should come with me to the meeting. I don't want you following me to the meeting place either."

"Crystal. I swear to God I would never lie to you. I don't know what you're thinking." Crystal turned and walked off.

"Wait a minute. Hold on a second. What's the deal?"

Crystal stopped again and turned back to look at John. He had never seen her with anything but a pleasant look or smile.

"Is it because of what the Greenpeacer told me? I swear, she volunteered that information. I couldn't help but think that maybe it had something to do with this mission you told me about. Crystal, I am not a spy!"

"It's all just too perfect." Crystal spouted with anger in her voice. "But now that I think about it, I am very insulted by the way you chose to weasel into my life." Crystal turned and began to quickly walk away. After a few steps she wheeled and exclaimed, "Do not follow me to the meeting. I have to report this to everyone, and they will not be very happy to have you around. I feel like such an idiot." Crystal had tears in her eyes as she turned and walked briskly away. John followed along.

"Crystal, you have to believe me! Wait!"

Crystal ran down the street so fast, John didn't even try and catch her.

"Crystal, please!" He knew he couldn't. It it wouldn't do any good anyway. John was devastated. Crystal turned the next corner and was gone.

John walked back to the train stop and sat down. His dreams and hopes, shattered. How was he ever going to convince Crystal that he wasn't some kind of a spy? He got out his PC and called Crystal's number. He got a message prompt. John hung up: he didn't want to just leave a message. He needed desperately to talk to her. Tomorrow was his only chance to spend time with her. They had made such wonderful plans. He had to convince her he wasn't lying, and he didn't have very much time.

John was numb on his way back to Berkeley, at a loss for what to do. He only hoped that the Chows hadn't been turned against him. As angry as Crystal was, what if she called and told them of her suspicions? This might tax Mr. Chow's faith somewhat, John thought.

But, God, what did I do? Let's put this into perspective. All I did was ask if what she was doing was connected to the project to neutralize radiation. I mean, that didn't seem to be a secret. If there is a connection, and I think there must be, that girl screwed up telling me. It was her fault, not mine. She was the security risk, he reasoned.

John thought that maybe he could find out something by

returning to the Greenpeace tent tomorrow, if there is a tomorrow. His faith waning, John called the Chows from the campus and told them that he would be heading their way shortly. He asked Mr. Chow if Crystal had called them and he said, "No, why?"

"I'll tell you when I get there."

The world was still a beautiful place, but John's mood had changed. He didn't enjoy the bike ride back to the Chow's house as he had the morning ride. Obsessed with thinking about how to get back together with Crystal put him in his own little world. There has got to be a way. Maybe Mr. Chow will have some idea.

When he got to the house, Mrs. Chow greeted him warmly and told him that they had already eaten, but there were leftovers in the refrigerator if he was hungry.

"No thank you, Mrs. Chow. I had something with Crystal at the festival."

"So you did make it to the festival. That's nice. Chen and I are playing bridge with some old friends in Vancouver. Come on in to the living room. We are about to finish."

John went into the living room and Mr. Chow said hello with a smile. "Yes. Hi, Mr. Chow."

John sat down and watched as they played out the last hand. He saw that the men were playing the ladies. The TV had life size pictures of the couple as well as the hand of his partner, as Mr. Chow had the contract. The Chows would play their cards, Mr. Chow would point at his partners hand, using the cursor to select a card to play, and Mrs. Mathews would play her card on her table, and all the cards would come up together on the center of the screen. The score was kept automatically, and Mr. Chow made the contract to win the game. They were laughing and carrying on like they were all in the same room. John thought it was pretty cool. After they said goodbye to their friends, John spoke.

"May I talk to y'all for a few minutes. Look, I don't know if you know anything about it, but Crystal is going on a mission for Greenpeace. It seems to be some kind of a secret. To make a long story short, Crystal seems to think I am some kind of spy."

"How did that come about?" asked Mr. Chow.

"I went to the Greenpeace tent today, and while I was talking to them, a woman there told me that the method they've developed for neutralizing radiation might be proven soon. I asked Crystal if that had anything to do with the mission she is going on, and she got suspicious of me and actually ran off."

"She ran off?" said Mrs. Chow incredulously.

"Well, she ran off and left me so I couldn't follow her to her meeting. It was totally unnecessary because I would have respected her wishes. She doesn't even want to talk to me anymore. I was keeping her company on her way to the meeting because it was the only time I could spend with her today. We made a date for tomorrow evening and were getting along great. All I did was ask her if that radiation thing was connected to her mission. I guess I shouldn't have been so curious, but, I care very much for Crystal. I was just hoping that there was some way that I wouldn't have to," John voice broke, "to not see her while she was gone. But I don't know how long I'll be here. I'm so confused." Tears began streaming down John's face.

The Chows were listening intently with somewhat serious expressions on their faces. They looked at each other for a moment as if trying to decide who should speak or what to say. John was nervous and worried. If they kicked him out, if they didn't believe him, what would he do?

"This must be an important and dangerous mission for Crystal to react with such fear," Mr. Chow said. "It is certainly not like Crystal to run away from anything. She has lost faith in your veracity again. Is there anything else you haven't told us that might have contributed to her loss of belief?"

"Not that I can think of, sir."

Just then the phone rang. Mr. Chow picked up his remote and had Crystal on the speaker phone.

"Hello, Mr. Chow. The reason I am calling is about John," she said with a shaky voice.

"Yes Crystal, he is here now and has told us about your loss of faith in him. As you can see, we have you on the speaker phone."

"I guess there isn't anything I will be telling you that I haven't already told to John. He is a fake, Mr. Chow."

"And how do you know that, Crystal?"

"I can't go into any details, but after talking to the rest of my action group, we are sure he was just using me to obtain information about what we are planning. Doesn't that make a lot more sense than his story about coming from the past?"

"And why do you think he would use such an unbelievable story, if he is a spy like you suspect?"

"I don't know. I guess some sort of psychological profile of me he obtained. I find that very insulting! Trying to take advantage of my trusting and caring nature."

John was dying to jump in and defend himself, to implore her to believe him, but he decided to let Mr. Chow go on.

"It seems as if your caring and trusting nature has left you tonight, Crystal. John is a very unhappy young man because you no longer trust him. From what both of you have told me, I see no conclusive evidence of his deceitfulness. Can you offer any real proof that he is not who he says he is?"

"He was asking about things that he should not know anything about."

"Yes, but he said that he was told that by a Greenpeace person at the festival. Have you checked on that?"

"Well, no. But Stuart said that he would talk to them tomorrow about security," Crystal replied.

"It seems that if you were trying to keep this secret, you wouldn't have made such a big deal about it. Now it looks as if John's curiosity is accurate."

"Just because I think John might be a spy doesn't mean he was right about anything. Look, sir, I have to go back to the meeting. I just wanted you to know about all the latest developments with John, as you were nice enough to let him stay with you."

John was encouraged that Crystal had said, "might" be a spy. At least she did have some doubt.

"We appreciate your call, Crystal. John said that you two have a date for tomorrow night. Perhaps you should tell him whether he can expect you to keep it."

God, John loved these people. There was a silence that gave John hope, then Crystal answered.

"No. NO! I can't take that chance. I have to go now. Good-bye."

"Crystal, don't lose your faith." John could keep silent no longer, but the click came before faith.

"Well, John. It seems that things have taken a very complicated turn. I must confess that Crystal's suspicions do offer us another explanation for what you are doing here."

"Please, Mr. Chow, don't you lose faith in me too." John was getting close to tears and his voice began to show it. "I am not any kind of spy."

They all sat there quietly for a few minutes.

"I thought that meeting Crystal was the reason I came to this time."

John told the Chow's the whole story about Faith and her death and what had transpired between him and Crystal, how Crystal fit the karmic pattern perfectly. Although he hadn't always believed in reincarnation, he now suspected that Crystal was Faith reborn. There was more silence.

"John. You have a place to stay here with us as long as you need it," Mrs. Chow said.

"Yes, John, do not worry about that," Mr. Chow added.

"Thank you so much. Do you have a voice stress tester, Mr. Chow? I'll gladly take one. I swear, I am telling the truth. Maybe I am crazy, but I'm not a liar."

Mr. Chow was silent for a moment, as if he were considering it.

"No, John. I will confess that I don't know just what to believe, but I am still willing to give you the benefit of the doubt."

"Well, I believe you." said Mrs. Chow. "Who could make up a story like that?"

"Thank you very, very much, both of you."

John told the Chows about his day. He showed them the PC he had bought, and explained how Mr. Patel had helped him set up an account. He told them about the festival and his new friend, Shashir.

"Mr. Chow, is it possible that the transmutation process can succeed? Do you think that radioisotopes can be transformed by some kind of soil bacteria, as the Greenpeace people say?"

"It has been proven to work with the low level waste, but there is no access to any of the more dangerous high level waste so that anyone can prove or disprove the theory. It would take a long time and be very costly. Many scientists say that more damage would be done than if we left the radioactive waste where it is. I suspect that the truth might lie somewhere in between the vested interests of the corporations and the hopeful enthusiasm of the Greenpeacers."

"So it is true that there is a bacteria that can transmute radiation at least at some level? That is amazing."

"Not so amazing, John. Organic life has great powers, or it could not have emerged or survived. The miracle of life is incredible. You know, John, back in your time people thought that the creation of life was something that happened at a particular time. I believe that the most common image was lightening striking some primordial pool and, poof! Life was created. Rather like the Frankenstein monster. Now we know that life is constantly creating and recreating itself in every pool and puddle on Earth, all of the time. We know that creation is a continuous process. This was demonstrated by the great scientist Wilhelm Reich almost fifty years before your time, and yet still had not been accepted by most scientists, or the masses. Such a paradigm shift takes much time."

"How did Reich prove that creation is continuous, Mr. Chow?"

"He sterilized some straw, and then put it in sterile water in a jar. Tiny protozoa formed in the jar, presumably from the decomposing straw tissue. Some scientist said they were from eggs or spores, though no one had ever seen such a thing, so he used coke, an organic material that could stand to be heated to much higher temperatures. Higher than anyone had ever seen any living forms or eggs survive, and still protozoa formed. It was replicated by many other scientists, but somehow was never included into the body of scientific knowledge. Creation is continuous. Miracles are a part of life. No, it would be more accurate just to say that life is a miracle, and we should never underestimate its power."

"Yes," said John hopefully, "and we should never underestimate the power of love, either."

GREENPEACE

After sitting quietly for a few minutes, Mrs. Chow said, "Let's have some dessert. John, please have a piece of fresh baked cherry pie with us."

"You folks are so wonderful and kind. I am incredibly thankful to have met y'all, and greatly appreciate your giving me your own son's room." John's emotion was showing. "I'd love to have some pie, thank you."

They went into the kitchen and the mood lifted as Mrs. Chow cut into the pie. Mr. Chow said that he had planted the dwarf cherry tree just four years ago, and this year it had produced enough cherries for three pies so far. John commented about how impressed he was with the number of people gardening nowadays.

"With a maximum thirty hour work week, more people have time to garden, and food is a major living expense, but I think that most of us garden because of the increased energy and vitality available from fresh food," said Mrs. Chow.

"Beverly is a really fine gardener with a magic green thumb," said Mr. Chow. "Back in your time people got used to eating very de-vitalized food. It was highly refined, mass produced, and loaded with chemicals. Food was grown without respect for the Earth and her future fertility, so their was no real connection between people and the Earth. Food was mined for profit."

"I used to use the same term, mining the soil," said John.

"Do you know, John, in your time miners did not even refill the mines they dug. It was actually a quite serious problem. The empty mines would fill up with water and leach heavy metals into the environment. I must say, John, people of your time did not show a lot of good sense in the way they treated the Earth."

"That's for darn sure. I was an environmentalist and a member of Greenpeace myself. That's the really unjust part of this thing. I would never sell out the environment. I knew it was crazy," said John.

"That is what happens when the people who are profiting from the destruction of the environment have too much power. Or we could put it another way, and say that if some people have too much power, they will inevitably make problems. We have made a lot of progress towards a more equitable sharing of power," said Mr. Chow.

"Like the Inheritance Share?" asked John.

"Yes. It was one of the most profound social changes since the advent of democracy here in the United States. A system that allows some to have vast unearned power just because of their birth will have many more problems than just inequity.

"I understand that, sir. Even though we had a democracy, people were so easily influenced by expensive television ad campaigns that with enough money, it was even possible to get them to vote against their own best interests. More sadly, though, most people didn't even vote."

"Nowadays, people are much more diligent about voting. Only individual citizens can contribute to a campaign, and only 500 IC per election. Between seven and eight each evening, all TV and radio stations that use the airwaves have to broadcast public information programming. During the election season, all channels have time for candidates and debates. Other times of the year, any organization that can get enough signatures on petitions can get a time slot during the civic hour to air their concerns. Some of them put together excellent documentaries, and a lot of the shows are very informative. People grew to enjoy the hour without commercial television coming into their homes, and I must say, it was great for teachers, as it created a good time for homework to be done. Eventually, most cable companies started preempting entertainment programming for the hour because it got them more family viewers."

"That's great. That is more like what the media should exist for. After all, it is the public airways. The expensive TV advertising campaigns we had during elections were mostly paid for by special interest groups. They manipulated the public with some emotional appeal instead of discussing the issues. Then everybody got into attack ads, saying terrible things about their opponents. It was incredibly negative, but it worked. The last election, all the candidates were on this huge death trip, all vying to be the most pro death penalty."

"Because of the high crime rate back then?" asked Mr. Chow.

"Right," answered John. "Even though it had long been established that executions didn't deter murder. I was waiting for someone to just say, 'kill them all, and let God sort them out.'"

"What? I don't understand," said Mrs. Chow.

"That was the slogan of the right wing mercenaries that the CIA paid to fight in anti-Communist wars," replied John. "They even had T-shirts with that printed on them."

"Incredible!" said Mrs. Chow. "You came from a violent and difficult time, John."

"I guess so. You know, I discovered what was probably the first use of that phrase while reading history," said John. "The Pope got a lot of German barons and other European nobles to go to the South of France to put down the heretics that were in a majority in many towns. The Pope promised them absolution, plus all the lands of the heretics they killed. They besieged Beziers, and told the city leaders that they would spare them if they would send out all the heretics. When the town leaders wouldn't, the papal legate was reported to have told the nobles, 'Kill them all, for God knows His own.' They killed about 20,000 men, women and children, though many were good Catholics who had taken shelter in their own churches. There were times that were even more violent than my time. You know, come to think of it, those heretics were Albigensians, who believed in reincarnation. Probably that is the explanation for why hardly any Christian sects have reincarnation as part of their beliefs. They were all wiped out."

"Isn't that incredible? You know, the root of the word heretic simply means free to choose. John, it is time that you started calling me Chen, and dropped the sir. I appreciate your respect, but you have never been my student, and we are friends now."

"Yes, John," added Mrs. Chow, please call me Beverly."

"Well, I feel honored. Thank you, sir, um, Chen. The pie is incredible, Beverly. Forgive me for bringing up all that negative stuff."

"Well, it was a part of your time, John," Chen said. "Nowadays, we no longer execute anyone, and we have much less murder. It sets a terrible moral tone for the state to be doing the very thing that it is trying to prevent."

They finished eating their pie and went back into the living room to watch a new movie on the television. It happened to take place in John's time period. It was the story of two young lovers who were a part of the democracy protests at Tienamin Square. John had been very tuned in to that event, and was highly sympathetic of the protesters. He had been aghast at the massacre that ended it, and he and Chen talked a lot about that time period as they watched the movie. John could add a lot of commentary about what it was like to live in those times, to have grown up with the threat of nuclear annihilation and then to see the end of the cold war. It seemed that Chen was impressed by John's depth of knowledge and feelings about that period.

The movie was a tragedy, in that the boy was killed in the final confrontation, leaving the girl to have his baby without a husband. She had a very difficult time, being jailed and forced to work in a factory making clothing for export under slave labor conditions, and having her child, a boy, taken away from her. It did manage a happy ending, as her son became an important leader in the subsequent movement that actually succeeded in bringing democracy to China. They were united, after almost a lifetime, back in Tienamin Square. Then the discussion turned to the difference between orientals and occidentals.

"It is like the East and the West are the two hemispheres of the collective human brain. The West is like the left hemisphere, and is more masculine, analytical, linear and material in its thinking," said Mr. Chow. "This is the Gemini twins of astrology, our own brain. The East is like the more feminine, imaginative, spiritual and mystical right brain. Independence is a characteristic of the West. In the East, it is harder for one to be different from the collective. Perhaps that is why it took longer for democracy to get to China."

"It is a wonderful thought," said John, "that the whole world is now democratic."

"It wasn't quite that easy, John," said Beverly, "because even with democracy there can be many problems. For instance, how big and how inclusive is the democracy? For a while, every little ethnic group wanted to flex its independence, after being a part of empires and big nation states for centuries. Then the need for greater cooperation caused political power to flow back toward the larger institutions, and ultimately the United Nations. After a few adjustments, the right balance of political power between the smallest units right up to the United Nations is sure to be found."

"So you don't think the Earth is there yet?" John asked.

"No, John, I don't think we've got it perfect yet. Perhaps there will never be a perfection of human culture. Perhaps it is just an ongoing process of cycles repeating themselves," said Chen.

"I certainly don't see it that way," said John. "I saw a lot of progress while back in the Twentieth Century, but since then to now, the growth and evolution are undeniable."

"Of course, you are right, John," said Chen. "But we Chinese have a very long history, and even golden ages come and go in time."

"I sure hope this one stays, and grows. Maybe those cycles are a spiral. An upward spiral. Chen and Beverly, do you think that the Com-Union has a chance at succeeding in their plans for taking over all communications and - let me just get to the point - do you think that they will succeed in creating a environment within which the consciousness of the oneness of all life can become the prevalent world view?"

"I think that it has already become the prevalent consciousness, but it doesn't necessarily have to lead to the lifestyle advocated by the Com-Union. Do you believe it is all one, John?"

John thought about it for a moment. "Yes."

"Well, so do we. It is already the prevalent consciousness around here," said Chen with a smile.

"If it is all one, and you think that God must exist, then it is all God." This was a revolutionary thought for John, and he expressed it with a sense of wonder. "If it is all God, why, then, anything could be possible."

"That sounds like a reasonable axiom, John," said Chen. "Perhaps that does offer some explanation of your amazing circumstances. I am somewhat scientific by nature, but I cannot deny the unexplainable."

"On that lovely thought I will say goodnight," said Beverly.

"I will join you. Goodnight, John. Do not worry about tomorrow. Tomorrow will take care of itself," Chen reassured him.

John felt good again. He was sure that the Chows believed him now after their long discussion about his time period. The world was so wonderful now, how could he lack faith? Somehow, some way, he would prove to Crystal that he was no spy, nor was he lying, and get her to keep their date. How could she think that he would be a part of some nefarious plan to stop Greenpeace from helping the environment?

He took a shower and then decided to do some of the yoga breathing exercises he had learned. He sat so he could do them while looking out of Lee's window as the almost full moon rose over the garden. After about five minutes of alternate nostril breathing, closing one nostril with the thumb and then the other with the ring finger, his arm got tired, so he just continued to breath deeply. He felt very elevated. The moon was very beautiful. He was full of joy, flooded with feelings of love for Crystal. He decided to send her that love, where ever she was, to let his love flow into her heart and fill it as his was filled. Surely she would feel it, a person as sensitive and conscious as Crystal. No matter what made her so paranoid tonight, surely she could feel his blissful love.

Then John had a flash of memory that really got his attention. He got his wallet out and looked between two of the pieces of ID in their translucent holder, and, sure enough, there was his 1992 Greenpeace membership card. He had been so broke all year he hadn't renewed yet for 1993. Surely, somehow, this would help him fix this thing with Crystal. Yes! Everything was going to be all right. It was late, and after a few more minutes, John drifted off to sleep.

The next morning, John decided to start the day with some more of that breathing, and even to try a little meditation afterwards. He could do the breathing all right, but when it came to the meditation, he was pitiful, or so he thought. Not having a mantra, he was trying to watch his breath, but his mind was so filled by thoughts of Crystal that he struggled to finish even fifteen minutes.

I guess when you are excited, even if it is good, you have a harder time meditating. I'll try again tonight, John thought.

John saw the clock when he got into the kitchen, and discovered that he would to have to keep moving steadily to make his ten am appointment with Shashir. Beverly was already in the garden, and Chen was doing Tai Chi on the front lawn. John squeezed up some orange juice and made some toast, thinking that he would bring some food home tonight or as soon as possible. Then he remembered the food he had given Ishmael's family, and smiled, thinking it was his karma to be receiving now. But he would get some food anyhow.

John said good morning to the Chows, and excitedly showed them the Greenpeace membership card he had discovered.

"I think this is a sign that everything is going to work out between Crystal and me somehow," he said.

"Well, I sure hope so." said Beverly.

"Me too, John," said Chen. "You have a great day."

He walked and took the subus to the trains, and had an adventure just going to the festival. People were so much more entertaining and happy now. There were musicians and jugglers performing in the train stations, and some even performed aboard the train cars. People actually talked to one another on the trains. Several asked him where he was from and if he were going to the festival. It seemed that his PC could usually determine the language being spoken, and would give John a translation.

John had to wait at the station for several trains to fill going to the festival, but it didn't take long, as they were running back to back. It was a very internationally flavored train ride during the last leg of the trip to the festival, standing room only, and everyone was already in a party mood. John was starting to get a little more excited himself.

There was more of a crush at the gate than the day before, as John was arriving closer to the opening time. All fifty meeting posts were jammed with people, and it took John a few minutes to find Shashir. He told John that Cynthia was also meeting them there, so they talked while they waited. Shashir was very taken with Cynthia. He had already made plans to travel back to Kansas with her and visit for a while with her family. They were going to take a bus train to Kansas, as that was the least expensive way to go.

"That's wonderful, Shashir. I'm afraid that my love life isn't going well. Crystal got paranoid last night that I was a spy or something. You know that mission she is going on? It must be illegal. Look, don't say anything about this if I get back with her. We were going to attend a ritual this evening, and then come here. Everything was going great until I asked one too many questions about her mission. That was a mistake. It's a long story."

Just then Cynthia arrived and gave Shashir a big hug and a kiss.

"Well, Cynthia, I could really use a hug today myself."

"I'd be happy to oblige you, John."

She gave John a sweet hug and didn't shy away from letting her voluptuous body press against his. It felt really wonderful. Then he and Shashir also shared a hug.

"It is very nice of y'all letting me hang out with you, even though I am a third wheel on a bicycle."

"It will be fun, and we'll meet lots of people. There are still a few unattached ladies floating around here John," said Cynthia.

"John has his heart set on Crystal, Cynthia. They are having a bump on the road of love."

"I am confident that I will straighten this thing out and still have my date with Crystal. As a matter of fact, I'm going to call her right after I visit the Greenpeace tent. If I can find the same girl I talked to yesterday I think I can fix this thing. Look, I don't want to cause y'all to miss any music or anything while I do this. Why don't y'all go on and enjoy yourselves."

"Nonsense, John," said Shashir, "we will give you moral support."

They walked as swiftly as possible, considering the crowds, to the Greenpeace tent. John looked everywhere, but did not see the same girl. He described her to one of the workers there. She said she thought it was Joan he was talking about, and that she was somewhere out there enjoying the festival. As John was leaving with Shashir and Cynthia he almost bumped into Stuart who was arriving. He looked at John intently.

"On another intelligence gathering mission?" Stuart asked sarcastically.

"Stuart, please give me a minute to talk to you. Do you know a girl named Joan? She is the one who told me that about, you know. I swear. Look, I know you care very much for Crystal, and..."

"What the hell do you know about me, or Crystal, or anything? Just who the hell are you anyway?"

"Please do not think so badly about my friend," said Shashir.

"Did he tell you guys the same ridiculous story about being from the past?"

"Yes, and I believe him," Shashir defended.

Cynthia hadn't heard anything about that yet, so she looked a little surprised.

"That's absurd. How can you believe something that stupid?" Stuart asked Shashir.

"You are Stuart. I am Shashir and this is Cynthia. I believe that if everything is God, so then everything is possible."

John was amazed that Shashir had said almost the same thing that he had concluded just the night before.

"Can you not feel John's heart? He is not a devious soul. You are a spiritual man, are you not, Stuart? Think about this carefully, and do not let your jealousy of Crystal's affection for John cloud your thinking."

"I am not jealous," Stuart shot back.

"Well, I can't say the same thing," said John. "I am envious of the long and loving relationship you have had with Crystal. I am jealous that she wouldn't go to the festival with me today, even though she said she wanted to, because of her love for you, Stuart."

"That was before she figured you out," Stuart retorted.

The emotion level had lessened and Stuart didn't seem so very sure. John had run out of things to say. He didn't want to gush out to Stuart how much he loved Crystal, how he had loved her, he believed, in another lifetime. He sympathized with Stuart.

"Stuart, you have a right to be completely skeptical of my coming from the past. Please don't think I am some kind of spy or something. I care as much for the environment as you do. I found this tucked in my wallet last night." John handed Stuart a card from his old leather wallet. It was his 1992 membership card to Greenpeace. Stuart looked at it and raised his eyebrows.

"Well, it could be a fake," he said while handing it back. "You're persistent, aren't you."

John smiled and said, "Stuart, after the miracles I've seen in the last two days, I just have faith that everything will somehow work out right."

John extended his hand to Stuart. He looked at it for a good ten seconds. He shook John's hand and said, "This doesn't mean I believe you."

John said, "That's OK, Stuart. Just believe that I would never hurt Crystal."

Shaking hands, looking each other in the eyes, knowing that they both cared for Crystal, John actually felt some affection for Stuart. John's spirit was really lifting as they left the tent.

"What is this about John being from the past?" asked Cynthia.

"I am sorry that I did not tell you," said Shashir.

"It is because I asked Shashir not to tell anyone, Cynthia. Please don't be mad at him for not telling you. It's not that I wanted him to keep anything from you, particularly. Let's sit over here on the grass and I'll tell you all about it."

John told Cynthia the whole story, except for the details of what he suspected about the Greenpeace mission.

"I'm probably not even supposed to know she is going on a mission. Please keep that in the strictest of confidence."

"God, John. Nobody has ever time traveled, as far as I know. The Star Voyagers claim that beings from other worlds have traveled to Earth in their astral bodies, but time travel is supposed to be impossible."

"Please tell me about the Star Voyagers." said John.

"They are people dedicated to communicating with other worlds." answered Cynthia. "Most of them dream about other planets that have humanoid life forms and civilizations. They have lists of hundreds of different worlds or realities or realms that many people have dreamed about independently of each other, yet they report the same things about them. Some of these worlds have tens of thousands of people having dreams or visions about them. Some of them have only a handful."

"So Star Voyagers are people who have been dreaming about other worlds?"

"Well, probably some people dream of other worlds who aren't a part of the Voyagers," said Cynthia. "And I think that some can astral travel in deep meditation."

"Star Voyagers," added Shashir, "believe that most of these other worlds are in psychic communication with each other."

"A lot of Star Voyagers hope to be reborn on another planet, or that's what they say," added Cynthia.

"So nobody actually travels using spaceships?" John asked.

"According to the Star Voyagers, a few species have made it far enough down the technological path to achieve inter-stellar travel, but the vast distances involved make such travel almost impossible. There are some very long-lived species, according to the Star Voyagers I know, that could make an inter-stellar voyage in just a few generations, but they say it has only been done a few times."

"Wow. And people have a hard time believing me. Has anyone from another planet ever visited here?" John asked.

"No," replied Shashir. "The mass phenomenon of dreams and visions of other worlds just started about twenty years ago."

"I continue to get my mind blown. Cynthia, please believe me. Do you have a voice stress detector on your PC. You can test me."

"Well, I do believe the Voyagers, though I've never dreamed of another world. OK, John. I believe you. Or at least I'm trying to."

"Thank you, Cynthia."

"Would you guys like to attend the ecumenical service at eleven? I sure would," said Cynthia.

"I'd really enjoy that," said John.

"Yes, Cynthia. After all this talk of other worlds and times, I think a worship service would be in order," said Shashir. "I am in great awe of the vastness of the Universe and the incredible miracle of cosmic life. I have always had some doubt about the Voyagers' claims, but after John's story, I am starting to believe. Perhaps they aren't just having mass hallucinations, or any of the other explanations that have been offered. It is an awesome thought, that we might someday be able to communicate with other worlds. Messages have been sent using frequencies given by the Voyagers, but the closest inhabited planets are over thirty light years away, so the message hasn't been received yet, nor have we received any from them."

"Well, if that is true, how is it that people can communicate with these other worlds?" asked John.

"In the astral plane, there is no time or space," said Shashir.

"And the Universe is filled with worlds having intelligent life," added John. "That is truly incredible."

"We'd better get moving, guys, or we'll miss the beginning of the service," said Cynthia as she stood up.

They all got up and headed towards the stage. The morning's program had been of spiritual music from around the world, and was being topped off by a large, mostly black gospel group that was really belting out the sound.

During a break, Shashir added, "No life forms can achieve communication with other worlds unless they are a united and peaceful race. That is why, so they say, that it is only recently that some humans have been in touch with other worlds. Our vibrations of disharmony and destruction created a veil that didn't allow good communications with us, until long after our last war."

"We were so much into material advancement in my time that we didn't even imagine that contact with beings from other worlds could be achieved through spiritual progress," said John.

They found a place where they were pretty far from the stage, but right next to the central isle. The gospel group had finished, and it was announced that the religious leaders would proceed to the stage down the central isle, so it should be cleared. Some very beautiful music started and they could see the procession heading their way. There were Christian priests in their robes, some swinging incense burners. Others appeared to be swamis or yogis, some wore the robes of Buddhist priests. Some looked like priestesses of old. There were Native Americans in full regalia. Others were Sufis or Muslim. John was very moved, and made almost ecstatic by the sight of so many different religious leaders all together in one spirit.

Each of twelve religions, chosen by lot, performed part of the service. It was obvious that they all had much in common. Everyone seemed to have bells, incense and candles, and each seemed to have a holy book. Everyone prayed, and most had chanting or singing as part of their religious observance.

Now, this is more like it, John thought. Religions honoring each other and celebrating the love for God they all share, instead of fighting or backbiting.

The Hindu priest led the whole festival in three Oms, and it was incredibly powerful to hear a quarter of a million people chanting together. John felt very uplifted.

He was surprised to find that when the stage rotated after the service, there was a whole symphony orchestra set up on the other side. They played the last movement of Beethoven's Ninth Symphony, and some of the choirs stayed to sing the ending with them. Shashir got out his pipe. He and Cynthia smoked some of his temple ball hash and handed the pipe to John. He was already feeling so uplifted he would have refused, but as they were being so nice letting him hang with them, he had a couple of tokes.

"Are you ready to rock and roll?" asked the announcer.

The loudest yes John had ever heard blasted back, followed by cheering. John asked Cynthia and Shashir if they were going to be there for a while, as he was going to a quieter spot to call Crystal. He had been very tempted to call her right after he saw Stuart, knowing that he wouldn't be with her, but now he believed the wait was a good thing. He had to have faith that Stuart's report to her would help his case. Maybe he had talked to Joan, or maybe he'd tell her about his Greenpeace membership card. The lovely spiritual service and beautiful symphony had calmed his nervousness. The hashish seemed to have given him confidence and positive energy, almost to feeling in a state of grace. He found a quieter space, crossed his fingers for luck, and asked for her number.

"Hello, Crystal?"

"Yes, John. I've been expecting you to call."

"Have you talked to Stuart?"

"Yes."

"Did he tell you he saw me?"

"Yes."

"Well, was he able to talk to the person at the Greenpeace tent who gave me the information."

"He said he talked to some of the staff, and they admitted that they had heard loose talk, and it was possible there was some kind of a leak. I did talk to the Chows. You have made some good friends there, John. Look, I am sorry about running off on you last night. I told you more than I should have, and then I got very afraid that my foolishness had jeopardized the success of this mission. I did get a disturbing communication yesterday. I can't go into it, but it made me tense and somewhat paranoid. A lot of people are counting on me."

"I understand, Crystal, and I am so sorry that I pressed you with questions that were none of my business. I just care so very much for you, Crystal. The idea of your leaving tomorrow is hard for me. Did Stuart tell you that I found my old Greenpeace membership card?"

"No, the Chows did. But Stuart did say that he wasn't sure about you one way or the other now. He thinks I should not see you because I shouldn't take any chances at this point."

"Crystal, please, from the bottom of my heart, please keep our date this evening. You said yourself that you may never see me again. I don't really understand any of this myself. The only thing I feel sure of is that we were meant to meet. Please don't end our relationship now. I won't ask anything about your mission. I don't want to know. I just want to be with you again. Please, Crystal."

"I want to see you again too, John."

John's heart leaped for joy. "Look, um, is there any chance that you could just come on down here and meet me?"

"No, John. It would be better if I finished packing and taking care of my plants now. Let's just keep to our original plans. I can't promise that we'll go back to the festival after the ritual. Stuart asked me if he could spend the night over here tonight, so we could get up and go to the train together tomorrow. He also suggested that you might come over and try and see me, or what we were doing, and he could be here to intervene. This was last night when we were sure that you were some kind of a spy. I have to talk to him when he returns."

"I understand."

"Where did you find your Greenpeace membership card?"

"It was between some of my IDs. Crystal, I'd never do anything

139

to hurt the environment or you. Please believe me." John wanted so much to tell her he loved her, but didn't want to intensify things any more than they already were.

"I am sorry I thought you were a fraud, John."

"That's all right, Crystal. It is very understandable, considering the circumstances. I am just so very glad that you will see me again. May I come over to your house and ride to the ritual with you?"

"Either that, or you could meet me somewhere so you could stay there at the festival longer."

"Remember what I said last night? I'd rather be with you anywhere than any place else at any time."

"I'm glad you still feel that way. We need to leave here by four-thirty, as I have a role in the ritual. Can you make it by then?"

"I guess I can wait that long. I am so happy. Thank you, Crystal."

"Thank you, John. I'll see you later. Good-bye."

"Good-bye, Crystal."

John was ecstatic. He jumped. He danced. He fell on the ground and looked at the sky with a silly grin on his face. When he got back to Shashir and Cynthia they were dancing with another couple, having a blast. John jumped right in. Between songs John told them that his date with Crystal was back on again and they all hugged. He told them that she hadn't committed to come back there with him after the ritual, but he thought that it would work out.

They met a lot of great people from all over the world that afternoon. The next band up was the first to play a style of music that was different from any John had ever heard, very spacey but rocking. They met some kids from Africa who were friends and fans of a group that fused ancient tribal sounds with rock. John learned a lot about what was going on in Africa. He found that the population had been greatly reduced at the beginning of the century due to droughts, famines and AIDS, but Africa had come back strong. It now had a stable population, and led the world in reclaiming deserts. He met a married gay couple, and found out that most gays settled down in a marriage. He did make a few waves with his questions, and though some people thought he was amazingly unaware of what was going on, most everyone answered and was friendly.

John was having a very good time, but he was also waiting anxiously for it to be three so he could leave to go and see Crystal.

When the time arrived, he made contingency plans to meet back with Cynthia and Shashir at nine at good old pole 25 and left.

John ran into Nan, the girl from Tibet, on the train out, and had a nice talk with her. She told him that most of the Chinese nationals who lived in the province of Tibet had become Buddhist, just like the native Tibetans. She was taking a break from the festival to see some of the sights of San Francisco. John recommended that she go to the park and see St. Francis and the wonderful Buddha in the Chinese tea garden.

John transferred to the Berkeley train, then to the bus to Crystal's neighborhood, and soon found himself walking up the street to Crystal's house. He figured that Stuart would be there, and he was beginning to be a bit apprehensive. Was she actually in love with Stuart? Things were so complicated. Have faith, he thought. Faith. That was the key to everything. He remembered that in one of his yoga classes he heard the teacher quoting his guru saying, "Your faith is God's grace." How did it go? Yes, it was a question. "What is God's grace? Your faith is God's grace." Didn't Crystal say the same thing the other day? John thought. He prayed that God might grace him with faith.

The Ritual

How can I not have faith? All life is a miracle from we know not where, so, added to my own personal miracle, you'd think faith would be a piece of cake, John thought. But it is easier said than done. Even after all these miracles, I still have a time with my negative thinking and doubt. At least I never think I'm crazy any more. Come on, John, it's a beautiful afternoon. Here you are at the end of the 21st Century, walking up a lovely street, going to see the girl you love.

Doubt seemed to flee, and he felt calm and serene. He was doing just what he was supposed to be doing. Everything was perfect. Stuart would probably become a very good friend at some point.

John saw Crystal's friend, Roger, gardening in his front yard, so he waved and said hello. Roger waved back, and asked John if he were going to see Crystal. When John said yes, Roger said to tell her hello for him. As John got to the house with the pot plants, he noticed that one of them had been nibbled down to the ground. There was a deer lying calmly in the yard looking quite content.

By the time John got to Crystal's pathway, he felt better than he had ever felt in his life. Even the clothing of Lee's that he wore, a pale blue pair of handmade drawstring pants and a seemingly hand woven, colorful, short sleeve shirt, felt beautiful and perfect. California still produced long, lovely summer afternoons. It was a tad hot, but dry and clear. Stuart was sitting on the front porch, and as John walked up he spoke.

"Hello again, John."

"Hi, Stuart." This time Stuart shook John's hand without hesitancy.

"I wanted to tell you that I now doubt you are some kind of

agent. This is an important mission that we are going on, and as you know, sometimes we Greenpeacers do things that are dangerous and illegal. Have you said anything to anyone about this?"

John thought for a moment. "I did tell Shashir and Cynthia that Crystal was going on a mission and that it was involved with her thinking I was some kind of spy. But I said absolutely nothing about any specifics of where y'all are going or what she might be doing. I don't really know much myself, except she will pass through Atlanta, and I didn't tell anyone that."

"Good. Thank you, John, and please do not say anything to anyone about this."

"OK, Stuart."

Stuart still had not returned a smile, but John was very happy about the vast improvement in vibrations.

"Tell me, Stuart, you're in the Com-Union. You must think that this perfect world with no money is really possible?"

"I know it is possible."

"It seems pretty impossible to me, but I must admit, I never dreamed the world could get this fantastic."

"You have to see it in a historic perspective, John. Humanity has been evolving, even though it often appears we're not, from the beginning of our history."

"I can see that, but I never really thought about what we would evolve into, probably because I didn't think we'd even survive. Almost all fictional portrayals of the future from my time were terribly negative."

"Well," said Stuart, "there is nowhere to go but to the perfect embodiment of the truth of the oneness of all life, or to eventual destruction of one kind or another. This choice has been reflected in many prophecies, which tend to be either apocalyptic, or have a vision of a world ruled by God, or God's chosen. We Com-Union people interpret this to be the Spirit of God living in us all. We think we are entering the final phase of human evolution, where we will be united as one on Earth, and in communication with all the other worlds with evolved life-forms in the heavens. Ask Crystal. Most of these other worlds of beings have evolved far beyond the credit exchange. It took a long time for us to get to here, and we still have a way to go, but we will inevitably continue to evolve."

John was listening attentively. "I really don't know how everything got to where it is now," he said.

"I can tell you how we got to where we are here on Earth. Back when we were going through the crisis, times were hard, and there were shortages of everything. Mankind was struggling to survive and had to do everything possible to prevent further calamity. We had to quickly transform from a consumer society that used up too much energy and polluted so grievously. And not just to a steady state environment, for we had great problems we had to address. We had to reverse all that ecological destruction and degradation. Healing the Earth took tremendous effort."

"I can imagine," said John.

"We humans can't take a lot of credit. The Earth herself is a self-regulating organism. For instance, she can use the growth and preponderance of certain types of plankton in the oceans to regulate weather conditions."

"How does that work?" asked John.

"Some of the many kinds of plankton in the oceans have a tiny molecular skeleton that survives their death, and can be drawn up into the atmosphere with evaporated water. Clouds cannot form, no matter how much moisture is in the atmosphere if there isn't dust or other specks of matter for the water droplets to condense onto. When the right plankton is blooming, their skeletons can supply the matter for the formation of clouds. This is just one way the Earth controls her temperature and weather conditions."

"That's incredible, but how does the earth control the growth of plankton?"

"It is not perfectly understood, but we know the Earth uses this and other mechanisms to regulate herself. She, herself, like a loving mother, deserves most of the credit for the rapid turnaround of the environment. The great regenerative power of life itself is a big part of what saved us."

"You mean, the Earth is like a living thing?" said John.

"The Earth IS a living thing, John," answered Stuart. There was silence for a moment as John took in that amazing new idea.

"Anyway, during the crisis period, times were hard, and for a long time there was a depression, as workers had to be relocated, retrained, and their workload eventually drastically reduced. We had already switched from an income tax to a consumer tax, so excessive consumption was further taxed in order to discourage it. Also, a lot of people were unemployed or under-employed for a long while.

"People started growing as much of their food as possible, and making or bartering for everything they could. It was an intelligent way to get by and to avoid paying taxes, which used to be much higher. It wasn't unusual for people to live without much money. The Com-Union started towards the end of this period, and the idea of doing away with credit exchange altogether seemed very attainable. People are using the independence that comes from owning a home and creating their own things, not just for beating poverty, but to liberate themselves and everyone else from a competitive, inequitable system. Once we take over all transportation and communications, it will be relatively easy for people to give up their accounts,"

"Well, I guess it isn't so far fetched, considering how far everyone has come. How does everyone get to own their own home?" asked John.

"From their share of the Inheritance Share," answered Stuart.

Crystal came out and John beamed as they hugged. John had never seen her with her hair down, and she looked very lovely, though she was wearing a pair of shorts and a simple knit shirt. She was carrying a bag in one hand and the hug was kind of short, but Crystal was smiling. She turned and gave Stuart a hug and he said, "Remember, we have to get up at five am tomorrow."

John was really beaming as they said goodbye to Stuart, and he and Crystal turned and left.

"Let me carry that, Crystal."

They headed down the path together.

"You sure are an old-fashioned kind of a guy, John," Crystal said with a smile. "We girls can take care of ourselves. This is my costume for the ritual. I don't want to be wearing my crystal tiara all over the Bay area."

"Crystal tiara, I can't wait. So where is the ritual?"

"Mount Tamalpais. Ever been there?"

"Yes, but every time I went it was fogged in. I've never seen it on a sunny day like this."

"It will be beautiful," added Crystal. "This is usually a very well attended ritual, being the Summer Solstice. Lady Denique will be the High Priestess, and she has a lot of fans. She is incredibly beautiful and powerful, yet still has a gentleness and warmth. She usually sings at the rituals and her voice is awesome. One problem is that she is such a popular singer that people who are not really pagans come to the ritual, just to see and hear her."

"You are a pagan?"

"Yes, but a reformed pagan. We don't perform any sacrifices, and I don't think any modern pagans do. I love all of the enlightened masters I've met or studied, but my favorite form in which to worship God is the Mother Earth. I guess that makes me a pagan, though maybe Goddess worshiper would be a more fitting term."

"You've met enlightened masters?"

"Well, one or two. I met a woman saint from India who was surely enlightened. I believe that Allastar, who was one of the founders of the Star Voyagers, is enlightened. I got to stay at his school for two weeks once."

"God, Crystal, I've got a hundred years of catching up to do. Look at that deer over there. I think he's stoned."

"Oh my", Crystal exclaimed. "Richard will be disappointed when he see's he lost one of his ladies. At least the deer didn't eat it all."

"There was an ecumenical service at the festival today. It was great."

"Yes, Lady Denique was there, but she didn't draw a role in the service. They can only represent so many religions in an hour. So have you been having a good time?"

"A blast. Especially since I learned I would see you tonight. From Stuart's remark I take it that you are considering staying out longer than just the ritual."

"Yes, I'm considering it." Crystal looked a little serious for a minute. "I have had to reevaluate my relationship with Stuart. I love him a great deal, but more like the brother I never had. I'm afraid I have been using him."

"You've always been honest with him, right?"

"Yes. But I shouldn't have let him spend so much of his time and life keeping me company. He should be looking for someone who can give him the kind of relationship he really wants."

"Well, I am sure that he would rather be with you, even like it is."

"That is what he always says. But that doesn't exactly make it fair."

They walked quietly for a while. John was very encouraged that he could cause Crystal to reevaluate her relationship with Stuart, and obviously she wasn't in love with him romantically. What great news!

"Crystal, what is your last name, and tell me about your family?"

"My last name is Silver. My parents live in Seattle now. I have a younger sister who has Down's Syndrome, and my mother mostly takes care of her. They could have terminated the pregnancy, but they chose not to, and they've never regretted it. Carol is an incredibly sweet being. My father is a fireman."

"Please let me carry that bag, Crystal, because I want to hold your hand."

Crystal shifted her bag over to her other shoulder, moved closer to John, and then took hold of John's hand. What a moment! John was so happy to get their relationship back to where it had been. They both walked along quietly. After a few moments, Crystal looked up at him and gave him a wonderful smile. John was ecstatic! But he was also getting an erection and he was afraid that Crystal would notice and it would ruin the moment. Think about baseball. Think of anything else. But he could feel a wonderful sensuous energy flow between them. John had never let himself actually fantasize about making love with Crystal, not any more than kissing her. They got to the subus stop.

"Two minutes to the next subus. Did you plan that, Crystal?"

"No. Just walked out of the house. They run every seven minutes this time of day."

"So tell me more about being a pagan."

"The Earth and the Sun actually give us our bodies, our lives. It just seems more natural, more grateful of me, to be worshipping them instead of some human being, or conceptualization of God. I love Jesus and Buddha and Krishna. I love a lot of the mythological gods and goddesses for what they represent and for all the faith and devotion so many humans have had in them. But my first love is for our blessed Mother Earth."

"Back in my time, a lot of Christian preachers would say you were a devil worshiper. The Earth and the Sun give you your body. They would probably say, what about the gift of forgiveness of your sins."

"Oh, there are still a few fire breathers out there. I never believed in original sin. Sin is just error to me. Eternal damnation has got to be the most awful concept imaginable. Like you said, God would never throw his own children into an eternal fire. I do believe in God's grace."

The subus pulled in to the stop and they got on board. John insisted on using his account to repay Crystal for his first train ride over.

"So, do you believe that Jesus's death on the cross paid for our sins?"

"No. I believe Jesus died on the cross so that he could demonstrate that death is not real. God's grace existed before Jesus's crucifixion. But if a Christian wants to say that Jesus died to manifest God's grace onto the Earth, I have no argument with that. As long as everyone in every time period benefits from it. When they try to make an exclusive thing out of God's grace, that I don't buy. Surely an enlightened soul like Jesus would give such a gift to all souls freely."

"So you don't buy the 'he that believeth in me' part."

"When Jesus said that, he was in a high state of universal consciousness. He was speaking as God, so it shouldn't be taken so personally. I think Jesus meant that anyone who believes in God can have His grace. Though it isn't stated in the Bible, I believe that no matter what name they have for God, or whether they ever heard of Jesus, they have His forgiveness. A lot of people were born before Jesus's time. Surely He would want them, and all souls, to be able to have God's grace in their lives. So if grace came from Jesus's sacrifice, then it was retroactive and all inclusive."

"Sounds good to me. Crystal, you are a Star Voyager. Would you tell me a little about them, if it isn't a secret or anything."

"Sure. Everything the Star Voyagers do is public knowledge. We don't want to have any secrets. The Star Voyagers were founded by a group of people who discovered that they were all having dreams about other worlds. Many of them were having dreams about the same worlds. We work to catalogue all worlds that over three people report dreaming about. Everything new anyone discovers is added to the information in the same way. Several people have to report it independently. We have compiled vast amounts of information about over two hundred different worlds with intelligent life forms. Some people are in psychic communication with beings from these worlds. Some of our data comes from people who remember incarnations where they were on one of these worlds. It seems that since we humans have become peaceful, some sort of negative energy field is dissipating, allowing this to happen."

"So you have dreams about other worlds?"

"I only dream and have visions of one planet. Vicomia Fernale."

"Vicomia Fernale. God, Crystal. Will wonders never cease? What's it like?"

"It is a beautiful world inhabited by very evolved beings who are human-like, but have the ability to photosynthesize energy directly from their Sun. They are beyond vegan. They won't even eat plants. It would be like eating their brothers or something, being part plant themselves. They have beautiful green leaf-like growths where we have hair on our heads. They take great joy in spreading their branches out and soaking up sunlight. They drink water and will eat fruits and nuts that fall off of trees and bushes. An incredibly gentle people, yet some of the most powerful species in the galaxy as they communicate telepathically and can understand the thoughts of anyone else. Even animals, to some degree. They only use spoken words for ritual and art like singing, poetry and plays.

Every once in a while I find myself in Muelf's, she is my connection to their world, mind when she is reading some other being's thoughts. Every thought comes to her in her own language and somehow I can understand her in my language. It's incredible. Those of us who are attuned to Vicomia Fernale are putting together a universal translator for all galactic languages."

"Amazing. You actually find yourself in the mind of one of these beings? So all the worlds y'all know about are in this galaxy?"

"No. Some don't even seem to be in this physical universe, but most of them are."

"So how is the universal translator coming along?"

"It is hard, slow work. We Vicomia people have to have endless meetings with people tuned in to other worlds and we have to know all about the species whose language we are working on. It's impossible to work on more than a handful of languages at one time. But the pace is picking up. We figure that in twenty or thirty years we may have a chip with most galactic languages in it."

"Well, what good will it be, I mean, if you can't physically visit them?"

"It will help many people who want to communicate with the beings they are dreaming about. And you never know about physically visiting. Many people have reported seeing beings from different worlds on the same planet. How that happens, we are still working on understanding."

"Did they travel in spaceships?"

"No one has reported seeing such a thing, but some people say that very advanced beings can travel in their astral body to another world and then manifest a physical body once they are there."

"Now that is an amazing concept," replied John.

It was time to change for the train to Marin County. John was getting used to the train and bus system in the Bay area, and had come to really appreciate it. It did seem like it was faster and easier to get around now, though a little more walking was called for. The public transportation provided an entertaining look at the people of this time, and John could notice the general improvement in everyone's mood, compared to the past. Most people seemed cheerful and readily smiled and talked to each other. Overweight people were actually rare. There weren't as many shabby looking people. Very few looked intoxicated, and even the folks with older or patched clothing looked contented. John thought back to the looks on everyone's faces in traffic on the freeway.

"I'm beginning to really like this world without cars, Crystal. It makes so much more sense."

"I've seen pictures of the days of traffic gridlock. I don't know how people put up with it."

"Having your own car is a powerful addiction. It gives you a lot of freedom."

"Yeah, but at what cost? It just wasn't possible for everyone on Earth to have a automobile" added Crystal.

"Back in my time, people thought we'd develop electric cars."

"We have them. But to give everyone an electric car would take so much additional power production that the ecological costs just weren't worth it. There would have to be power plants everywhere, many times more than in your time, not to mention all the mining and manufacturing to create all those cars. There are over six billion people alive today."

"In my time, mostly only people in the wealthier countries had cars."

"That wasn't very equitable, or sustainable. Nowadays, we don't have a world where a quarter of the population uses up most of the resources and does most of the polluting, leaving everyone else to suffer the consequences. It's easy to understand why peace wasn't common."

"We were pretty screwed up." John was beginning to feel a little defensive for coming from such a backward time. "You had to live with a lot of injustice and insanity. The Cold War was really crazy."

"Yes, and it is still causing problems."

John realized that Crystal was probably referring to her coming mission. The toxic legacy of his time was now going to separate them. He could tell that Crystal was somewhat apprehensive about the mission, and it made him feel a lot of love for this sweet, innocent healer who was going to take some kind of risk to make the world a better place.

"Thank God for idealistic people from all generations, who sacrificed to raise humanity a little higher," said John. "In the last century we had the suffragettes, the labor movement, the civil rights workers, the ecologists." John took Crystal's hand. "Crystal, I admire you so much."

She smiled at John. "You're right, John. It has always taken a little sacrifice from some good hearted souls to move us forward. Maybe some day, sacrifice won't be called for. If we can clean up this radioactive mess, I believe that humanity will be able to solve the rest of our problems and take our place in the galactic community."

"That is an interesting thought. Is that what the Star Voyagers think?"

"Yes. Who would want to visit a world that was loaded with radioactive contamination? Or a people who would allow it, and who still had violence and inequity?"

"Isn't there some inequity on any of these worlds you know about?"

"None of these worlds has any real poverty. Beings are on different levels of spiritual evolution, but some living in splendor and luxury while others suffer hunger and poverty, no. There are some beings who have achieved interstellar travel with physical spaceships,"

"Cynthia told me about them," said John.

"Supposedly, some of them have been known to try and create empires, but the difficulties of inter-stellar travel pretty much prohibit anything more than just scouting missions. We believe these species have exceeded the rational range of technological development, and they are not highly regarded by the Star Voyagers. We are pretty sure that there have been robot vehicles that have visited earth."

"Maybe that explains some of the UFO sightings back in my time. I haven't seen obvious signs of poverty nowadays, like we had in the past."

"Right, though we do still have some living extravagantly."

"Isn't that acceptable, if not necessary, to create an incentive for accomplishment?"

"Acceptable, but not perfect. I know a lot of people who are willing to work hard and take risks to further humanity's evolution. Is it too much to ask, for some to work hard, take risks and maybe even sacrifice to move humanity ahead materially? Shouldn't that be reward enough?"

"Yes, it should be, but in my time everyone was so totally fixated on money."

"The consequences for not having any were so much worse then, I can understand that. Unrestrained greed and self-interest running the world is just not a sustainable system. Things got worse and worse until it failed."

"Thank God the failure didn't destroy everything," added John.

"It came darn close, and certainly caused a tremendous amount of suffering. The amount of sacrifice and hard work it took to straighten everything out was incredible, and is still going on."

And thank God for wonderful people like you who will do it, thought John. Even though I can't bear the thought of your being in danger. Enough had been said about this. It had changed the mood to a more somber one and John wanted to change the subject.

"I really want to help with completing the cleanup of our world, Crystal. Um, what is this ritual we are attending going to be like?"

"This is a reformed Pagan ritual. We don't evoke any of the old goddesses of antiquity. It is a more straightforward approach. Once humanity could see our world from space, it was time to evolve away from gods and goddesses as metaphors for the Earth and other cosmic energies. We could simply worship the Earth herself as a living, breathing reality, our Mother. Here is where we get off and catch the bus for the top of Mount Tam."

Another couple had come up to them and said hello to Crystal, and she introduced John.

"John, this is Angelo and Marie."

"Hi, it is a pleasure to meet you."

"And you, too, Brother," said Angelo.

"Hi, John. Crystal, are you assisting the ritual today?" asked Marie.

"Yes, and I feel quite honored."

A lot of people got off another bus and joined the crowd at the bus stop. "Looks like they have them running about every five minutes. We might not get on the next one," said Crystal.

Many of the people waiting at the stop were wearing robes, even though it was a somewhat warm afternoon. Marie lifted up her robe and flapped it around in order to cool herself. Angelo took his off to reveal a pair of shorts and a T-shirt underneath.

"That is why I carry mine and change up there," said Crystal to everyone.

More people came over to greet Crystal, and John met about a dozen of her friends as they waited until a second bus took most everyone left at the stop. This bus ran above ground, but otherwise was just like the subuses. The ped ran next to the road for much of the way. It was a festive mood going up the mountain. John was happy to see that they still had the same little winding road up. The day was perfect, and the redwoods beautiful as they passed through them. When they got up top, John could sometimes see a beautiful view of the ocean, though there were a lot more trees than John had remembered.

"Did they plant a lot of trees up here, too?"

"Oh, yes," answered Crystal. "I haven't been to a ritual up here in a long time. I usually attend the one on Redwood Hill, where I met you. I met Lady Denique when I did healing work on her daughter. We became good friends, and she asked me to assist her today."

"So what will you do?"

"Not much, really. I hand Lady Denique the things she needs as she needs them. I told you that I called Mr. Chow today. He really likes you, and though he finds your story amazing, he doesn't have a better explanation for how you know so much about the past. Also, I think I dreamed about the angel last night again. I woke up slightly after midnight and remembered that there was an angel in the dream, but I couldn't quite remember details. Let's just say it left me with a warm feeling about you."

"Very interesting. It sounds like that angel is my best ally, because it has helped me twice with my relationship with you. I wish you could remember it better. I'm glad you called the Chows. We saw a great movie last night about my time. Did he tell you?"

"Yes. I feel badly about doubting you and checking up on you, John."

"Don't, Crystal. God, the last thing I want you to do is feel badly. I'm sorry I pressed you about the trip. Let's just take it from the top and start over."

They both smiled at each other.

"And here we are at the top," said Crystal.

They got off the bus with a big group of people, most of whom headed the same way.

"We have about a half mile walk to get to the ritual site." Angelo and Marie joined them and they all started singing.

"The Earth is our Mother, of her we take care.
The Sun is her lover, whose light we all share.
Share the Earth and know her worth.
Share the Light and it gets bright.
Sharing and caring, caring and sharing,
Doing what is right."

After a couple of times John joined in. The little procession was getting happier and higher all the time. Everyone was in festive clothing. Colorful robes were the most common attire, with some togas as well. People were carrying flowers, and many wore them in their hair. Someone with a drum, and then a flute player caught up with them, and soon people were dancing up the path. John and Crystal were beaming and held hands as they skipped along, sometimes stopping so that he could spin her around. He put his right arm around her and they waltzed until Crystal's bag slipped off of John's shoulder. He grabbed it about an inch from the ground, looked at Crystal with a grin, and said, "Didn't you say there was a crystal tiara in here?"

"Yes, and it's about time I put those things on. I'm just going to step into the trees and change. Be right back."

For a moment John thought about sneaking a peek, but he quickly dropped that notion. He was so filled with happiness and mirth as he waited. An almost constant stream of people danced and frolicked up the path, and it was a very amusing sight. John had been to the Mardi Gras when he was in college, and it was fun, but played out in filthy streets filled with empty beer cans and trash. This was a beautiful woods and there wasn't a beer can to be seen. A few people did have wine skins, and he did catch someone squirting a red stream into his girlfriend's mouth. No one seemed drunk, but everyone seemed to be having a fantastic time. He saw a few folks passing a beautiful, feathered pipe. He had enjoyed smoking with Shashir, but he had been on such a natural high since this whole experience began that it seemed totally unnecessary.

John heard Crystal returning from the woods. When he turned he saw her with the afternoon sun behind her, and the sunlight shining through the crystal tiara shot rainbows all around. Her dress was to her ankles and full, with long pointed sleeves, all in shimmering white satin. When she changed direction it swirled out and rainbows flashed around on it. John was stunned. Her long blond hair, with the light behind it shone like a golden halo around her face. John felt profoundly that he was looking at a living goddess.

As she got closer, John could see that a large blue gemstone hung around her neck on a silver chain. At six feet away, he could see that her eyes outshone it. God, she was beautiful!

"You look like a goddess, Crystal. Your outfit is stunning."

"All women are the Goddess, John."

"Again, I find myself underdressed."

"You look very handsome, and nicely dressed. Is that some of Lee's clothing?"

"Yes."

"I thought they looked familiar."

John offered Crystal his arm and they continued into the clearing, which had no statue, but a fantastic view of the ocean. It contained hundreds of people, with more arriving all the time. Even with all the outrageous outfits, Crystal seemed to get a lot of attention from everyone. There was a small makeshift altar set up in a prominent place, and they headed towards that as Crystal ran a gauntlet of greetings and compliments. John couldn't help but feel a lot of pride to find himself with such a prominent lady. Standing by the altar was a stately woman of about forty, wearing a headdress with two natural crystal points emerging from beautiful feathers. Her gown was made of cloth, but had the appearance of colorful feathers.

Her smile broadened when she saw Crystal. She stepped toward them as Crystal let go of John's arm to give her a hug. Now that is a good hug, John thought as he watched for a long moment. Crystal introduced him to Lady Denique, and John had but a moment to look into her beautiful, bronze face before she embraced him. It was just as long as the one she gave Crystal, and John almost melted. She was a big, full-bosomed woman, and John was actually mildly ecstatic from the warmth of her body and spirit. As they separated John said, "Wow," and staggered, weak-kneed, back a couple of steps. The ladies both laughed heartily at that, and Crystal said, "John, I need to go over things with Lady Denique. Just find a nice spot and I'll see you after the ritual."

John could see that all the space up close to the altar was already filled with people, so he went around to the back and decided to stand back there behind everyone and just take it in. He could see a fellow heading his way who was fanning a large shell full of smoking leaves, causing the smoke literally to engulf the person in front of him. When the fellow got to John, he asked if John would like to be smudged, and John said sure. The smoke didn't especially smell good, and John didn't quite understand, but it did seem to lift his energy a bit as the smoke dissipated. When in Rome, he thought.

Everything quieted down for a few moments and then John discovered that he couldn't hear so well back where he was. Crystal had said something. Everybody started to chant Om. First it was in unison, and then the Oms started at different times until a continuous vibration of Om was created. John joined in. After about five minutes, Lady Denique raised her hands. She held a wand with a crystal emerging out of some feathers in one hand and a feather fan in the other. The chanting died down and he heard Lady Denique's powerful voice say, "I cast our circle of love and light." Then she said that they would now call the directions.

Everyone got up, and John discovered that now he couldn't see very well either. They were facing away from the ocean, and he could hear a person calling.

"I summon the East, the energy of air, of awakening, of Spring, of illumination. Hail East. Be with us now."

"Hail East," everyone repeated with arms up stretched.

They turned towards the South, and he heard someone else say, "I summon the South, the energy of innocence, of the Summer, of fire, be with us now. Hail South."

"Hail South," again everyone responded.

They turned towards the sea and he heard someone say, "I summon the West, the energy of introspection, of the Fall, of water, be with us now. Hail West."

"Hail West."

They turned to the North and someone said, "I summon the North, the energy of the Earth, of Winter, of logic, be with us now. Hail North."

"Hail North."

Lady Denique spoke again. "It is fitting, that at this time, at the turning of the seasons, we gather together to thank and honor all of the energies that give us life. God's cornucopia of abundance is overflowing within every heart whenever we give thanks. Our life is a precious gift beyond all measure. We do not fully comprehend, nor could we ever fully thank, the myriad powers that bring us together here today. Billions of years ago, stars were born, lived out their lives and died the fiery death of supernovas to create the elements that make up our bodies. Our Mother Earth, our Solar

System, are made from the recycled bodies of these stars, ancient beyond all antiquity."

"Hundreds of millions of years ago, plants struggled out of the sea, wet nurse to all life on Earth, and climbed up onto the land, creating a beachhead for all life to follow. For countless eons, creatures were born and died, lived and evolved, and their and bodies came from and went back to the Black Mother, the organic Earth, the slim layer of living soil from which all terrestrial life is brought forth. We thank each of these beings, from the mightiest of suns, to the smallest of bacteria, for the great sacrifice of their lives in order for us to have these bodies we now grace. We take joy from the knowledge that our own deaths are not in vain, for life springs anew from every atom within us."

Crystal handed Lady Denique a bunch of large sticks of incense. She then took a candle from the altar and lit them.

"To the air we offer this sweet fragrance, in thanks for the rain, the gentle breeze that cools us, the breath that keeps us alive." She waved the incense sticks around.

Crystal gave her a bowl that she held deftly in her right hand, and then Crystal gave her a pitcher.

"To Water, so essential for all life, we offer this wine, gift of the vine and our labor." She poured some wine from the pitcher into the bowl. "This bowl will be taken to the sea and merge with that great goddess, as the rain and rivers all must."

She gave the bowl back to Crystal and after putting it back on the altar Crystal handed her another smaller bowl.

"To the Earth, from which we all arise, we offer this cornmeal in return for the gift of our bodies. There is no way we can but give a token back for now, but we will all offer back our bodies in a way that will enhance your fertility at our deaths." She poured a circle of cornmeal on the ground.

After returning the bowl to the altar, Crystal gave Lady Denique a slender, flaming torch.

"To Fire, the element of passion, of movement, of change, we offer a special gift." She lit a fire in a large caldron placed in front of the altar. "We give to the fire, and ask the fire to receive and transmute, our greatest fault, our most vexing weakness, our most stubborn error."

John noticed everyone putting their hands together in the prayer position in front of their foreheads. After differing lengths of time, the people took their hands from in front of their foreheads, and opened them in front of their mouths with the hands still together, like they were holding something. They then blew as if they were blowing something towards the fire. He got the idea and quickly put his hands together in front of his forehead. What is my worse fault? He pondered. Doubt? Fear? No, doubt, doubt that he deserved the wonderful things that were happening to him, doubt that he was worthy. He put his hands down in front of his mouth, opened them up and blew the doubt away.

Within a couple of minutes, everyone was finished. Lady Denique raised her hands again with the wand and feathered fan and said. "O power of life. O mighty forces of the Cosmos. Know that we know. All life is one. God is one. We are all one. To worship you in any one form is to limit you, and for this we ask your forgiveness. To worship you now and not worship you always is foolish, and for this we ask your indulgence. And to think that you need or want our worship is but another mistake. Yet we trust in your love like a child."

"The Earth on which we stand is our Mother, and the Sun which lights the day is our Father," she continued. "We thank you. The black eternity of space, the womb of all creation is our Grandmother. The mighty Pran, the cosmic energy, the life force is our Grandfather. We thank you. And we thank you for the greatest gift, the most amazing of gifts, our free will. Free to love, free to give, free to join in the creation, we are the most blessed of beings."

Then Lady Denique started to sing a song that John had never heard before, nor could he understand the language. It didn't matter, for her voice was the most wondrous he had ever heard. The whole ritual had been a very high experience for John, and he found himself filled with the sweetest of emotions, incredible gratitude for this day, this life, this wonderful world. Tears of joy streamed from both eyes. He wasn't the only one moved to tears, for it seemed that many others were having the same kind of profound experience.

He was almost entranced as the directions were dismissed, and each was thanked for their presence. At the end they all stood with their arms around the people on either side of them and sang.

"May the blessings of God rest upon us.
May Her peace abide with us.
May His presence illuminate our lives, now and forevermore."

They sang it three times, and then there was silence for a few moments. John could see that most people had their eyes closed.

"Our circle is open but unbroken.

May the love of the Goddess be ever in your heart.

Merry meet and merry part, and merry meet again."

After Lady Denique had said it once everyone sang it three times. Then everybody started hugging. John had never hugged so many people in his life.

SOLSTICE FULL MOON

The hugging went on for at least ten or fifteen minutes. There were so many people and the hugs were so heartfelt and long that there was no way that John could hug everybody. Then people started talking and milling around visiting with friends. Some were leaving, and some were sitting down in little groups and taking out food. John made his way over to Crystal and Lady Denique, who were still hugging a few folks. John waited as the last people in line exchanged hugs and greetings.

Then Crystal turned her attention to him and said, "What did you think of the ritual?"

"It was wonderful, really moving. And I never got so many hugs at one time."

Crystal smiled. "Lady Denique has invited us to share the meal that her husband Mario, prepared. He's a famous vegetarian chef, so we'd be foolish as well as impolite to refuse."

"Sure. That sounds great."

They followed Lady Denique over to where Mario had spread out a large blanket and already had a fancy picnic basket opened. It contained plates, cups, utensils, napkins, everything they needed for a picnic for six people. Crystal introduced John to Mario and their two teenage daughters, Sandy and Ruth.

"John, would you lead us in a grace?" said Lady Denique.

"OK," said John, a little surprised by the idea. They all held hands in a circle, and for a moment John was silent. He was searching his mind for an appropriate prayer.

"This is a Sufi blessing. I believe it's called Nazar. O Thou, sustainer of our bodies, hearts and minds, bless all that we thankfully receive. Amen."

Amens and smiles were all around. Mario put out some mushrooms that he and the girls had found in the woods the day before and he had marinated with herbs. John found them to be delicious. The next course was a pasta salad. Everyone talked about the ritual and how well it had gone.

"John, Crystal told me that this was your first ritual. What did you think of it?" said Lady Denique.

"I was raised a Catholic, and they are not short on ritual."

"Me, too." added Mario.

"This was the first pagan ritual I ever attended," John continued. "I really found it uplifting. When Crystal told me she was a pagan, I think my old Catholic programming clicked in, and it made me uncomfortable. Now that I have been to the ritual, I think that thanking and even worshipping the Earth is a wonderful idea, especially considering how greatly she was disrespected in the past."

"I know what you mean, John," said Mario. "I had the same problem when Denique and I fell in love. My parents were very upset. They told me that it wasn't enough just to love Jesus, and follow His commandments to love God with all your heart and your neighbors as you love yourself, something we both have no problem doing. They said that you have to put away all other gods. I told them that they had made a god out of money. We didn't talk for three years. When Sandy arrived, we had a reconciliation of sorts. We never could get them to fully understand our non-dualist philosophy. How we believed that everything is God, that God is immanent in the creation and could righteously be worshipped in any form. They still think God is masculine, and that we'll probably go to hell."

"Well, right now certainly seems like heaven to me. This pasta salad is really great, Mario," said John.

"Yes, it is wonderful. Thank you so much for inviting us to join you," said Crystal.

"It is our great pleasure, and you are very much welcome."

"How have you been doing, Sandy?" asked Crystal.

"Really well. In two weeks I will be re-tested, and if this one comes up clean, Dr. Franks says we can assume that we've got it beat."

"I can tell you right now, Sandy. You are free of any abnormality. But you should go ahead and have the tests run."

"Sandy says that I give the treatments as well as you do, Crystal," said Lady Denique.

"I'm sure that you will soon be better than I am, Lady Denique. We know your voice heals and inspires. I wish I could project healing through song like you can."

Mario brought out some lovely little golden brown pastries filled with spinach and onions. He took out a bottle of golden wine that he said was a gift from the private stock of a vintner friend. At first Crystal declined, but Mario pointed out the festiveness of the evening and insisted that one glass would do her good. John took some as well, and Mario offered up a toast.

"To a summer filled with love and inspiration."

Glasses clicked, and they all drank.

"This is wonderful wine," commented John. "What is it?"

"It's my friend's own creation, and he hasn't found a name for it yet. As a matter of fact, he wants my help in that area. Anyone have any suggestions?"

"Let me have some and I'll give you a name," said Ruth.

"No way, Child, not for a few years," said Lady Denique.

"It is wonderful," said Crystal. "How about God's Golden Gift?"

"Fine Gold Wine?" adds John.

"Not bad. Not bad at all. I'll give him your suggestions."

"Lady Denique." John spoke. "I was wondering about the part in the ceremony where you said something about offering our bodies in a way that will enhance the Earth's fertility. What do you mean by that?"

"Embalming people with chemicals, then sealing them in metal caskets buried deep in the Earth doesn't allow for our bodies to be reabsorbed by the living soil. Now that we recycle all of our sewage into fertilizer, this is the last step, the proper disposal of our bodies, in ending humanity's waste of organic matter that should be returned to the cycle of life. It is good to respect a soul's mortal remains, but we need to recognize that the body isn't the person."

"How do you think we should deal with people's bodies?" John asked.

"Mario and I are going to be buried in pine boxes and have trees planted over us."

"It's going to be a nut tree in my case," said Mario.

Everyone laughed heartily.

"That makes a lot of sense," said John.

It seemed that Crystal hadn't said anything to anyone about him being from the past. John was glad, and decided to be careful and not say anything that would suggest it. Mario served some sliced strawberries for desert and told Crystal that the whipped cream he had made came from a dairy that did not allow the male calves to be sold, so perhaps even a vegan could have some. She still declined. Mario refilled her wine glass before she could say no. John could feel the wine a little himself and wondered if Crystal could. Perhaps it was somewhat mischievous of him to offer another toast.

"To our wonderful host and fabulous cook, Mario, and his beautiful family." John holds his wine glass high.

Crystal did take another couple of sips. It was delicious wine.

The Sun was slowly sinking towards the sea, and a cool breeze stirred the grass on the hill. Crystal asked John to finish her wine while she went back into the woods to change back into her casual clothing.

"I wish that we could stay up here and watch the sunset and the full moon rise," said Lady Denique, "but we must get back home. We have a full day tomorrow."

They began packing the picnic things into the suitcase-sized basket. Mario tried to get John to keep the last third of the bottle of wine, but he declined with many thanks. When Crystal came back, they all said good-bye and hugged again. What warm and wonderful people, John thought. The idea of running off to the festival seemed rather silly to him at this point. Why share Crystal with all those people? If he were never to see her again, he would rather have some time with her by herself. And what better place than up on Mt. Tam on such a beautiful night.

"Crystal, do the busses down the mountain run later?"

"Yes, why?"

"Because I think I'd rather spend some of our precious time together up here. We haven't had much time to really get to know each other. Let's stay for the sunset and moonrise."

"I like that idea, John, and to tell you the truth, I really should get back before the end of the festival. Can we just go home after the moon comes up?"

"Sure, Sweetheart." John had never used a term of endearment with Crystal before. It just slipped out, no doubt due to the loosening effect of the wine. She didn't seem to mind.

"I know a place where we can see both sides of the mountain. We can see the sun set over the ocean and the moon rise from the other side. It is about another half a mile walk. Do you want to go there, or just stay here?"

"That sounds great. A little hike after that wonderful dinner would be perfect. Thanks so much for letting me come to this with you, Crystal."

"I am enjoying your company very much, John."

"You sure have a lot of great friends, and it is obvious that you are very well liked and respected."

"There is always a good group at our rituals. I kind of like the smaller group that meets over on Redwood Hill, but the ritual up here is always wonderful. There are a lot of pagans in Marin County. There is another, even larger group that meets by the ocean in Bolinas, but they are more Bacchanalian and drink a lot of wine."

Crystal and John were heading away from the clearing toward a narrow path through the trees. As they entered the woods, John took Crystal's hand.

"Are you going to let me carry that?"

"OK, John. I don't mind being a little old-fashioned."

John took the bag from Crystal and put it over his shoulder on the side away from Crystal. Instead of taking her hand again he put his arm around her waist. It felt so good to have his hand on her hip. Crystal reciprocated and John was ecstatic. They walked on silently with arms around each other's waists for a long while. John knew that this was a rather meaningful escalation of their relationship, and couldn't help wondering just where it could, or should, lead. Every time he had touched her, it thrilled him and filled him with love and warmth. It did lead to another erection, as their hips rubbed with every step they took. It felt so good. He wanted so much to hold her, to kiss her.

"So tell me about yourself, John. You know a lot about me, now that we've been spending time together. I'd like to know more about you."

"What would you like to know?"

"Tell me who your heroes are."

"My heroes. This is one I have thought about a lot. They were all revolutionaries, visionaries, and unfortunately, most of them outlaws, at least some of the time."

"Outlaws? Now you've got my interest," she said.

"In chronological order. First, Jesus of Nazareth. What a loving, giving, inspirational being. He selflessly healed the sick, taught the people, even raised the dead. He had the incredible faith it must have taken to go to the cross, knowing that it was necessary for His spiritual purpose." John was starting to get a little emotional, and a tear ran down his face. He realized that his faith had been restored. He did believe. "The fact that He triumphed over the terrible combined forces of a corrupt church, a totalitarian political order, a decadent monarchy and a faithless people and rose from the dead," John's voice rose as well, "It's just fantastic." John was tearing and could tell Crystal was moved as well.

"I guess I let what some Christians have done cause me to forget that Jesus was truly a beautiful and divine being. I love Him too, John. As Mario said, it is too bad that just loving Him and following His commandments isn't enough for so many Christians. They have to condemn everyone else. Oh, well. Maybe some day they'll learn. So who else?"

"My next hero is Thomas Paine," stated John.

"I know about him, he wrote *Common Sense* and *The Crisis* during the Revolutionary War. 'These are the times that try men's souls,'" she quoted.

"Right. Very good. His writings were essential for the emergence of America. Do you know any more about him?"

"Not really."

"He actually enlisted as a regular soldier, but the army had the good sense to take him out of the ranks. Paine continued to be a revolutionary after the revolution. Thomas Jefferson said 'Where liberty is, there is my country,' and Paine heard of this and replied with, 'Where Liberty is not, there is mine,.' Then went to France and helped with the French Revolution. Though he was not French, he was made a delegate to the National Convention and was the only delegate who voted against the execution of the king. That is probably one of the reasons he ended up in the Bastille. The other was that Paine was against Robespierre and his party. They were taking people out and guillotining them the whole time he was imprisoned, and he never knew when it would be his turn. He was scheduled to be executed and a miracle saved him. The door to his cell had been closed by mistake and the guards couldn't see the number four that was written on his doorstep to signify that he was the fourth person to be taken to the guillotine that day. A few days later Robespierre was removed, so he was saved. He was imprisoned for months, and when he was released, he made it to Ben Franklin's doorstep and passed out. I imagine he had a terrible case of post traumatic stress." John always enjoyed talking about Tom Paine, who always made him feel revolutionary and defiant.

You have very interesting tastes in heroes. I like them, and I thank you for sharing them with me."

"So what about you Crystal?' Who are your heroes"?

"One of my favorite people is Giordano Bruno. Ever heard of him?"

"No."

"He started out as a Dominican priest, but he was almost tried for heresy and left the Order. He was a brilliant theorist, but he lived in the Sixteenth Century. There wasn't much intellectual freedom then. He was excited by Copernicus and the discovery that the sun was the center of the solar system. He took that thought a little further and hypothesized that perhaps the stars were also suns, and perhaps they even had planets circling them, not unlike the Earth. He even proposed that there might be other souls on them. This was a great heresy then, and way beyond the comprehension of most everybody. They were still into burning witches and such. We credit Bruno as an early Star Voyager. We're not sure if he was the first person to have that idea, of other planets having life on them, but he's the first one we know of."

"Wow," said John. "I've never even heard of him".

Crystal continued, " He was lured back into Italy, Venice, to be exact, by a noble who claimed he wanted Bruno for a teacher, but who was actually in cahoots with the Catholic Church. Bruno was taken to Rome and lived in the Vatican's dungeon for about six years where he was tortured. He confessed and recanted. But like Joan of Ark, he couldn't live with his recantation and so in sixteen-hundred he was condemned to be burned at the stake. He had his tongue pulled past his lips and pierced by a nail, and another nail through his cheeks, so he couldn't speak on his way to be burned alive." Crystal's voice broke as she continued. "That cruel cross of nails silenced one of the greatest minds that ever lived. After he was burned, they pulverized his remains into powder and threw them into the river, so not a relic remained."

"That's incredible", said John. "I'll never go into a Catholic church again."

"There have been some wonderful and enlightened Catholics, John, so I wouldn't go that far. Many priests have also died trying to help people. Anyway, Bruno's writings have lived on and his legacy is alive in the Star Voyagers. We revere him."

"Incredible," said John. "I thought it was pathetic that almost no one attended Tom Paine's funeral. He had made a lot of enemies when he wrote "The Age of Reason", as he had expressed a lot of problems he had with the Bible. Some people have called him an atheist, but right in the beginning of the book he states, 'I believe in one God and one God only'. I think he has had a profound influence on me. A lot of the church's dogma didn't work for me after reading Paine".

They had been walking uphill for a while, and were about to break out of the woods into a high clearing.

"We're almost there," said Crystal, and grabbed his hand, "let's run." And they ran together, laughing the last 50 yards and into the clearing. Sure enough, there was a place where you could sit on the grass and see both the ocean, and the hills over Marin County, to the East. The sun was low enough that the sky began to glow. Lights were turning on in the towns down below. They sat down on the grass across from one another, Crystal to the South and John to the North.

"We both seem to like tragic figures, John. We should let the past go, for now."

"Let me add just one more thing." added John. "Those wonderful souls we talked about. Now I can see that their sacrifices were not in vain. That makes the whole thing so much more positive. They would have gladly given, no, they actually did gladly give their lives to further mankind's evolution."

"And bless them for it. That sounds like a healing, John." Crystal was giving John that super sweet smile that always melted him. They sat there smiling at each other for half a minute and the space between them seemed to thicken and come alive, the energy was actually visible. What was this? John thought.

"I think I'm still feeling that wine, John, but I'd love to chant OM with you and meditate together for a while. How about if we face the setting sun, chant OM nine times, and do an open eyes meditation on the sunset?"

"OK." That wasn't exactly what John had in mind, but it sounded like a nice, high idea. John followed Crystal's lead and turned to face the sunset.

"Have you meditated before?'

"Not much, but I think I have the general idea. Just try and still your mind and have it focused on one single thought, image or word."

"You got it."

"Are we going to try and Om together or just at our own pace?"

"What would you like?"

"Together."

"OK. Ready. I'll count. Lets inhale. Ommmmmmmmmmm."

After the first couple of Oms their voices started to harmonize very beautifully. It was like an ocean of Oms washing upon the shores of their consciousness. Long beautiful Oms, with Crystal starting and ending each one, then the delicious silence between as they slowly inhaled. John had no idea how many they did, but he was sure it was many more than nine. And he didn't want to stop either. About that time, Crystal paused: the silence was beautiful and full, full of love and clarity. Amazingly, John stilled even his racing thoughts about Crystal. There was sun. There was ocean. There was love. It was natural for the sky to celebrate with reds, golds and purples.

This is the best meditation I ever had, thought John. Oops. John again focused on the beauty of the sunset. The sun's sinking decent into the ocean was perceptible. The colors deepened. Time existed only as the sun's movement in the sky. As the sun settled slowly into the ocean, ripples of red orange light and color flowed in waves from that sweet union of fire and water. Wow, WOW! thought John. The moment was so blissful. The satisfaction of seeing that magical merging of opposite elements was deep. Profound. It might have been the most profound moment in John's life. Beyond contentment to perfect peace and joy.

Once the sun had completely disappeared beyond the horizon, John found it harder to still his mind, for the perfection of the moment was having Crystal there with him sharing it. He turned to look at her and she was doing something with her hands, going swiftly from one gesture to the next with fingers interlocked. She ended up with fingers interlocked except for the index fingers which were extended together, with wrists crossed and the index fingers touching her forehead between her eyes. She then seemed to take a deep breath and turned to John.

"That was the best meditation of my life," said John.

"I enjoyed it tremendously, but I did have a hard time stilling my thoughts," answered Crystal. They both seemed to be in a pretty high state. Crystal got up and turned around.

"Look, John. The moon is just coming up over the hills."

John got up and went to Crystal's side. The moon was as orange as the sun had been, and to see it coming up after just seeing the sun set was kind of odd, like it didn't take any time for the thing to get around the Earth and time had shifted twelve hours forward. The moon's ascension quickly became the moon, and what a moon. John amazed himself by letting out a loud wolf call. Crystal turned and laughed and said, "John, we don't do that any more. Someone might really think you are a real wolf."

"That is wonderful. Absolutely wonderful." John put his arm around Crystal's waist again and they stood there looking at the moon for a while. John was quite unsure what to do. Crystal spoke.

"We should get back down before it gets too dark. We don't have a flashlight."

"We don't need one, We have the moonlight."

John had turned to look at Crystal. She was smiling a Mona Lisa small smile. He bent down and touched his lips to her's. She did not withdraw. He turned slightly and put his other arm around her. He felt a sweet moisture as their kiss deepened and their mouths moved. John pulled Crystal to him, and he felt her body full against his. The moonlight, the moment, was the perfect fulfillment of his fondest wish.

John felt his erection strengthen against Crystal's body. It felt so good he was close to orgasm. Her hands were rubbing his back. He felt her tongue touch his lip. God, he loved her so. He gently moved his tongue into her mouth and tasted and felt the delicious exchange of energies across these wonderfully sensitive and nerve rich organs. It was a powerful kiss. Their tongues explored and delighted. He could feel every part of her body. Her perfectly sized breasts. Her trim waist, so sculpted yet soft. Her precious mound of Venus against his incredibly hard erection.

Suddenly she moaned slightly and he was filled with mental confusion. God, he wanted her so! He wanted her more than he had wanted anything in his entire existence. He slowly ended the kiss, put his cheek against hers, and they rocked slowly together. It was a long and wonderful hug, with their bodies still so close, and their arms and hands gently rubbing each other's backs. John separated from Crystal slightly and looked into her moonlit eyes. He loved her so deeply. He could take no chance with this precious gift.

"I guess we better head on down," he said.

"Yes," she answered.

John picked up the bag and put it over his shoulder. They took a couple of steps down the path. When John took Crystal's hand, he stopped and their eyes met again. He took her other hand in his and said. "Crystal. I love you. This moment has been the most wonderful of my life."

"I love you, John. I feel like I've known you for a long, long time. I am amazed at the power of my feelings for you."

John had tears filling his eyes. The love and gratitude he felt at that moment were incredible. She had tears flowing down her beautiful face as well. They both laughed a somewhat nervous laugh as John again took her into his arms. He felt the tears between their cheeks and it was so sweet. When one reached his mouth it tasted like ambrosia. This hug was different. The sexual content had gone, and only a sweet and peaceful love remained. After a couple of minutes the tears had ceased, and each taking a big breath, they headed down the mountain arm in arm. John started to sing.

"If you want your dream to grow.

Take your time, go slowly.

Small beginnings, greater ends,

Heartfelt work grows surely.

Day by day, Stone by stone,

Build your future slowly.

Day by day, you'll grow too,

You'll find heaven's glory."

When he started for a second time Crystal joined in. Within a couple of verses she was singing along. It was true. Their voices seemed to harmonize perfectly. The woods were darker, but enough Moonlight was filtering through that they could see the path well enough to navigate it. After six or seven verses John stopped and said, "Our voices harmonize so well. Can you even believe us, Crystal? What a miracle." John didn't want to bring up Faith again, but he believed that Crystal was she, and that she thought so as well.

"What is that song from, John?"

"It's from an old movie about St. Francis of Assisi. Donovan wrote it. Did you ever hear of him?"

"No."

"He's got some great stuff. I think the songs he wrote for the movie about St. Francis were definitely some of his best work, but I believe that the movie company and the record company he was contracted to couldn't reach an agreement, and it was never released as an album. That was back in the album days."

"Record albums. Vinyl records right?" she asked.

"Right."

"I'm really surprised that we had that place all to ourselves tonight, of all nights. It's a beautiful and popular spot."

"Crystal, to quote another Twentieth Century singer, 'You have to believe we are magic.'"

GOODBYE CRYSTAL

When John and Crystal got back to the big clearing there were still some people left there. John remembered Shashir and Cynthia, and told Crystal that he should call them and let them know what was going on. John put on the little earpiece and got Shashir on the phone.

"What is happening, my friend?" said Shashir.

"Crystal and I are having a wonderful time up here on Mt. Tamalpais. The ritual was a really high experience, and Crystal and I just got finished watching the moon rise."

"Yes, it is just becoming visible here, and very beautiful. I am getting the impression that you two are not going to come to the festival."

"Yeah. It is already getting late, and Crystal does have to get up at five am tomorrow. There wouldn't be much left by the time we got there, anyway. What are you going to do tomorrow? Are y'all leaving right away?"

"No. We are going sight-seeing tomorrow, and will not be leaving until evening."

"Can I go with y'all?"

"Of course, my friend. We'd be happy for you to join us. Crystal will be gone, right?"

"Yes, I'm sorry to say, I'll be alone."

John looked at Crystal as he said this and could see she wasn't very happy at the thought. He certainly wasn't.

"We will have a good time. Cynthia wants to say hello."

"Hi, John."

"Hi, Cynthia."

"I kind of thought you two wouldn't make it back. The bands have been great, but we are starting to get a little tired of crowds and lines for the restrooms."

"I'm very glad we can do something together tomorrow, Cynthia. I'm looking forward to getting to know you better."

"Likewise, John. Tell Crystal good luck for me."

"Here, you tell her."

John handed the earpiece to Crystal. Crystal listened for a moment and said, "Thank you very much. I hope we meet again."

When John got the earpiece back, Shashir was on it again. They arranged to meet the next day at ten AM at Market and Powell by the cable car stop.

"I'm so glad that you will get to spend some time with your friends. It is so amazing that you sponsored his great grandfather, and so good of you," said Crystal.

"It was only twenty dollars a month. It was very enjoyable. I got some very nice letters from Shashir's grandfather. Once he sent me a lovely color drawing of a parrot."

Crystal stood up. "I wish we could just stay here, but we had better head on down."

There were few people left up there. One group had sleeping bags and seemed to be ready to spend the night under the stars.

"Yes. Maybe next time we can bring up sleeping bags like those folks and spend the night."

They headed down hand in hand. The mood wasn't as joyous as the trip up the mountain. In a short while they would have to say good-bye to each other for too long. Everything between them was working out so wonderfully. She had kissed him. She had told him she loved him. Now she was leaving. Why? If everything else were so perfect and magical, why did she have to go?

"I don't suppose there is any way that you could.....God, Crystal, I am going to miss you. You're the reason I'm here, the way I see it."

Crystal thought for a moment, then smiled and said. "John, I'd love it if you stayed at my house while I'm gone. You could come over and move in tomorrow. If Stuart wasn't sleeping on my futon, I'd say you could stay tonight."

John's mood brightened. "That would be great, Crystal. I know I'd feel close to you in your beautiful home. I will take care of things for you."

"I'll call Roger and tell him."

Crystal called Roger and told him about John's staying there. She asked Roger if he would teach John how to take care of her plants and garden. Roger agreed, and with that accomplished, they were smiling again.

"I keep a key under the flower pot on the left side of the front steps. I'll show you when we get home. So, John, tell me some more about yourself. What were your plans before this happened?"

"I was going to help reform the medical profession. I thought that doctors should be much more concerned with keeping people healthy instead of waiting and intervening when they were sick. I was going to charge people a flat fee for care when they were well and help them for free when they got sick. I wanted to work without malpractice insurance in order to keep the cost down and help create a totally trusting relationship between me and my patients. Mr. Chow said that you ask a lot from your patients. You get them to exercise, eat a proper diet, meditate and do positive affirmations. My plan wasn't as ambitious, but I was hoping to do something similar."

"It's a great idea, John. I don't know how well that would work, because my patients are usually very sick when they come to me, and that gets them highly motivated. Once they are well, some of them keep up the practices, but a lot of them do not."

"Yeah. My roommate David said it would never work. Back in my time, everyone ate meat three times a day and few exercised. And as you know, they rode cars everywhere. There was a lot of room for positive change. There were a lot of powerful forces promoting meat-eating. You wouldn't have believed the TV commercials back then. Fast food restaurants spent billions promoting unhealthy food and huge proportions. It was like a contest to see who could come up with the most completely unhealthy burger."

"I can't imagine living back then."

"Perhaps that is why you left," replied John.

"John, I have thought a lot about your fiancé, Faith. I still can't say I believe I was her. Can't say I wasn't, either. Though I have had a few psychic readings, I try not to dwell too much on possible past life scenarios. I've got a lot of friends who are all caught up in their supposed past lives, and I think it takes you away from fully living the one you are in now. Chances are, I'll continue to be sort of an agnostic about that. I know I feel very close to you, like we've been together for a long time, but there could be other explanations for that.

"Like what?"

"Well, you are a Pisces sun and my moon is in Pisces. That is a very classic connection for a man and a woman, and it makes for a feeling of natural masculine/feminine affinity. Once Carl Jung, the famous psychologist, picked the married couples out from an equal amount of randomly matched couples simply by using that one factor. His success rate was far beyond what chance would predict. If we compared our horoscopes, I bet we'd find that we had a lot of other good astrological connections."

They were back to the bus stop. The folks already waiting there said that it would be about ten more minutes for a bus. As there were light and benches inside the clear glass shelter, Crystal asked John if he knew his time of birth. John couldn't remember the exact time that he had seen on his birth certificate. He told Crystal he thought it was 5 something am. Crystal asked for the date and place, and he told her March 8, 1970, in Atlanta.

"I'll be there Tuesday morning. The bullet train I'm taking is an express, and only stops at Salt Lake City, Denver, and St. Louis. It can hit four hundred kilometers an hour. It runs suspended on a magnetic field."

"They were just developing that technology back in my time. Don't they have airplanes any more?"

"Yes, but they mostly only fly over oceans. We don't have enough oil left to fly planes around like in your time. They polluted a lot and were noisy anyway. Here comes your horoscope on my computer. Let's see. Aha! I knew it. Your Sun conjuncts my Pisces Moon. Your Moon and Venus are also in Pisces, and they conjunct my Venus there. God, you have a lot of Pisces! Mercury is there, too, and the Moon and Venus are trine Neptune in the beginning of Sagittarius. That is unusual, to have a trine from planets in two dissimilar elements like water and fire. You also have Mercury Square Neptune."

"What does that mean?"

"Well, it sure explains your idealism and powerful emotions. You have a lot of psychic sensitivity with all that Pisces and Neptune. The Venus and Moon trine Neptune is wonderful and romantic, and can bring an ideal love. As it conjuncts my Venus, it is a very loving connection between us." Crystal looked up at John and smiled. "I expected our charts to compare nicely, but I must admit, they fit together really wonderfully. I'm calling my house and will get a print out of your chart made on my printer. Phone on, Thena, call home." Crystal looked more serious for a moment. "I forgot

Stuart. The phone will only ring once before the computer gets my instructions and downloads." Crystal put the PC to her ear. "Hi Stuart. I was just sending John's horoscope to my computer for a printout. We are at the Mt. Tam bus stop, heading home. See you in a while. Yes, it's been very nice. I love you too. Bye. Thena, copy, store and print chart."

Crystal gave John a somewhat unhappy look. "God, John, my life has gotten so very complicated."

John put his arm around Crystal, and she leaned her head against him. "If I said the same thing, it would be a gross understatement. But, I'm really glad."

"So am I, John."

They sat there together quietly, thinking. The bus arrived in a few minutes, and soon they were heading back down Mt. Tam with a bunch of happy pagans joking and talking. They were sitting in the back in their own space, trying to be happy with each other's company, but knowing that what they had found together would soon have to be put on hold. John had many questions he wanted to ask Crystal. Where was she going? Why did she have to go? Was she still planning to stay a celibate, and just what did that kiss mean? He didn't think it was the right time to be pressing her with such questions. He should be happy at the tremendous progress they had made, support her completely in her mission and be patient about their relationship. She said she loved him. That should be more than enough for now.

John did have this one nagging thought. Why did he pop into Crystal's world just before this mission? To have found his love in another century only to lose her again was an incredibly negative thought. He just couldn't think that one. He had to have faith. All of a sudden, he was gripped with fear. Everything was going great with Faith and then the bottom fell out. Well, he sure couldn't share that one with Crystal. All she needed now was him piling on his fears. John started praying. He asked God to remove his fear and restore his faith. He implored God to keep Crystal safe on her mission.

"I'm going to pray for you every day Crystal. Many times a day. I'll be so glad when you come home."

"Me too, John. If this weren't so very important, I'd stay. But it is, John, so pray for our success, too."

They were down the mountain and had a train waiting for them. As soon as everyone was on board, it took off at a rapid clip. Now John was sorry that the trains were so darn efficient. He knew that they would be in San Francisco in minutes, and then a quick ride to Berkeley and a subus home. The walk would be the best part of the experience. John thought of a way to broach an important topic.

"Crystal, have you thought about, um, do you want to some day have a family? You know, children?"

"I wasn't planning on it. My dream is to be able to communicate fully with beings from other worlds. There are Voyagers who have successfully attained a virtually constant communication with one or more beings from other worlds. Most of them are celibate, and though some have children, most say that they only had sex for that purpose. I have occasional dreams, and some fleeting experiences in meditation, but I am far from the level of connection some advanced Star Voyagers have. We believe that only people who have attained a high degree of spiritual perfection will be able to establish a strong and continuous communication, and so far, that is the way it has been. That is the way it seems to be for the beings from other worlds, and they are all a lot more advanced than us."

"Then it is possible for one to have a family and be a Star Voyager?"

"It seems that way."

John had to fight back a powerful urge to ask her to marry him right then on the spot. "I hope that I can lead a pure enough life to be able to keep up with you, Crystal. I know you are going to make it."

"I haven't been able to make a lot of progress in that direction lately. I was getting closer and closer for a while, but now I seem to be on a plateau. We also don't know how long it will take humanity to clean up our act the rest of the way. We are in good communication with many worlds, though. Muelf, the one being I have been in touch with from Vicomia Fernale, knows a lot about me and our world. I have actually had dreams in which we sat and talked telepathically. That was so cool, as you would say." She laughed a little laugh and John Joined in.

"I so want to be able to communicate with her at will, like the head of the Star Voyagers, who can communicate with several people on two different worlds. Well, neither he nor Muelf knows how long it will take for the Earth to clear from the remaining negative energy so that communications will be better and more universal."

The train was over the Golden Gate and into downtown San Francisco. They got off and headed for the Berkeley train.

"I'll call you when I get into Atlanta," she said.

"You know, I was born in Atlanta. It would be very interesting for me to go there and check up some on my parents. Maybe I could find out something about myself, like if I ever got back into the past again. I can tell you, I don't want to go back."

"John, it isn't a good idea. Believe me, if I thought it were, I'd really love for you to be there. I'm only going to be there from Tuesday until Thursday morning. I probably couldn't spend any time with you. We are just going to have to be patient."

They got on a train for Berkeley and were quiet again. They were lucky to get a seat just before a flood of people who seemed to be returning from the festival got on board. He put his arm around her, she laid her head on his shoulder, and took his other hand in hers. The train was quite crowded and noisy. They just sat quietly, holding each other, feeling the warmth and energy of each other's bodies. John turned his head slightly and kissed Crystal on the forehead. She looked up at him, squeezed his hand and smiled.

"So there is really no way for you to call me regularly, Crystal?"

"I'm afraid not. We will be carrying some phones, but as soon as we use one our position can be plotted. I really don't think any one would come after us, but I just can't chance it."

John somewhat forced a smile. "Well, call me every day until you leave Atlanta, OK?"

"I will. So what do you think you'll do until I get back?"

"I'm not sure. Perhaps I'll go to my med school and see if they have any records on me. I'm a little apprehensive about the idea. I'll be hoping I'll have disappeared in 1993 and never returned. I don't know what I'll do if I find a record of, say, my finishing med school. Maybe I should just leave that whole thing alone."

"You had better not disappear on me and go back, John."

"Unfortunately, I had no control over the first time, and don't know how I could stop it if it happened again. All I can tell you is, I think I'll stay off of that goddess hill."

The train pulled into the Berkeley stop and they got off. Checking the schedule, they saw they had only two minutes until the next bus. They walked together arm in arm towards the next stop.

"Enough of this seriousness. No matter who, no matter when, no matter where, no couple has any more than right now, the present moment, anyway," said John.

"We are together now, let's enjoy this time together," said Crystal."

"Now we have more to celebrate than just the Solstice." added John.

They were smiling again. Their steps energized, and they were at the stop just in time for the bus to pull in.

"Let's plan what we will do the next time we are together," said John.

"Great idea. What do you suggest?"

"How about a long camping trip. How about Yosemite?"

"Great idea, John. I haven't been in years. I power glided there with a lot of friends a few years ago. That was an exciting trip because one of the guys was doing a power dive and his glider folded and broke in the middle. He fired his ballistically propelled parachute and landed softly, but it scared the heck out of us all. It was still a fantastically fun trip. You know, they don't let cars in Yosemite anymore, and it is a biker's dream."

"One thing I'm going to do while you are gone, Crystal, is get in better shape. I'm going to ride every day. I know I'll never be the biker you are, but hopefully I won't slow you down too much. I guess I could use the motor if I can't keep up. I'll bet Yosemite is fantastic without all that traffic."

"We can ride across it and back. I think I can be gone that long once I check with all my patients' progress. I haven't taken on any new cases because of this trip."

"All right! That sounds wonderful." John put his other arm around Crystal and hugged her closer to him in their seat, and she squeezed a little closer. Smiles were beaming again.

"What a miracle. What a wonderful miracle! Why should I question my amazing transport to this time? Nobody knows where we all come from or where we are going. I don't even know why there is something instead of just nothingness. All life is an amazing miracle."

Crystal was looking up into his smiling face. He kissed her on the forehead again. "I love you so much, Crystal."

"I love you, John."

They rode together, melted into each other for the few minutes it took to get to Crystal's stop. This was the part of the journey John was looking forward to. The moon was somewhat higher in the sky, and the evening was perfect. You could see some stars in the sky, as the street lights were under the cover of the bike and pedestrian lanes, and so the night sky wasn't artificially illuminated. They walked together slowly up the street, hand in hand. After about a block John turned her toward him.

"John. I haven't kissed anyone like I kissed you in a long time. It was wonderful, but...I don't think we should again. Not now."

That took John by surprise. He looked into her moonlit face, and at her beautiful lips. God he wanted to kiss her. He stood there, trying to think of what to say.

"Please don't take this the wrong way. It is just that our relationship is so new. Our feelings are so powerful. I've been a celibate for five years. It just wouldn't be right to start something now."

John thought for a moment. She was right. It just wouldn't work to make-out all the way up the street, and then, being totally aroused, what would they do? Even if Stuart weren't staying at Crystal's, she probably wouldn't, shouldn't make love with him tonight. He didn't even think he was ready for that.

"Sure, Crystal. I understand."

They started back up the street. John fought off the temptation to discuss the celibacy thing right then. He was confused. Probably she was, too. Don't rush this, he thought. Think celibate yourself. But that kiss. It enflamed him to think about it. I will not rush another love. No. No. Never again. Don't think about the kiss.

"What are you thinking about John?"

"I was just thinking that I'm sorry if I have been trying to push you past where you are comfortable, as far as physical intimacy goes. Of course I find you incredibly attractive, I love you, and I'm a young man. Please forgive me."

"No, no, John, please don't apologize." Crystal turned him to her and hugged him. John returned the hug and they stood rocking gently for a moment. "Everything has been perfect. You've been perfect." She drew back slightly to look him in the face. "I don't know what wonderful lifestyle will develop from our relationship. I know that I'm very happy you came into my life. Though it is difficult to leave, and sometimes love turns into an arrow in the heart, like when you are separated from your love, the joy of love is well worth the price."

"I sure feel the same way, Crystal. Some people consider love an addiction. Some think marriage is a limiting prison. I disagree. As you pointed out, the family is the backbone of civilization. If we honor the family, then we have to honor romantic love, for it is the force that creates families, and the glue that holds them together. If the family is sacred, then so is romance and making love. I glory in being in love. Romance is a sacred and civilizing force and thank God for it."

"All right, John! You've really got that Venus Neptune trine going tonight. I'm beginning to feel it would be downright uncivilized to not fall in love."

They both laughed and hugged again. They started back up the street, hand in hand with a little bounce in their step. Crystal started telling John a few things about some of her plants. She told him that she had an aquarium in her bedroom, and that would be the most complicated thing to keep up, as it had a lot of finicky fish in it.

"So, I should sleep on the futon in the living room?"

"No, John. Make yourself at home and please sleep in my comfortable bed."

Richard was sitting on his front porch smoking what John assumed was marijuana.

"Hi, Richard." They walked over to the fence. "Out here trying to keep the deer away, now that he's tasted your goodies?"

"Nah. Just enjoying a little of last year's. You guys want some?"

"Not me. Richard, this is John, a new friend of mine. He will be staying at my house while I'm away for two or three weeks."

Richard had gotten up and walked over to his side of his front gate. He shook hands with John over the gate and asked him if he'd like a toke.

"I'll have one," said John, not wanting to be unfriendly. It was strong pot, and John couldn't hold it in for very long. He coughed and said, "Wow, that is powerful! We saw the deer in here earlier. It looked really stoned. Now I see why."

Crystal watched with a smile and laughed when John coughed out the toke. "Richard is well known for his talent in this field, John. Always take little tokes when you smoke with him."

"Yeah, I see what you mean. Thanks Richard. That's enough for me. I hope to get to spend some time with you."

"Me as well, John."

"Good night."

"Have a good trip, Crystal."

"Thank you, Richard. Good night."

In a few moments they were at Crystal's path. There were lights on inside her house. John figured that Stuart was waiting up for them.

"Would you like to come in and have a cup of herbal tea?"

"Sure. I'd love it." John was amazed at the power of that one toke. He was getting rather psychedelic.

They went inside the house, and Stuart was sitting at the dining area table, putting things into a day pack.

"Hi," she said.

"You're back. And it is only Ten thirty. That's great!"

"We can sleep on the train tomorrow, Stuart. How about a cup of tea?"

"I just had some chamomile, thank you."

John felt some compassion for Stuart, as he knew how much he loved Crystal. John was glad, for he knew that Stuart would take good care of her.

"Good evening, Stuart," said John. "You missed a great ceremony and sunset."

"We had supper with Lady Denique and Mario. It was a very lovely ritual," said Crystal. "I love the way Lady Denique is so straightforward."

"Yes. I like her approach a lot more than the priestesses who summon up a lot of arcane old goddesses. I believe that this completes packing." Stuart was buckling down the flap on the day pack. Then he put it into one of two medium size hand trucks there in the front room. "I'm going to make up the futon and get ready for bed."

"We'll stay in the kitchen."

John followed Crystal into the kitchen and she closed the door to the living room and dining area.

"Excuse me a minute," said John, and he went back through the door. "Stuart." John spoke in a low voice. "I don't know how dangerous this mission is, but I know you will take good care of Crystal. Thank you for loving the Earth, even if you don't love rituals, and for loving Crystal." Stuart returned John's smile, and took his hand. "As a matter of fact, thank you for not liking rituals." They both chuckled as they shook hands, Stuart shaking his head gently.

Stuart looked John in the eye for a while and then said, "You're welcome."

John went back into the kitchen. Crystal was pouring hot water into two cups. They both sat down at her small kitchen table and looked across it into each other's eyes. John was determined to not let himself become negative or sad. Crystal was smiling gently and looking at him lovingly. His small smile broadened. What was there to say? They had this moment, and they seemed to choose to spend it in silent communion. Occasionally one of them would look down to remove the bag or stir the tea. They sat, looking into each other's eyes, even as they slowly drank the tea. The second hand on the clock on the wall turned around and around, ticking off each second with precision. It wasn't a timeless state, time was all too real, too fleeting.

"Now I'm definitely going to have to go to the bathroom."

Crystal laughed.

John got up and went. He was so very glad she was letting him stay here in her wonderful home. He felt really confident of her love for him. A lot different than just last night, he thought. When he finished, he went back to the kitchen, and Crystal suggested they move to the front porch. Crystal turned the light off, and they sat on her little porch swing in the moonlight. He put his arm around her, and she once again laid her head on his shoulder. Again they sat quietly for a while.

"We will be at Glacier Point in Yosemite on the next full moon, John, and it will be even better than this one."

"Yes, because we won't have to separate after that one."

Crystal got up, lifted a flower pot, and showed John the key. "Not that I lock my doors much. I do try to keep them locked when I'm gone for a while. The key is for friends, as I can lock and unlock my doors by voice command."

John knew that this was the moment. He held her in his arms and they hugged so tightly. This time he eased off slowly. He looked again into her blue-green eyes. "I love you with all my heart and soul. I'll be counting the days until I am with you again."

"I love you, John."

"Call me as often as you can. And as soon as your mission is completed."

"I will, John."

They hugged again for about a minute, shared a sweet but brief kiss, then John released her, turned, and walked away. When he got to the end of the path, he turned and saw her in the moonlight. She was watching him, and when he turned, she blew him a kiss. He grabbed it out of the air, and pressed it to his lips with love and tenderness, then opened his hands as he had done in the ceremony, and blew it back to her. She caught his kiss, and pressed it to her heart. Slowly he turned. An incredible wave of emotion swept over his whole being. It was the ultimate in bittersweet. As he walked down the street, tears fell. Richard wasn't on his porch. John was alone with the moon.

THE NIGHTMARE

John walked slowly down Crystal's street. What an incredible adventure the last three days had been! He knew that he was very blessed to have made the amazing transition to this wonderful future. Life was so much better, he probably would have wanted to stay even if he hadn't met and fallen in love with Crystal. But he would miss many people, his parents, aunts, uncles and cousins. David and his other friends from school and work. The best and only explanation for his situation was the concept put forth by Mr. Patel that he had been in a very high state and invisible for the hundred years. If that was what happened, then going back was out of the question. Time travel seemed unlikely to him.

Perhaps being invisible isn't such an impossible idea. His yoga teacher had said that if all the matter in his body were compressed to just one bit of matter so that all the space between molecules, and all the space within atoms were removed, what was left would be a tiny speck too small to be seen with the naked eye. He thought that to be absurd when he heard it and almost got up the courage to tell the teacher. That was one of the excuses he had used to justify to himself his quitting the class. But months later he saw a movie called "Mindwalk," in which a physicist said that there were relatively vast distances between nucleus and electrons within atoms, and that most of any object was empty space. John realized that the teacher's idea was probably accurate.

The movie also suggested that there was a lot of doubt about the physicality of any matter, as particles seemed to blink in and out of existence, rather like the whole Cosmos is supposed to do in the bang, bang, bang version of the big bang theory. John looked up at the moon and shook his head. How can I expect to explain my situation when we can't even explain why or how the Universe is here?

When John got to the bus stop, he saw that he had almost eleven minutes to wait, and it was already after eleven o'clock. He called the Chows and got Chen on the phone. Chen said they would probably be in bed when John got there, but they would leave the door unlocked. He told Chen about his day. Chen was very happy that everything with Crystal was straightened out and that they had such a good time together. John told him that Crystal had invited him to stay at her house while she was gone.

"That is very nice, John, but feel free to stay here with us if you don't want to be alone."

"I'll probably visit y'all often," replied John.

After telling Chen about his plans for the next day, John and Chen said good-bye. The subus was pulling in and John got on board. He decided to rerun his date with Crystal in his mind. He progressed rapidly to the kiss. That surprised him. Crystal was surely feeling the gold wine. His mind couldn't resist the thought that if he had pressed it then, she might have even made love with him. Conceivably, he thought but he was glad that he hadn't. It was a golden moment and very romantic. It was also very public. They could have gone into the woods. Enough of these sexual thoughts. He didn't, they didn't, and it was perfect... Unless something happens to Crystal. No, even if Crystal didn't make it back from the mission, they had done the right thing.

The fact that he and Faith had at least experienced making love before she died certainly hadn't brought him any happiness or peace. Perhaps it should have. Though somewhat awkward due to their inexperience, it was beautiful and pleasurable all the same. And they really did love each other. Besides, Faith would have died anyway. So even if they had waited until after the diagnosis, would that have been any better? Her parents couldn't have blamed her leukemia on their making love then. But how enjoyable could it have been if they had had the stress of her illness to contend with? Maybe everything was perfect just the way it was. That was a peaceful thought, one that he had never had before.

He got off the bus and was soon at the Chows' home. Beverly had washed his clothes, which were folded on top of the dresser in Lee's room. John took a long shower and went to bed. He got back up, went to the window, knelt there and prayed. "Thank you God for the wonder of the day, the bliss of love returned, and the kiss. Please, please protect Crystal and Stuart and everyone on their mission. May their mission be filled with light, be successful, and may they return home soon and safely." Then he went back to bed. Sleep absorbed him rather quickly.

Crystal is running through a pine forest. She looks terrified. She is running as fast as she can. Her shirt is torn open and her bra is showing. Dogs are barking in the distance. Crystal catches her left foot on a root and falls with a sharp cry of pain. She quickly comes to her feet and tries to run again, but her left foot is hurt, hobbling her progress. Pain and fear mark her tear-stained face. The dogs are getting closer. Crystal stumbles again. She rolls over onto her back and rubs her ankle. The barking is much closer. Crystal looks around and spies a tree. She drags herself to it, crying and in pain. When she gets to the tree, she uses it to pull herself to a standing position. She turns to face whatever is chasing her.

John awoke, his heart pounding, his face sweaty. My God, he thought. What an awful dream. It was so real. So vivid. Was this a warning? Crystal is in great danger!

She can't go on this mission. John got out of bed, went into the bathroom and washed his face. Fear seized him by the throat and left his mind swirling. The paranoia he had been fighting of this wonderful dream turning into a nightmare seemed to have materialized. Not again. Not again, please. Don't have brought me here to just suffer through this again, he thought.

John went into the kitchen. It was just starting to get light out, and the Chows were not up yet. It was a little before 7 am. John went back into Lee's bedroom and put on his own clothes. He sat on the bed thinking. What should he do? He could tell her and implore her not to go. What if he told Crystal and she was still committed to going anyway, and it just made her more frightened? It was just a dream. But the dream was so real! If he told her about it, the worst that would happen would be that she would be more careful. She might not appreciate his telling her. She might even think he made it up to keep her there.

If it was prophetic, then he must tell her so that if she does go through with it, she will be somewhat prepared. There was no way he could know if it was going to happen or not. Better she think him paranoid or manipulative than let her go off and get into trouble like that. He had to tell her. He got his PC and asked it to call Crystal. He got a message of her telling everyone that she would be out of town for about three weeks and would be out of communications for that time. He asked his PC to call the train station and found out that the bullet train to Atlanta had left at 7 am and the next one would leave at 9, but it was booked up, and so was every one for the next four days. He could leave at midnight Thursday.

That wouldn't do! John could hear the Chows stirring and was glad that they were up. When Chen got out of the bathroom, John asked him if they could talk for a minute. He told Chen about the dream and asked him what he thought he should do. Chen said he wanted to think about it and they went into the kitchen. Chen started making some espresso. Beverly entered and John told her what he had dreamed.

"I'm very worried. I know that this mission they are on is dangerous, Beverly," said John. "What do you think I should do?"

"John has already called Crystal. She has left and so has her train. She doesn't have her phone forwarded, so there is no way to get in touch with her for now," said Chen. He joined John and Beverly at the kitchen table with his espresso.

"Perhaps you are making too much of this, John. It was just a dream. Very few dreams are actually prophetic. I don't think I've ever had one. You might frighten her if you tell her this," said Beverly.

"I've thought of just those things, Beverly, but it seems to me that it would be better to err on the side of caution. Perhaps telling her could help her to avoid a really bad situation. Knowing Crystal, I doubt if she would give up the mission just because of a dream I had."

"Probably not," said Chen.

"She is supposed to call me tomorrow when she gets into Atlanta. I can tell her then."

"There you go, John," said Chen. "It never hurts to be extra careful. It sounded like Crystal was running from some dogs?" he asked.

"Yeah, but the way her shirt was ripped seemed to me to have been caused by someone grabbing her right here," John puts his hand to the upper part of his shirt at the neckline, "and ripping it open so all the buttons tear off. I could see tearing at the place where the buttons were."

With that John got to his feet. "I'm going over to Crystal's house and see if I can learn anything. Do y'all know how to get in touch with Stuart's family?"

"All I can tell you is his last name is Parker. I'm not sure where he lives," said Chen.

"Me neither," added Beverly.

"God. There are probably a lot of Parkers. I'll stay in touch with you and let you know if I learn anything. Look, um, it seems like the crisis of the day with me. Y'all have been so kind and helpful. I am sorry for all the agitation I've caused you."

"You have been very stimulating, John, but there is no need to apologize."

"Yes," said Beverly. "Now don't get all worked up, John. I'm sure everything is going to be all right."

John trotted to the subus line. He thought a mile a minute all the way to Crystal's about what he would do with each different scenario he could imagine. It was obvious he wasn't going to have much peace until this thing was resolved. All he could do now was wait for Crystal's call, tell her, and hope that she wasn't essential to the mission and would not go. While not a great idea, it was the best he had. The fact that his whole relationship with Crystal was so magical and amazing just added to his belief that he had seen something important in his dream, that there was a reason for it. It wasn't just paranoia.

John was out of breath when he finished power walking uphill to Crystal's cottage. He had to sit on the porch for a while to catch his breath. What a charming place she had. What a dedicated and high soul she was, to risk herself to help clean up the Earth. John went inside not knowing exactly what he was looking for or where he might find it. He went to her computer desk, sat down and thought. He looked over at her printer, and it still had three faxes in the tray. His horoscope was on top, and under it were copies of newspaper articles from the Augusta, Georgia, news service.

It was about how a gang of criminals that had been using the Savannah River Plant off-limits area as a hideout had recently escalated their criminal activity. For years they had raided the local population living on the edges of the off-limits area, mostly stealing food and supplies. People had been threatened, but they had hurt no one. Then things changed when a new man, who was very large, had joined their gang. In the preceding six months there had been many rapes attributed to the gang. The latest case was on June 7th. That was only a couple of weeks ago, John thought. Four men raped a mother and her sixteen year old daughter right in front of the father, who had been badly beaten and bound up.

A couple of half hearted attempts to round them up had failed, stated the article. What was needed was a large coordinated search requiring hundreds of police officers. During each of the prior searches, the men just retreated deeper into the more radioactive part of the area and escaped. There was some debate about whether they should be brought out and at what cost, as many experts thought that they must surely succumb soon to radiation poisoning.

The article, dated June 19th, gave John cold chills. That was the day he arrived. Probably Crystal got it the day she ran away from me, he thought. He looked at the other article about the last incident and the people had reported that the men were accompanied by two large dogs. Now he was sure his dream was prophetic. John was really scared. What could he do? What should he do? He was upset and on the verge of crying out loud. He got down on his knees to pray. Immediately a calm and positive thought relieved his mind. He was not going to lose Crystal this time. He knew the reason he was there: it was to save Crystal from this.

"God, give me the strength," he prayed, "the faith and the ability to save Crystal. Please, God. Keep Crystal safe until I can find a way to get there with her. I just can't believe that You brought me here only to lose her again. No God is that cruel. No! I've seen the miracle of a world saved, I know You will help me save Crystal. And thank You, God. Thank you for bringing me here so that I can save her." John rose, feeling a powerful inner strength and resolve. Now he was certain why he was there.

After a few moments reflection, John decided that just waiting there and telling Crystal about the dream wouldn't do. Surely he was supposed to play a more active roll in saving her than that. He needed to get himself to Georgia and the Savannah River Plant, intervene in this nightmare, and turn it back into a dream. Was this all just a dream? That idea resurfaced. Could be, John thought. That is just as good an explanation as my really being a century ahead. It just didn't make any difference. Even if this was some amazingly long dream or vision, he needed to save Crystal anyway. John took a big breath. The extra stress of the dream was cracking the seams of his mental stability. It was not easy to accept the situation he was in.

John decided that this was the right time for some meditation. He sat down cross-legged on the floor, then decided he needed a cushion under his behind. That helped to get his knees lower to the floor and caused his back to be straighter. What would he use as a focus? John went back to the yoga classes he had attended. What was the peace mantra? Om shanti. Yes, that's it. God's peace. He deepened and slowed his breathing. Om, shanti, shanti, shanti. A long Om on the inhalation, and three shantis on the exhalation. After a few minutes it seemed to be working very well at calming and quieting his mind. He stayed with it until his right leg got numb and complained. When John opened his eyes, he was much more centered and much calmer.

John figured that he couldn't just leave the dream on Crystal's answering machine as a message. He needed to have Crystal call him while he was heading towards Augusta. How in God's name would he find Crystal?

John searched his mind for what he knew about the Savannah River Plant. Uncle Bob had told him all about it. He had attended a protest where Jackson Browne had played music for the protesters who were going to get arrested the next day. Bob said it was the best Jackson had ever sounded. Jackson told the protesters that his songs meant a lot more to him, singing to them.

The Savannah River Plant was the place where the Department of Energy ran a reactor that made plutonium for nuclear weapons back during the Cold War. The government had sacrificed safety many times during the arms race, from atmospheric testing of bombs, to allowing and covering up leakage from many weapons plants. The method they used to get the plutonium was to take fuel rods from this reactor and dissolve them in acid. Then somehow they removed the plutonium, but they didn't know how to re-solidify the highly radioactive, so hot it is self boiling, liquid acid. This was a terribly unstable form to store high-level nuclear waste in, but no doubt it speeded the production of nuclear bombs. What an incredibly diabolical witches' brew it was. What would you expect would be the by-product of building doomsday weapons of mass destruction, John thought.

Uncle Bob said that they just put this stuff in giant steel and concrete tanks that needed to be stirred all the time so they wouldn't boil over. Many of the tanks had already sprung leaks and the only solution they had was to build new tanks and pump it into them. Unfortunately, they would have to keep on doing this every twenty or so years for the ten thousand years it was dangerous. John had to agree with Bob that it was hard to imagine people doing that for longer than recorded history. Inevitably, radioactive waste would end up in the Savannah River, in people's wells and all over the area.

John wondered if they had ever found a way to do something with that hot, radioactive liquid acid. Crystal said that the place she was going had to have the off-limits area enlarged more than once, so he assumed they hadn't. John decided that he would try and access Crystal's computer files and see if he could come up with a person in Georgia to contact Crystal through. He got Thena up, and John was surprised to find that she recognized and remembered him. But she would not give John anything without a password, and Crystal had given him none. After twenty minutes of trying, he gave up.

The only thing John could think of was to try to find some Greenpeacers in Atlanta or Augusta. That seemed unlikely, as probably not many of the members knew about the mission. Surely the officers knew, but why would they tell him? This wasn't going to be easy at all.

John could see that it was after nine now, so he called Shashir. For some reason he couldn't connect. Then John got a great idea. He found that Thena would give him access to the phone numbers Crystal had listed for quick dial. He found two in the Atlanta area code. What a great clue! He copied them down and put them in his wallet. As John didn't know just what to do anyway, he decided to head on over to San Francisco to met Shashir and Cynthia. He really couldn't do much more at Crystal's. Before leaving he left a message for Crystal to call him. John then took off for his meeting.

THE GIFT

By the time John was at the Market Street stop in the city, he still hadn't been able to figure out a good plan. One idea was to rent a car and drive straight through until he got to Georgia. In the old days, it wouldn't take more than about forty-five or fifty hours of non-stop driving. He'd have to have help for that plan, but it would potentially get him there by Wednesday night. Another idea was to find some alternative mass transit to Georgia other than the bullet train.

John was ten minutes late, but found Shashir and Cynthia in line for the cable car still a hundred yards from where they would board. He joined them in line and they all hugged.

"I see the cable cars are still a popular tourist attraction."

"Yes," answered Shashir, "we thought we would go ahead and get in this long line. So you have said good-bye to Crystal for a while?"

"Yes, she left this morning at seven."

"We are going to have a lot of fun today, John. We plan on seeing Fisherman's Wharf, China Town, and Telegraph Hill," said Cynthia.

"I'm not sure that I'll be able to spend the whole day with y'all. I had this incredibly frightening and vivid dream of Crystal being in trouble. I'm convinced that she is in great danger if she goes on this mission, and I am supposed to go and help her, actually, save her."

"God, John, you're just too much!" said Cynthia.

"Here," said John while handing them the copy of the article he got at Crystal's. "In my dream she was being chased by dogs."

Shashir and Cynthia looked at the article together. "You're going to have a real hard time getting any transportation out of San

Francisco now that the festival is over. The only way we got a ticket for Shashir was using the exchange at the festival. Two brothers had come together, and one of them found a lady friend. He was going up to the Mendicino coast with her for a while."

"Do any airplanes still fly across to Atlanta?"

"No, John. Not for a long time."

"How about if I rent a car and drive straight through? Is there any chance y'all would help me drive as far as Kansas?"

"You don't understand John," said Cynthia. "It isn't like in the old days. Most of the interstate highways are for bus-trains or commercial trains. There are very few places where you can use them. Cars drive on secondary roads. And even if you got a battery service so you wouldn't have to wait for a charge every few hundred miles, it would still take several days just to get to Kansas."

Shashir was listening attentively with a serious look on his face. "John, do you even have a good driver's license?"

"You're right, Shashir, I don't. I'll just have to find something."

"Maybe we can get you on the tube train. It's expensive, but it goes eight hundred kph in a vacuum tunnel. There are only two operating now, and they go from LA to New York City and Seattle to Miami. Cynthia got out her PC and dialed up the central transportation line. She found that all tube trains and bullets were booked up for two or three days. She checked for anything going east and couldn't find a thing. She checked going to LA and then east, with no luck. She tried anything out of San Francisco anywhere, and couldn't get out of town, except for a family emergency, until Wednesday.

"How about renting a car and driving to Sacramento, then going east?" asked John.

Cynthia tried again. She could get a train out of Sacramento Tuesday night, but that wasn't a great improvement, as it would cost a whole precious day.

"How fast are these bus-trains, anyway?"

"You can forget about locals," added Cynthia. "They stop at every exit. Interstates run about a hundred and forty kilometers an hour out on the open highway, but they have to stop for a half hour in each major city. Ours makes about eight stops, and with slowing down in cities, that takes some time. We arrive in Kansas City at one am on Wednesday morning."

"So even if I could get a ticket out on your train, I would still only have about a day to get the rest of the way to Atlanta. She said she was leaving there on Thursday morning. Please don't say anything about this mission to anyone. I'm not supposed to know about it and it could get them in trouble if it got out."

"Don't worry, John, Cynthia and I will keep your confidence well."

"Right, John," added Cynthia.

"Oh, by the way, John," said Shashir, "my grandmother called and said that the person who sponsored my great grandfather was a woman named Sally Rogers, but he did have a man sponsor at first for a short time. That was probably you, don't you think?"

"I guess I could very well have been," said John with a small smile.

It was their turn to board a cable car, and soon they were heading up Powell Street with a bunch of happy tourists and a bell-ringing fun-loving driver. There was nothing John could do but think. He wasn't exactly having fun. He was feeling a little guilty about laying this trip on his friends, considering all the circumstances. He tried to smile and be a good companion. Cynthia and Shashir were almost ecstatic and were having a great time. When they got to the wharf, it was packed with sightseers. John saw that they still sold seafood and was glad they still had some sea life to catch.

They left Fisherman's Wharf and hiked over to Telegraph Hill. The city was so different now, with the ped going everywhere and the streets filled with parks, fountains, swimming and wading pools, and tennis, basketball and volleyball courts. It was easy to see just how much space people had given over to cars in the past. On the way, Shashir asked John to tell him about the dream again. John described the dream in detail. Cynthia and Shashir could see how it fit with the article he had found at Crystal's.

"I can see why you are so concerned, my friend."

"I hope this doesn't sound stupid or egotistical, but considering all that has happened to me, I just feel sure that the dream was really a warning and this will happen to Crystal. She is such a wonderful person, so sweet and gifted and caring. We were doing great together. We shared a kiss under the full Moon last night. I told her that I loved her, and she said she loved me too. God, I love her so much."

Shashir and Cynthia were both moved. "I have a wonderful idea," said Shashir. "I will take the train on Wednesday night, and let you have my ticket for the train tonight. If that is all right with you, Cynthia?"

John beamed with hope.

"Well, sure, Shashir, if you are willing to do it. It's OK by me."

"It is just too much to ask, Shashir. Too much. You two shouldn't have to go separately. Where would you stay?"

"I'm sure the Patterson's would be happy to put me up for two more days. We've been having a very nice relationship. Yes, I would very much miss riding with Cynthia. She is a dear, sweet soul and we have been having a great time together, but I could be back with her in three days. It is not too big a sacrifice to make for someone who helped my family so much."

"Hey, it was just twenty dollars a month, and I did it for less than a year before I flashed to here. Even if I did begin helping your great grandfather, someone else did most of the giving."

"It does not matter how long you helped. If something happened to Crystal, I could never forgive myself. Actually, I am very honored to be able to help repay my family's debt. You must get to Crystal and save her from this menace. I am happy to help. And maybe now you can begin to really have a good time until we head for our bus-train."

"You bet, brother. God, Shashir, I just don't know how to thank you. Cynthia, would you please find out if I can get a train out of Kansas City to Atlanta? How about a bullet?"

"I'll see what I can come up with, John. I'm very proud of you, Shashir. You are a truly wonderful man."

Cynthia laid a really nice kiss on Shashir. In a few minutes she had booked Shashir on the Wednesday night Bus-train, and John on the 10 am bullet train out of Kansas City to Atlanta. It made six stops and didn't go straight there, but it got him to Atlanta at midnight Wednesday. John was very happy. He felt a tremendous love for Shashir. Cynthia told John that he could stay at her family's farm sixty miles northwest of Kansas City, and still be able to make it back in time for his train if he left Hiawatha on the 8:30 am train. Her father would be picking them up in his truck outside of Kansas City and driving them home to the farm.

The level of camaraderie had gone way up, and they all were having a really great time together while they hiked down through North Beach to China Town. By the time they got there they were starving. They had a late lunch at a Chinese restaurant on Grant Street that had almost two hundred vegetarian entrees and no meat at all. They discovered that it had a Taoist Temple upstairs from it, and checked it out after dinner. As they stood in front of the altar,

Shashir led them in a prayer for John to be successful in rescuing Crystal from whatever tribulation she might be facing. John had a tear roll down his cheek at the thought of just how kind and accepting Shashir had been with him. At this point, it was all too apparent just how much he had needed a friend who believed in him. John gave Shashir a long hug and told him with tears in his eyes just how much his friendship and generosity meant to him.

"Just one thing I ask of you, John. You must keep Cynthia and me posted on what is happening."

"Deal," said John, "I'll call y'all every day."

John realized that he wouldn't have any time to go back over to Berkeley before the train left at seven. He called up the Chows and told Beverly the whole story of how he had found the article at Crystal's and how he was sure that he was supposed to go to Atlanta to find Crystal, and make sure nothing happened to her.

"Your friend is so generous, John," said Beverly. "You go and be very careful yourself. Chen and I will be praying for your success."

"If by some chance Crystal calls, please tell her to call me on my PC number. I'll leave it up to your judgment what to say about any of the rest of this stuff."

"We'll be glad to give her your message, John. As for the dream and how it fit with the article, we'll leave it up to you to tell her about that. I hope it is just a coincidence and nothing like that happens to her."

"Me too, Beverly. But I just can't wait around and take the chance."

"I understand, John. Good luck."

"Thank you so much for everything, Beverly. Please give my thanks to Chen and say good-bye for me. I'll call you as soon as I know any more."

"Please do. Good-bye, John."

It was starting to get late. John figured he had about an hour to shop for some clothing and a suitcase for himself. They all went to a department store by Union Square and John bought a couple of changes of clothing, some jeans, and a couple of pairs of short pants, as he was going back to the south. He got some athletic shoes, as he wanted to be ready for anything, and the toiletries he'd need. Shashir had fun buying some American clothing. John was finding his funds getting dangerously close to allowing only for a one way ticket for him.

Cynthia and Shashir had already put their bags in lockers at the main subway transfer, so all they had to do was stop off there before going to the station. Shashir had connected with the Patterson family, and they had happily consented to his staying with them for two more days. Shashir was good at winning people's hearts. At 6:30, they were all heading for the train station. John was incredibly excited. His confidence level was very high. Surely he would somehow get to Crystal before anything could happen to her.

John bought Shashir a ticket for the Wednesday night train. A quick calculation made his predicament official. After paying for the bullet train from K.C. to Atlanta, he wouldn't have enough money for any kind of return trip.

"I'll ride a bicycle back to here if necessary." John said, but he was a little concerned that he was using all his funds on an idea he had gotten from a dream. He could think of no other course, though. Just to wait was unacceptable to him.

John gave Shashir another sincere and heartfelt hug when he and Cynthia were ready to board the train.

"I guess I must have been doing something right to have such a wonderful friend as you've been, Shashir. I'll never forget this."

"It's not such a big deal, John. I'll be with my sweet Cynthia again late Thursday night. We will have a wonderful weekend together."

The bus train had a locomotive the size of a large bus, but with tires instead of steel wheels on tracks. It pulled ten bus size cars all linked together. John was told that each car had computer controlled steering that followed the lead of the locomotive, so it could even snake through a series of turns.

Cynthia and Shashir shared a very nice, long kiss and hug. John and Cynthia boarded and found two seats together. Shashir soon saw them through their window and gave them a big smile, waved, and blew kisses as they pulled out. The bus train was rather ponderous, and took quite a while getting to the edge of the city. Once it got on the open road, it made its way up to a pretty good clip. John could see that they were on the old interstate highway. The only difference was a very well-made fence on either side of it. Cynthia explained to him how there were now good fences that protected people from the wildlife and vice versa.

"That's a very good idea. I used to think that that would be the only way to protect animals like elephants and rhinoceros from straying off of preserves and getting poached. You know, back in my day a lot of animals were almost pushed to extinction. Well, a lot of species were, but I mean some of the more magnificent animals that everyone knew about, like pandas and tigers."

John told Cynthia about his poem, *I Stand with the Tiger*, and asked her if she'd like to hear it. She said yes and he recited it for her. She said she loved it, but it was hard for her to relate to that time.

"It is a good thing there were people like you back then, or there wouldn't be a lot of these species left."

"I can't take a lot of credit. I never got the poem published, but I wish more people from that time could have heard it."

Cynthia told John a little about the changes that had taken place in the areas that they would be passing thorough on their way to Kansas City. The biggest change was the massive Prairie Common that had been created out of parts of eight states in the region. The draining of the aquifer in the region ended farming with irrigation, so only plants adapted to the area could make it. Instead of using the land for farming and cattle, it had been given back to wild species like bison, antelope, deer and elk. At first, the common was expected to be a major source of meat, and it had been determined that they could actually get more from these well adapted species than from cattle, with a lot less destruction to the land. And a lot better quality meat, as these animals had much less fat than cattle. In the last fifty years, more and more of the natural predators, like wolves, cougars and bears had returned, while at the same time people were eating less meat.

"My dad thinks that in twenty or thirty years there won't be much of a hunting quota left," said Cynthia.

"So people still hunt?" said John.

"Yes. My grandfather was a hunter and then a game warden. It is very hard to get a license to be in the hunting lottery. You have to be an expert shot, and be very knowledgeable about wildlife, ecology and the laws regulating both. Most people have to take the test two or three times before getting a license. Hunters are kind of an elite group."

"Back in my time, anybody could get a hunting license and go out and start shooting animals. A lot of cows and people were shot too. Growing up in a rural area, most of my friends hunted from when they were ten or twelve years old. I tried it a few times. You can get really bloodthirsty running around in the woods looking for something to kill. The truth is, I'm still haunted by some of the animals I shot."

"I could never kill anything. I was so glad when my grandfather became a game warden, because they're not allowed to hunt. It's kind of a conflict of interest. I cried one time, when he brought a deer home while we were visiting."

"In my time, if you couldn't kill you were not considered a man. I wrote a poem about that, too. Do you want to hear it, while we're in a poetry space here?"

"Sure. So you're a regular poet?" she asked.

"Not exactly. These are about the only poems of mine I can recite.

I Don't Want To Kill

I am a man, but I don't want to kill.
To me it's surely not a thrill.
But I've been taught this all my life
that as a man I must take a knife
or gun or other weapon mean
and turn into a killing machine.
In most every movie I have seen,
in every man's book or magazine
the message comes through loud and clear.
To be a man you must have no fear,
and be able to kill without a tear.

Men must kill, young man you see.
Men must kill so that we can be free.
Men must kill so we can eat.
Men must kill or know defeat.
Men must kill so we can be white.
Men must kill so we can be right.
Don't let Commandments, or the Golden Rule
turn you into such a fool
that you would dare to think or say,
it doesn't have to be this way.

I am a man but I don't want to kill.
Of death and destruction we've all had our fill,
but the murder and mayhem are going on still."

"Wow, John, I can't say I like it as much as *I Stand with The Tigers*, but it was good. God, it was so much different back in your era. We have a hard time imagining what it would be like to live with all that crime. The murder rate was so appalling during the late nineteen-hundreds. So many people had guns."

"So what's it like nowadays? Can individuals still own guns?"

"Yes, but they are much more regulated than in your time. All guns have to be fitted with a hand grip that will only allow the registered owner to be able to fire it. The registration includes a ballistics test, and that is kept on file. There are heavy fines for owning an improperly registered gun, or for altering the ballistics, as that had helped a lot to eliminate the poaching that was a real problem years ago."

"Very smart. So you can be tracked down by your bullets."

"Yep."

"I saw in the library at Berkeley that there are still almost fourteen hundred murders a year. Obviously better controls on guns has helped a lot, but people still are killing people."

"Yeah, and it's mostly people killing family members. Pretty sad isn't it."

"I guess there will always be some crimes of passion, as long as human nature isn't perfect," added John.

"Well, it's gotten a lot better. Much better than back in your time."

"That's why I want to stay in this time."

"What would prevent that?"

"I don't know, except I had no control over my coming here, so I might not have any control over whether I stay or not."

"You think you might just flash back?"

"I guess it could happen."

John and Cynthia went to the dining car to have some supper. John was enjoying his time with her, though it did make him a tad guilty that he was the one getting to travel with her instead of Shashir. Cynthia was very lovely, even with her freckles. Her figure was fabulous. She was warm and vivacious and perhaps a bit flirtatious.

It seemed to John that all the women of this era were better looking. Perhaps it was just that most people were healthy and not overweight. Everyone looked so much calmer and relaxed, friendlier too. People would look you right in the eye and say hello with warm smiles. It was normal to introduce yourself to people you met. I guess if you are healthy, happy, calm and smiling you were nice looking no matter how God stuck your features together, John thought.

John and Cynthia went to the club car and were sharing a table with a couple from Poland who had attended the festival and were heading to Illinois to stay in the home of a couple they had met. They exchanged tickets home with each other. It had been a spur of the moment thing and the Poles were having second thoughts about it. Cynthia assured them that they would enjoy the American Midwest and that everyone would be friendly and treat them like family.

After their meal they went back to their seats, lowered the backs and settled down to see if they could get a little sleep. It was starting to get dark, and they enjoyed a beautiful sunset over the Central Valley up past Sacramento. John was tired but found it difficult to sleep. Soon Cynthia had her head on John's shoulder, sleeping soundly. It felt good to have a woman so close to him. Her warmth and scent were so pleasant. John was very happy that his self-imposed exile from the feminine was over. He had been so lonely in the last year since Faith had died but he just couldn't bring himself to be with another woman.

Was Crystal really Faith? Probably he would never know for sure, but he believed it. Maybe someday she would as well. It didn't make any difference so long as she loved him. That kiss. Surely some of Crystal's sexuality that she had suppressed for so long had been awakened by his love. He was so filled with gratitude, for Crystal, for the Chows, and for Shashir and Cynthia. Mr. Patel had helped so much. Surely he would get to Crystal in time. For what seemed like hours, John enjoyed a dreamy reverie of pleasant memories from his three days in this wonderful time before he finally fell asleep.

John arose on the sofa in his apartment in San Francisco. Within a few seconds he realized that he is back in the past! He is shocked to find himself back there with his vivid memories of Crystal and his adventures in the future. He is numb for a moment. The realization that it must have all been a dream saddens him profoundly. It had been so completely real and Crystal needed him! He let out an anguished cry, but then he awoke.

"John, are you all right? You must have had a bad dream," said Cynthia.

He was on the train with Cynthia. Whoa! What a disturbing dream! He felt the utter despair of finding himself back in the past. It had only been for a moment, but the emotion was so real and intense. He told Cynthia about the dream and its rather negative effect on his consciousness.

"You are really attached to staying in this time."

"Yes, and I really, really love Crystal."

"Well, I have a hard time believing you would just vanish. You had your head on my shoulder for the last couple of hours. You feel very real and solid to me. I can understand your not wanting to go back to the Twentieth Century. The early part of this century was a pretty intense time. I've always been amazed by how bad they let everything get before they started changing it. But maybe you're needed back then."

That was a thought John hadn't had. It made him think for a few moments. Maybe it was his destiny to return to the past somehow. He didn't like the idea much but he had to accept it. That was his real time, where he spent almost all of his life. He took a deep breath and let it out with a sigh, then smiled at Cynthia.

"You're right, Cynthia. I have to try and not count on staying here. It isn't my real time, though I very much want to be here. You know, even if I did go back, it wouldn't be as bad because I know what the future holds, and I know it is good."

They had passed through a giant field of wind turbines in the foothills and now that they were through the mountains and in the Salt Lake area, John could see a very large array of mirrors as far as the eye could see.

"What is that?" John asked Cynthia.

"That is one of the worlds largest solar concentrator systems." answered Cynthia. "It produces enough power to supply a good part of the Northwest."

"Wow, pretty impressive. I read about the Tower of Power experimental solar concentrator, and what a great success it was back in the early eighties. That's nineteen eighties, and I wondered why they didn't start building them back then as they said it produced more power than they expected."

The bus train was pulling in to Salt Lake City, and John got a good look at the skyline. It was all green, as if it were a city of those charming tall, steep mountains of China. Here and there the morning light would reflect off a glass window showing through the trees and bushes, giving the buildings the look of mountains filled with crystals. It was incredible. He could also see elevated trains running between these modern mountains of foliage. It was different from any futuristic city he had ever seen, more like a hanging garden than space age skyscrapers.

Cynthia explained to him that old fashioned glass enclosed buildings were energy gluttons and very un-ecological. Most of the older buildings in cities that got hot in the summer had a facade of steel planters added to the outside. All newer buildings were built with automatically watered foliage on the outside. The trees and bushes actually produced fruit and nuts, and provided habitat for animals. Studies had shown that there were more wild animals living in cities now than ever before. Naturally, the temperature and energy consumption in cities had gone way down, due to all the plant life.

John got Cynthia to help him check to make sure his PC was in the receiving mode, so that there was no chance of missing a call from Crystal. He was pretty anxious about that possibility. Cynthia assured him that he would get any incoming calls, but John wanted to actually make a test call to his PC, so she called him. His phone rang.

They got off the train for a while in Salt Lake City, which was supposed to have one of the most beautiful transportation hubs in the world. It was rather awesome. A huge saucer-shaped building with a ceiling almost two hundred feet high in the middle. It contained more stained glass than John had ever seen. The works were of monumental proportions. There was a two acre park in the middle, complete with mini mountains and waterfalls. John went right to a public phone and called his PC number to double check. Sure enough, it rang. They bought some fruit, then spent ten minutes walking around in this park-like area on beautiful paths with bridges and fantastic flowers, all under a massive central skylight. Then they had to run to get back on board the bus train.

They spent the morning getting to know one another better and looking for wildlife. John learned all about Cynthia and her family. She planned to attend nursing school after a couple of years of being young and free. She explained to John how each young person's Inheritance Share could only use for specific purposes. Everyone got enough to afford an excellent and complete education. If you went to expensive schools, there wouldn't be as much for you to buy a home or to start your own business.

"Money used from the fund to buy a home or start a business can never be used for any other purpose. If the house is sold, the profit could be used for anything but the original capital to buy, or put a down payment on the house could only be used for that, or for a business or education, so the money would be put back into your pool.

"I think I understand," said John. "You get a certain amount from the Inheritance Share, and you can spend it either for college, or to buy a home or start a business, in any ratio you please, but you can't just buy a house or business, sell it, and then spend the money."

"Right, it stays in the fund. Hardly anyone rents, and almost no one is homeless."

"That's a real improvement. A fantastic improvement. Everyone gets equal opportunity."

"Not completely. Kids from wealthy families do get more stuff than less well-to-do kids. But after your children are twenty-one, you can't give any money to them."

"But up to then you can?"

"Up to two thousand IC a year, and you can buy your children a lot of things. Parents can also personally pay college tuition and expenses until the child turns twenty-two. Otherwise, the gift tax is high and heavily graduated, except for spouses."

"What if your child is sick or needs special care?"

"We have good medical care for everyone so there is still no reason you would have to give your children extra money."

"The other side of equal opportunity," added John, "is that you don't have to compete with people who have a lot of money and power just because of their family. There was this guy back in my time who inherited a pet supply fortune. It was over sixty million. His company already had a majority of the market but to him it wasn't enough. His company told all the pet stores that if they sold any other brand but theirs, they wouldn't sell them their brand any more. I guess that is a good example of using inherited wealth to overcome competition."

"Yes, and some of the people he was trying to squeeze out might have had some good ideas or innovations, or at least lower prices. People still manage to get rich and powerful though, John."

"Yeah, I guess that's good though," he said.

"It depends on how they did it. There are still scam artists. A lot of these corporations are not serving the public interest very well. Lots of people still try to get around the Inheritance Share by giving their kids money under the table. Those people are the exception, though. It's pretty obvious to most people that everyone's better off now than before the Inheritance Share."

Cynthia told John that she was going to first become a nurse and then a midwife. That was her real interest.

"It is so much different birthing babies nowadays. In your time they brought the baby out into a bright room and spanked them if they didn't start breathing immediately. Then the baby was separated from the mother. We have the baby in normal light, then give it a little bath and give it to the mother. If the mother doesn't have any problems we leave the baby with her and just assist. People who have a lot of physical contact with their parents grow into much healthier and contented, adjusted adults."

"While we are on the subject of having babies, back in my time the world population was exploding. How was it brought under control?"

"In the beginning of the century, population growth was slowed by the droughts, famines, and epidemic diseases and the difficulties everyone was going through. It was still a problem that caused all our other problems to be worse, so it was recognized that policies had to be implemented that discouraged people from having more than two children. As more people were lifted out of poverty and the recovery got under way, the population quickly stabilized. Security is by far the best form of birth control. Feeling secure about the survival of your children, and about your personal welfare."

"That makes sense," said John. "What policies were put in place?"

"We have some incentives that work to keep people from having more that two children. Each parent can only leave one full share of the Inheritance Share. You get one-half from each parent. If you have more than two children, or your spouse has, the share for those children is reduced proportionately. If you have a lot of children then they don't get as much to start their life.

"That doesn't seem fair, for the kids to suffer for what the parents did."

"That's true, but nobody would vote for someone with ten kids getting as much for each child as those who are more responsible world citizens and only have two. Parents get a twenty-five percent reduction from their tax rate if they have dependent children. If they have more than two children, they lose all of it, so that also discourages larger families."

"Wow," said John, "that is intense. I don't think people would have stood for that back in my time. That would have been considered the worst kind of government meddling."

"They hadn't gone through the crisis. Something had to be done to keep the population under control. This system is a lot better than the forced abortion or sterilization so many countries adopted during the crisis period," answered Cynthia. "It works very well, and few people have more than two children."

At eleven o'clock, John started to get worried. By noon he was very upset. Why hadn't he heard from Crystal? Did she call him? Maybe Stuart or the others didn't want her to. Maybe she had thought it over and wasn't ready for a relationship with him. He decided to call her house and the Chows and see if he could find anything out. Cynthia told him he ought to wait untill they got in to Denver to call as he should give Crystal more time.

It was a little after two when they got to Denver. Though John called, he couldn't tell if Crystal had called her house or not, but she sure didn't leave him a message. He wished he had thought to ask her to. When he called the Chows, Beverly said that they hadn't heard from her. All John could do was try to relax and wait, or call one of the numbers he had for Atlanta. He wasn't quite ready for that move yet.

They spent a lot of time traveling through the Prairie Common that afternoon. Cynthia explained how the animals now used the underpasses as migration routes. They saw an amazing amount of wildlife. John was excited to see several golden and one bald eagle, a large grizzly bear in the distance, and herds of bison, elk and deer. As there were antelope, too John was moved to sing that old standard, "Oh give me a home where the buffalo roam and the deer and the antelope play." What a different world! The sight of the wild animals returned lifted his spirits and helped restore his faith that everything was perfect. Everything would be all right.

Then the prairie gave way to farmland, golden fields of wheat mixed with greener crops. John saw that though most farmers still had tractors, others farmed with draft horses and even oxen. Cynthia told him that her father preferred horses and really loved his teams. John was looking forward to seeing their farm and a bed would be incredibly welcome this night. He saw a lot of buildings that had a slanted roof down to the ground on one side, with a bank of windows on the south side. There were still a good number of older looking homes, though most of them had greenhouses or sun rooms added to the south side. Cynthia told him that they lived in an original solar eco home from 2033.

When it got dark, Cynthia got out her PC and they put on their ear plugs so they could hear some of the music from the festival and some of her favorite groups. She invited him to join her in the smoking car for a little of the hashish Shashir had given her but he decided that he should stay straight until this whole thing was over. She was back in a few minutes looking dreamy eyed. John was curious about this smoking car. This legal use of marijuana was really different. Cynthia played a lot of different bands for him. It was a real education in the new music. Many did sound like the old rock and roll. She even had some reggae.

THE FARM

John and Cynthia had been dozing for a couple of hours when the bus-train pulled into the station at Kansas City. John gathered up his one little bag and helped Cynthia with one of hers. Soon they were in the transportation hub and making their way to the train that went to the north parking area. It wasn't quite as magnificent as Salt Lake's, but very nice. In a couple of minutes they were on a train for the short ride to the parking area. Cynthia was excited about being back home. She had so much to tell her friends and family. She especially looked forward to introducing everyone to Shashir. John thanked her again for letting him come in place of Shashir. By their conversation, John could tell Cynthia was very taken with Shashir and she was already planning a trip to Bangladesh.

"Cynthia, I'm a little too tired to go into this thing about my being from 1993, so would you mind not saying anything about it until tomorrow morning?"

"Sure, John. I understand, and if you don't want to bring it up at all, it's OK with me."

"Thank you. Tomorrow would be all right. I just remembered. I thought to ask you if your parents knew about my coming and then I forgot."

"Oops. Me too. They're expecting Shashir."

Cynthia's father was waiting at the stop, looking very much a farmer with his overalls and straw hat. He was very happy at his daughter's safe return and was surprised to find that she was with John, not Shashir as he'd expected. His name was Malcolm Stanwell, and told John to call him Stan. Cynthia explained to him how John was desperate to get to Atlanta to see his girlfriend before she went on a long trip, so Shashir had been nice enough to trade tickets with John.

"I hope you don't mind him staying with us, Daddy. I'm sorry I forgot to call you and tell you about it."

"That's OK. John is welcome to spend the night. He'll have to take the seven-forty bus to Hiawatha to get the eight-thirty train to K.C.. That'll be cutting it close, getting to that ten o'clock bullet."

"It'll work just great, very little waiting. The trains are very punctual around here," added Cynthia.

"Y'all are great. Thank you so much for the hospitality, Stan. Cynthia says y'all live right up against the wildlife forest."

"Yeah. We live way back, right up against the deep woods." They all got into the front seat of Stan's six passenger pick up. "It's ten miles straight through to the next farming strip. As a matter of fact, our property is surrounded on three sides by the forest. It's only ten miles across but this strip is over three hundred miles from north to south. We live in a little valley and have hills on three sides of us. It just made sense to include them in the national forest in 2029. Look in the glove box and you'll find a map of the Midwest."

John took out the map and unfolded it. The whole Midwest was striped like a tiger from north to south, with long strips of national forest and wilderness. Maybe as much as half the Midwest was now in forest or prairie. It seemed about every third one was called a wilderness area. "Does this wilderness area mean no hunting or logging?" asked John.

"Sure, son. That's why our place is so special. We're next to the biggest wilderness strip in the whole region, and see up here, in Iowa? It connects this large area with this other strip that goes all the way to Canada. If you put it all together with all these other little branch shoots, it's over nine thousand square miles of connected wilderness."

'What kind of wildlife do y'all have?"

"You from the South, John?"

"The Atlanta area, originally."

"You sure have a deep accent."

"You too Stan."

They all laughed.

"We've got deer, possum, raccoons, black bears, a few griz running around, coyotes, wolves, foxes, mountain lions, bobcats, lynxs, minks, eagles, elk, and an occasional bison wanders down. We have just about everything."

"That's great, Stan. You think we'll see any on our way to your farm?"

"The fences are real good around here, John. Not in the road, that's for sure. When we get almost home, we run along side the wildlife fencing for a couple of miles. We'll probably see some with this moonlight."

John told Stan how Cynthia had told him he farmed with horses. Stan explained to John why he loved horse farming, even though it is a lot of work.

"You got to love horses or forget it, John. But if you're willing to do the work, you can make more money than a tractor farmer. He's got natural gas or electricity to buy to run that tractor, then he's got to buy compost, if he can find it. Most farmers won't sell their manure for nothing, so he's got to get it from a sewage recycler or from the Mississippi delta dredges."

"What are the delta dredges?"

"You don't know about them? They still sell offshore, ocean bottom sediment. It's not like in the boom days of the replanting. My grandfather went down there and worked during the time when they were hauling hundreds of barges of sediment a day back to the Midwest. We'd have never recovered from the dusters without it."

John could see he was getting in over his head so to avoid having to explain his ignorance, he changed the topic to the local road system. He sure had a lot to learn. The roads were virtually empty at almost two in the morning and it was a pleasant ride in the moonlight to the farm. Once, in a turn, he thought he saw a pair of flashing eyes in the woods, but the forest was pretty thick and he didn't really see anything.

"You wait until your bus ride into town tomorrow," said Stan. " Look right back there where the creek crosses the road and I guarantee you'll see something in the clearing by the creek there. You can see more at dawn than any other time."

Soon they were at the Stanwell's little home. When they pulled in, John could see that it was very much like many of the homes he had seen from the bus-train. The south side had a solid ten foot high wall of windows flanked on either side by what appeared to be sliding shutters. Then the roof sloped down to almost earth level at the north. John walked down the steps from the front porch to the house and he found that, as he suspected, it was mostly underground.

All along the south wall there was a great room with a sloping ceiling eighteen feet high at the windows. The west wing held the kitchen, and the dining area was right in front of that. The east wing was a large living area with a small round metal fireplace standing on a wide, short pedestal. It had a saucer shaped hood over it with a stovepipe leading all the way to the ceiling. John walked over to it and as it was empty he could see that the pedestal was some kind of an intake pipe with a regulator on it. It must be pulling air from the outside when there's a fire, so as to not be sucking cold air into the house through cracks, John thought.

From a line of five doors along the north wall, Mrs. Stanwell emerged wearing a robe. She gave Cynthia a hug, and was introduced to John. "Please call me Nancy," she offered. Cynthia told her about the ticket switch, and she and Cynthia went right to work turning the couch into a bed for John.

"Now, John, you can use the kids' bathroom. It is the second door on the right. It's almost two thirty, so we all better get to bed," said Nancy.

In a few minutes John had brushed his teeth, taken a quick shower, and was lying on his bed. He liked this house. It made a lot of sense to him. The ceiling looked to be quite thick when he was coming down the stairs so he figured it was very well insulated. Being under ground, he was very comfortable, if not a tad cool, even though it was rather warm outside.

I bet it gets nice and warm with all that solar gain in the winter, he thought. Those shutters are probably sensor controlled. What a sensible design. It seems to be made mostly of concrete, stone and glass, except for the ceiling and roof, which look conventional. Those are building materials the Earth has plenty of. They can probably heat this thing with a few sticks in the winter if the foot thick ceiling is all full of insulation. What would be the point of going to all this trouble and not insulating it, he thought.

John tried to still his mind. The moon was starting to peek in the window. He thought about his beloved Crystal, and their time together on the mountain. What bliss! He wondered why he hadn't heard from her. With a little luck he might just be with her tomorrow night. Then he said a prayer for Crystal, Stuart, and all of the folks on the mission, hoping God wouldn't mind if he didn't get up and kneel down. He was about to ask to be with her tomorrow night, but instead just prayed, "Thy will be done. Amen." By God, I'm not going to let anything happen to Crystal, he thought. Sleep came slowly.

211

He awoke to find Mr. Stanwell making some coffee. Stan told John to just stay in bed, as it was six-thirty in the morning, and he could catch another thirty or forty minutes sleep if he wanted to. John was relieved not to awake to a disturbing dream for the third morning in a row. He had some fleeting memories that he thought were about Crystal and were positive, but he couldn't really bring them into focus. He did feel peaceful and positive for someone with only four hours sleep in a bed in the last two days. Stan offered him a cup of coffee which he graciously accepted.

"I get up a little before Nancy and go feed the horses. It's a nice time of my day. I love the horses and the mornings. They sure love to get fed."

"You were telling me about why you like farming with horses last night," said John.

"I love working with the teams. My grandfather started breeding this stock over sixty years ago. He was one of the first in the area to return to horse farming. It is the only way to have a self-sufficient, well managed farm. We put a portion into oats and hay, and we get enough fertilizer to maintain our soil fertility, what with manure crops and all."

"What kind of manure crops, if you don't mind my asking?"

"Clover and soybeans mostly. We never plant over half in cash crops at any one time."

"You can still make it on that?" John asked.

"I'm a pretty successful farmer. I've added eighty acres to this piece in my lifetime. I was a little concerned about Alex, that's our son, being able to take it all over what with the inheritance tax and everything, but as there is no tax on the first three hundred thousand, so put with his inheritance share, he should be real close. He's a great worker, and he knows the farming business better than most old hands, so I'm sure he'll be able to get the financing if he needs it. He's in the Army in one of the U.N. divisions. They don't ever see any fighting. Hopefully, they never will again. It pays to keep them up though and they do a lot of relief work. With what he'll save during his tour and his Inheritance Share, he'll be all right. He's going to use some of the Army money to put himself through the two year agriculture program at the local junior college."

"What if someone's willing to pay more than him?" asked John.

"If they're willing to pay over ten percent more, then they'll get it after Nancy dies. Can't do nothing about the market. I tell you this,"

Stan turned and looked John right in the eyes, "nobody can run a more efficient farm than my boy. That ten percent from the Family Preferential Act will help a lot. I doubt if anyone will bid more than ten percent over Alex. Nobody can use this land for anything but farming, you know?"

"Really?" said John.

"Oh yeah, the Farmland Preservation Act. I got to go out and feed the teams. You want to come and help?"

"Sure. That would be great."

Stan had two teams of draft horses and a couple of extras. They were beautiful, and had really nice, big stalls. They were happy to see Stan and waited impatiently as he fed one after another.

"You can get some oats from that bin, John. I feed these in the same order every day, oldest first, and every day Mable and Sugar bitch at me. I tried mixing the order but that just made it worse. Then everybody bitched at me. You'd think they'd learn I'm going my fastest."

"Do y'all have any cows or pigs?"

"Pigs! Lord no! Those things stink to high heaven. I don't even eat the stuff. I had a dairy cow for a while. It was all right until she finally had a bull calf. It was her fourth. They've got it down to one male in ten nowadays. Anyway, nobody wanted to raise up that bull calf, and we got stuck with it. There was no way the women were going to let me sell it for slaughter. I kind of thought about setting it loose in the Wilderness. Some folks do you know, especially up in the dairy regions. It throws the whole natural balance out, though. Anyway, we took care of that bull for nine years until it was struck by lightning while standing under a tree and died. It ate more than any of my horses and was a terror if you tried to cross his pasture. We sold the cow after a couple of years of putting up with old Pancho."

"My brother-in-law has a dairy in Wisconsin where they keep all the bulls and only breed enough to replace the herd. It's called an animal sensitive dairy. Ever heard of them? Their products cost over twice as much as regular dairy products. I don't know how anybody affords it but he says he can sell all he can produce. The company he sells to gets over twelve IC a half gallon for frozen yogurt. Amazing huh? We pretty much gave up dairy after our bull experience. Soy milk's better for you anyway."

"So what do you grow mostly, Stan?"

"Wheat, beans, oats, hemp, and a little corn. Three hundred and forty acres with about one hundred and seventy in cash crops. This year we are growing wheat and hemp. It is good to have at least two different things going. Its a lot of work."

"Hemp. You mean like marijuana?"

"Fiber hemp. It's not much good for smoking. Nancy used to grow some smoking hemp in our vegetable garden when we were younger. We quit when the kids started getting up. Didn't want to encourage them none. These overalls are made out of hemp cloth. It's much stronger than cotton and lasts almost forever. All paper products have been made out of hemp since the tree cutting moratorium."

"What kind of price do you get for wheat nowadays?" John asked.

"Wheat closed at fifteen forty IC a bushel yesterday. If it gets to sixteen, my broker will be selling my whole crop."

John had discovered that though other things were similar in price to his time, food was considerably more expensive. But, look at the way they're doing it, John thought. In harmony with the Earth, and all organic. He was looking at an unusual piece of equipment.

"What is this, Stan?"

"That is a no till planter. It just plants the seed without turning over the soil and exposing it to a lot of erosion."

"You use any pesticides or chemicals?"

"You really are a city slicker, John. There haven't been any chemicals used on farms in over fifty years. We have integrated pest management without any chemicals. Shucks, son, where'd you hear we used chemicals up here?"

"I'm sorry to be such an idiot, Stan. You're right. I don't know anything about modern farming."

"Let's go into the house and get some breakfast. The women should have it ready by now."

"What is the roof of your house made of? I see that the barn is mostly steel."

"Actually, steel and aluminum. So are the beams in my roof, and there's galvanized steel on top."

"Is that whole ceiling filled with insulation?"

"Oh yeah. They built these old eco homes better than anything today. Had to, back then. It was the beginning of the recovery. That is an R forty-nine ceiling."

"Wow! Does it stay warm in the winter?"

"You bet. Cool in the summer too. Most of the time we leave the shutters open. That is triple pane glass in those south windows. The sun can't make it in from May till September."

"I saw the moon last night."

"Yeah, the moon can just peek in on occasion this time of year."

They were back inside and Nancy was setting the table for breakfast.

"Good morning, John. Cynthia is taking a shower. You like pancakes?"

"I love them."

"These are buckwheat. They do have egg in them if you are a vegan."

"No, I'm not quite that pure."

"Now chickens are different, John. All you have to do is eat all the eggs and no roosters," said Stan.

Soon Cynthia came out of one of the rooms pushing an elderly lady in a wheelchair. John was introduced to her grandmother. Cynthia sat down next to her grandmother and began feeding her. John assumed she had suffered a stroke, and was partially paralyzed. They were all having a great breakfast of pancakes with honey, homemade apple butter, and fried tempeh. John really laughed when he saw that. David had said that moldy soybeans would be a hard sell. Yet here they were in the middle of the midwest on a farm.

Cynthia proceeded to tell her parents all about the festival and what a wonderful time she had with Shashir. John added some comments about Shashir's great spirit and kindness.

John learned that he would have to be at the local stop a quarter mile away to catch the van to Hiawatha. Soon it was time for him to leave and, after saying good-bye and thanks to the rest of the Stanwells, he gave Cynthia a hug and a thank you. He told her he would call them up Saturday morning with a report and promised to call Shashir sometime that day. It was still early in San Francisco. Cynthia checked the home computer for the van schedule, and found it to be within a minute of being on time.

Cynthia walked with him to the stop. John could see how beautiful their farm was, with forested hills on three sides and a small orchard of fruit trees in the side yard. They had a partially underground greenhouse next to the horse barn. Several beehives dotted the orchard. What a wonderful scene! A picture postcard farm. Nancy had made him a tempeh sandwich for the train, and he had gotten a half gallon bottle filled with water from their well.

The Stanwells shared an entrance road to their farm with another farm, the Christiansons'. When they were passing in front of the Christiansons' house, John saw a truly amazing sight. It was a little child with wild blond hair, wearing a nightshirt and carrying a bucket, who was being followed by several animals - a large, black and white cow and her calf, a couple of sheep, and a full-grown mountain lion. John's jaw dropped. The child got to a few chickens and started throwing out corn.

"That's little Isaiah," said Cynthia. Old Seven is tame as a house cat. They've had him since he wandered out of the wilderness half starved as a kitten. Isaiah, how are you doing today?"

The child looked up at Cynthia and John, put the bucket down, smiled and waved.

"Isn't he adorable? The sweetest little child."

John looked at Cynthia and said, "Isaiah?"

"Yes. You managed to get the perfect scene with Isaiah actually leading the animals. They've had Seven since before Isaiah was born, and planned it that way. Cute, huh."

"Yeah. What does Seven eat?"

"Big cat chow that is a mixture of soy, grains and fish meal. Old Seven never did have much of a hunting instinct."

"Will wonders never cease," mused John.

They continued down to the main road. John just had enough time to tell Cynthia what a wonderful home and family she had, when the bus pulled up. Another hug and he was on board the bus to town.

It was a smaller version of the subuses in the city with seats for eighteen passengers, two seats on one side and one on the other. It was about half full. In the back, there was the rack for bikes, and in the front for carts and the larger trucks. John learned it ran every thirty minutes. Sure enough, when they got to the creek John could see several deer down in the clearing. After about fifteen minutes of curvy roads they got to a larger two lane highway with a covered ped. There were stops at regular intervals but most were empty. At one stop, the driver got out and helped a very elderly lady with her cart, and then helped her into the bus with patience and smiles. John saw a lot of folks walking or riding bikes on the ped. Some people got on, and a few got off, so by the time they got in to Hiawatha they had fourteen passengers.

John found out from the driver where to catch the 8:30 train to K.C., and made it with fifteen minutes to spare. He decided to use the time to call Crystal, but couldn't reach her. John left another message for her to call him. It was too early to call the Chows or Shashir, what with the two hour time difference. Soon he was on the train to Kansas City. It was very modern and fast but stopped several times on the way. John got to the hub in K.C. at 9:50 and rushed to the bullet train. He barely found a seat when it took off. Once it got out of town it really accelerated and soon was going so fast that it was almost impossible to see things close to the track.

He decided to wander around. The dining car was full and very attractive, with large windows and skylights. Behind it was the smoking car which also had a coffee and tea bar and sold beer and wine after noon. There were not a lot of people in the car. Some were smoking tobacco or marijuana, and the majority were drinking coffee or tea. Intake vents hung over every table, and they seemed to do a good job of pulling the smoke out. John decided to hang out there some, as the car had skylights and a much better view than his seat.

He sat at an empty table but was soon joined by a couple from Israel, Jerry and Fatima Myer. Jerry was wearing a Star of David around his neck. They were very friendly, and John was quite interested in what had happened to Israel since his time. He didn't want to confront the whole issue of his time shift though.

"So how is everything in Israel nowadays?"

"Prospering like never before," answered Jerry. "The pace is a bit hectic. We've been enjoying the American Midwest. It's so much less crowded than Israel. Everyone is so friendly, and they're very hard working people.

"What is the primary industry in Israel now?"

"We don't have much industry, mostly farming, banking and tourism."

John was watching as Fatima rolled a hand made cigarette out of what looked like tobacco. She was wearing a sweatshirt that said U. J. I..

"What does U. J. I. stand for, Fatima?"

"University of Jerusalem International."

"What's it like?"

"Big. It has the most ethnically diverse student body in the world. Only about fifteen percent of the students come from Israel and Palestine. Every single nation and ethnic group is represented."

"How does it attract all those students from everywhere?" John asked.

"For one thing," answered Jerry, "as you've probably heard, they award a scholarship to at least two students from each ethnic group. But the main reason is because it's the best school for international affairs in the world."

"Cool."

"Cool? What does that mean?" asked Fatima.

"It's an old slang term for good."

While Fatima completed her deft rolling of a cigarette, she asked John if he wanted her to roll him one and he declines. When she finished she put it in her mouth and Jerry held a match to it. She took a big drag and held it out to John.

"Want to try a puff?" she asked.

"No, thank you. I'm not much into tobacco."

Fatima let out her puff in a cloud of smoke. "It's not so bad if it's organically grown." She passed the cigarette to Jerry. "We were given this tobacco by a wonderful couple we met on the trail who grew it themselves. It's legal to buy tobacco in Israel, you know."

"No, I didn't know that."

"Where are you from, John?" she asked.

"Outside of Atlanta, originally, but I've been going to med school in San Francisco."

"Did you go to the festival."

"Yes. It was my first."

"How was it?" asked Jerry.

"Great. I didn't see it all but I had a super time. Met some great people, too."

"That's the best thing about the festivals," said Fatima. "I went to the Jerusalem festival in eighty-five, though I was only seventeen."

Fatima and Jerry each had a few drags and then put the cigarette out.

"We've been hiking the wilderness trail from Canada to north Missouri," Jerry said. "It was really nice considering the forest is mostly just sixty years old. We saw lots of wildlife. Now we're going to try and do as much of the Appalachian Trail as we can before winter. We don't expect to make Canada, though."

"That sounds like a great summer. So how could y'all afford to take all summer off?" John asked.

We both teach."

"Super. What do y'all teach?"

"Fatima teaches conflict resolution at U. J. I. and I teach science at a high school."

"I'd love to go to Jerusalem some day," said John.

"You really should. It's the most interesting place on Earth," said Jerry.

"I guess I'll go back to my seat and try and nap for a while. It was great meeting you."

John went back to his seat. He leaned his seat back and soon dozed off. The next thing he knew, they were pulling into St. Louis. It was approaching noon. John got off and called Crystal's number. She didn't answer so John left a message for her to call him. *What the heck am I going to do in Atlanta tonight? If she's leaving at seven-thirty, I'll have precious little time to find her unless she calls me.*

John called Shashir and did reach him. He was excited about leaving for Kansas that evening. John told him he hadn't been able to get through to Crystal, but that otherwise his trip was going great.

"You're going to love the Stanwells' farm. It is beautiful."

"Yes. Cynthia is going to take me for a backpacking trip in the wilderness. How is she doing?"

"She's beautiful, Shashir, and she likes you a whole lot. It was so nice of you to help me. Thanks again."

"Stop thanking us, John. You are very welcome. You just find Crystal."

"I will. I'll call you Saturday morning when you're at the farm. I love you, Brother."

"Much love to you as well, John. Good-bye."

It was time to board the bullet. Soon it was off again and shortly it was crossing the Mississippi River. John couldn't be sure, but he could swear that it wasn't as muddy. *Now that was a change. I guess better farming practices had made the difference,* he thought. Soon after that, it was up to speed and heading for its next stop, Evansville, Indiana. The train passed through woods about half the time and then through farmland, with the scene changing about every four or five minutes. The woods were mostly a blur of eight foot high chain link fencing. When it opened up into farmland, he could see a lot farther. John was amazed when he realized that he hadn't seen a single cow yet. Oxen yes, but no cows. Just then a pasture with a few dozen head flashed by. *Probably a dairy,* John thought.

The conductor passed through, so John asked him if it were possible to get a phone call on his PC on the train.

"You should be able to."

The rest of the day passed as fast as the scenery. They stopped in Evansville, Louisville, Nashville. John was thinking they ought to call the train the "Ville" Express. When they reached Chattanooga John decided to get off and eat something, as he hadn't eaten since about 2:00 when he had his sandwich. The city of Chattanooga had been made famous by the song "The Chattanooga Choo-Choo," so the train station was separate from the rest of their hub. It was done in an historical motif, with old train cars and both Civil War and World Two artifacts abounding. It was almost 11:00 and John decided he had to call one of the numbers he had gotten at Crystal's if he wanted to reach anyone before they got to sleep. He dialed the first number.

"Hello."

"Hi. My name is John Berry and I'm a friend of Crystal. It is extremely important that I reach her before she leaves for her trip."

"Crystal from Frisco?"

"Yes. Do you know where she is or her phone number?"

"And you're who?"

"John Berry. I'm a new friend. I'm in Chattanooga and on my way to Atlanta."

"Hold on a minute."

There was a somewhat long silence.

"Crystal can't be reached right now. I'm sorry. Good-bye."

"Wait. Don't hang up. What's your name?"

"If you don't know, why should I tell you?"

"It is very important. Will you see Crystal before she leaves?"

"I have no idea when Crystal's leaving or where she might be going."

"Please. I'm in love with Crystal and I believe she shares my feelings. I think that she will be in great danger if she goes on this mission."

"I don't know what you are talking about. Good-bye."

She hung up. John called the other number and got a message saying that Ralph would be out of town for about two weeks, and wouldn't be able to be reached. John was frustrated. He called the other number again. When the lady answered he spoke.

"Please don't hang up on me again. Please tell Crystal to call me as early as possible tomorrow. Please."

"If I see her, which I doubt. I'm trying to get some sleep. I'm putting my phone off. Good-bye."

Soon he was back on the train speeding across north Georgia towards Atlanta. He was tired when he got off and decided that he'd just have to spring for a room. There were several hotels within the hub. The room was expensive but John was too tired to care. He caught a quick shower and watched the news channel for a few minutes before he went to sleep. President Samantha Smith was at a trade conference in Africa. It was to lay the groundwork for a new treaty that would finally bring Central Africa fair and balanced trade. John woke up at 2:35, and turned off the television. Before going back to sleep, John got out of bed and prayed on his knees to be able to reach Crystal the next morning. Then he prayed for her safety and the success of their mission. He asked his PC to give him a wakeup call and found that it would do it. It took him a while to get back to sleep.

ATLANTA

John woke up at 6:45. He had been dreaming about being at Stone Mountain with his parents. They were having a great time until they started hiking up the back side. Then his dad started breathing heavily and coughing. They had to stop and rest and when his father got his wind back, he lit up a cigarette. Well, that dream had really happened, John remembered. He went to the bathroom, washed his face and shaved. By then it was 7:00.

John was getting very antsy. If Crystal were going to call him before 7:30, then it would have to be very soon. He was dressed and sitting on the bedside. Then he thought to call his PC from the room phone to see if it was working OK. It went through. He quickly hung up, not wanting to tie up his line. Seven-thirty came and went. No call.

Damn, John thought. What's going on? He didn't know what to do and it was making him very nervous just sitting there waiting. He decided that if he didn't hear from her by 8:10 he'd call her house and then that woman he talked to last night. At 8:10 he called her home, and there was no new message. He called the number for the woman. He got a recording saying April and Edgar weren't home. She could be reached at work at 899-2837, extension 2232. He called the number and a recording answered, "New Fidelity Insurance Co., if you know the extension of the person you are calling, enter it in now. If you wish to speak to an operator press zero."

John pressed in 2232 and after several rings got a message saying that April Ciceroni was not in, and he could leave a message. April Ciceroni, I'm just going to go and see her in person. Then she can't hang up on me, he thought. He called again and got an operator who told him the address on West Peachtree Street. It was 8:25 and John decided that he'd wait till 8:35 just in case someone's watch was on the wrong time or something. He got his stuff together and was ready to leave at 8:35.

He went down to the lobby and into the transportation hub. Atlanta had a massive hub, a little different from the other cities. More fountains and water added a lot of beauty. The building he was in had a giant triangular window two hundred feet high on the south side with incredible modern art stained glass pieces interspersed with clear glass. The structure was a three-sided wedge, sloping down to a point at the north end. This is sort of like the eco homes except much larger, he thought. They must get a huge amount of solar gain through that window in the winter. It was the biggest window John had ever seen, and through it he could see mountains he knew to be buildings, that were rectangular, stepped, and pyramidal in shape. It appeared that all the buildings in Atlanta had the foliage cover.

He got on the subway that went up West Peachtree Street and before he knew it, he had missed his exit. He got off at the next one and decided to walk the four blocks instead of riding the train back. He needed time to think, and besides, he was really curious about Atlanta.

When he got to the street he was amazed. He had been on this street many times, but it was very different now. The street itself was covered with a tree canopy except for a few areas over the open lanes. The covered lanes were very large and had glass roofs every other twenty paces so you could still see the amazing valleys and canyons of foliage-covered buildings. He saw flowers all up the sides of the buildings, and peaches, cherries and green apples on many of the trees. There were birds and butterflies everywhere. Lots of hummingbirds added a beautiful touch, not normally found in a downtown area. He was in close proximity to the old interstate highway yet the street noise was very moderate. He could see bus-trains and what appeared to be cargo trains running on one side of the highway and covered lanes sharing the other side with delivery trucks and service vehicles.

Just then an ambulance sped by. It was going fast and didn't have to slow down as it was easy to maneuver on the uncrowded service road. Though the siren was on, the foliage seemed to be absorbing a lot of the sound. So, thought John, one reason for the lack of noise is that the greenery absorbs sound instead of reflecting it. I bet a lot fewer people die in ambulances with no traffic to fight.

The air smelled sweet from hundreds of magnolia trees in blossom. I'll bet it stays much cooler downtown now, he thought. Of course. Why didn't anyone think of this in his time? He had always loved the fact that Atlanta had more tree canopy than any other city he'd ever seen. Now it was really incredible. He found the building he was looking for, a huge pyramidal affair that took up a whole large city block at the base and went steeply up for at least a couple of hundred feet. The lobby was a smaller pyramid with a beautiful fountain in the middle. The directory said that New Fidelity was on floors eighteen through twenty-two of this twenty-six story building.

I'll just go up and tell a receptionist I'm here to see April Ciceroni, he thought. He took an elevator up to the eighteenth floor, and went to the receptionist's desk. He said he was there to see April Ciceroni and asked where her office was.

"Is she expecting you?"

"No."

"I'll just ring her up and tell her you're here. And what is your name, sir."

That wasn't John's favorite idea, as he hoped to surprise her so she couldn't avoid seeing him or have him thrown out. "I'm John Berry." John figured he had screwed up.

"She is away from her desk right now. Would you like to take a seat and wait?"

"Um, I need to use your bathroom."

John was directed to the bathroom and waited there for someone to enter. In a couple of minutes a fellow came in.

"Do you know April Ciceroni?"

"Yes."

"Could you tell me what office she is in?"

"Yeah, 2232."

"Thanks," John said.

Damn! I should have figured that out. I'm not thinking very clearly. It must mean the twenty-second floor. John went back to the elevator and went up to the twenty-second floor. He got out and soon found room 2232. The door was open so he walked right in, but the room was empty. A sliding glass door on the outside wall led to a railed walkway with a floor of metal grating. Only a screen door was closed. John marveled, a screen door on an office building. He slid back the screen door and looked out. There was a woman standing at a corner about 30 feet away with a cup in her hand. That might be her, he thought.

John went outside on to the walkway. It was about four feet wide and had what appeared to be large planters all along the outside. In many places John could see through the trees and bushes and over the mountains of buildings all covered with greenery, running right off into the distance. There were blueberries on many of the bushes and cherries on the dwarf trees. When he got up to the lady, he could see that she was watching a pair of falcons feeding their three young in a nest they had built on the outside of the planter.

"That's amazing. Hello, are you April?"

"Yes. Who are you? Don't tell me. You're Crystal's friend."

"Yes, have you seen her?"

"No, but I did talk to her. After your call last night, Ed and I decided to call Stuart and Crystal and tell them you had called. When they found out you were in Atlanta, Stuart got paranoid. They had already told her that she shouldn't call you. After everyone conferred, it was decided that Crystal certainly couldn't call you now. It was too great a chance. She called me and told me about this because she didn't promise them she wouldn't do that. She told me that if I talked to you to tell you that she appreciates your concern, and she still trusted you, but you really shouldn't have followed her to Atlanta. I can tell you that they are gone now."

"Gone? Where? Damn, I guess she's mad at me."

"I'm sorry John. I can't tell you.

John told April his whole story of how he had gotten to the future and had fallen in love with Crystal, the story about the dream and then he showed her the article. She seemed to accept it and kept a rather serious look on her face.

She took the copy of the fax and said, "Yes, I sent this to her. I regretted it afterwards as it didn't make any sense to frighten them. They wouldn't change their minds. Crystal said that you are from the past. That seemed to wig everyone out and I must say I have a hard time with it myself. They know all about the raiders in there. I hoped they'd wait or find another site, but that idea was voted down."

"Then they are going to the Savannah River Plant?"

"Did I say that? As much as I might want to help you, John, I just can't tell you anything else."

John got down on his knees. "Please April. I love Crystal so very much. I'm going to look for her anyway."

"Get up, John. Come on."

John stayed on his knees. "Please help me get to her before anything happens to her," John pled with a break in his voice and a tear in his eye. April seemed very moved.

"Get up, please, John. God." April took hold of John's shoulder. John got back to his feet.

"You are really sure that she is in danger? God, John, this is serious. I'm really worried about them too. We've all been following this story for months. It's the biggest news around these parts. But I'm sworn to secrecy."

"April, can't you tell me anything that would help me? Is there any chance of catching them before they actually get into the Plant area?"

"They'll be in Augusta by ten-thirty and they are heading right off. There is no way you can catch them. The best you could do would be to take the next bullet to Augusta at ten. But by the time you get there, they'll probably be gone."

"Can you tell me where they plan on entering the area?"

April looked somewhat taken back. "I'm really glad they never told me, John, because it would be a total breach of trust to tell you. What if Crystal is wrong and the majority of the group that didn't want you to know are right? You could just call ahead and have them arrested. It is a two to five year confinement for violating a rad-toxic area. You already know too much."

"So you can't help me any more? Can you at least tell me how they are going in?"

"Well, they are taking mountain bikes."

"Can you think of anything else that you feel you can tell me that might help? All I want is to go with them and protect Crystal."

"She's got a lot of protection. There are a dozen people going, and several of them know martial arts."

"I don't suppose they have any guns, though?"

"Of course not. They are all committed to nonviolent protest. It could be totally misconstrued if they had any weapons. You're not planning on taking any, I hope."

"No. I swear," he said.

"I can't stop you from going, John, but I wish you wouldn't. There is probably a greater chance of you causing problems than being of any help."

"I don't think so, April. I know I came to this time for a reason and I believe it is to save Crystal. After that vivid dream, I can't just sit around. What time do you have?"

"It's nine-twenty-five. You have to leave now if you hope to catch the bullet east. John, you be very careful, and good luck. I hope to God you're wrong. Andrew said that they'd almost for sure not see the outlaws as the place is over a thousand square miles. Do not say anything I told you to anyone. Don't say anything you suspect about this mission. You understand?"

"Don't worry, April. Good-bye, and thanks. I'm sure I'll find them. I have to."

John raced out the building, back down to the street, then to the subway and just made the train. The clerk told him he'd gotten the last available ticket. A minute after he got on the train, it took off for Augusta. What was he going to do? He needed a good map of the area in South Carolina and if possible the Plant itself. He'd have to get a mountain bike if he was to have any hope of catching them. He wished he was in better condition. School and waiting tables in a smoky restaurant hadn't been very good for him.

It will take too long to do the research, John thought. I don't have time to go to libraries or ask around. I've got to get to the area as soon as possible and catch up with them if I'm going to save Crystal. They can't make me leave. They're nonviolent. All I want to do is protect Crystal. But I do want so very much to be with her. Could it be that my desire to be with her has led me to this? If I do catch up with them and nothing happens, they could all be really angry with me. Crystal, too. I could ruin our relationship forever. I could be stranded in Georgia with very little money, no friends and no Crystal. God!

John closed his eyes and started the Om shanti meditation. Yes, it was pretty crazy to chase all the way across America after a girl because of a dream. But, look at the situation. He was in the future by some strange means. What was crazier than that? He brought his mind back to Om shanti. He was too excited and anxious to meditate, so he started to pray. "God, please help me to keep my faith in myself and this mission. Please help me to take the right path to be able to find Crystal before she gets into any danger. Please protect Crystal and her companions on this dangerous mission they have undertaken because of their love for the Earth." John repeated this prayer for a good while when he heard someone speak to him.

"Is this seat taken? I was in the smoking car when we left."

"No, sure."

"Hi. My name is Norman Rockwood."

"John Berry." They shook hands. "It's a pleasure to meet you, Norman."

"Likewise, John. Where are you from?"

"I'm originally from outside of a little town north of Atlanta. Have you ever heard of Free Home?

"No. Can't say that I have. I'm from a small town south of Augusta down on the edge of the Savannah River Rad-waste area. Jackson, South Carolina. Ever heard of it?"

"No, but I've heard of the Savannah River Plant." John was amazed at the coincidence. "I hear y'all are having a real problem down there due to a bunch of outlaws."

"I'm afraid so. Jackson is already almost a ghost town due to the contamination. I'm supposed to be twice as likely to get cancer for living there. But hey, I have a small mansion and a real nice, big yard and I live a very healthy life, except for a few cigarettes a day. Most of the heavy radiation is down stream. They're talking about extending the area all the way to the mouth of the river now. It's already ruined fishing down there. Now with those outlaws getting worse, I guess Jackson will end up losing even more folks. Some families have already left."

"How come they haven't gone in and gotten those guys?" John asked.

"Oh, they've tried. But until they get enough full radiation suits, they can't get the law to really stay in there long enough to track them down. They just go further back in to where the radiation is even worse. It's going to eventually kill them but they're in too deep to come out now. They'd spend the rest of their lives in jail and they're all contaminated already. That's why they're so damn dangerous. They know they are doomed anyway."

"How long has this been going on?"

"You know, there have been petty criminals hiding out in the rad wastes ever since they sealed it off. These guys weren't too bad until the big one with the illegal shotgun joined up with them. They've been raping as well as stealing ever since. I guess about a year now."

"What do you think is going to happen with them?"

"Everybody around me is registering for guns. I guess sooner or later someone's going to get killed. The trouble is, no one man or family is a match for four armed men. There is more chance of getting yourself killed than killing them. But ever since Mr. Rogers was beat up and his wife and daughter were raped, everybody is getting armed. There was a lot of talk about us putting together our own posse and going in and getting them but the law wouldn't let us. Almost did it anyway. Some of us know that place." Mr. Rockwood looked around, and lowered his tone. "I used to go hunting in there when I was a kid, some of my friends, too. No game wardens in there."

"How would y'all go about it?"

"As long as we stayed off the road we felt safe. Hell, there is only one road through that place. Old Highway 125. It still runs right up to it, but it's been destroyed and heavily barricaded at the edge of the plant. Where it hasn't been destroyed they felled trees across it for miles. You have to get several miles into the plant to hit decent road again."

"Isn't there any other way in?"

"Not unless you want to walk through thick woods all the way."

"Well, it seems that it wouldn't be that hard to get those guys if they use the road," John said.

"My feelings as well. It seems the authorities just want to wait it out until they're all dead. They didn't want to do nothing about the plant and now they don't want to do nothing about the bad guys. Worthless bunch of bureaucrats, if you ask me. My grandfather told them that they'd end up losing the whole river all the way to the coast if they didn't do something way back when they started this crap. He was totally right."

"Have you heard about the method Greenpeace has to transmute radiation?"

"Yes, we're real interested in that. But they won't even let them test it. It's because they're afraid it'll work and they'll have to get off their asses and do something, if you ask me. It wouldn't be an easy task cleaning up that mess now that they've let it leak out all over creation. But they could at least get the big concentrations of it so as not to have any more leaking out."

"Wow! What a mess." John racked his brain trying to think of more questions he could ask Mr. Rockwood that would help him.

His prayer answered, John realize he needed to head for Jackson when he got to Augusta. There was a good chance he would be found by the authorities, due to the manhunt going on. Surely the Greenpeacers know all about this. How would they get in? If they are bringing bikes, it is likely that they plan on using the road at least some. There is a good chance that they wouldn't get in without being detected themselves.

"So what are you heading to Augusta for, John?"

"Would you believe I'm a journalist working on a story about these outlaws? You're the first person I've met from the area." That just came out of John's mouth before he could think about it. Not a bad idea, though.

"Don't say anything about me ever going in there. The law is pretty serious about that," said Rockwood.

"Why should they much care if anyone wants to risk his own life and health going in?"

"That's not the worry. They are afraid that someone will get a hold of some nuclear material, like the nuclear terrorist did."

Some journalist he was, John thought. If he asked any more about that he'd surely blow his cover. He didn't like the idea of lying to Mr. Rockwood anyway but this was a dire emergency. Mr. Rockwood pulled out a briefcase, opened it, and took out a small PC.

"I need to do some work, John. I'm an investment broker and I've got a lot of stuff to look over since attending the conference in Atlanta."

"Sure, Mr. Rockwood."

"Call me Norman."

"Thanks. One more thing if you don't mind. Just what is the government doing to protect you people?"

"Oh, we do have extra State Troopers and some FBI but they can't protect every home along the whole area. It's just a waste of time unless they're willing to go in and get them, or let us go."

"Would you actually go in after them Norman?"

"I've got a lot of friends who are hunters and let me tell you, they really want to go get those guys. If it was a large, well-led posse, you better believe I'd go with them."

John let his seat back and closed his eyes. He figured that he'd get a mountain bike in Augusta, try and find a good map, some food and maybe a good knife, then he'd head for Jackson. The idea of coming up against armed and dangerous criminals scared the hell out of him. He promised April he wouldn't take a gun, and he probably couldn't get one in a day with no identification and what he'd heard about registration. He never much liked dirt bikes and the funky noise they made while they were tearing up the woods, but he wished he had one now. And a 357 magnum. Well, he could just forget about that. Pretty stupid idea anyway.

The scenery was streaking by very quickly. He saw in the pamphlet for the train that it hit 280 kilometers an hour. John decided he'd better get something to eat. He sure had to keep his strength up. Four armed and dangerous men, was he crazy? He went to the club car and got a couple of biscuits and a large glass of orange juice. His mood went from worse to grim. He somehow hadn't confronted the reality of breaking the law and going into a waste area without any protection. Hell, going into the woods for possibly many days was intense enough. Then there were the men.

John thought back to his dream and ran it over and over in his mind. It was a pine forest with a few hardwoods. There had been no roads or anything much to help him find it. He hadn't seen any men, only heard the barking of dogs. John tried to decide what he'd do if he found Crystal's group. If they didn't see him, he could perhaps follow them without being discovered. That way he could help them if they got into trouble without ever letting them know he'd even come. Probably not a bad plan. He'd have to take a lot of food too, as Crystal had said it would take about two weeks. The whole thing seemed very difficult, if not impossible and crazy.

John remembered the fear and pain on Crystal's face in the dream. Why, oh why, did this have to be? Ours is not to reason why, he thought. Ours is but to do or die. *The Charge of the Light Brigade.* His mission seemed just as foolish as charging into all those cannons but he just couldn't turn back. He had come too far, a century of time, and across the whole country. "God, give me the strength and the faith to save Crystal."

Soon he was in Augusta. John got off the train and looked up a bicycle store. He called the store and got directions. It was just one bus ride. Augusta was just as covered with foliage as Atlanta had been. He remembered what it looked like in the spring when his family visited. It was very beautiful then, with all the dogwoods, wisteria, azaleas and red bud trees in bloom. It must have been awesome then because it was very nice now.

When he got to the bike store, he was disappointed to find that his remaining 167 IC wouldn't even get him a good bike. All the mountain bikes, even the ones without booster motors were over 300 IC. He explained his financial status to the clerk and he was told that they just happened to have a used mountain bike in pretty good condition, with no motor, for 100 IC. He took it. They also had some outdoor equipment, so John got some insect repellent, a large pocket knife, a flashlight, a compass and a day pack to put everything in.

By the time he got to the grocery store he only had nineteen IC left to buy food. How was he going to afford bus fare to Jackson? John bought a loaf of whole wheat bread, a jar of peanut butter and a jar of jelly, a bag of sunflower seeds, two gallons of distilled water, and some fruit. What with the modern food prices, that only left him three-fifty-five IC, and he was skeptical he'd get to Jackson with that. He found out from the clerk where to catch the subus to Jackson, got on the bike and rode there. It was now almost 3 pm and it was very hot. When he got to the stop he asked some of the folks waiting for the subus how much it cost to get to Jackson, and they told him five IC.

"God. I only have three-fifty-five. How far can I get on that?"

"Not much past Bench Island."

"How much do you need, son?"

John turned and found that it was a large, distinguished looking black man asking him. "Only about a credit and a half."

"All you got is three-fifty?"

"Yes sir, I'm afraid so."

"You got people in Jackson?"

"No sir." John didn't know what to say, so he stuck to more or less the truth. "I'm trying to catch up with some friends on a bike tour. If I can get back with them, I'll be all right. But if I don't get the subus to Jackson, I might never catch them."

"Keep your money, son. I'll pay your bus fare."

"Thank you so much, sir. I'll be happy to pay you back if you give me your address."

"Just stop calling me sir and pass the good deed on to someone else, OK?"

"You've got a deal. You are too kind. My name is John Berry."

"Brad Johnson, pleased to meet you." They shook hands just as the subus pulled in. It was set up a little differently. You entered your destination at the turnstile and it dispensed a little round paper sticker with a number on it. John put his bike in the rack, and went up to sit down by Mr. Johnson. He could see that the other passengers were wearing their stickers on their shirts, so he stuck his on.

"You'll be in Jackson in about forty minutes. This subus makes a lot of stops. It probably would have been better for you to have waited five minutes more and taken the express but then I couldn't have paid your way."

"This'll do fine."

"Where are you from, son?"

"Ever heard of Free Home, Georgia?"

"No."

"I've been living in San Francisco for a couple of years going to medical school."

"That's great. We can always use more doctors. I can remember back when they wouldn't even make house calls. That was back before the Inheritance Share started helping everyone go to college. If we keep educating a lot of doctors, we can keep them competitive and serving the public interest better. I guess it will eat up most all of your share going to medical school. What kind of doctor do you hope to be?"

"A general practitioner."

"Good. I'd think that would be the best kind of medicine. You get to know folks and stay with them all their lives."

"Yeah. I like that idea too," said John.

"I might have been a doctor myself if there had been the Inheritance Share back when I was going to school. I ended up working at the disassembly plant in Augusta for forty years. It wasn't so bad, and I did feel that the work was useful and positive. We did contract disassembly for a lot of different small companies. As soon as they'd get big, they would start doing their own. I'm surprised that anybody would want to ride over by the Plant area."

"Because of the outlaws?" John asked.

"Right. I wouldn't get too close to it if I were y'all."

"It was very kind of you to help me."

"Well, son, I try to do a good deed every day. Would you believe I learned that way back in the Boy Scouts?"

"Yes, sir. Oh, I'm sorry, Mr. Johnson."

Their subus was now out of Augusta and resurfaced above ground. John could see that there were a few automobiles mixed with the occasional trucks and busses.

"That's OK. Your mom raised you right. It never hurts to be polite. Yeah, I was a pretty good Scout, and made Eagle. I got my manual out twenty years ago and even though I was over fifty, I started trying to live by it again."

"Let me see if I can remember," John said. "A scout is thrifty, cheerful, reverent, kind, brave, loyal, friendly. I'm afraid I can't remember them all. I remember 'Do a good deed daily,' but I can't say I ever seriously tried it. I got lost on my five mile hike, and never even made second class.

"Oh no. Well, John, you can still be a good scout. It's not to late."

"You're absolutely right. I'll seriously try to do a good deed daily."

"This is my stop. Good luck finding your friends, John."

"Thank you, Mr. Johnson. I'll need it. Good-bye."

John thought, so he wasn't such a good Boy Scout. He was going in after Crystal, bad guys or not. He seemed to find a measure of inner peace. Everything was just perfect. He had almost the perfect amount of money. He had gotten the ticket he needed due to a friend's love and generosity. Now here was another perfect stranger helping him. There is a flow here, John thought, and whatever my fate, I must follow it.

DARK NIGHT

John was soon in Jackson. He bungied his small bag to the rack, put on the day pack, got on his bike and headed down old Highway 125 towards the border for the plant. When he was out of town less than a mile, the ped ended and he had to take the open road in the hot sun. He heard something behind him, and turned around to see a State Trooper had come up right behind him. His car was so quiet that John hadn't heard him, and it startled the hell out of John. The trooper was passing him slowly, giving him the once-over. John smiled and waved at him, and he sped up and went on down the road towards the plant. He had been sure he was about to get stopped.

Whew! John wondered if the Greenpeacers had gotten caught. They are a dedicated and smart group. They've probably done a lot of reconnaissance. I had better worry about myself. I still don't have a map of the place.

Many of the houses along the road appeared to be deserted. When he got to a sign that warned that the road was closed in a mile and was a dead-end, John got off his bike and took it into the woods and underbrush. He headed towards the Plant area, and found the going tough. He had to carry his bike most of the way, and it took him what seemed like hours before he got to the cleared area along the fence line. The two gallons of water were really heavy. He cautiously approached the clearing, looking both ways. He thought he saw a police car in the distance in the direction of the road but by now he was almost a mile away, as he'd walked on an angle away from it.

John could see a very formidable eight foot high chain link fence with three strands of barbed wire on it. They probably kept it well maintained, he thought. All he could do was keep heading away from the road, staying in the woods. His only plan was to get in, get back to the road, and head on down it looking for the group. John had gone about two hundred yards when he saw a hole under the fence.

They didn't even repair the fence, John thought, or this is a new place. The hole looked old, and wasn't big enough for his bike, but he could get himself and his bags under it. John checked to see if the police could possibly see him and not seeing any, he stood up. He still couldn't see any cars or people.

John went back across the clearing to the woods and found a small downed tree about two inches in thickness. He went back to the fence and stuck it in the chain link about three feet high. Then he got his bike, and walked up the slanting little tree until he was up against the fence. He hoisted the bicycle up and though the space between the top of the fence and the first strand of barbed wire. When he got to the handlebars he wiggled them through, and then hung the bike over the other side of the fence by the handlebar. Then he jumped down and took the dead tree back to the other side of the clearing into the woods. He crawled back through the hole, then took his bike off of the fence.

He was quite proud of himself for overcoming that barrier. He sat down on the forest floor for a few moments. He had overcome a long list of obstacles to get here, and now here he was, sitting inside the Savannah River Plant Rad-waste Area. Awesome, he thought. This could very well be a hole used by the bad guys. There did seem to be a faint trail leading in. John took out his pocket knife. It only had a four inch blade. He sure couldn't see himself tackling those men with this, and the idea of sticking it into someone disgusted him. Perhaps he could protect Crystal nonviolently somehow. This is a good time for a prayer, John thought. He got to his knees, and prayed out loud.

"God. I don't want to hurt anyone. I just want to protect Crystal and her friends. They are so good and idealistic for doing what they are doing in the face of such dangers. Please help me to help them. Please help me save Crystal or anyone else from any harm. I pray that I don't have to hurt anyone to do it but I must use whatever force is necessary to help them. Give me the strength and courage to help them. The best thing is if you could just keep the men away from them somehow. Keep them far away, on the other side of the area.

I ask humbly in the name of Jesus and in the name of the Mother Earth, who the Greenpeacers are here to help. Amen."

John put his bike on his shoulder and started walking at a slant towards the road. It was hard and awkward. He took the bag off of the rack and used his belt to attach it to his waist and started off again. The going was even more difficult inside the plant area. He had to climb over downed trees every few yards, as the forest floor was littered with them. His PC said it took him almost two hours to get to the road. It was still so full of downed trees that he could only ride a few dozen yards before having to get off and carry the bike over the next impediment. He was really wearing out and it was starting to get dark. The Sun had set behind the trees.

John was hungry and running out of energy so he decided to stop, eat, and rest. He went back over to the woods until he felt he was protected from detection from above and settled down to make some sandwiches. The mosquitoes were starting to come out, and John was very glad he'd brought the insect repellent. John ate his sandwiches and some of his fruit. He was already down to about three or less quarts of water in one of the gallons, and he knew that in a few days he'd be drinking radioactive water if he didn't find the group. But there was no way he could have carried two weeks of water. He wondered how the group were going to keep supplied. Trust the flow, he thought.

He gathered together a lot of pine straw and made himself a nice bed. I'll probably get a million ticks and chiggers he thought, and sure enough, he pulled a tick off his leg a moment later. The insect repellent didn't seem to stop it but it helped a lot with the mosquitoes. John wished he could start a fire, but it probably wouldn't be wise nor did he think to bring any matches. He heard something rustling the underbrush, and felt the hair stand up on the back of his neck. His body tensed up. In a couple of moments he could see it was a large skunk heading his way. He stood up and the skunk stopped. John didn't know what to do but the skunk did. It turned around and took of in the opposite direction. Whew! John felt his heart racing, his body filled with adrenaline.

There didn't seem to be many birds in his area. Perhaps animals can somehow sense the danger of the place, he thought. John settled back down and thought about his whole adventure since he arrived in the future. What a trip it had been! Tomorrow he'd have been there only a week, but it seemed like ages. So much had happened.

He had learned so much. When it became dark, he put on a long sleeve-shirt and laid back on his bed.

As the last light faded from the woods and the crimson sky turned to black, John felt his mood make a parallel shift. Perhaps it was exhaustion. After such an incredible week, culminating with his cross country journey, he had every right to be burned out. Surely that was part of it, but it was the black of the woods that allowed every doubt and fear that John had pushed to the back of his consciousness to emerge and flood his mind. Fear could swiftly move into a panic if he didn't get it under control.

What in God's name was he doing in the deep woods of this long abandoned old radioactive relic of the nuclear arms race? Just how much radiation was there and was he risking his life and future health? How did he think he was going to protect Crystal from four armed and dangerous men with a pocket knife? He must be crazy to think that this would work. John remembered back to his childhood. He had never had a single fight or even struck anyone in anger, in his whole life.

His father had been very unhappy with him when his neighbor, who was a year or so younger, had given him a black eye and John didn't fight him. He knew that he deserved the black eye for verbally haranguing the kid with a lot of profanity all afternoon in front of his friends. The punch had sort of straightened him out. His dad thought that he should have fought the kid and though he didn't say it, implied to John that it was cowardly that he hadn't defended himself.

Then he remembered an even deeper trauma. One of the family dogs had puppies and then went out on the highway and got killed before it had even nursed them. Despite their best efforts, they couldn't keep the little puppies alive and one by one, they died. No matter how much they tried to feed them, it didn't seem to be enough, and they had sucked each other's feet raw. When there were only two left, his mother asked John to put them to sleep by asphyxiating them with the car exhaust. John was 11 or 12 years old and his dad was out of town for a while. He took the puppies' little box outside and put it under the car's exhaust with a blanket over it. He turned the motor on, and sat there listening to the puppies cry and whimper for what seemed like an eternity. It got to where he just couldn't take it any more.

John stopped the engine and removed the puppies. When he took them back inside, his mother was furious with him for not completing the job. She angrily scolded him and called him a coward. That had a powerful influence on him and his poem, *I Don't Want to Kill*, was one of the results. Unfortunately, the puppies did die shortly thereafter and he did believe, at the time, that he was a coward. If he were still a coward, maybe he'd just freeze up and be unable to save Crystal. John could think of nothing worse. And then he did.

Maybe I'm really dead, and this is HELL! Maybe having sex with Faith, and then...oh God, maybe I did commit suicide and I just don't remember it. That is a mortal sin!

Panic, fear and confusion engulfed him. Of course! This is an after death experience! That explains everything!

I blew it! Hell, he thought. Oh my God! I'm in hell so I can lose my love all over again? Why? I was a good person wasn't I?

John's breathing was very rapid. His heart had taken off, going a mile a minute. A deep cold terror chilled him from his toes to his crown. I am dead and this is hell! There was nowhere to run. He realized he had no escape. His heart was still there though, beating so fast he thought it would burst. My heart is still beating, so I am alive, he thought.

If I'm not dead, surely I'm going to die now. Or maybe I'll get killed trying to save Crystal. Total failure, and then total annihilation. John lay there for a few minutes, fully expecting his heart, which seemed to be beating faster than it was possible to maintain, to stop at any moment.

I'm alone and scared. That would be even worse. Being alone in the blackness, alone and filled with doubt and fear and guilt. Being alone and scared forever. At first, the ultimate in solipsistic paranoia filled his being. His panicked, speeding mind seemed to stop for a moment. His heart was going so fast that John was sure the next thought would cause it to burst. The next thought was monumental. I can never really be alone because God is always here! Wooh!

His heart was beating faster than it ever had. John sat up straight. Then in a flash, somehow, by some amazing mental leap, John realized that he would never be alone. I am one with it all, and it is all one, John thought. He saw through the great mystery, the great paradox. I am an individual, a mortal, and yet one with the whole of creation. I am one with God and eternal, all at the same time. No brilliant lights and colors flooded his consciousness. No bliss and ecstasy filled his being. Yet deep within, he felt peace. A quiet calm slowly began to grow.

I am a good man. I love God. I love our Mother Earth and I love life. I am not dead. I don't remember cutting myself because I didn't; I couldn't. I'm not crazy, either. Nobody goes crazy like this, with a coherent reality for almost a week. No. No, this is real, this is really happening. I really am in the year 2095. I don't know how, but I'm here. And I am in love. I haven't known Crystal long, but I know she is a good person and I love her deeply. I have seen the wonder of a world transformed, a world that works, that is getting better and healthier and more fertile by Man's efforts, not being destroyed by them. This isn't some dream or something. The world is at peace and the animals and the natural wonder is returning.

His heart rate having slowed considerably. John was starting to get a grip on his feelings. He got up and fumbled around in his pack for his flashlight. When he turned it on, sure enough, he was still in the same woods.

John sat with his back straight, consciously slowed his breathing, and started the Om shanti mantra in his mind. It was hard to stay focused on it, so he started chanting out loud. After twenty or thirty minutes he had regained his composure somewhat. Wow, he thought, what a bunch of negative thoughts. But strangely enough, followed by a deeper realization of the oneness of all life than I have ever had. Even more so than after the bliss experience. Perhaps that was what they call, "the dark night of the soul?" I am no coward; I'm here, aren't I? Somehow, I'll save Crystal, even if it kills me. I don't know what death is, but surely it isn't a hideous plot to break your heart and spirit? Maybe it is the end, but not some hell of fear and guilt and nothingness forever.

John decided to review the whole experience in his mind from the start to the end. Then he could perhaps regain the faith and confidence that had abandoned him so suddenly and completely just a few minutes before. That's a good idea, John thought. He laid back onto his pine straw bed and put his hands behind his head. Now let's see. Actually, it had all started with a dream. Yes, he thought, it had all started with that dream about Faith. John started reviewing the whole experience, beginning with waking up after dreaming of Faith last Saturday. He got to his date with Crystal and the ritual and he found himself smiling again. Soon he was asleep.

John awoke the next morning at first light. A few birds were singing. John got up, did his toilet and was disgusted he didn't bring any toilet paper. He couldn't wash his hands with his precious distilled water either. Leaves and his pants leg acted as TP and a hand towel. He started scratching and found what must have been fifty chigger bites under his arms and around his pants line and crotch. He ate all his grapes and headed off. This was his chance to catch up, by making this early start.

For a while it was ride, then get off and climb over old dead trees. Then he broke through to where there were no longer felled trees but only the occasional tree that had fallen in the road due to natural causes. He came upon one tree trunk that was about ten inches high and lying flat on the road. John saw what looked to be fresh sprocket marks on it in two places. Like someone had ridden a bike over it, but the larger front sprocket had dug in as it climbed over the log.

Aha, John thought. It was the first sign he had of them. It made his heart leap. He noticed a few little branches that seemed freshly broken as well. As John hadn't seen any signs up to this point, he decided to spend a few minutes seeing if he could find where they had emerged from the woods. About fifty yards back he found a few more broken limbs on trees by the edge of the road. There were trees right up to the road's edge as no one had cut the sides of the road for many years. He followed the trail back into the woods a few dozen yards and could confirm that there was a trail leading into the deep woods on the opposite side of the road from the way he'd taken.

If they came this far through the woods, then they must have taken longer than me, he thought. Not necessarily, as they might have known an easier route to this place. He made himself two more sandwiches and ate an apple. He planned on saving the sunflower seeds till he was out of the more perishable bread and jelly. John got back on his bike and rode with renewed vigor. After a couple more hours he was really wearing out and knew he had to stop and rest and drink some more water. He was about to get off the bike when he heard a shot followed immediately by the sound of dogs barking.

Cold chills ran up his spine. This was it! he thought. Paralyzed by indecision and perhaps fear, he wondered if he should ride on down into whatever was happening or should he be more stealthy? He decided to be cautious and quickly hid his bike in the woods. He started running down the edge of the road, sometimes in the woods and sometimes on the road. He still didn't see anything down the road which curved off to the right.

He stopped to catch his breath after about two hundred yards, and when he did, he noticed that the barking sound that had been directly ahead of him was now more off towards the right. As a matter of fact, it seemed to be moving from front right toward more due right. John knew he had to head towards the barking. He started running through the woods as fast as he could, but he was already out of breath and getting very scratched up from the tree limbs. He tripped over a downed tree and fell to the ground, got back up and staggered off again toward the barking. He was really giving out. Then the barking became even more intense and seemed to stop moving.

Pushing his out-of-shape body to its maximum, John started walking, trying with each step to catch his breath. After a few seconds he started trotting again, gasping for air. The barking was quite close. Suddenly a very large and obese man in overalls came into view and then John saw the dogs. The man was with them at the base of a tree and he was putting one of the very excited animals on a rope. John kept on moving towards them, hiding behind trees as much as possible. In a few more steps, he could see up into the tree, and there was Crystal! She had managed to climb up the tree, but she was only about ten feet off the ground. John's emotions erupted. First, into intense gratitude for having actually found Crystal there OK. Then came an amazing fury at the dogs and man, and lastly the stark fear for Crystal's life and his own safety. What if the dogs got wind of him?

This was a very large man. Well over six feet tall and, though somewhat fat, a giant of probably over three hundred pounds. John was behind a thick tree not more than thirty feet from the scene now. What should I do? I am five feet ten and a half and one fifty-five, I can't take on that guy, John thought. And besides, he's got a damn shotgun!

The man was tying up the other dog. Then he was trying to lead them both away, though they were still lunging at the tree. He pulled them a few yards away to another tree and tied them to it. They were all enthralled with Crystal and hadn't noticed him yet. The giant looked incredibly huge when he stood between John and the tree. John's heart was racing, his mind running out of control.

"You can come on down now. They're tied up and won't hurt you. It won't be so bad. You might like it," the obese man offered.

Crystal didn't move. She then shifted her head out from behind the tree, and John suffered a pang when he saw her tears and blood-stained face. "No way I'm coming down."

"You better come down, or I'll shoot you down."

"You can shoot me but I'm not coming down."

He lifted his gun. It appeared to be a pump shotgun.

"I said come on down now. I can cut that tree right off below you and cut you down. If you don't want to get shot or hurt, you better come on down," he ordered.

John was frantic! He knew that the decision of when to act was being taken out of his hands. He had to do something quick. He looked around and didn't see anything big enough to knock the huge man out. He saw a rock about the size of a tennis ball on the ground at his feet. In an instant, a plan came to him. He remembered the story of David and Goliath. He quickly took one of his sports shoes off and removed his sock, then put the shoe back on. Thank God for the speed of Velcro. He put the rock in the sock. He heard a shot. The giant had shot the tree a foot below Crystal. John stepped out from behind the tree and walked swiftly and deliberately towards the man. He shot again, and it seemed to weaken the tree. Crystal saw John and her expression turned to total amazement. The giant saw that and was wheeling around just as John got up to him.

WHACK!

John had struck the man as hard as he could with the rock in the sock, right at the left temple. He fell over like a falling tree. John stood there for a moment, surprised that the giant had actually gone down. He wasn't moving. Then he looked up at Crystal, her mouth hung open with amazement. The dogs strained at their ropes. John picked up the shotgun and removed the man's hand from it. He worked the pump action and found it empty. No custom hand grip that he could see, though. He pulled the trigger and it clicked. He put the gun against the tree, looked up at Crystal and smiled a strained smile, while still gasping for breath.

"Come on down, Crystal. It's OK."

"What are you doing here? How did you find me? Ouch! I hurt my ankle. I think I sprained it."

Crystal was moving down the tree towards John's waiting arms.

"I know," John said.

"You know! What's going on? Oh, John!" She had gotten far enough down that John could take her in his arms and lower her to the ground. She turned around, favoring the hurt leg, and hugged John so tight. He returned the embrace with the greatest sincerity and feeling of his life. Crystal was crying. John was rocking and comforting her. "There now, it's OK."

They embraced for about a minute as Crystal became more

composed. She then looked him in the face and said, "God, John. You saved me."

"That is why I'm here, Crystal," John's eyes filled with tears, but there was a smile on his face. "To save you, and praise God I did. Are you hurt? You're bleeding!"

"It's just a scratch." They embraced again for a moment then Crystal pulled back and said, "The others…"

"What happened with them?" John asked.

"We were ambushed by these guys, just when we were in sight of some building at the plant. They all had guns. They made us get off our bikes and lined us up. This monster seemed to be in charge, and when he got to me he said, 'What have we got here, and ripped my shirt open. Stuart was next to me and he grabbed the man. While he was struggling with him over the shotgun, I turned and ran like hell. I heard a shot," Crystal's eyes flooded with tears again, "but I didn't look back. God, John, I'm scared Stuart might have been shot. I think a moment after that they let the dogs loose and they started after me. I ran for about two or three minutes and sprained my ankle. Then I had to climb this tree and just managed to get up it before the dogs got here. They had me treed for a few minutes, then he showed up."

"So everyone else has been captured?"

"Yes."

John picked the shotgun up and told Crystal to put her arm around his shoulder. "We need to tie this guy up and see if he's got any more shotgun shells."

They walked cautiously over to the man. His eyes were slightly open, and so was his mouth. There was a bruise on his temple and a little blood coming out of his left eye.

"Oh God! I might have killed him. Oh God."

John knelt down next to the man and put his hand on his throat. The dogs fiercely strained at the ropes and John was very concerned about them. He pointed the empty shotgun at them with no effect. "I don't feel a pulse, Crystal." John put his hand in the man's right front pocket and sure enough, there were several shells in it. He quickly took them out and loaded the shotgun, then put a shell in the chamber. "Let's get out of here before I have to shoot a dog."

They started off in the general direction of the group.

"What are you doing here, and how did you find me?" Crystal asked him.

"I had a dream the morning you left that you were being chased

244

by some dogs and were scared and in danger. I saw you sprain your ankle and crawl to the tree. It freaked me out but you had already gone. When I went to your house, I found the article about these guys, and saw that they had dogs. Shashir gave me his ticket to Kansas, and I spent all my money getting here. April in Atlanta told me you still trusted me but couldn't call. But when I told her my story, she did tell me y'all were on mountain bikes and did kind of confirm that y'all were heading in here. I went to Augusta and bought a bike and some supplies with the last of my money. Someone had to loan me the money to get from Augusta to Jackson. Then I just came on in here looking for you."

"Incredible." Crystal stopped walking and turned to John "I'm totally amazed by you, John. I thank the Goddess for you and I love you. Thank you." She hugged him again, and they shared a nice, but short kiss.

"You're very welcome, my Love. I guess you've probably figured out that I really love you."

They both managed a little smile.

"I do get that impression." They turned and continued to walk towards the road. "We need to be very careful now. We're getting close." Their pace slowed and they hunched over a little. "God, John. I don't see them, but what's that in the road? Oh, no!"

Crystal pulled away from John and ran with a limp towards the person lying in the road. John was taken by surprise, and certainly didn't want to run out in the road without a little reconnaissance. But he had no choice now, so he put the shotgun to his side and followed her, looking and pointing in all directions. John didn't see anyone.

"It's Stuart!"

John arrived at Crystal's side as she turned Stuart over, tears streaming down her face again. He had blood coming from his left ear. John knelt down, took Stuart's hand, and felt for his pulse. It took a couple of seconds for him to find it. It was weak, but he was alive.

"I've got a pulse!" he exclaimed.

"Thank God! Thank God!" Crystal was wiping away the matted hair and blood. John took off his T-shirt and gave it to Crystal.

"Here. I don't see a bullet wound. Especially not by a shotgun." I think he was hit, look." John showed Crystal the butt of the shotgun. It had a small bloodstain. John tried to collect his thoughts.

"I wonder where they took everyone?" The group's bikes were still on the ground where they left them. "You stay here with Stuart. Let's move him into the woods. Come on. You get his feet."

They picked Stuart up and carried him about fifty feet into the woods on the other side of the road. "I guess I'm going to go and look for them. Stay right here if possible, so I'll know where you are." He bent down to kiss her. She had cleaned the blood away from Stuart's ear and John could see that it was bleeding both externally and internally.

Crystal looked up apprehensively. "What are you going to do?"

"I don't know, won't, until I find them. This shotgun works. We can't let them hurt anybody else."

"Be real careful. Oh, John." They kissed a sweet little kiss.

"I've got to stop this bleeding. He's lost a lot of blood." Crystal's attention returned to Stuart. John trotted off, shotgun in his right hand.

This is incredible! I feel like Rambo, with my shirt off and this gun. I can't believe this myself! Oh, man, it's not over yet, John thought. I've never even hit anyone and now I've probably killed a man. Well, I know now for sure that I am no coward. There just has to be something really worth fighting for, he thought as he trotted cautiously down the edge of the road.

Suddenly John saw them up ahead and ducked out of sight along the side of the road. He saw them before they had seen him. They were marching the Greenpeacers into a cluster of buildings. John headed for the back side of one of the buildings, placing it between him and the bad guys. They told everyone to lie down on the ground with their hands on the backs of their heads.

"Not you two women," one man said.

Uh oh, John thought.

"Leave the women alone!"one of the men exclaimed.

"Shut up before I blow your head off. Jerry, you take the first turn watching em. This time we're gonna have a while to enjoy ourselves. Ah reckon old Buck is having a good time with that young one, unless he had to shoot her. I hope not. I'd like a little of that for dessert."

This is good, John thought. Only one of them guarding the prisoners. That's a good opportunity. John realized he'd have to act quickly if he was going to save the women.

"Look, guys, we're gay. We're married. We're not going to be any fun," one of the women pleaded.

"Well, maybe that's because you never had a real man."

"Please. We have children."

"Children huh, which one of you got a dick? Get on in there. Now. I'm not fooling."

John worked himself around to the side of the house away from the talking, and peered around the corner. The guard was standing about fifteen feet away with the group lying on the ground between him and the other men. They were following the women inside the building across from John. He took a deep breath. Can I really do it? If he hesitated he might lose his chance for good. He tip-toed out to the fellow and put the shotgun against his back.

"Don't talk, Don't move or I'll blow you in half. Now, drop the rifle." The man hesitated for a minute, and then dropped his rifle on the ground. "Get on the ground just like them." The man got down on his knees, then on down and put his hands behind his head. The Greenpeacers closest to John had looked up. He put his finger to his lips. A couple of them got up and came to John. More of them looked up and were signaled to be quiet. One of them grabbed the rifle. They alerted the rest of the group. John told them in a quiet voice to watch the man. "Who wants to help save the women?" he asked. All of them raised their hands.

John told three of them to stay with the prisoner. The rest of them headed toward the building with John in the lead. They heard scuffling inside. John stationed himself along the front wall next to the door. The noise from inside got louder. Someone screamed. At least one of them was busy, John thought. He realized he might very well have to shoot. John swallowed hard. He jumped in front of the door in a crouch, with the shotgun pointing inside. To his amazement, he saw two partially nude women standing over two men, who were lying on the floor. One man was out cold and one was in an arm and wrist lock, down on his face. The woman who wasn't holding the other man down had a rifle. She pointed it at John and pulled at the trigger. Nothing happened, and in a second more Greenpeacers were in the door and she realized that John was not a bad guy.

"Wait! It's OK! he's on our side! We got the other one."

"Thank God this rifle didn't fire."

"What about Crystal?" asked the women holding the man down.

"She's all right. She's with Stuart down in the woods," said John.

"Who the heck are you?"

"I'm Crystal's friend, John, from the past."

Hero from the Past

"You're John? The guy who called April and Ed?"

"Yeah. Let's see if we can find some rope or something and get these guys tied up."

"Incredible! I'm Andrew. This is Fran and Shirley. Fran is a Tai Chi master, and Shirley is one of her best students. How'd you ladies get the best of them?"

"This one," Fran nodded to the man she was holding in a wrist lock, "took the rifle from his friend and I made my move. For that split second, when he was holding both rifles, he wasn't in a position to shoot. I caught him with a kick to the knee and he dropped them both."

"That's when I got the other one from behind by the leg and pulled him right down on his face. Luckily, he was knocked out cold. Then Fran and I got this one under control," said Shirley.

"Fantastic," said John. Somebody take this shotgun. Be careful, it will shoot for anyone. All these other ones look like they've got the key hand grips."

"Thank God, or I might have killed you," said Shirley, who was putting her shorts back on.

"I'll take it, John." Andrew took the shotgun. A moment later one of the group found an extension cord, and they started tying up the conscious man.

"I'm going back and let Crystal know that everything is OK. She's probably worried sick." John got a big grin on his face. "Pretty cool, ladies, everybody. I'll meet everyone later."

"Cool?" said Shirley, looking at Andrew.

John laughed as he turned and went outside. He saw two of the men were sitting on his captive. "All right! Crisis over. I'm going to Crystal."

"Is she all right?" said one of the fellows.

"Yeah, she's fine and Stuart's alive but hurt."

John hurried back up the road with a couple of the Greenpeacers following behind. John was elated. An incredible joy filled him and he ran as fast as he could. He was gasping when he got to Crystal. She was smiling to see him again. He knelt down next to her and after gasping for a few breaths said, "Everyone's all right. We got the other bad guys."

Crystal's small smile turned to unadulterated joy and she hugged John's neck and kissed him on the mouth. They were laughing when they separated but in a second they both turned their attention back to Stuart. He was still out though the bleeding has stopped.

"Stuart's our only casualty. God, Crystal. I'm going to have to go back and do something about those dogs and check on that man. Maybe he's still alive somehow."

The other two fellows arrived. "Crystal. How's Stuart?"

"He's hurt bad, Rex. I'm very worried about him. We have to get him to a hospital and get some x-rays of this concussion. Get Andrew, and let's see if we can call for a helicopter."

"God, Crystal. I don't know."

"We have to. Did you guys capture those men?"

"Yeah, Fran and Shirley got two of them. Your friend is really too much. You've got a lot of guts, John. I'm Rex Harold."

"A pleasure, Rex."

"I'm Chris. I'll go get Andrew." Chris ran off back towards the rest of the group.

"What happened, John?"

"We were lucky. Two of them were going to rape Fran and Shirley so they left one guy to guard the prisoners. They didn't know about me. When I put the shotgun in the guy's back, it didn't take him long to figure out what was going on. God, I'm glad I didn't have to shoot him."

"Fran and Shirley got the other guys," said Rex. "John here was going to save them, and jumped in the door with the gun. Shirley would have shot him if the rifle she aimed at him would have worked. Thank God these other guys had legal guns with key grips."

"Thank God! That's incredible! John, you're a hero."

"Not any more than Stuart, and he's the one that paid the price."

"I feel he'll be all right. It might take some time though," said Crystal.

Andrew and a few of the others had arrived, and Andrew concurred with Crystal that they had no choice but to call for an emergency air lift. Though that would totally blow their cover, it could mean life or death for Stuart. They also had to turn the prisoners over to the authorities.

"Maybe since we got these guys, they'll be a little lenient. John, where is the other one?" Andrew asked.

"Back there in the woods where the dogs treed Crystal. I think we'd better take the shotgun. I'm afraid that big one is dead. I hope not, but I don't know."

John found the thought of having killed someone quickly took the edge off his joy. Andrew called the local 911 operator, and they had quite a conversation. He had to hold while she called the other authorities. After about five minutes, she got back on line. Soon there would be a medical helicopter, and within the hour the police would be getting some army helicopters to come and pick everybody up.

By this time the rest of the group showed up with the three men. Their hands were tied behind their backs and Fran was leading them by a rope that tied all the men together around their necks. It looked kind of brutal but they couldn't escape without choking themselves. One of them was limping badly and one had a big knot on his forehead.

"That'll teach them to mess with a lesbian," said Fran with a big grin on her face. "I told them we were gay just to distract their puny little minds."

"We're the last women they'll mess with," said Shirley.

The bad guys looked shameful and kind of pitiful. They also had some signs of radiation poisoning, some open sores and hair loss. They all stood around in the middle of the road.

"Look, people, the police will be here shortly. It's not too late for some of us to bug out. Fran and Shirley, you have kids. You should take your bikes and gear and split now. We only need a few of us here to watch these guys. I'm staying," said Andrew.

"Me too," said Crystal."

"If you're staying, I'm staying," said John.

"Perhaps you don't know how serious a crime it is to enter one of these places. It's a minimum of two years confinement. That's not as bad as prison but it's serious. Rex, you go. All of you who have children should split. And anyone else who wants to."

Nobody was leaving. The group tightened around Andrew.

"We started this together, we will finish it together," said Fran.

"Yeah." Everyone was nodding and agreeing.

"Look, guys. We can't afford to bail everyone out. Please. You six with children, please go."

"These guys know we were here." Fran nodded in the direction of the prisoners.

'Yeah, but they won't say anything, will you?"

"Screw you. Where's Buck?"

"I think screwing anyone is out of the question for you guys," said Andrew. "Come on ladies. Rex. Larry. Frank. Jack, do it for your kids. We also need to get our radiation suits and Geiger counters out. They'll confiscate them when they arrest us. We need them for possible future missions. Do you think you can take all of them?"

"We'll get them out," said Rex. "But they will probably find out about us anyway."

"These guys aren't credible witnesses," Andrew replied.

Soon, Fran and Shirley and the four men were re-packing their bicycles. In a couple of minutes, they hugged everybody, and got on their bikes.

"Hit the woods at the first sound of a chopper. Stay out of sight for today." Andrew turned to John. "Last chance, John. Maybe you ought to hit it."

"No. I don't have children."

"OK, Brother. We'll get you bailed out somehow." Andrew hugged John, smiling. "Hey, you were really something. How'd you deal with the big one?"

"Like Goliath, a stone to the temple. Will you come with me to check on him and the dogs?"

"Sure, John. Do you think we need the shotgun?"

"Well, probably not. But let's take it to be on the safe side. The dogs are tied up. I don't know what we're going to do about them."

"Maybe we can get the police to take them to the Humane Society. They're probably pretty poisoned too," said Andrew.

John, Andrew, and a fellow named Britt, headed off into the woods. Andrew was curious as to just how and why John was there and John told him the gist of the story on the way.

"A dream. And it really was accurate. Wow! You've got a lot of guts and determination, John."

"Not guts. I was scared shitless. It was my love for Crystal."

"She is something, isn't she."

They were getting to where the dogs and the man were and what John saw filled him with pathos. The dogs had gotten loose. One of them was licking the man's face and one sat at his lifeless feet. Tears came to John's eyes. Dogs love even a sadistic rapist, John thought, but even those terms lost their meaning when confronted by another human being lying dead. When the dogs saw them they barked and retreated away growling. The three men got closer to the fallen giant. With ulcers on his ankles and most of his teeth missing, he looked so very pathetic.

John started to cry. His crying got louder and more emotion filled and he went to his knees, then sat on his haunches with his hands to his face and just bawled.

"I didn't want to kill him. I just wanted to save Crystal. I knew when I put the rock in the sock he might die."

"Hey, John. You did the right thing," said Andrew.

"I was so scared of him. I knew I couldn't fight him."

"There was no other way. He would have killed you, Man, and then raped Crystal."

"He really hurt Stuart," added Britt.

Andrew and Britt knelt beside John, each with an arm around him. He wept softly for a little while longer, then gaining his composure somewhat he said, "I guess there was no other way. Will you guys pray with me?"

The men got up on both knees and put their hands together. "God, we pray for the soul of this man, our brother still. We know You love all of us struggling souls. Please forgive me for not having the faith and strength to subdue him without killing him." John's voice broke slightly. "And thank you from the bottom of my heart for helping me to prevent him from adding another black mark on his soul." That thought comforted John greatly. "Thanks for saving Crystal." John was filled with an extraordinary mix of powerful emotions. Tears and a smile spread across his face as he said, "Thank you. Amen."

They all stood up and approached the man closer. The dogs made one growling lunge in their direction then backed away even farther. Britt checked for a pulse and then closed the man's eyes.

"He would have soon died a very painful death due to radiation poisoning," said Andrew.

They could hear a helicopter approaching.

"Those dogs are going to get hung up with those ropes dragging from around their necks. I wonder if they'll let me take them."

"If not you, Britt, nobody. Andrew turned to John and added, Britt is very good with animals. He's a vet."

"Good. Look, guys, I'm going back to Crystal."

John walked back towards the clearing, and Andrew soon joined him. The helicopter could be seen taking off through the trees. When John got back to the road, he was told that Crystal had gone with Stuart in the helicopter. His heart sunk but he knew it was best. She was a healer. Besides, he didn't want her to go to jail.

"They wouldn't have put us in the same cell with her anyway. It's not to late to change your mind and bug out, John."

"Crystal's not running from the law and neither am I.

"Are you like, no shit, from the past?"

"That's right. I'll have been here a week tomorrow."

Andrew was shaking his head. "Now that's a hard one. Maybe those Star Voyagers aren't crazy."

"I hardly believe it myself. But now I know why I came here, to save Crystal."

"Well, you sure as hell did," Andrew said with a smile, and then it was smiles and hugs all around.

"Stuart and I saved her together" John said as he hugged each in turn.

They all got to be pretty good friends by the time the helicopters arrived. John told them the whole story of his amazing trip. They told him of their plans to survey the spread of radiation at the Plant, retrieve a small amount of high level waste, dilute it into a large compost, and inoculate it with the culture of the rare, radiation transmuting organism. They would come back in a year to see if it was working. They were confident it would.

It took almost two hours before the helicopters carrying the state police and FBI finally arrived. It was no wonder they had never captured the men. John was told that most police were low budget due to the small amount of crime. Most didn't have their own helicopters.

The officers had mixed feelings about the whole thing. The state boys liked the Greenpeacers a lot. John claimed his membership. The Feds were a little more hostile. They were the ones who would have to arrest the Greenpeacers for entering a rad-waste area. They got the state police to bring out their bicycles and the dogs that Britt had managed to lead back out of the woods. Then they loaded them all into a helicopter and off they went. The guys explained to John how the criminal system of that time worked.

"All law enforcement officers wear video cameras that have to be on the whole time they are on duty, so everything they do is recorded."

"That's a great idea, but I suppose the police hate it," said John.

"Not really," answered Andrew, "because they still get to have a private life. The video recordings protect them as well as the suspects. It's actually a very prestigious job. You have to have a degree and special training and they make good money."

Andrew continued, "Only violent or repeat, non-violent felons are ever put in jail. If you didn't use violence, you pretty much only go to jail if you are terribly incorrigible and then not with the violent felons. Most are under house confinement and either have to report in front of a picture phone several times a day, or, if that doesn't work, wear an electronic ankle bracelet. Their wages are garnished until they pay off their victim totally so a big theft could mean a lifetime pay back as there is no bankruptcy protection for crime related debts. The criminals also pay for the administration of the program."

The police were incredulous of John's story of downing Buck Jakes, the 6 foot, 3 inch, 345 pound man who was after Crystal. They had wanted posters with the descriptions of the men. John was so glad that he didn't know just how big the guy really was. When he confronted him he appeared gigantic and that was the reason John had struck him as hard as he could. They hardly managed to get him in a body bag. A reward of twenty thousand credits just for information leading to their capture had been offered. At first some of the guys suggested that the authorities keep it but Andrew said "Not so fast. Greenpeace can use it."

They had decided the only thing they could do was tell to the truth, not answer any questions about anyone else being involved and make a plea for legal testing of their method to transmute radiation. They were taken to the federal building and brought to some showers so they could decontaminate themselves. Then they were given overalls to wear. After that, they were interrogated. They all stuck to their plan. No one said anything about the others or the equipment they carried out. About five hours into the interrogation, they got a phone call from the governor of South Carolina thanking them for the capture of the four men. He especially wanted to talk with John about his downing the giant.

John felt very uncomfortable, as he was prodded to brag about the whole thing. He told the governor that he felt grateful for saving Crystal and for bringing the criminals to justice, but he deeply regretted having to kill a man to do it. He said good-bye, then he handed the phone back to Andrew. After a couple of minutes of mostly listening, Andrew handed the phone to one of the FBI men who said, "Yes, Sir," several times before saying good-bye. The tone and deportment of the FBI interrogators improved greatly after that. After that call, they completed the rest of the interrogation in about a half hour.

Andrew reported that the Governor said he would pardon them of any state crimes and was working on getting them pardoned from all charges. They were just about to get to sleep in their cells when they learned they'd been bailed out on their own recognizance due to the Governor's influence. They discovered that they had many lawyers scrambling to represent them for nothing.

A little problem arose when the police couldn't find any record of John. He told them the straight truth and they were, of course, incredulous. After about a minute's pause, one of the lawyers made the case that they had to let him out, records or not, because he wasn't wanted for any other crimes.

When they got outside, they found that it was a media frenzy. They were the men of the hour! Bombarded with cameras and shouted questions, John felt overwhelmed. Andrew, media-wise guy he was, made a fantastic, impassioned plea for legal testing of the Greenpeace method for transmuting radiation. Then he gave John credit for the capture of the men. John really wasn't ready to talk about the whole thing. He whispered that to Andrew, who announced a press conference for 10:00 am the next morning. Then they left in an official vehicle provided by the Governor.

It was all quite exciting but John just wanted to find Crystal. They were told that Stuart had a serious concussion, and the doctors were contemplating surgery to lessen pressure on his brain. After several phone calls, Andrew finally got through to Crystal, who was still at the hospital. She had been given twenty-four hours in which to come down and be officially booked and bailed out. She told them that Stuart's condition hadn't changed. It was 2:00 am and everybody was very tired. John got them to bring him to the hospital and the rest of the crew went to a wealthy member's house there in Augusta.

When John got inside the hospital, he found Crystal in the

waiting room of the emergency wing. She smiled widely, grabbed John around the neck with both arms and hugged him tightly.

"I'm so glad you're here. And I mean that in every way possible. I feel so bad about flying off and leaving you there, especially after you said you'd stay because I was staying."

"I understand totally, Crystal. You did the right thing staying with Stuart. I love you."

John pulled his head back and looked into her blue-green eyes. "Isn't it all just amazing? I told you I've always been amazed that there is something instead of just nothingness, so why should we be amazed at anything? But I am."

"I am, too. How you ever found the courage to come after us is incredible to me. Why I had the wonderful karma to have you come from the past to save me, to have a person like you to fall in love with, I'll never know. I love you very much. You are a real knight in shining armor."

"No," said John, "I never want to fight another man again. And, God help me, I sure never want to kill a man again."

"Oh, John. I know how much it pains you that the man is dead. But you were so brave."

"It wasn't courage, Crystal. I was terrified. It was love for you. I pray that that act didn't mar my karma. I did it without thinking because I didn't have time to think. I did feel a lot of anger and a lot of fear. I just saw the rock, flashed on David and Goliath. I took my sock off, and after that I had to act instantly."

"You made nothing but good karma John, heroic good karma."

"I was not going to let him hurt you. I know I had God's help. I hope that doesn't sound too egotistical."

"No, John. It sounds honest. I agree."

"How is your ankle? I see they put a bandage on it."

"They said it was a mild sprain and I shouldn't have to use crutches, just stay off of it as much as possible. It doesn't hurt much."

They talked a while more about getting back to California and their Yosemite adventure. Crystal filled John in about how they were watching Stuart overnight to see if such intense surgery as opening his skull was going to be necessary. She said she thought she had given him as much as she could give, and came out to sleep some. After a while they fell asleep in each other's arms. John was in an exhausted bliss.

At first light, a reporter woke John and Crystal for an interview.

John asked them to please leave them alone. They'd be at the press conference at 10:00 am. The reporter asked him if it was true that he was from the past. John looked at Crystal. Two more news types arrived, one trailing a cameraman.

"I'm going to see if I can find out the prognosis on Stuart, John. I'll be back," Crystal said.

John sat up, rubbed the sleep out of his eyes, and found himself confronting four news people and a camera, with a bunch more reporters and more cameras and microphones on the way. It was looking like the story of his being from the past was overshadowing both the capture of the outlaws and their mission. That was what most of the questions were about, though some were about killing the giant. John sat there stunned for a few minutes not saying a thing. The crowd of reporters grew. They finally stopped shouting questions as he refused to say a word.

"There will be a press conference at ten. I am not answering any questions until then. I'm sorry y'all wasted a trip down here but get the hell out of here, OK? This is a hospital and we have a very sick friend in there who is the real hero of this situation. That's it. Now, please, go!"

They bombarded him again with questions for about three more minutes while John sat silently. Finally, a hospital security guard got them all to leave. He came back, shook hands with John and told him how much he admired him. It was great, but a bit overwhelming to John.

Crystal returned and said that they thought Stuart was out of any danger and they were not planning to operate though he was still unconscious. She said that they were going to let her work on him for a while, so John said he'd just stay and meditate. It started out very poorly as his mind was racing a mile a minute as to what he'd say at 10:00. He stuck with it and after about twenty minutes it got better. He started calming down. Crystal came back about fifteen minutes later.

"Stuart is safe. We can leave."

"I've been stalling the reporters by saying we have a press conference at ten. I have no idea how to handle this, the whole coming from the past thing."

"Just tell them the truth. What else can you do?"

"Head for the hills." John suggested with a smile. "God Crystal, I just want to be with you."

"I promise, we'll stay together."

"I'm going to call and talk to Andrew about this press conference."

John called Andrew and awakened him. He suggested that Crystal and John come on over so they could eat some breakfast and meet beforehand. He was both happy and relieved to hear about Stuart. John and Crystal headed out for the meeting. This was one time John wished he had a car as they had to transfer twice to get there. It still only took about forty minutes. The few blocks' walk at both ends in the early morning beauty, with the birds singing and the morning light at sunrise, were quite lovely.

When they got to the house, everybody was just rising and getting themselves going. Crystal and John took showers and they were given clean clothing by the hosts. As Stuart seemed out of the woods, the whole group was filled with a sense of jubilation. They had hoped that their capture of the men would soften their treatment for entering the rad-waste area, but they didn't expect the Governor to get them out. Nor did they expect to have lawyers calling constantly, volunteering to take their case. The phone never stopped ringing. Their own lawyer was arriving at 8:30, so they waited until then to start the meeting.

They enjoyed a great breakfast of fresh fruit and pecan waffles. The lawyer arrived and they got down to business.

"John, this is our lawyer, Emerson Pierce," said Andrew.

"Pleased to meet you, Emerson."

"So you're the guy from the past. Can you prove it?"

Emerson was a big man with reddish hair and a mustache, and he was looking at John somewhat skeptically through his glasses.

"Probably not. I don't blame you for not believing."

"Oh, it's not that. This thing about you is a two-edged sword. On the one hand, the media is going nuts, and we'll get even more coverage than we would have normally. On the other, it detracts from the points we are trying to make, and if you're shown to be a liar, it will reflect badly on the whole group and mission."

"I was sort of afraid of that myself. Not to mention that my first inclination when a bunch of reporters started shouting questions at me about being from the past and slaying the giant was to head for the woods."

Just then they were told that media people were already hanging out outside.

"I'm sure that ultimately I can prove it because it's true. There must be records. I have some ID."

"If it weren't for John, we wouldn't be here. We'd be in the woods with the women at the least raped," said Andrew.

"Be that as it may, it's going to be a major distraction to the main point, which is the need for legal testing and a way to end this long-lived nuclear terrorism perpetrated on the world's people and animals. No offense, John. You are a hero and deserve the status," said Emerson. "But…"

"Hey, no offense taken. Frankly, I have no desire to get in that media spotlight."

"I'm thinking that maybe John should get lost for a while. Then we could have our cake and eat it too. We have that tantalizing story to excite the media to a frenzy, and we'd have time to present our case clearly without the distraction of getting into John's story. Whenever John surfaces, maybe in a few days, he'll get more attention than he will probably be able to stand," said Emerson.

John looked at Emerson again for a long moment, trying to figure out if he had believed him or not.

"That sounds great to me, except for one thing. I really want to be with Crystal."

"What do you think, Crystal?" asked Andrew.

"I want to be with John." Crystal looked at John with a lot of love. "I'll do whatever is best."

A reporter was bold enough to ring the doorbell, and the host had to run him and the others off the property and back to the street.

"Maybe John and I should go away for a while. I know we'd both rather and it seems it might help the mission," Crystal offered.

"There's already a lot of popular support for our position on trying to solve the long term radiation problem. This thing with this great, heroic, made-for-the-media story, might just help us put it over the top. I've already talked with the Governor's office and they said their senators are ready to reintroduce a bill authorizing sanctioned, legal testing of our method. It would be better if John were a part of the group but I guess we can't have it both ways."

"I am a member of Greenpeace," said John, handing his old membership card to Emerson.

"Wow! Too much! Greenpeacer from past saves mission. This is going to really be big. John, you better get a lawyer and an agent and I'd love to work with you."

It was decided that John and Crystal would split for a few days. Chuck, the host, let them have the use of a cabin in North Carolina close to the Joyce Kilmer Forest. John and Crystal were elated. He was actually "heading for the hills," and everyone thought it was best. Chuck had a car at the north parking building and gave Crystal the keys. Luckily she knew how to drive, since John didn't have a current license. They decided to distract the media with a large group exit out the front while John and Crystal slipped out the back.

They went back by the hospital so that Crystal could give Stuart one more treatment. He seemed better, though not conscious yet. They were hoping to get Fran, who had her own form of energy healing from her Tai Chi and Chi Kung training, to continue to work on him.

Then they went by the Federal Courthouse so Crystal could get booked and released on her own recognizance. Crystal was in and out in ten minutes. They were both treated very nicely by everyone. The people of South Carolina had received a disproportionate share of the nuclear problem and they appreciated anyone who tried to remedy it. The Federal authorities were beginning to think that their charges would eventually all be dropped.

Then they took a subus to the huge, eight-story parking garage where Chuck kept his car. He had a ground floor, enclosed garage space that even had a private bathroom. They got the car, a beautiful red convertible with the top already down, and were soon off for the mountains.

HEAVEN

John was ecstatic. Here he was, heading out into the North Georgia countryside with his dear, sweet Crystal. It was a beautiful summer day. Chuck's electric car was very fine. No one would be told where to find them until they were ready. It was beyond a dream come true. John never imagined or even dared to dream so many incredible yet wonderful things could happen to him or the Earth and humanity.

"This car is really great. It's so quiet and yet still quick to accelerate. It was really super of Chuck to loan it to us," said John.

"Yes. This is about the finest car made. Chuck is very well-to-do for someone of his age. He's a great investment broker, and he made his money by investing in companies that were the most democratic and forward thinking. He's working with Greenpeace to put together a non-profit corporation to develop the radiation transmuting organism and then manage the cleanup. The Com-Union will be involved. It will be much cheaper than the figures the anti-cleanup people have put out."

"Having a car in this time is a lot like people having a boat in my time. Chuck's garage is like a boathouse. It seems most everyone out here in the countryside has a garden," said John.

"Yes. Food does cost more today, but people can make a living with a small plot of land if they work it right. I get some of my produce from a man who makes a living with a few shovels, rakes and hoes. Most food is grown locally, and not shipped everywhere from just a few states like in your time."

"I met a farmer in the Midwest, Cynthia's father, who was worried that his son wouldn't be able to take over his farm. He thought his son was a good enough farmer and would probably have the money together what with his Inheritance Share, but he wasn't sure. I guess if you get really rich, like Chuck, your son would never be able to afford your business."

"Not necessarily. If you really learned the trade from your dad and seemed to have the ability, you might get the financial backing necessary to take it over. It does happen. Chuck bought that huge old home because it used to belong to his grandfather. It made his father very happy and he shares it generously, using it for many civic functions. He had to buy a large array of solar voltaic collectors because it uses more energy than a one-family home is allotted."

"If all electricity is produced sustainably, why can't people have as much power as they want? Why is it limited?" asked John.

"Because all power production, even the most ecological, has some environmental costs," Crystal replied.

"I heard that windmills kill bats and birds," John responded.

"Yes, and all power production requires land that some species uses. Chuck got together with some friends and they pooled their inheritance shares and started a very successful investment business without compromising their ideals to do it. He is quite a guy."

"I guess that is the strength of the Inheritance Share system," said John. "It makes people earn power and position by demonstrating their ability to handle it, instead of just being someone's kid. You know, back in my time there was a collapse of the whole left wing of the political spectrum. Communism had fallen all over the world and the right wing was winning the elections here in America. It seemed that everyone had learned that the free enterprise system was by far the best and most productive. Here in America, it was obvious that welfare didn't work. Giving people money just didn't work to really improve their lives. I always thought that the government ought to give needy people training and a job. People didn't want to pay taxes that were just given to people who didn't work. Yet the same folks who were so down on giving someone a few hundred dollars a month in welfare, turned around and gave or left their own children fortunes."

"Nepotism has been a very hard thing to rise above. We see putting an end to vast inherited wealth and power as the culmination of a long evolution from a ruling class to real democracy and egalitarianism. I can't knock getting something for nothing as I am grateful for my share of our inheritance."

"Well, that seems fair," said John. "Everything has to be passed on to the next generation eventually. I always thought it wrong that someone like Ishmael, the kid I adopted through Big Brothers, was born on this earth and owned nothing. Didn't even have a place that he could be without paying someone. So many people were born into poverty back in my time. Though many still managed to make a success out of their lives even against those odds, most didn't; and many ended up involved with crime. Everyone who wants to can go to college now, and most people own their own homes. I think your system is a huge improvement."

"I am not one to comment as I never finished college," added Crystal, "but nowadays most kids get great educations because everyone knows that they will be able to afford to attend college."

"Has corruption in government been eliminated?" asked John.

"Pretty much. Back in your time, most everyone would fudge, under-report or otherwise cheat on their income taxes, yet they expected the government to be honest. Accounts and the consumption tax eliminated that. Corruption in government was eliminated partly by the transparency of the credit system, partly by getting so much money out of the elections and partly by people really getting involved, studying the issues and the candidates and voting intelligently. This system, with everyone using accounts instead of money, would be terrible if the government were corrupt. In the beginning, there were some problems with that. The attempt by the Bell administration to pressure people with threats to cut off their accounts led to the rebellion that got everyone voting. We have over ninety percent voting nowadays. The same collective sense of responsibility could probably succeed in getting us to an even higher level of social evolution, like the Com-Union advocates. But even the Com-Union people use their Inheritance Share and the credit exchange to buy houses and a array of the new high efficiency solar voltaic systems before they take off their account bracelets."

"That makes a lot of sense. Maybe they're not totally crazy," said John, smiling. "Back in my time, computer hackers could break in to any system and mess with it. Isn't there a lot of computer crime with this system and maybe voter fraud as well?"

"No, because we have super encryption now so unauthorized people can't gain access to anything they shouldn't be in. We have very good safeguards to protect accounts and peoples' privacy."

"I need to call Shashir and Cynthia. I told them I'd check in this morning."

John put on his ear piece, got his PC to call their number, and soon had Cynthia on the line.

"You guys are famous. We heard all about you capturing the criminals. They are saying you are supposed to be from the past and everything. You really saved her, John! I'm so proud of you. Here is Shashir."

"Hello, Brother."

"Hi, Shashir. Your sacrificial gift was essential and successful, my friend. I just got there in time. I mean almost to the second."

"I am so very glad. You are a hero, John. We saw the news conference live. They said that you were the main person responsible for the men's capture, along with Crystal's friend Stuart and two women who were not available. Everyone wanted to know where you were."

"I'm on my way to the mountains with Crystal. Can you believe it?"

"That is most wonderful. You have the fabulous time you deserve. And John, I will pray for the soul of the man whom you had to kill."

"That's very kind, Shashir. I have, too. You know I'm in heaven, my brother. When we get some long range plans worked out we'll let you know. Maybe we can visit on our way back West."

"That would be very nice, John. Give our love to Crystal."

"I sure will. And you give my love to the whole family there. They're great folks, huh?"

"Oh, yes. We are having a very good time."

"Good-bye for now, Shashir."

"Good-bye, John."

"Shashir and Cynthia send their love, Crystal. It was really something for him to give up his ticket and his ride to Kansas with Cynthia just because of a dream I had. Thank God he did!"

"He is incredibly loving and kind. Let's do go visit on our way home."

"Crystal, do you think we could go by Ball Ground so I can pay my respects to my folks? I know the church cemetery they had a plot in. We had to go to Gainesville to get to a Catholic church so they are supposed to be in the one by the little Baptist church where I used to go to Vacation Bible School with my friends. They wanted to be buried close to where they had lived. I guess it's the right thing to do, even though they've probably been gone a real long time."

"Sure, John. That's a very nice thought. We'll get some flowers. You went to Vacation Bible School?"

"Yeah. My folks were glad to get rid if me and I had several friends who went to the church, which was right down the road. I got saved every year. Being a Catholic, too, I really had my bases covered."

John and Crystal had a good time that day. They were really enjoying each other's company. Crystal told John much about her life and youth and John did the same with her. It seemed so natural and perfect for them to be together.

"Crystal, can someone be a Star Voyager if they haven't had any dreams about any other planets or anything?"

"Sure, sweetheart. Anyone can be a Star Voyager. All it takes is the interest. There really aren't that many of us who seem to be in touch with other worlds, considering the number of people on the planet. "

"Tell me more about what y'all have learned about these other planets." Being back down South seemed to bring the southern out of John's accent.

"Well, most of the beings we're in touch with stand erect and even have some sort of opposing thumb. That does seem to be universal. The idea of our being created in God's image is right, in that this form is widespread all over the galaxy. There are many variations on the humanoid form, but there are other more unusual races as well. Some beings have energy forms beyond physicality, according to some Star Voyagers reports. Some beings have obtained great consciousness without having humanoid forms.

"One race of beings looks very much like the ideal of angels, with beautiful wings and lovely human forms. They are a very advanced, very pure race, with great powers and great love. They are thought to live on planets near the center of the galaxy, though no one knows for sure if the planets are spiritual or physical. They help beings all over the Milky Way. The angels don't interrelate much with the beings on the more advanced worlds, as they are usually busy helping souls on worlds that are still cut off by negative density fields. Angels seem to be able to go anywhere. Not even anyone in the Star Voyagers knows how they come into being, as they are thought to be sexless, or even how they manage to be able to travel to other worlds. It is thought that they are here to help souls evolve, perhaps to help keep the karmic scales balanced somehow. We believe that their main method of operation is to amplify a soul's faith."

"Then they are the instruments of God's grace because our faith is God's grace," said John with a big smile of elation.

"Yes, John, that is a very fine point."

"So, Crystal, how many angels can dance on that point?"

"A little philosophical humor," Crystal said with a wide smile.

"Very little, I'm afraid," said John, chuckling.

"You know John, one theory about where angels come from is that when two people love service to others more than anything else, to where it is their greatest joy, and their love for each other is very great, their souls are bound together in some way and form an angel."

"What a lovely thought.."

"It is, isn't it," replied Crystal. After a short pause she continued.

"Many of the other races have great powers but none is using this greater power to oppress any of the others. The density of negativity keeps un-evolved beings from even tuning into other worlds. Some of the more advanced beings have no trouble tuning in to less evolved species like us, even through the negative density fields. Many of these beings spend time assisting the evolution of the struggling souls and races on other worlds, using dreams or mental projections. Many of them just have wonderful lives filled with love, art, adventure, and travel. Some can live for a very long time."

"That is wonderful, Crystal. It sounds heavenly. Literally. I wonder if I'll ever be able to tune in to other worlds."

"I'm sure you will, my love, if you want to."

The bucket seats in Chuck's car kept them somewhat apart physically. The first time they stopped to answer the call of nature, John finished first, so he leaned up against the car and waited for Crystal to return. When she got back, he took her in his arms and kissed her lovely mouth.

John's passion rose quickly, and again he entered her mouth with his tongue and found Crystal enthusiastically joining in a sweet and wonderful, warm and moist dance of ecstasy. The kiss lasted for many minutes, and the hug that followed was long and sensuous. John was weak-kneed again, and it was good he only had to turn around and get in the car.

In a while they stopped at a station where they could charge their car's batteries. Some major improvements in battery technology had occurred since John's time. Batteries could power even a large car like Chuck's about 250 miles. Recharging them only took twenty minutes. The car was big but seemed to be light weight and only went to a 100 kilometers on the speedometer. Again they shared a long and sexy kiss before leaving. John was very aroused and he thought that Crystal just had to be as well.

It took them until 3:00 pm to get to the little church cemetery where John's parents were. They had stopped in town and picked up a bouquet of flowers. Sure enough, John found his parents' graves. It was very strange as the tombstones were so old, they looked almost as old as his grandparents'. John had been an only child so there were no other children or descendants buried with them. Crystal and John knelt by the grave, and John could see by the dates that his father only lived eleven years after he left, and his mother eighteen. Both had died relatively young.

"My father smoked way too much. And they both ate a very unhealthy diet, way too many double cheeseburgers. They were both a good bit overweight. Do you know that when I left, one third of the population of America was obese?"

"Too much! A real epidemic of obesity," replied Crystal.

Sadness suddenly overtook John. A few tears fell from his eyes, as, still kneeling, he said a prayer for his parents' souls. He was sorry he wasn't there to help them when they needed it. He thought of how much it must have hurt them to lose their only son. But he felt no remorse about coming to the future, as it had been so important for so many people. It had perhaps even saved his own soul, as he was getting beaten down by the hardships and sadness of his times. Would he have killed himself if he'd have stayed? He could never know for sure, but in his heart he didn't believe he would have. John ended his silent prayer and looked over at Crystal, who was also kneeling and praying.

"Please know, dear Mother and Dad, that your hurt and sacrifice in losing your only son was far from in vain," prayed John. "And know that the character you helped me to develop was put to good use. Thank you both. I love you."

"Great Goddess," said Crystal, "thank you for giving these souls life. Thank you, Mr. and Mrs. Berry, so much for the gift of your son, John. I know that you have found peace. I so wish that you could know what great good came from the disappearance of your son, and what a hero, and wonderful soul he is. May the blessings of the great Goddess be upon you as you make your journey home to the One." Crystal opened her eyes and looked at John. "Perhaps they will receive some great good in their next incarnations to balance out their loss of you."

They both got up and slowly walked away. When they got to

the edge of the cemetery, they kissed again. It was as if seeing his parents' graves had awakened some primal instinct to propagate his gene pool. He was very aroused, and he could tell Crystal was, too. He thought about just discussing it all with Crystal, asking her if she was ready to abandon celibacy. It sure seemed that way. He wanted so much to make love with her, to merge totally with her. He already felt one with her.

"Crystal," John asked after their third passionate kiss, "will you marry me?" John got down on his knees. Crystal seemed somewhat surprised. "Please, Crystal, marry me. Please, say yes. You know how much I love you. I think you love me, too."

"I do, John. Very much. Yes. YES!"

John got up, hugged her and swung her all around. "Let's do it today. Right now. I had some friends who went to a little town called Ringgold and got married in one day. It's not far from here. God, Crystal. I want you so very much. I love you so much. I want you to be my wife tonight, when we stay together for the first time."

"This is very sudden, John. But it feels right. I'm so aroused. I want you so very badly. It's like five years of suppressed sexuality has flooded into me. Ever since our full moon kiss, I haven't been able to get making love with you out of my mind. In the *Bhagavad Gita,* it says, 'When one lets one's mind dwell on objects of the senses, from thus comes attachment. From attachment springs desire. Desire fans to fierce passion. Passion breeds recklessness, and then the memory, all betrayed, lets noble purpose go and saps the mind, until purpose mind and man are all undone.' I know I had a good purpose for my celibacy, but now it doesn't seem nearly as important as my love for you."

"Gee, Crystal. When you put it that way, it seems like I'm sort of corrupting you. I don't really want to do that. I know I want you and love you, but I don't want you to give up any of your ideals for me."

"John, destiny this powerful can't be escaped. Feelings this strong cannot be denied, and they are not supposed to be. Just because we love each other and get married doesn't mean that we have to turn into sex maniacs. I believe I am destined to join with you and I very much want to, but we can do it in a way that keeps it holy and doesn't sap our energy."

"What do you mean?"

"Have you ever heard of sacred sex?"

"No, I don't think so."

"It is the practice of using the sexual energy to achieve higher states of consciousness instead of just having orgasms. You join in sexual union without ever releasing your semen. We would only do that if I was fertile and we wanted to have a child. No energy is lost; energy is only gained."

"That's the same thing as Tantra, right," John said.

"Yes, exactly."

John got thoughtful for a few moments. "I've got to tell you. I'm not sure I could do it." John was a little hesitant to share all his feelings with Crystal, but he knew he must if they were to have the kind of relationship that he wanted, one with total honesty and openness.

"The first time Faith and I made love, I had an orgasm within a few seconds. It was only the last time we were together that she even had an orgasm and we had to do it twice to achieve that. That is one of the reasons I felt so bad about the whole thing. She died," John was getting a little emotional, "and she didn't even get to enjoy it all that much. It was almost like all she got was the guilt."

Crystal put her arms around John and rocked him gently. She spoke very softly in his ear. "I'm sure that Faith enjoyed making love with you very much even if she didn't have an orgasm every time. We women can enjoy the love and sharing part greatly. You were young and inexperienced, John. You can't judge your ability as a lover from your first few experiences. You were dealing with all that youthful pent-up sexual energy. Don't worry a bit about you and me. I don't expect you to be perfect. It's going to take a lot of practice for us to be able to have a righteous sacred sexual ceremony. All I would like is a commitment to the general idea of keeping our sex sacred."

"You have that, Crystal. That sounds absolutely wonderful. Perfect." John separated enough so that he could look in Crystal's eyes. "We'll get it down if we have to practice night and day." They were both laughing and joyous.

It was a celebration driving up to Ringgold. They found when they got there that their celebrity had preceded them. The folks at the little wedding chapel figured out who they were and got tremendously excited. Even though it was late on a Saturday, the fellow at court records issued them a license. They really got off on John's old ID and said it would be the first wedding ever of a 125 year old, though they did have a 108 year old man just last year. A local florist provided flowers for Crystal to carry and put in her hair. The mayor of Ringgold was called and he and his wife came over to be the witnesses. They took a lot of pictures of the wedding with all of them together and promised to send copies to Crystal's house.

"It's our house now, John," said Crystal to John with a sweet smile on her face. John was beyond proud and happy.

The mayor insisted on taking them all out for a wedding dinner at the best restaurant in town. They had a great, festive dinner with champagne and many toasts. The people at the restaurant made a wedding cake out of two cakes they had on hand and everybody in the place celebrated with them. They just managed to leave before several reporters arrived. The reporters were going to chase them but the mayor got behind their cars and wouldn't let them out.

John called the folks at Chuck's house and he told them that everything was going fantastically. He learned that Stuart was conscious but experiencing some short-term memory problems. He couldn't remember the last few days. A national network had done a call-in poll and an overwhelming majority of the electorate wanted testing of the transmutation method. Almost as many were willing to pay for the clean up of all radioactive sites. It seemed that the Greenpeacers, too, had succeeded beyond their wildest expectations. With sanctioned testing, the results would come quickly and couldn't be refuted.

Emerson told John that offers for exclusive interviews with him were now in the six figure range. He might even be able to get him half a million. He was overwhelmed. They amazed and delighted the Greenpeacers with the news of their marriage.

Just enough light lingered to make the very scenic drive up to the cabin. They passed through the beautiful Ocoee River gorge and a lot of great North Carolina scenery. When they got to the cabin, they discovered fantastic views from the deck that held a large hot tub with a water massager. That sounded wonderful to both of them and they soon were naked and in the tub. John was thrilled seeing the beauty of Crystal's nude body. She wasn't voluptuous, more athletic and trim, her breasts not large but not small. She had a very trim waist, powerful thighs, and a very strong, tight behind. He needn't be ashamed of his trim, but not very well developed body. It was his heart and soul she loved. It felt perfectly natural being naked with her.

The day faded from sunset red and purple to reveal the starry sky. After enjoying the massage on their backs, tired from a whole day in the car, they turned it off to enjoy the night sounds. Lightning bugs added a sparkling brilliance to the beauty of the night. Frogs, crickets and other evening creatures filled the airwaves with rhythmic vibrations. John and Crystal had kept away from any physical contact. It wasn't planned but it seemed a natural space, since they planned to have a controlled sexual experience, rather than just letting their passions sweep them into something.

"Crystal, tell me more about sacred sex. How do you do it?"

"It's simply the idea of making a ritual out of the sexual experience. Usually people do a variation on the traditional practice of partaking of something representing the five elements. It's from the Indian tradition so they have Fire, Earth, Air and Water plus Ether. It's because you are using the five senses to heighten your meditation experience, your search for God consciousness. You try to see your partner as a representation of God or the Goddess. You sanctify in your mind the yoni and lingam, which are the Sanskrit names for the vagina and the penis. You try and recognize the oneness of all things and the ceremony itself uses the senses to help you actually feel and experience the oneness. You make a meditation out of the experience and only use enough motion to keep an erection."

"Are you supposed to enjoy it? Do you have any foreplay? And if you don't have an orgasm, how do know when it is time to stop?"

Crystal smiled and tilted her head back. "Oh, yeah. Sure, you're supposed to enjoy it. You should enjoy it tremendously. It's just that you don't let the sensuous, physical side of the enjoyment be all there is and you don't let it sweep you along to an orgasm. You experience a different kind of a climax, or crescendo might be a better word. It can be a profound experience of oneness, or a great peacefulness, or perhaps a truly enlightening experience."

"It sounds like you've done it before. Have you ever made love with anyone, Crystal?"

"Yes. I had a lover when I was seventeen. He was older and quite a famous musician around the bay area. Actually, my desire to change our lovemaking in this direction might have been why we broke up. He was unfaithful to me and when I found out, he used the few times we had tried sacred sex as part of his excuse. He wasn't ready for it. How about you, John? Anyone other than Faith?"

John was kind of embarrassed. But then he wanted total openness, didn't he? It seemed intense telling his sexual history to a once celibate. "Well, I made love with a few ladies, always with condoms. I did have oral sex with some ladies who I didn't have intercourse with. I thought it was much safer than even sex with a condom. I hope you don't think I'm, well…" John was really embarrassed now, and Crystal could tell.

"There is no need for embarrassment, my love. I petted to orgasm with several of my steady boyfriends. Nowadays we don't think that it is bad to have, or give someone you care about, an orgasm. It's actually known to be quite healthy as a matter of fact. People are clear on the distinction between behavior that leads to orgasm and behavior that can lead to pregnancy or disease."

Somewhat shocked, he had to quickly reassess his ideas about sexuality in that time, not to mention his ideas about Crystal. Did Crystal actually give them… John asked himself, then quickly thought, you really don't want to know that. What an automatic double standard the male mind can create, he thought.

"The first time I actually made love without a condom was with Faith. And there has been no one since her. I've had a blood test, and I don't have HIV, or anything else."

"Me too."

Crystal got out of the tub and put a towel around herself. John felt his erection coming back.

"I'm going to make us an altar by the fireplace. It's too hot to have a fire, but it's a very nice space and the stone hearth there is just the right height. I'll put some candles in the fireplace. Let's save the champagne they gave us for when we are with our friends."

John smiled broadly. He didn't have to ask if tonight was the night. "That sounds simply beautiful." He got out the tub and followed Crystal in through the screen door. "I'm going to the bathroom, Crystal. Be back in a minute."

John was incredibly high. He brushed his teeth, combed his hair, and put on a pair of short pants. Chuck's cabin was very nice without being ostentatious like his home. I guess if you're an investment broker you need an impressive front, John thought. He looked at himself in the mirror for a few moments. He could hardly believe his incredible change of fortune. It was still him looking back but he did feel very changed. The sadness, yes, and even the guilt, had slipped away. Instead, a man in high joy looked back at him tonight. He said thank you to God. He said it to himself in the mirror for the awareness that he, like all beings was one with God, was truly beginning to penetrate his consciousness.

He walked back into the living room. Crystal had made a beautiful altar on the hearth with flowers from their wedding and many candles. There were two glasses filled with what looked like water and a silver bowl filled with a small bunch of grapes from the fruit basket they had been given. Incense was burning, filling the air with a wonderful floral fragrance. He could see she had put something in the fireplace shovel that was lying on the hearth. Crystal had spread a beautiful quilt on the floor in front of the fireplace, and with the plush pile carpet, it was quite soft.

John couldn't help noticing that Chuck had a very large telescope in one corner of his cabin sticking through a domed and obviously movable ceiling. He walked over to it, took the cover off of the lens piece and looked in. He couldn't believe what he saw! Crystal would have to see this.

John saw a light on in the other bathroom. He closed his eyes, and started the Om Shanti meditation to calm himself. He felt so incredibly energized that his spine seemed to vibrate. He realized he was actually shaking somewhat. The mantra did help. He slowed his breathing even more and put a smile on his face and the intensity seemed to come under some control. In a minute the bathroom light went off, and Crystal came into the room.

Her hair, unbraided for the wedding, held the floral head piece she'd been given in Ringgold. Otherwise, she was naked. She was so truly beautiful to John that he was sure he was seeing a living Goddess. John was awestruck for a moment. She was smiling and joyous and came over to him, standing by the telescope.

"You have to look in here Crystal. It is the most romantic thing I have ever seen in my life, that is, next to the way you look right now."

"Really?" Intrigued, she looked through the lens.

"Oh my! They are so beautiful. Do you think they are twin stars, revolving around each other?"

"Yes, Crystal, I think so. They are so close, and there are no other stars by them. I've heard of twin stars, but I never heard of a pair where one was distinctly blue and the other clearly golden."

"How did you find them?"

"I didn't; they were just there."

"Probably Chuck has an explanation for this but I can't help still seeing it as a miracle." Crystal looked at John with a look of joy and awe. "Sort of like a wedding present from the Cosmos."

She turned and walked over to the altar area. John took off the shorts he realized he still had on. They took seats on the floor a few feet away from each other.

"I see you as a Goddess, Crystal. Truly." There were tears in his eyes. "My heart is overflowing with incredible love and gratitude."

"Let it flow upwards to your crown, my love. Let us begin the ceremony with partaking of the fire element by burning these herbs and letting the smoke consecrate our bodies. It is a purifying ritual."

Crystal lit the sage and cedar in the shovel from the fire tools. It burned for a minute and then Crystal gently blew out the flame. A thick smoke rose and she used her hand to wave it in John's direction. As the smoke surrounded him, he felt a calmness settle over his being. Crystal handed the shovel to John and he surrounded her with smoke. She waved her hands, taking some into her face and then touched the back of her wrists to her forehead. John put the shovel down.

Then Crystal took the little bowl holding the grapes. "These grapes are the fruit of the Earth. They allow us to partake of her essence." Crystal took three grapes, put them in her mouth and then handed the bowl to John.

"Thank you Mother Earth for the gift of these grapes and these bodies." John also ate three grapes.

"Let us invoke the air element by doing some pranayama, breathing exercises. Let's just do the most simple and straightforward, the complete yogic breath. Just sit with your spine straight and fill your lungs slowly from the bottom to the top, taking about seven seconds for each inhalation and exhalation."

They began the deep rhythmic breathing, and from the first breath, were in perfect unison. John looked into her eyes deeply. He looked upon the beauty of her form. He knew the purity and generosity of her spirit. He loved her so very completely. The moment was perfect. After about five minutes they resumed regular breathing.

"And now the water." Crystal handed one glass to John and took the other herself. John was thirsty and had a very dry mouth, so he quickly drank all of his water. Crystal did too. They both laughed heartily at that, for they knew of each other's nervousness. The laughter eased it considerably.

The laughter slowly settled into broad smiles. "For the element of ether we could just meditate for a few minutes. It will help us raise our energy and calm and center our minds," said Crystal.

"OK. I'm going to meditate on 'God is Love'."

"Then Love, my dear, is God."

They closed their eyes and straightened their postures. John was trying to stay focused on "God is love," but it was very difficult. He put Crystal sitting there naked across from him in his mind to go with the mantra and it seemed to work. All other thoughts slowed and lessened. He was making good progress towards totally stilling all thoughts but that one. That God is Love, and Love is God, and Crystal is both. He felt a hand on his knee.

John opened his eyes. Crystal, knelt on one knee in front of him, gently stroking his thighs and looking deeply into his eyes. John's lingam swiftly rose to full erection. He came to his knees and they kissed a long slow kiss. It was transcendental; the exquisiteness of the sensation of her mouth on his, her body against his, her firm young breasts pressed against his chest. After several minutes her tongue entered his mouth and he again joined in the dance of moist tongues sensing, feeling, loving each other.

Fully erect to the bursting point of hardness, John surprisingly felt under control, even with Crystal's warm, sensuous body pressed against him. Her hands slowly rubbed his back, and gentle scratching felt wonderful and electric. After reciprocating on her back, John brought his right hand around to the side of her left breast. She moved back slightly, though still kissing him passionately, allowing him greater access to it.

John slowly ended the kiss and then looked into Crystal's face and said, "I would very much like to kiss your beautiful breasts, my love. I see them as manifestations of the Goddess. Just as the mountains give the streams and rivers to the plains below, I see your breasts as divine beings, actually giving us our bodies in our infancy and giving us beauty and pleasure in our adulthood."

"My dear, sweet love, you may do anything you wish to do."

John laid Crystal back on the quilt. After giving her another kiss on the mouth, he kissed his way slowly down her throat to her breasts. A sweet sigh came from her lips as he kissed one, then the other, first with reverence, and then with a measure of passion. He circled her firm nipples with his tongue and heard longer, deeper sighs.

He longed to kiss her yoni, for he saw it as a great Goddess that gives life to all humanity. As divine, the gate of life that suffers so in the travail of birth that she duly deserves any pleasure that can be given to her.

He kissed his way down her firm stomach and took a full minute to get to the hair at the beginning of her most sacred of places, where life can flow forth. John thought with true reverence that every human ever living, even Jesus and Buddha, came through that magical gateway. He felt tremendous love for the yoni. He gently separated her legs and lowered himself to where he could comfortably kiss this sacred being. He pressed his lips against her fragrant yoni and felt the soft, hairy lips form a cross with his. He kissed them again and again, and then within one deep, long kiss he gently parted her lips with his tongue and tasted the sweetness of her nectar. Crystal moaned loudly, opened her legs a little farther and brought her right hand to his head. His kisses explored deeper and her fingers gently stroked his hair.

After several minutes, leaving her once moist but now wet yoni, John kissed his way back up to Crystal's mouth and another of those sweet, deep kisses. At its end, Crystal rose to a sitting position and spoke.

"I forgot to tell you that usually the ceremony is done in a sitting position, the woman astride the man." She reached down and touched his lingam. "I love your lingam as the ultimate manifestation of the masculine creative force, the fountain of life."

John took her hand from his lingam and said, "I think, being out of practice, we had better forego much stimulation of my lingam."

"I understand, Darling. John, before you enter me, I want to tell you that even though I don't think this is my fertility period, it was probably last weekend, I'd greatly love to have your child. Please do not feel any pressure to perform, or to not come, or anything, sweetheart. I love you. Whatever happens will be perfect."

"Thank you, my Love. I'm ready, and if we go slowly, I think I can keep it under control. How should I sit? Cross legged?"

"Right, darling."

John sat cross legged and straight, and Crystal got close and lowered herself onto John's lap. One arm was around John, and with the other hand she guided John's lingam to her wet lips, and then inside her yoni. It took a full minute for her to bring his lingam fully into her. The whole journey was wonderful, exquisite, sensuous beyond compare. It was like he was on the brink of having an orgasm but never quite did. Once fully inside, she stopped and settled down to a sitting position on his lap. She looked into his face and kissed him. Their tongues completing a connection bringing even greater physical ecstasy. John thought he might lose control. He ended the kiss saying, "Let's close our eyes and meditate for a while."

John closed his eyes, and before long he found himself swiftly sinking into the light and colors dancing in his mind. His body was in complete ecstasy and it was so deep. Suddenly his torso jerked backwards with a start. Crystal looked him in the eyes and asked, "what is the matter, my Love?"

"I was in a very high state of bliss, the colors came, they swirled and danced. Then all of a sudden I was afraid that I was slipping back into the same place I was in when I was transported to this time! I was afraid I was going back!"

They sat quietly for a moment.

"John, my darling. I'm having the same experience but I think it's wonderful. It is what I've been searching for in my meditations all my life. You're here in my arms. Let go of your fear. Let the oneness take you away. When the experience is over, you'll still be here in my arms."

John looked at Crystal's sweetly smiling face. He loved her so much. He knew that the moment was perfect beyond, well, almost beyond belief. He knew that even if he had stayed in the past, he still would never have known where he came from and where he was going. Whether it was to go back to the past, or merge with God forever or even become an angel with Crystal, whatever God and Life had in store for him he would graciously accept. Even to becoming a pair of twin stars like they had seen tonight.

"Perhaps I still wonder, Crystal, if you and I will be together tomorrow?"

"Have faith, John. We were meant to be together."

"I do, my love."

At that moment, he knew that the oneness was beyond John and Crystal. The oneness that would merge them with each other would also merge them with all of life. John returned her smile. He knew that he must continue. He must transcend his fear.

"I love you," said John.

"I love you, my Darling."

John closed his eyes again. His erection had abated considerably so Crystal gently started moving back and forth. It felt good, so very, very good. Slow, deep strokes in and out of her wet yoni. His lingam quickly rose again to full erection and then it felt even more wonderful. They shared another deep and sensual kiss. John felt himself getting close to the edge of orgasm. The kiss ended. John turned his attention to the exquisite, slow but steady strokes going deep into her being. Crystal was vibrating, and moaning softly in a somewhat broken voice, then she stopped again. She wanted to stay in control.

John found it easy to still his mind and experience the totality of the complete oneness with Crystal, the deep love and satisfaction filling him. In a few minutes it was back. The overwhelming bliss that filled his being, the transcendental sounds and incredible colors. The brilliant-beyond-description light. There was no up, or down. There was no day, or night. There was no time, but all time. No thought, only love and oneness. There was only Love.

I Stand with the Tigers

I stand with the tigers as they make their last stand.
I stand with the tigers against the ravage of man.
I stand with the animals pushed to the wall.
The rhinos, the pandas, I stand with them all.
I stand with the great apes. The gorilla's my kin,
and I wouldn't want to live in a world they're not in.

I stand with the wolves, the she-wolves and cubs
against steel-jawed traps that would leave just a nub.
I stand with the whales. I stand and I weep
over all of their blood that was shed in the deep.
I stand with the elephants, noble and bold,
who are killed for their tusks that are hacked off and sold.

I stand with the animals. I love one and all,
and I think to myself, surely this is Man's fall.
We're burning the Garden. We're cutting her trees.
I stand and I beg; I plead, people **stop, please**!
Yet my heart knows that this won't be enough.
If we stand with the Tigers, we'll have to get tough.

For this is our last stand. We're all on the brink.
We just have to stop it, and take time to think.
We must face the truth that we're killing ourselves.
We must learn to treasure our planet's true wealth.
It's not in the gold hidden deep in her soil.
It's not in the steel and it's not in the oil.

It's not in possessions that these things will build.
What good is it all after everything's killed?
What joy in a world if we're in it alone,
With her beauty destroyed, and our hearts turned to stone?
Oh, we might still live on, but surely not well.
For our Garden most fair we'd have turned into hell.

From *There is a Tomorrow Redux*, by David Nazar
Please visit: www.reverseglobalwarmingnow.org